MERDE AND MANDARINS: DIVINE BREATH

KIND HEARTS AND MARTINETS BOOK 5

PETE ADAMS

OTHER BOOKS BY PETE ADAMS

Kind Hearts and Martinets series:

Book 1 – Cause and Effect

Book 2 – Irony in the Soul

Book 3 – A Barrow Boy's Cadenza

Book 4 – Ghost and Ragman Roll

"We cannot heal the wounds we do not feel"

S R SMALLEY

By now many would have realised that Martin, the Border Terrier, is based upon Charlie the Dog - unfortunately, I mentioned this to him once and he became quite star-struck, wearing sunglasses even if the sun is not out:

ACKNOWLEDGMENTS

A.J. Griffiths-Jones, author – Miika Hannila of Creativia, who responded so speedily and enthusiastically.

FOREWORD

Dr. Samuel A. Mudd was the doctor who treated John Wilkes Booth, who had broken his leg jumping onto the stage after shooting Lincoln. Dr. Mudd set Booth's leg and was later sentenced to life in prison for aiding and abetting an assassin – he was a doctor and he claimed, "He treated the body in front of him". It took 137 years to clear his name.

It is this story that inspired my character, Sigmund Merde, *Ghost* in my previous book, *Ghost and Ragman Roll*. Sigmund Merde, and the spirit of all doctors that *treat the body in front of them*, regardless of who it is or the consequences, moves on in this sequel. It seems such an alien concept in this day and age, where we allow self-interest, politics and other modern day influences, survival even, to colour what we know we should do; what is proper: I believe this has been the driving force behind my novels, social fairness. My books are humorous, but, as Peter Ustinov said, *"Comedy is a funny way of being serious"*.

A Mandarin, in the political context in Britain, is a high-ranking Civil Servant, perceived to be outside political control. The name said to have come about because their elaborate language is often as hard to understand as Chinese; likely deliberately so.

"Civilisation is a stream with banks. The stream is sometimes filled with blood from people killing, stealing, shouting and doing things historians usually record. While on the banks, unnoticed, people build homes, make love, raise children, sing songs, write poetry and even whittle statues. The story of civilisation is what happened on the banks.

WILL DURANT

"Whittle statues?"

PETE ADAMS

PROLOGUE

J<small>ONATHAN</small> C<small>RUMB</small>, <small>A DISTINGUISHED</small> C<small>IVIL</small>
Servant, the Permanent Secretary at the Ministry of
Defence and a key Whitehall Mandarin, was on his
second circuit of St James's Park in London. He
jogged every working day at lunchtime. Like clock-
work, at one pm, he could be seen jogging around the
park, come rain or shine. Since his heart attack, he
had religiously maintained a rigorous fitness regime,
lost his tubbiness and all evidence of a sedentary,
comfortable lifestyle, achieved not just from his considerable salary and perks.

He jogged – ordinarily an anathema for this man, and
indeed this type of man; *outside with the Plebs?* –
and, after some time of practicing the art, for he
treated it as if it were an art form, he jogged with a

spring in his step and a sense of wellbeing you ac-
quire through having dodged a bullet, and when he
told people this, only he knew he did not just refer to
his heart attack. He did continually place a hand over
his heart, though, it was only natural, but the monitor
would register any unusual, potentially troublesome
warning signs.

He had an in-depth knowledge of classical music, en-
cyclopaedic, some might say, but on his runs he listened to pop music, which was unusual for a
Mandarin of this stature, but he liked it, having
picked it up by listening to his children's popular
beat-combo stuff. So, imagine his confusion when his
Duran Duran track switched unexpectedly to
Shostakovich Piano Concerto Number Two, the
second movement, a particularly elegiac, lyrical and
emotional refrain. Crumb eased his pace and looked
down at his chest where the iPod had bounced rhythmically with his jogging step and to that of the music,
but was now still, providing no popular musical beat
to run by.

He felt the thud, no pain, but immediately registered
the crimson staining that grew like an ever-expanding
red ink blob through his white vest. He clutched his
chest and the remnants of the music machine as he
dropped to the pavement with a shocked look on his
face, and eventually others around him shared that
look of horror. It was a cold, early December day,

bright sun but frigid air, and people hurried around the park on personal missions, too cold to be strolling, eager to be where they were going, and dressed for the winter weather. However, though they may have wished to avert their eyes in the time-honoured English manner, they could not avoid noticing the jogger drop to his knees. It took a while before anyone reacted. People were not cognitive of such events in London, even though there had long been terrorist incidents. It was the British way; it didn't exist. After a brief time of inanimate shock and awe, people screamed and dashed for cover, heading this way and that way. After all, what do you do? Hide? See to the victim? Think of yourself? And wasn't this the way people had become? *Bugger everyone else?*

Crumb, hunched on the tarmac in a kneeling foetal pose, coincidentally took in the crisp scene of the Royal Park, the bandstand, birds and the winter bare trees, as though he were newly born and only just become aware of his surroundings. He sensed life's essence draining from him. Nobody was running toward him, they were all escaping – all, that is, except for a skeletal form in a morning suit, a shadow of a man who knelt beside him. He took Crumb's head in his hands and laid it gently back to the pavement, unfolded his Civil Service legs and whispered into the Mandarin's ear, 'Life is for living, and everyone should live and enjoy life. The pleasure of life is not just for the privileged few, and it is not for the privileged to manipulate life, or to dictate how others should live it. It is time to make amends.'

That was it, other than a parting word: 'I have to go, you will be okay, a true near miss. Remember it.' At least this is what Crumb thought he said, or meant, because it sounded remarkably like, "ner bet yeg bun coten nechtmiss, mush", the frontier gibberish of the parting words, indelibly stained in his memory. It was a special skill of Crumb's, to remember exactly what was said to him, and so he was able to repeat it, word for gibberish word, to the police.

———

Quentin Bryant, Permanent Secretary to the Home Office, a most senior Whitehall Mandarin, had serious palpitations after hearing the news of Crumb via a phone call from Archibald Pointe-Lace, known affectionately as Buttonhole to his Eton boyhood chums, and stalwart members of the St James's Gentlemen's' Club, Bumblin'tons. It didn't make sense... well it did, and they thought it could soon be significant, but chose to ignore that sense for the time being.

Pointe-Lace further reported that in the hospital, Crumb had been mumbling incoherently about the second movement of the Shostakovich Piano Concerto Number Two. Crumb wasn't known to have leanings towards Moscow, was he? He was one of us, wasn't he? However, as Permanent Secretary of Defence, these things needed to be run up the Civil Service flagpole, to be batted around, and not to do so, was not cricket.

So those Mandarins in the know thought seriously; at least nobody was thinking of them. *Poor old Crumb*, expressions of faux concern; however, was this coincidence? Maybe, but not likely? Does Buttonhole have this buttoned up? When was their next embroidery meeting, and could this wait?

———

PROFESSOR ROY ROGERS, Head of the Faculty for Strategic Defence, Military and Cowboy studies at the University of Portsmouth, had watched the news conference and thought their friend may have overstepped the mark. But wasn't that just like Jack, and wasn't he just a little pleased he had? He considered calling his colleague in the Faculty of Political Sciences, but didn't have to as Professor Will Manfred called him.

'Feck me, Roy, did you see Jack on telly?'

As close drinking pals of Jack Austin, though they drew the line at sharing the bathwater with him, both espoused *Cod-Irish* as an ordinary manner of speaking.

Will Manfred was a political academic who had his students examine not only the concept of politics, constitutional law, contemporary societies and so on, but principally, he tried to instil in all his students an ability to think for themselves. He encouraged them to deconstruct doctrinaire politics and look deep into government, to the controlling seat of power in Britain, the Civil Service, and especially the White-hall Mandarins. He was not there to churn out career-minded, political nonentities; he wished to create open and fertile minds, to educate, inspire, and to illuminate a pathway of free thought.

His students, when eventually they went out into the world, could argue and debate their true beliefs and comprehend others, and were not afraid to change their minds if a convincing argument won the day. They were free thinkers, not groomed to be party politicians, not educated in pertinacious tripe you can get from a book, and were especially coached not to be seduced by party political dogma. They left Professor Manfred as philosophers. His students had resolve in their heart and soul. Politics was not a job, but a way of life, and not their own life, but the lives of everyone else who would have to live with the consequences of their thoughts, and ultimately, their actions.

Beth Mayhew had been a student of Manfred before she was believed to have drowned in a Jet Ski accident on the Solent, just off Portsmouth. She had, though, survived, and had later been found embroiled in a fascist plot, not a philosophy shared by Will Manfred but, when she was in his seminars, he did enjoy debating with her. Beth was bright, a one in a thousand mind, and he had felt confident that her breadth of comprehension would balance as she matured. But it didn't. She did not mellow.

'I did see him, Will,' Roy answered.

'Well?'

'Well, I imagine it starts now, but in truth, hadn't it already started, and I see he mentioned *My-loft*,' and they both tittered, thinking of their police detective friend, Mr Malacopperism, knowing who he meant, but not who *My-loft* was.

'He means to track him down, you think?'

Will sighed, an audible breath down the phone, 'Yes, that is exactly what I think, but what does that mean for us? I suppose Jack will brief us? I bloody hope so, because I feel a right lemon, and not a little exposed. You at C&A's later?'

Roy replied he would meet Will and most likely Jack, too, in the Crown and Anchor, their local pub, later.

———

IT IS a painstaking process to unravel brainwashing, primarily because, for the technique to have succeeded so well in the first place, the victim needed to at least have sympathetic views, and Beth Mayhew did have serious right-wing views. However, she was responding to treatment by specialist psychiatrists, (Jack Austin called them *Trick Cyclists*), under the overall supervision of Dr Jim Samuels, a Harley Street Trick Cyclist and, unknown to most people, the head of a discreet MI5 division. Daily hands-on work was being done by Dr Jackie Philips, at the request of her good friend, DCI Jack (nicknamed Jane) Austin, police detective, retired. Did he retire? He may have just flounced out in a hissy fit after the press conference; after all, he considered himself a prima donna copper, and thus, Mr Malacopperism was a consommé flouncer. And, if he had retired from the police, had he retired from MI5, as he had already done previously, and also not really; clear?

Beth was a wealth of knowledge, making her useful to some and a danger to others, something Jack Austin was aware of.

———

KEITH BANANAS LIKED to think he was an East End of London gangster, but was actually a lanky, gangly, twenty-three-year-old thug from Hither Green, in South London, who had the look, with goofy teeth contained by thin, parallel, crusty lips, of a Hillbilly retard. His eyes swivelled like a ventriloquist's dummy and looked in different directions, contributing to his shifty appearance, though an asset when looking out for the police.

"It's Keef and I'm not from 'Ivver Green," he would say in a spiky London accent, estuarine, not cockney, and if you called him Keith, you would get a bunch of fives in the face, and we're not talking actual bananas, though that really was his name. Having said that, he did have a "A lardy-da, Uncle Josh, posh aunt, what lived in Sowfsea, a poncy bit of Portsmuff on the sowf bleedin' coast of England, innit."

The aunt was Lady Francesca Blanche-Teapot and, unknown to many, she had been born a Banana. She had been a wheel tapper at Hither Green shunting yards, before she married Sir Reginald Teapot and was elevated to the aristocracy and a life of leisure; this latter assertion she refuted unequivocally, arguing she was a very busy-body. There was no disputing it, and what would be the point, as one did not dispute points with the Duchess, as she was known locally. The Duchess knew what was what, don't you know. She did, however, have a soft spot for her nephew and the whole Banana family, from whom she hailed, not that you would ever know or be informed of this fact. The soft spot was more of a blind spot, which was very much the way she viewed life, and people for that matter, especially if they, or life, happened to disagree with her point of view on matters.

Keith Bananas visited his aunt on a regular basis, had done so ever since he was a juvenile delinquent. We know this because Detective Chief Inspector Jack (Jane) Austin, retired (we need to check on this), observed it thus. Well, his wife, Detective Superintendent Amanda (Mandy) Austin did, and happened to mention this to her husband who later claimed, "It was him what noticed it, so shut yer trap." But what they both knew was that the said Mr Bananas was on the *"To watch list"*, and not just the Metropolitan Police (London) but also MI5, and since Mr and Mrs Austin were indifferently attached to MI5, in an inept monkey spy way, it was duly noted.

———

Mandy was worried about her husband; was he in meltdown? Jack Austin suffered from Post Traumatic Stress Syndrome and often behaved in an irrational manner, but always with a semblance of lucid thought. She had thought interesting him in gardening would help, but it had backfired, in a way that could only happen around Jack Austin, getting the neighbourhood up-in-arms about his landscape designs, and now, apart from all of his other distinct mannerisms, he was behaving as if he was Captain James T. Kirk of the USS Enterprise. It was amusing at first, especially as his empty eye socket had wrinkled, sunken skin with the look of an inverted Klingon Cornish pastie. And this was her chaotic but lovable husband, Jane, and was he retired, or was his performance in the press briefing simply consommé flouncing, after which he had disappeared, though she had a shrewd idea where to look.

ONE

'MAY I JOIN YOU?' HE LOOKED UP, NODDED, AND she sat. 'How long have you been sniffing the Dogs Bollix?'

His one eye swivelled accordingly, he thought his wife beautiful. He shrugged, he was good at shrugging. 'Kirk out,' he said.

Mandy had seen this before, though not the *Star Trek* shrugging, although she had seen his shrugging before, often associated with equivocation. Sometimes he would pour himself a Jameson's and swirl it, sniff it, put it to his lips, but not sip, and here he was sniffing, not sipping, the Dogs Bollix, an ale second only to his favourite London Pride, and doing it very much as he would with his Irish whiskey.

She looked across the C&A's narrow, intimate bar and saw, as she expected, perched precariously on a stool too big for him, the dishevelled short-arse, Bernie 'LeBolt' Thompson, Portsmouth Evening News crime reporter, who was here following the chaotic conclusion to the press conference, looking to get some news crumbs off Jack's broken emotional table. Bernie looked at Jack then swung his gaze to Mandy, who gave him her best *Leave my man alone* stare in return.

The skinny runt of a reporter averted his eyes to the table in front of Jack and his untouched, and only sniffed, Dogs Bollix, and shrugged himself; as far as shrugging went, it was pretty amateur. She also expected to see Roy and Will, the people Jack was probably waiting for. She decided to wait with him. She didn't expect to see Della, though, in an extraordinary way she hoped she would, but it had been a tough day or two, Jonas had picked up a couple of wounds from the shoot-out in the cemetery, and must be wondering what he had gotten himself into with his cockney sparrow.

Bruce, the burly oaf landlord of C&A's, a gentle soul, brought Mandy a drop of cry and tonic and waved away the charge, asking, 'You okay?' A gruff voice which suited his ox-like, beery frame. 'Saw the news conference, been hearing all that happened, and Sponge Bob's been in, moanin' on and on about Jack, how he'd not owed him one, or something like that. His lifeboat is all shot-up and he's at a loss as to how he was going to explain that to the RNLI.' (Royal National Lifeboat Institute).

Sponge Bob was the local lifeboat skipper, and Jack had recruited him and his lifeboat, calling in a nonexistent favour, to assist in the rounding-up of a brutal horde of Fascist thugs someone had coordinated sufficiently well for them to act as a small militia. They had been attempting to take over the secret military command bunker, known as the Glory Hole, in Portsmouth. This plan had been thwarted by Jack Austin and Della Lovington. Della was a Detective Inspector, down from the Met in London, but also MI5, and coincidentally, she thought she had resigned but hadn't. Della did, however, think Jack should retire, and had told him so several times, much to the chagrin of the more experienced and uglier of the two cockneys.

Mandy was exhausted and looked it. It had been a hell of a few weeks for her, too, coordinating the police operation, being in the thick of it, being shot at, and eventually rescuing Jack from a fireball sea, off Sponge Bob's lifeboat, that Jack called *Thunderbird 4*. She was grateful for some small mercies in that they had moved from *Thunderbirds*, where everybody wanted to be Virgil, onto *Star Trek*; no argument, Jack was Kirk. Mandy knew she was someone, but couldn't be bothered to find out who, likely O'Hurra she thought, subconsciously playing around with her ear.

Bruce knew all this. He knew about Jack and Mandy, and knew he was bloody Scotty, engineering up the beer and dilithium crystals (cheese and onion crisps) and didn't expect an answer from Mandy. He patted the shoulder of the handsome, long-suffering, over a short period of time, police Detective Superintendent and wife of Chief Detective Inspector Jack (Jane) Austin sitting in front of him, and disappeared back to the bar of his deadbeat, but homely, local pub.

Mandy took a sip from her drink and placed it on the table. The ice lumps chinked and alerted her to how quiet it was in the saloon bar of the pub that had the look of Fag Ash Lil's boudoir. None of the locals looked at or cared about the decor, it was a quintessential English Pub; no music, occasional hubbub, people looking at each other, not the wallpaper or the beer-sodden carpet, or Fag Ash Lil for that matter.

Mandy massaged her chin, and Jack observed; he liked to watch her fondling her face. He was an ugly, overly large, cockney barrow boy, and if you didn't comprehend rhyming slang, it was not his problem, communication not being one of his stronger suits, which was probably why Mandy was O'Hurra. Mandy, aware her husband was watching her inti-

16

mate facial movements, allowed her index finger to slip into her not insubstantial nose, rattled it around and waited for a response. She was an elegant, handsome, fifty-five year old woman, "a real woman," Jack said of her; his Sophia Loren of Portsea Island. All bollocks, but she liked him saying it, though she did worry she should have had her brains tested and also gone to Specsavers, as she had married the truly bonkers, ugly, cockney barrow boy spiv.

He turned his good eye and scrutinised her nose-rattling antics and could not resist a smile; she caught him, and he tried to recall his serious face, but failed. She had her man back, thank the Lord, she thought, the feckin' eejit, and just in time, too, as Roy and Will came into the pub, looking sheepish; perceptive and intelligent men, she thought.

Mandy knew enough, also, to know these two academics were more than just good friends of her husband. They were the conduit by which Jack had communicated with Ghost; he'd not said as much to her, but he knew she knew. Wherever Ghost had been in the strife-torn world, the three of them had intermittently been in touch and acted as a home front, or rear-guard, for the extraordinarily talented, though disgraced, trauma surgeon.

As a Professor of Politics, Will Manfred was often seconded to Fact Finding missions into these hot-spot parts of the world, and Roy, a Professor of Military Strategy, would be on those trips, presumably advising on the military risks should the UN need to be involved. Who they both fed back to, apart from Jack, she could only guess, as Jack had not said. He would tell her eventually, and she bided her time; she had, after all, only just found out about Ghost. Mandy was a shrewd woman and her husband knew this. He called her a smart biscuit; she thought he meant sharp cookie, but maybe not, as she often felt like a Jammy Dodger.

'Bollix?' Jack shouted, making Mandy jump, and the transformation from the slumped, ugly elephant to an animated, and overtly bonhomie-fuelled, charging rhinoceros, caused him to bump her sideways as he jumped up to get in a round of drinks for his friends, his balls being at risk of dropping off if he didn't get in first, the twat. So because of these daft masculine rituals, she was now sprawled, like a dozy cow, across the pub banquette seat.

'Bollix yerself, Jack!' Will shouted back, nudging him into the table, worried for his own balls, Mandy imagined, as she righted herself, balanced and steadied the table of glasses like a consommé juggler.

'Bollix, you bollix. Bruce!' Roy shouted, hand gesticulating that it was he who would be buying the first round.

Bruce knew these men only too well, and smiled; 'Three Bollix then?' and they tittered at the incongruity like kids at the back of the class, as Bruce poured from the real ale tap. Bernie oozed nearer, like an infectious bacteria on the bar surface, and coincidentally caught the eye of the landlord. 'Cheese sandwich, Bernie?' Bruce called, allowing a sideways grin to Mandy to show he was in wind-up mode.

'Fuck-off, Bernie, bollix to a bollicking cheese sandwich, everyone knows you can't trade a drink for food. Tell him, Bruce, as a landlord you should know that,' Jack exclaimed, and looked like he was fully supported by the professors.

This was a long-standing, and likely to continue as such, wind-up, as just the once, Bernie had asked for a cheese sandwich on Jack's round. It was as if the whole of civilisation had collapsed if Jack's reaction had been anything to go by, and so the ritual had been continued. Mandy had told him to let it go and it would end, eventually, but in her heart she knew there were some things you just can't tell children, especially those at the back of the class; they will never learn.

Bruce did his mental maths and arrived at a total for the round. 'Dilithium crystals, Bernie, lager?'

'What?' Jack was dumbfounded, speechless, although Mandy knew this would only be a temporary condition. It was not so much the cheese sandwich, or the feckin' cheese and onion crisps, or even Jack would feel he was buying the gutter press a three-course meal; she knew what it was and anticipated the reaction with a degree of mischievous relish. 'Fucking cotton candy, pansy-arsed, daft lager...' Jack looked to the professors, and like Laurel and Hardy, which was just how they both looked, they nodded agreement and said, "Fuck off, Bruce" in unison, like they always did. Will, whom Jack called Stan, spoke in a squeaky voice and added an animated scratching of his head, while Roy fiddled with an imaginary tie he watched bouncing on his rotund beer belly.

Grinning benignly, Bruce unmoved by the wobbly ogre frame of Jack and the unlikely clever bonce comedy duo, plonked the pint of lager on the counter beside Bernie and told Jack the cost of the round.

'How much? How much?' Jack's regular rejoinder, more energetically espoused this evening because of the injustice attached to the order than the subsequent tally. 'Your round, Ollie,' Jack said and, hitching his trousers in a harrumph manner, he took his Dogs Bollix to the table, mentally grabbing his balls so they remained attached whilst multitasking a gentle fondle. Meanwhile the mild-mannered rotund Roy (Ollie) Rogers placed his hard-earned Hi Hoh Silver onto the bar with a generous smile across his wobbly chops, and nudged Bernie with his pansy-arsed lager, so it spilled onto his already disgusting, gutter press trousers, for good measure.

Everyone in the bar had enjoyed the contretemps, including Bernie, who applied a nicotine-stained grin and directed his supersonic, grimy, grey-hairy, fag ash lugholes to listen into the discreet conversation at the pub table. A conversation he would not be invited to attend, but that would not stop him eavesdropping, even though he knew he would get the droppings, as and when Jack needed it broadcasting; anonymously attributed, naturally.

Mandy was on Fred Alert, as Jack's one eye, so recently morose, was now energised. She could see the puckered skin that sank into his vacant right eye socket, twitch, and the iridescent silvery vertical scar that stretched from his forehead onto his aged, wrinkled, liver-spotted cheek, wobble and pick up reflected light. It was as if the traumatic scarring to his face was a beacon to portray his emotions, of which the incongruous man had many, not least crying at the drop of a hat. However, this was his *Give me gyp* twitch, as apparently his nan in Stepney, the East End of London, used to say. Probably all bollocks as well, as his explanation varied every time, but this was her man, and she was his trouble and strife, and there was no doubt that the recently sullen, contemplative husband of hers was now also on Fred Alert.

Bernie, the stick thin, diminutive, grubby reporter just two fags away from having to walk into the pub with his drip stand on wheels, edged closer. Mandy gave him a frigid stare, a head gesture, and Bernie moved back to his sandwich, cheese and onion Dilithium crystals and Nancy boy beer; he may be a revolting gutter press journalist, but he was no fool.

Jack noticed Mandy's gesturing to Bernie. 'Thanks, luv, this is not for Bernie,' he said, his non-drinking hand on her thigh, where it should be. It was a thing they had, and she liked it, his overtly dirty-old-man sexual nature, and his desire for her, not only physically but emotionally and spiritually. She loved him and he loved her, and they could not get enough of each other. However, she also knew something serious was about to happen, as his hand left her thigh, which had been at advanced liberties position; ordinarily, she wouldn't let his hand rise so far, so early in the evening.

'Right, my round, Bollix?' Jack shouted, as if Ollie and Stan were in another city, and, swinging his glass around like a Ouija board tumbler, he advanced unsteadily toward the bar, barging past the academically gifted comedy duo.

See, she knew her man, and knew something serious was going to happen, in that he was about to buy his round, but she cautioned him nonetheless: 'Jack, the Queen?'

Stan scratched his Laurel head, responding to the stare from Mandy, and so the three socialists, not quite Republican, stood and toasted her Majesty with the dribbles of ale that remained in their glasses, but, before they could sing the National Anthem, *For she's a jolly good fella*, they were completely thrown into a purple perplexity as Mandy rolled on the banquette in energetic mirth, so much so that Jack's trailing dirty-old-man hand fell off its current station and assigned task, feeling for her bra strap outside of her shiny, silky blouse.

'What?' he asked, irritated. He was enjoying feeling her shoulder and imagining what lay beneath, and the other two musketeers also thought, *what?*, and looked to Mandy's now exposed bra strap, aware of what was happening, as Jack had spoken his thoughts.

'You daft bugger, we're meeting the Queen tomorrow, and I don't think she would like your ugly, hungover face quite as much as I do, my love.'

Jack'tangnan and Ollie Porthos looked like they'd just noticed Cardinal Richelieu order a cheese sandwich and a pint of lager before they could run him through. Jack and Ollie turned to the other musketeer, who scratched his head in a thoughtful silent film reverie, his *I need to spill some beans* face on.

'Something to say, Stan?'

'I've heard from Ghost and he is going to the Palace tomorrow, and furthermore, he has no invite. You know he will get in,' Stan reported, sighing. 'I think you need to speak to a few people, Jack...' he looked at Mandy, '...or you?' (They knew Jack and Mandy were associated with MI5, not whether they were retired spooks or even still in the police, so there's no point in asking the professors, but I am sure we will find out later as the story progresses; my money is on he's still in, but a nod's as good as a wink to a blind bat (spook talk, that), don't you know, and I do; *I know things.*)

Mandy pulled out her bat-phone and blindly called Father Mike and informed him of Ghost's intentions. Father Mike was a Catholic Priest and longstanding friend of Jack, as well as being his conduit, and now also Mandy's, in MI5. He would sort it as well, but she did wonder what Ghost was up to. Jack didn't seem bothered. Did he know something, she mused, smiling to herself, wondering if Ghost had a morning suit, as she further recalled the fiasco that had occurred the last time Jack was at the Palace (*see A Barrow Boy's Cadenza*). Jack had been awarded the George Medal, and his dog, Martin, the scruffy ginger Border Terrier, the George Bone. For tomor-

row, she had at least got Jack a morning suit that fitted, having on the previous occasion, ruined the
Prime Minister's and attended the ceremony wearing
an ill-fitting suit provided by Prince Phillip. To rub
salt into the Duke of Edinburgh's wounds, Jack had
not returned the suit, but had auctioned it off to provide funds for the children they had recently rescued
from a paedophile ring. She imagined they would
have some explaining to do at the Palace tomorrow.

'You wearing your green dress and Jackie's cream hat,
love?' Jack had moved on, round of drinks purchased,
his balls secured.

'Yes,' a despairing lilt, 'I will explain to the Queen I'm
wearing the same dress as before, because you like me
in it.'

'She'll understand, love. Tell her I fink it brings out
the green in yer mince pies and goes well with your
raving Barnet. Shite!'

'What?'

'Me tan brogues went into the sea.' He relaxed,
which signalled he had a contingency plan, and she
decided not to enquire. The Queen had seen him before in an ill-fitting morning suit with his tan brogues
that had juice, so she relaxed as well; with Jack, you
have to take relaxation wherever and whenever you
can, and the Queen knew this also.

TWO

DELORES LOVINGTON, DELLA TO HER FRIENDS, was a Detective Inspector in the Met; and if you believe that, you'll believe anything. Having said that, up until quite recently, Della herself thought she was a DI in the Met elite, Serious Crime Unit, who are often thought to be a law unto themselves, and if you knew Dynamo Della, you would have to concur. Aside from the fact Della was a petite blonde woman, strikingly beautiful, and the exact opposite of Jack Austin in looks, age and gender (though Jack did think he was good-looking and Mandy thought he was a tart), even Jack Austin had to admit Della was his dopy-banger, by which Jack meant doppelganger. Della was Jack's spirit and essence, a cockney sparrow, except he wasn't a bird, he was a tart, and if that did not seem so incongruous, she, to all intents, could be Jack Austin personified. She was the epitome of the cockney barrow boy, but a sparrow; a lady spiv, and Mandy had more than once wondered if Della was not another of Jack's long-lost daughters; after all, she would not be the first to appear on Mandy's horizon.

Della, after leaving university, had been recruited by Jack into MI5. Jack was never an action man spook; he was a liability if he was ever allowed out into the field. However, he was a mustard analyst with an ability to see the bigger picture, think laterally and to conceive strategy. Della had worked closely with Jack in her early days at MI5, which contained, or at least defrayed, any fall-out to Della's caustic cavalier style. The Teflon coating which was always there for Jack Austin, ironically, seemed to rub off onto Della. However, the wheels came off for her when Jack returned to Portsmouth, and after a while of, "Brick shitehouse, wanker, bureaucratic, pillock nonsense," as she put it, quoting *Mary Poppins*, Della resigned, or so she thought, to a fast-track graduate programme in the Met.

Jack Austin returned to Portsmouth CID where he set up a benign unit called the Portsmouth Community Policing team, which, on occasion, did exactly what it said on the tin. It was a stroke of genius on Austin's part, one he rarely got credit for, he would argue; a team of cowboy coppers who gelled, there to look into anything MI5 thought needed looking into, in Portsmouth, a south coast of England city of Naval, Military and Commercial strategic importance. The team functioned as a police unit, but under the radar it did a lot more, and over time, some of the team had been recruited fully into MI5.

Mandy was in, as she was now married to Jack, and this did elicit a lot of sympathy for the woman. Of the rest of the team, there was Jo-Jums, Detective Inspector Josephine Wild, a consummate copper, a mumsy figure with the sharp acuity that allowed her to run, under Detective Superintendent Bruce (now Mrs Austin), the Community Policing Team, the MI5 unit, while Jack settled back to being a consulate; people thought he meant consultant, but he had also said he was an Insultant, which was more than likely what he was. There was Frankie, the computer whizz, and of course Alice, Jack's newly found, long-lost daughter who, although only just returning to service after an horrendous facial injury in a dog fight, was in because she had to be briefed on just who her dad really was, apart from being an ugly, jumped-up cockney barrow boy, which everyone knew; you couldn't keep that a secret, even in MI5.

In all of this, it would be remiss to exclude Martin, Jack's scruffy ginger Border Terrier, who had also recently been decorated by the Queen; a rub-down with the *Sporting Life* and two coats of emulsion, is what Jack told everyone. But it was a bravery award, The George Bone, which he received at an award ceremony where Jack received his George Medal, though Mandy argued that whereas Martin had been brave, Jack had won his medal for being a feckin' ee-jit, and it said this on the citation, but only because Mandy had written that in, in pencil.

Martin now lived with Meesh, a little girl of about eight, whom Jack had rescued from a paedophile ring where, apart from being serially abused, the tiny, cherub-like girl had witnessed her mother being mur-dered. She was recovering, Martin an ever-present life stay, and living with the Splifs, a huge Roman Catholic working class family, who had taken Meesh in and gave her something she had never had before, a home, family, and unconditional love, albeit mas-sively chaotic.

————

'ALLY ALLY IN,' Della called out as she stepped into the CP (Community Policing) room, 'where the feck's tosspot?' she referred to Jack. 'He still up wiv the bleedin' Queen, Gawd bless her little cotton socks?'

Jo-Jums looked up from her immaculately organised desk. 'Della, nice of you to drop in, I take it your brains are all fucked out now?' Jo gave up her best sideways look, knowing Della had left a scene of carnage at Fort Cumberland, The Glory Hole, and the Bank's family crypt in the Eastney cemetery. It was a chaotic scene of bloodshed that she and her doppelganger, Jack Austin, had caused almost single-handedly, and, like her mentor, Jack, Della had left the scene and all of the admin work to others, to clear up the inordinate mess, following what the papers were calling the modern day equivalent of the Battles of Waterloo and Trafalgar.

Della's excuse was she needed to get her brains shagged out by her new fella, Jonas the Gypo, who unfortunately had sustained a bullet wound or two in the melee, but that was never on Della's radar, whose caring genes were a little lacking in substance. That was it, and she could not see any holes (except the bullet ones in Jonas's thigh and upper arm) in the logic and, when pressed, neither could Jack, who of course had also left the scene with his errant Superintendent wife, to get his one remaining, non-Alzheimer-affected, brain cell, shagged out, one presumed, as her Majesty would say.

The Community Policing Team could barely disguise their attenuated mirth, eagerly awaiting a witty response from the beautiful and quite amazing cockney sparrow. Della had only been on the team for a short time, and had already fashioned her indelible stamp; not least the recent blitzkrieg. The mayhem in the office was admin butchery, which everyone took on and was used to, because they had worked with a cockney barrow boy for some time; Della was just a better-looking addition to the team.

'Not a bad rogering as Gypo shags go, Jo-Jums sweet-'art, but Jonas was carrying a few injuries that, to be honest wiv yer, were just scratches, so I had to do most of the work. Still, isn't that always the way with geezers, eh?' She flicked her head, 'A woman's lot, I suppose,' and Della went for wander around the cavernous, tired old room, inviting Jo-Jums to join her. 'It can be so refreshing,' she said. (*Pride and Prejudice* – I told you she had known Jack Jane Austin for a long time.)

The hall-like room was voluminous, even as it was, divided in half by an old wonky, bi-fold screen that had the *Time Team* researching as to when the doors had left their guide tracks; the best guess was shortly after the Romans, *I Austinus* arrived. Della strode like she owned the place, swerving past Jack's deck chair (you moved that at your peril), and ruffled Nobby's hair. She had a satisfied smile on her face, even if "*She had to do all the bleedin' work round 'ere,*" and that included her Gypo as well.

The Gypo in question was Jonas Sexton, now a firm fixture in Della's life, and he had only himself to blame on that score. The landlord of the Gravediggers pub, opposite Eastney cemetery in Portsmouth, was a cosy, old-fashioned, local pub Jonas ran as a micro brewery, while his sister Pansy, the female equivalent of Hagrid but with no beard, ran the bed and breakfast above the pub with her partner Angel, who was not unlike Della in size and beauty, but more cherubic in appearance, and most certainly in behaviour.

Jonas, Heathcliffe out of *Wuthering Heights*, which was how Della described him, insisting he was "definitely not a bleedin' Gypo as she couldn't stand Gypos", had hooked up with Della in the most extraordinary circumstances, which of course you would expect, as it was a rare positive spin-off from one of Jack Austin's hare-brained schemes. Jack wanted Della down in Portsmouth and re-recruited, so to speak, and it was lust and love at first sight for the cockney sparrow who had been sent down by the Met fraud and murder squad to observe Sebastian Sexton, the youngest of the Sexton siblings, who was Asperger's, on the autistic spectrum, and lived in a cemetery.

Della was following a lead on the slaughter of the Head of the Military, the Cabinet Secretary and Government Chief Whip, and a man they called Pomerol, in a house just off Whitehall and Pall Mall, in London. John Sexton, the chairman of the City of London Merchant bank Cedric James, and husband to Beryl, father of Jonas, Pansy and Sebastian, had his fingerprints all over the conference room. However, he could not be *fingered* for the crime, as at the time he had been brokering a deal with the financial doves of Europe, which eventually rescheduled Britain's debt over a more manageable seventy years.

John Sexton bought the cemetery and the Gravediggers pub at the insistence of Seb, their name being Sexton. John, Beryl and Seb lived in The Old Sexton House, and Seb, a computer genius, great problem solver and code breaker, worked out of, and rarely left, the Sexton's shed, which had been fitted out as a state-of-the-art computer suite, courtesy of Jack Austin and MI5; Seb was one of Jack's big successes, a natural, and did all the problem-solving for Jack, who was very busy looking like Captain Kirk.

Father Mike O'Brien was O'Hurra, though Mandy erroneously though she was. No, he had appointed Mandy as Spok, and if you looked under her long, raven black, glossy hair, you would see a set of pointy ears, though Jack recommended that if you wanted to survive the subsequent Vulcan death grip, it would be best to take his word for it – most people did, and with a pinch of salt, "Like what Fireguard (we think he meant Kierkegaard) would do," Jack would tell them.

So, Della had come to Portsmouth to observe this family and Seb in particular, but had been captivated by Jonas, which Jack saw as a bonus as it would keep Della in Portsmouth, right where he wanted her. She hated being manipulated, and manipulated by Jack Austin was number one up there on her number one hate list, and she had many lists and Jack was on most of them. However, she could now stay down and appear to be seen reluctantly dragged, kicking and screaming, back into the MI5 fold, her excuse being she was shagging a country yokel, also her excuse for emigrating from the Smoke. "No self-respecting Londoner would ever want to leave London, you see," she would explain, but only Londoners understood this.

Jo-Jums stood, hands on her childbearing hips, which had been called into action four times, her children still all school age, and she watched as Della strode about the space she considered her domain – this woman has no shame. 'Della, debriefing notes on yesterday would be helpful.'

Della stopped her pacing. 'Unless Jack has described to me somebody other than you, Jo, I would guess you already know evryfink, right?'

Jo-Jums was not a woman to be pushed around, either. 'How would I know, until you have told me all that you know? It's a lot like us interrogating prisoners. We know that they did it, but sometimes it comes in handy if we ask a few questions to get to the salient points, like, what the feck happened?' Jo had her feet firmly planted, her stance and fixed face challenging; water off a sparrow's back for Della, who continued circling, unabashed.

'Yeah, see where yer coming from, sweet'art, but I'll leave that bit to you if you don't mind, darlin', that's admin. I'm more concerned about that bird, Beth Mayhew.' Della paced some more, metaphorically scratching her arse, a lot like Jack does when he's thinking, only he doesn't do it metaphorically, but meteorologically; he had a bum like cumuli nimbus, and frequently demonstrates this with thunder and lightning.

Jo allowed time to drift, but curiosity eventually got the better of her. 'What about Beth Mayhew?'

'What's what about Beth Mayhew?' Della replied mischievously.

Jo saw Della had not only managed to wind her up, but had also successfully circumvented her original questions. 'You said you were worried about Beth Mayhew... Or are you mainly worried that Jonas, the feckin' Gypo, is injured and can only lie there while you do all the work?'

Della turned on Jo. 'He's not a fuckin' Gypo!' Miraculously, she calmed. 'Alright, he might be a Gypo...'

and she lolled her head like a lovelorn sparrow, '...but he don't live in a feckin' caravan or sell lucky 'evver,' she thought, then recalled he had some heather in his bedroom; shite.

'So, he has lucky heather, does he?'

Della had her answer for Jo, and waving her Julie Andrews, *Climb Every Mountain* hands, quickly responded, 'Yeah, it's for cooking, see?' Face saved, she made a mental note to chuck the heather out. Bugger the luck bit, and it might not have been that lucky; she'd missed her period.

'Della, Beth Mayhew?'

Almost as an inconsequential thought, Della replied, 'Yeah Jo, she's coming down 'ere. I'm gonna put her up in our bed and breakfast, well, Pansy and Angel's bed and breakfast. The safe gaff's blown, you knew that, didn't you? And you knew Jack, the feckin' tosspot, wanted to allow it to be blown, probably blew it himself,' she said, acknowledging a light bulb moment. 'He'd arranged for Jimbo to follow the turnip bad guys. Anyway, I've countermanded it 'cause he's wrong, see? To be 'onest with yer, gorgeous, I fink he's lost it good an' proper,' and she sloped her head and grinned to assert just how right she was.

'You countermanded, Jack?' It was then that Jo noticed all of the room focused on the conversation between her and Della. 'What about Del-Boy?' Jo asked, pursuing her point with animated vigour. Del-Boy was the MI5 field officer attached to the monkey spanner spies.

'Del-Boy, that feckin' girl's blouse, what does he know about the price of fish, except he probably knows now as Jimbo is bringing Beth down,' and then Della seemed to have another light bulb moment. 'That's what I wanted to say when I came in 'ere, I knew there was something. Jo, expect a call from Del-Boy, and while you're at it, put some people on the Gravediggers, will you, babes, and I'll be yer best friend.' She explained, not that she needed to, 'In case we need a bit of back-up while I'm fuckin' Jonas, and, as I'm doin' all the bleedin' work, I can't be expected to do surveillance, naturally.' She applied her smug sparrow face and pursed her beak. She'd ended her dawn chorus and was likely thinking of whistling *Dixie*, Jo thought.

Jo was dumbfounded as Della shaped to leave. 'You off? Nice of you to pop in.'

Della stopped at the door. 'Sorry, Jo, but I'm as randy as a fuckin' rabbit from Sainsbury's, so even if I have to sit on top and do it all meself, I've just gotta go an' get me brains fecked out again,' and Della departed, leaving Jo standing with her hands on her expansive hips.

Nobby, a Detective Constable, and coincidentally the Chief Constable's son and now partner to Jack's new daughter, Alice (*honestly, you need to read the previous books – for heaven's sake, do I have to do everything around here?*), spoke up and gestured with the phone in his hand.

'What is it, Nobby?' Jo-Jums replied, irritated, venting some of her frustration on the young lad.

It was wasted, however, as Nobby giggled conspiratorially with the rest of the room, the phone in his hand, 'It's Del-Boy, for you.'

THREE

KEEF BANANAS HAD BEEN SUMMONED BY
Fingers, and this worried him. He expressed his concern to his second-in-command, Shitlegs, whose real
name was Dave Lillicrap, and whose main attribute
to being appointed second-in-command, apart from
being as tall, skinny, and dozy-looking as Keef, was
his innate propensity to follow Keef's orders.

'I ain't done nuffin', so why'd I get a bleedin' summons?' Keef asked, scuffing the toe of his Doc
Martens in the dried soil around the base of Fingers'
shed, knowing this could mean trouble. Who'd be a
baddy? Apart from you get to wear black hats.

Shitlegs looked at his esteemed leader in a goofy, in-
comprehensible way. Although good with a knife in a
fight, Shitlegs was, ironically, not the sharpest knife

in the drawer. He had drainpipe jeans, like everyone else in the Banana gang (except for Jeremy who had tired Saville Row Chinos), and his grubby pants showed above the waistband in a revolting but fashionable manner. He wore a black tee-shirt two sizes too small, that may have been another colour at one time, and it had writing on it: *Shit Happens – down yer leg*; more irony.

Brains, who had an unfeasibly large shaved head, making him appear like a bowling ball atop a skittle pin, declared, 'It's not a summons from a court, it's just Fingers wants ter see yer.'

Brains was Brian Bates, but as he had a library card and half a GCSE... well, you get the drift. However, Fingers, who had now stepped out from within the shed, was indeed a master criminal; a legend in his own opinion, and was responsible for coordinating the masterly devious and diabolical acts the Banana Boys got up to. At least he thought so, and this is what he told people, even undercover police, but generally everyone knew he got a note from his mum telling him what to do, and the undercover police knew this as well. He was called Fingers, not because he had built up a reputation as a master safe cracker, though he did look like a Ryvita, skinny, with a Swedish crispbread, pockmarked complexion, but because he had six fingers on each hand, and he knew how to use them; he had the cleanest nose in all of Hither Green.

The Banana Boys usually met behind Fingers' dad's shed. Fingers' dad had disappeared a long time ago, and this shambling timber shanty was known as Fingers' dad's shed because it is universally believed Fingers' dad is buried beneath it. Seems he took exception to his wife shagging the south London criminal cognoscenti, who truly were master criminals, and not, as is often erroneously thought, the name of an Italian ice cream parlour. A common mistake, and one Fingers' dad is thought to have made, and as a consequence, had been beaten into a Mr Whippy Ninety-niner, a flake shoved through his heart, buried with dirt sprinkles on top, and then a shed. It was also widely believed he should have shut his mouth and settled for the black hat, which most also agreed would not have suited him as an officer in the Council Tax department of Hither Green Borough Council.

'I've 'ad a note from me mum,' Fingers said nasally, nervously jumping around and shrugging his shoulders, as is the hyperactive style of most shifty, naughty boy delinquents.

Brains and Shitlegs tittered. 'What?'

Fingers was irritated; not unusual, as Tom Jones, who as far as I am aware, did not know Fingers or his dad, but may have a black hat, would sing.

'Your mum?' Shitlegs said to Fingers. Shitlegs took his position as second-in-command and Banana spokesman seriously.

'Yeah, wot's wrong wiv that?' Fingers responded, flexing all twelve fingers, ready to make them extra wide fists.

The tittering grew, and Brains momentarily stopped his own shoulder-shrugging and feet-shuffling, as he thought he needed to get things moving along. His bus would be here soon, he had to be home for his dinner (lunch to you and me) and his mum was a tad south of the loving caring Fairy Mum you see on the telly. Brains knew it didn't do to let his fish fingers get cold. That, and he was scared of ghosts, and this shed was bound to have a ghost; stood to reason.

'We fort you got your instructions from Big-Knob, that's all?' Brains wobbled his head to reinforce his point, recommenced his own Ali shuffle, and embellished this with a gangstery-looking, nervy eye twitch.

'Big-Knob speaks to me mum and she tells me, see,' Fingers responded, looking angrily at Brains, not happy he had mentioned fish fingers. For a hoodlum, he could be quite sensitive.

'You'z sure Big-Knob's not just some bloke your mum's shagging?' Keef asked, adding some depth to the conversation, looking up to the sky, and knowing also that nobody knew who Big-Knob was, or whether he even existed, and then if he didn't, who was actually ordering them about. Fingers' mum?

Fingers got all upset. 'Me mum shags master criminals, it's what she does – der,' and he spread his spindly arms and waved about his extra-large mitts, in order to emphasise a point he considered should have been obvious.

The Banana Boys had forgotten that. They were each in their own way a lot like absent-minded professors, insomuch as they had a lot to think about, and quite often, the salient features of life on the street passed them by; charming when you think about it.

'What's Big-Knob want us to do, innit, anyways?' Brains asked, drawing on all the reserves of his demi-GCSE in arse-scratching, thinking he could also use a few extra fingers himself to dislodge some irritable detritus he was sure was a few days old now and he knew, instinctively, it should be removed; maybe he could have been a doctor?

Fingers drew himself up to his full pockmarked crisp-bread five-foot-two, and looked up to the contrastingly tall, moronic Banana Boys. 'Get yerself down ter Sowfsea now and get some bleedin' guns...' and he gestured with a few of his spare fingers to a white Transit van that had seen better days, '...in yer toffee-nosed aunt's gardin' and bring back some lolly as well, bowt free grand should do it.'

Brains knew this would mean trouble, and cold fish fingers, though he was careful not to speak out loud about his dinner. 'Why now, Fingers?'

'Cause Jack Austin's at the bleedin' Palace today and we can do it wivowt 'is nosy cow of a missus lookin' at us,' Fingers replied, convinced of the logic of the case, as well as mentioning, by way of a general conclusion, that it was an instruction passed on by Big-Knob, probably just before he went upstairs to shag his mum, everyone else presumed.

'What time is it?' Shitlegs asked, aware his mum would have his dinner (lunch) on the table soon.

'Wot's that got to do wiv the price of fish?' Fingers replied, edgy.

'Ow'd you know I was 'avin fish fingers?' Shitlegs responded, too late to stop his galloping gob.

Fingers dobbed him one in that errant mouth. See what I mean about being a baddy? Apart from the black hats.

'Just get yerself down there and do as yer bleedin' told,' Fingers finished off, and went back to clearing out his nose; he'd recently had a cold, comes to us all if we wear only a T shirt in the middle of winter, and it was an uphill struggle keeping it free of bogeys; life could be tough if you wanted to look hard.

'Who's drivin'?' Brains asked, thinking they should maybe get the show on the road. He was the clever one, and he discarded all thoughts of cold fish fingers.

'I'll drive,' Shitlegs said.

'You drove last time,' Brains said.

Fingers flicked a boulder bogey at Brains. 'You feckin' drive, just get on wiv it,' and the Banana Boys made their way to the van, Brains with his smarmy victory grin beaming through crooked, goofy teeth.

'If he's drivin', then I get to choose what we listen to on the radio, innit?' Shitlegs said.

Keef stepped in as Top Banana. 'Shut it, we're listening to Radio Four. Jeremy likes Radio Four, don't yer, Jeremy?' Keef looked at the only Banana that didn't look goofy or retarded. He radiated a posh persona to accompany his refined name.

Jeremy nodded affirmation of his preference for the intellectual radio channel, and Keef followed this up with, 'I wants to listen to *Desert Island Discs* anyways, before the *World at One*, innit,' and so it was agreed. Shitlegs drove and they listened to talkin'

45

radio all the way to Portsmouth. See what I mean about being a baddy – no lunch, and talking radio!

———

JIMBO HAD REPORTED to Del Boy that he suspected the safe house was being watched, and broke the bad news that Della had told him he should 'Pop Bef down ter Sowfsea'. Jimbo was an excellent mimic, besides being an outstanding MI5 minder. Del-boy was the MI5 field officer he reported to, and Del reported on to Dr Jim Samuels, the head of this section.

'She's recovering well. Extraordinary when you think about it, this brainwashing stuff,' Jimbo said in a conversational manner.

Del-Boy was irritated. He had a lot of time for Jimbo, but instinctively knew he had allowed him to associate with Jack Austin for too long, and furthermore, he was not comfortable with Della ordering people around, although he could see the sense in moving Beth Mayhew. Jack, and now Della, were viewed a little like nuclear radiation fall-out; you had to stick to the safe doses, and extended contact could be dangerous – a lot like sharing the bath water, Mandy had once openly opined, and to her surprise, everyone agreed.

'What?' Del-Boy had asked, never having shared the bath water with anyone except his mum, on a Sunday evening, just before *Sing Something Simple* on the radio, a banana sandwich, and an early night for school in the morning.

'What I mean,' Jimbo elucidated, 'is the girl who had ordered the beating-up of her dad was one nasty bitch. I hated her...' Jimbo said, of this daughter of Brian Mayhew, former Professor of Politics at the London School of Economics, a beloved daughter who was thought to have drowned off Southsea beach in Portsmouth. However, Beth had just dropped off the radar and become involved in the Fascist group that had sought to take over the Glory Hole subterranean, military command bunker in Portsmouth, to wreak what havoc MI5 could only guess at for the time being. A guess, until Beth could tell them the aims of the group, for it was becoming clear she was not a foot soldier, but an integral cog in a malicious hierarchy, and one that logically must still exist, although significantly weakened following their recent losses.

'Now though,' Jimbo continued, demonstrating a little emotional attachment to the terrorist girl, 'we can see beneath the surface. She was a girl who had allowed herself to be steered along a particularly deviant course,' Jimbo said, realising the interrogators and psyches were doing a similar brainwashing exercise, to not only bring the young woman back to a semblance of normality, but to take her the other side, to the polar extreme. In this way, it was thought she could help them. The irony was not lost on Jimbo, but he chose to ignore it. It was also thought they could not allow the observation of the safe house, leading MI5 back to others in this chain of deviant command; Jack's idea of course, and already Del-Boy and Jimbo suspected this had the hallmarks of a Jane Austin leak. Della knew it was a Jane Austin leak, because she knew Jack, and she had reacted; nobody leaks on her.

So, Jimbo was on his way to Portsmouth with Beth.

FOUR

Sigmund Merde didn't want to be here; what was he doing here? He didn't want to be anywhere, though he would prefer to be anywhere but here, but, he needed to be here. He leaned against the wall, hard, as if he were trying to press himself into and through the masonry, fingering the flock wallpaper as he did so, the nap, expensive, posh; he rubbed it like he used to do with felt and suede when he was a boy. His mother had given him some felt squares to stop him carrying his father's Hush Puppy shoes around with him, like a lost kid with a dog, and it was a comfort, and he still had one of the almost bare cloths. It had gone with him everywhere. His daughter also liked to do it; not that he had seen her in a very long while, and he wondered if she still sought that comfort. He wondered if she ever missed

49

him, and did she still have his spare felt square, the only thing he had been able to pass on to her?

She had been seven when he was taken, charged, found guilty, released on appeal, lost his medical licence, which, after a long time, had been reinstated; too late. He'd missed the last bit, because, after his wife had left him, taking their daughter away, and exasperated with the bureaucracy and the powers-that-be in their Ivory Towers, making decisions based not on facts or strength of belief, but bowing to popular public opinion, or what the banks or corporations wanted them to believe, whether right or wrong, and through their mouthpiece, the newspapers and media, he left the country.

Will Manfred had informed him later of his reinstatement and the return of his medical licence when they had met in Beirut, but by then he had his new life, doing things for people who appreciated it. Sigmund Merde went to wherever they needed his specialist medical skills; trauma. He was good; the very best, people had said, not that this saved him from disgrace, and wasn't that just like people? His mistake, if it was a mistake, was that he had used those skills on a terrorist who earlier that day had blown up a coach full of children. The terrorist, Ben Ali Azim, was thought to have survived after being treated by Sigmund Merde at his home, which would mean he was still out there somewhere, still plying his evil trade.

Merde didn't like that, but what was he supposed to do? He told people he was only doing what any doctor would, or should, do, "*Treat the body in front of him*", but his name became, ironically, *Shit*, and that was it. He often wondered what his wife had told his daughter, to explain why she had no dad. Did she think him a disgrace? Did she even know he was alive, or who he was? She would be fourteen now; a young woman.

'When I was little, I used to do that, Dr Merde. I find the texture and the sensation at my fingertips irresistible. My father, the King, did not approve.'

Sigmund looked at the Queen. She looked kind, understanding, with warm eyes that could not avoid gazing upon the red splatter staining on his morning suit and shirt. She sought an answer, so he answered.

'Sert net bin blerdy nutsplosh, yer materney,' Sigmund answered, and continued to worry the flock wallpaper.

The Queen had been briefed about the late guest at the Palace reception, this man of legendary magnificent skill and courage, a man who had turned his back on life in the *civilised* world. He had been in Iraq, Libya and most recently Syria, wherever his specialist skills were needed for ordinary people who needed help, but never expected it. He had been known as *Ghost*, an ephemeral *Pimpernel* like character, as he appeared to have the ability to drift, wraith-like, in and out of war zones unseen and unscathed, plying his merciful trade. He told anyone who could understand him, as he had also given up *civilised* language and spoke only a personalised Gibberish Esperanto, that he had only returned to this farce of a country that called itself civilised, because Jack Austin, whom the Queen knew only too well, had pleaded with him to return. He'd done enough, and there was unfinished business Jack wanted him to pursue, though with Jack Austin you never got a straight request.

The Queen could sense the man's pain and suffering as she looked upon Ghost's skeletal guise, a skull popped atop a tall, though hunched, bag of bones, held together by sun-scorched, leathery skin; old before his time, thin, straggly black hair atop a face smudged with a permanent charcoal five o'clock shadow.

'I'm so sorry, Dr Merde, I am not sure I understand you?' Ghost's Esperanto was not unlike the Jack Austin frontier gibberish. The Queen continued, undeterred by her lack of comprehension. 'I have, however, noticed you have not eaten. Can I ask someone to bring you something?'

Siggy looked at her, his sickly sallow eyes brimming; he had a permanent watery stare, glassy eyes that swivelled in a stationary head. 'Mench net dat feckin' shoite.' He may be an infamous Ghost, but he knew Jack Austin, and so naturally could speak Cod Irish, frontier gibberish, in a flourishing Esperanto manner.

The Queen looked around her, decidedly uncomfortable, and sought the only person she could think to help. *Heaven help one,* she thought. Her Majesty could roll her eyes and flick her head into the air and still keep the crown on; pretty amazing when you think about it. Practice, I suppose, though Jack said it was tied on with string, which was tucked under her Alice band, which was actually a cornet; the Royals loved ice cream, though generally eschewed the flake out of the head when at a function.

Mandy nudged Jack, who was distractedly looking back at his bum, so his "knickknack poncy food", as he called his canapés, nearly went flying. She did notice he securely held his champagne glass that incongruously sloshed an amber liquid. London Pride ale. They knew Detective Chief Inspector Jane Austin at the Palace. 'Go help Siggy and the Queen, Jack,' Mandy instructed, gesturing her head to where the Queen and a confused Equerry stood, 'and why do you keep looking at your bum?'

'She seems okay to me,' Jack said in reply, still distracted, wondering if he could change his feckin' champagne flute for a pint glass; he never could play an instrument, though he was very musical on a pint glass, and if he had practiced, he knew he would be a true proficient after a few pints. He chuckled to himself, thinking like Lady Catherine de Burgh out of *London Pride and Prejudice*, one of Jack's favourites (not Lady Catherine of course, she was a stuck-up, miserable mare), he would tell anyone who foolishly asked. Jack got his musical talent from his nan who used to play the tambourine with the Salvation Army in Bermondsey, South London, a century ago; remarkable how it lasted, really. 'You either have it or you don't,' he would say, speaking his thoughts.

'Listen, you bozo, you have no musical talent, and I'm convinced her Majesty knows no frontier gibberish,' Mandy responded, stating the obvious to Jack, who was still looking at his bum, and so missed Mandy flamboyantly gesturing head and hands toward Johnny, the Equerry, who in turn, was trying his best to interpret the gibberish, scratching his head and getting splinters from his posh woodentop skull.

Jack stopped looking at his backside, which coincided with his search for a pint glass, and as he scanned the reception room he could see the Queen wore a confused frown; not crown, that was quite clear and not at all confusing, Jack thought, amusing himself. He was quite amusing, to himself, and often made himself laugh. 'What a wag I am,' he would say, reinforcing his self-esteem that, believe it or not, hovered quite low, often on the floor; the effects of Post-Traumatic Stress Syndrome, PTSD, the psychiatrists said, not that Jack agreed with them. To him, the way he felt, and as a consequence behaved, was his mid-life crisis, which, if he could add up correctly, meant he would live to be at least one hundred and twenty, and he was quite pleased about that.

'You are not a wag, you're a bozo, and heaven help me and those in our care home if you live to be a hundred and twenty. Now, go and help the Queen, please,' Mandy repeated, menace in the "please".

'Heaven will help us, darlin', we have a Papal Blessing – der, (*See book 4 – Ghost and Ragman Roll*), and I was looking at me bum to see if it looked big in these round the houses,' and he left Mandy open-mouthed in astonishment as he went to rescue the Queen, as incongruous as that sounded here in Buckingham Palace where they were surrounded by soldiers, albeit they were in tart clothes as Jack Austin had wittily observed, unaware he looked a tart himself in his elephant's-arse morning suit, with tan leather brogues that were crippling him. The shoes were killing his plates of meat, he had explained to the Queen earlier, because he'd left them in the oven overnight to dry them out, and it was now like wearing a pair of cardboard boxes. Not that this would deflect Jack Austin, as he set about reintroducing juice back into the dehydrated clodhoppers.

Mandy did reflect, however, on the total incongruity of his attire, knowing his bum would look big in anything, and reflected on her life and all that had happened in the very short time she had been intimate with, and then married to, Jack Austin. They had been instrumental in relieving the country of gobshite politics, as Jack called it, which was in fact a complex conspiracy to bring the country to its knees, fiscally and spiritually, and it had very nearly succeeded. Then she thought, why was she reflecting when she should be over there, rescuing the Queen herself, not from Ghost but from Jack, as she saw him put his arm across the shoulder of the Monarch, and being a consommé lip reader, saw him lift the crown a bit so he could whisper a suggestion into the Royal ear that they should 'maybe bugger off somewhere for a pint and some proper grub.' She meant consummate, but, as everyone knows, if you share the bath water with someone you can catch some very nasty things, like *Austin Malacopperism*; a rare disease, but getting less rare. How many people bathed with Jane Austin? Probably Darcy, maybe even Bingham, but definitely not Wickham.

'Baths are dangerous, Mandy,' Father Mike said, and she realised she had also been caught speaking her thoughts out loud, as well as all the other *feckin' eejit* stuff Jack did, but she loved him; didn't she? Maybe she should not bathe with him quite so much? Give her eyes a rest as well, and she tittered to herself at that reflected thought.

———

BETH MAYHEW WAS NOW on her way down to Portsmouth, having been held and treated in an MI5 safe house in the Hammersmith area of West London. Jackie Philips travelled up from Portsmouth on the train and visited Beth three or four times a week, to reinforce the programme of treatment that had been showing signs of success; Jackie becoming a female anchor that was intended to be a mainstay for Beth while she readjusted to a normal life – whatever that may hold for her in the future, as she had been instrumental in some diabolical acts that needed to be answered in a criminal court, unless MI5 could use her, naturally.

Beth was talking of her involvement in what was believed to be a fascist conspiracy, and Jackie worried that the twenty-two-year-old former student of politics was showing no remorse; she needed to work more on this if they were to redress the balance of her mind. This was Jackie's priority, but she knew Jack Austin wanted more, and she batted him away in her consummate way. Dr Philips knew Jack Austin well, but had drawn the line at sharing the bath water with him. Jack never lost any sleep over this deprivation in the bathing department, as Jackie, who was a tall and lithe, attractive, mid-forties black woman, was gay. "She is from the Isle of Lesbos after all", he would say, though he did think she might reconsider her sexuality if she did take that bath with him – least this is what he told Mandy, who drew on all of the spiritual sustenance their Papal blessing could provide, before clumping her dozy husband.

He didn't even lose sleep when Mandy told him of the reports that the Hammersmith house was being watched, and she wondered, not for the first time, if he had leaked the whereabouts of the house. Her husband was, after all, a *consommé leaker*, and she did wonder if she should maybe get him into incontinence pants.

Jackie or Mandy, or even Jack for that matter, at that time, did not know that Beth was en route to Portsmouth.

FIVE

MARTIN TURNED HIS NOSE UP AT THE DRIED FOOD that was *good* for him. Meesh thought he looked funny; not the result the small, intelligent, Border Terrier wanted, and he shrank back into his wiry, scruffy, ginger hair and applied his sulky face that he had learned from Jane Austin. Martin, in addition to being an accomplished actress, was a small dog with a massive heart and, like his former master, Jack Austin, the terrier lived in his own dream world where he was bigger, braver, and better looking than he actually was. Having said that, the Queen had recently awarded Martin the *George Bone,* a dog bravery award, and later that same day, as if to prove to any doubters, he had chewed the bollocks off a particularly nasty pirate, Captain Pugwash RN, who had shot at his mistress and master outside the Albert Hall.

Martin had been particularly annoyed with the errant naval officer, not just for wounding Amanda, but principally for delaying the Prom concert he had been looking forward to; Tchaikovsky's Violin Concerto, and played by his favourite soloist, Alexander Pantsoff. Well, there was an orchestra, but Martin ignored them; he was a typical dog in that respect, though he was not averse to weeing up the rostrum, which he viewed as his territory and felt that, on occasion, he needed to mark it so other dogs who enjoyed classical music would be aware.

Looking up at the waif Meesh from his bowl of balanced and healthy, shite, dog food, Martin gave the little girl his best *so what can I tell yer* look, and woofed, *d'yer fink it's easy?* He was a dog who was always ready, at the drop of a lead, to go to New York and so regularly practiced his best Brooklyn Jewish whenever he could. So, you might say, this was a dog who was as bonkers as his former master, and the fact that former master and hound were to be reunited very soon, ought to have sent waves of vigilance around the City of Portsmouth at least, if not further afield, and Jack had wanted to take Martin to the Palace with him. He could see nothing wrong with the notion, and although Martin wasn't a horse, though he did eat like one, even shite dried food, Jack thought the Queen had taken a shine to Martin and as The Duke of Edinburgh was very old, he would likely have forgotten that Martin had wee'd on the trousers of the Duke's morning suit; but then, seen in a providential light, the Duke did look a lot like a rostrum.

Martin also loved *Pride and Prejudice*. Jack had explained to Prince Philip, as the Prince wafted his trouser leg with a practiced amount of flare (not flares – heaven forbid, Royal flares!) that Martin was just marking his territory and as most of the people at the palace were posh, their noses would be higher in the air than normal people so they would likely not smell anything. "Ipso facto", he had concluded, using Welsh, in case Phil wanted to tell the Prince of Wales.

Mandy had, however, put her foot down, and since Jack's size twelve feet stuck out at a quarter to three, it landed on his already dodgy and directionless toes. Jack had argued that since Martin was to spend a fortnight with them, it was not unreasonable his former dog should accompany them to the Palace. Meesh and her newly adopted huge family, the Splifs, were off on a much needed Christmas holiday; funded by Jack and Mandy, as the Splifs, Gail and Mickey had not a brass farthing to rub together. Jack, distracted as always, argued that if Gail had rubbed her legs together a bit tighter, they might not have eleven kids, to whom they now added the newly adopted Meesh.

"But that's Roman Candles for you", Jack would say knowledgeably, speaking as a Roman Catholic himself and having married a Catholic, in a Catholic cathedral, and received a Papal Blessing, and this perplexed a lot of people as Jack Austin told whoever was crazy enough to ask and even those who could not give a toss, he was C of E (Church of Egypt), and their principle faith was Denial (De Nile), *naturellement*, aah so, ipso facto in facto, as the Nippon Welsh say.

Jack had thoughtfully replied to the Holy Father, thanking him for the blessing, mentioning they had put it on the mantelpiece behind the clock and Mandy was going to get a frame for it but kept forgetting, and requesting the Pope not bother replying if he was going to advise Mandy to rub her legs together too tightly. He signed off, *S'laters, from your old Arsey (RC) mucker, Jane.* And this was the explanation as to why Jack always intercepted the post, in case the Pope replied and had ignored his request about Mandy keeping her legs together. But he needn't have bothered, as the Pope e-mailed a response to Mandy, not mentioning her legs, as Popes were not aware that ladies had legs or even naughty bits, and recommended a local loony bin that Father Mike and Jack could go to, to be safe, and spiritually sound. He was thinking of the people in Portsmouth being safe and sound, concerned that if word got around that Jack was a Roman Catholic, the church would start to haemorrhage members.

Martin was also a Catholic, but Meesh was not thought to be, not yet, anyway. Nobody knew anything about the girl. Jack had rescued her from a sordid house run by Nazi paedophiles, a house that had been her torture chamber and where she had witnessed the murder of her mother. Jack and the girl had bonded from the moment he had hugged her filthy, skeletal and naked frame to his body and taken her from the house, and it was the natural earth-mothering instinct of the Hagrid-shaped *Angel of bandit territory*, Gail Splif, who had offered the girl something she had never known before; a safe home, a family and, most importantly, unconditional love. It was a huge, very much non-bandit, loving family, and within this Splif council house, set in the middle of bandit territory in Portsmouth, Meesh had been absorbed naturally, and felt very much a Splif.

The psychiatrist, Jackie Philips, kept a continual careful eye on the waif, always concerned for the trauma the little girl had suffered – not that Jack could see this, as he felt the girl was "bleedin' marvellous now" (said in his posh voice – he used posh talk to trick cyclists – they expected it, they had GCSE's and things), and surprisingly the girl did seem to be okay. Meesh had responded to the cockney oaf, Mandy's reassurances, and the Splifs' love; the girl felt safe and cared for, but it was Martin who had become her life raft and emotional anchor.

There was an irony there, as Martin had previously been Jack Austin's dog, following the recommendation of the police trick cyclists that he should have an ever-present pet, to help calm his notorious bouts of berserking; the mist would rise and Jack would completely lose control. However, there was no evidence Martin had helped on that score, as the dog would, more often than not, wade in to support his master whenever the occasion arose. Martin, although intelligent and perceptive, refused to accept he was a mollycoddling, pansy-arsed hound, as he told the vet trick cyclist. He was, in point of fact, an action-packed police dog, and he also knew that he was a spook, which would of course explain everything, but he could not tell anyone about this, especially a vet; anyone who would squeeze a dog's anal glands had to be treated in a circumspect manner.

He had mentioned it once to a bitch he had met and since he was, what they call in the spook dog world, intact, he had wanted to bring his new lady friend home to meet Jack and Mandy, and maybe, well, you know what I mean. Although Jack was all for it, Mandy was not happy with the parentage of the bitch and considered a cross between a Border Ter-

rier and a Rhodesian Ridgeback would not necessarily present a particularly satisfactory outcome,
even though Martin had arranged for an orange box
and assured them he could remain steady behind his
bitch while he did the biz, so to speak.

Martin had sulked, just as Jack did after he had read
the e-mail from the Pope; Mandy had been too late to
erase the bit where the Papal Father had signed off,
*God Bless and keep your legs together, for the sake of
all humanity*. The Pope didn't realise it was not relevant advice as Mandy was well and truly into the
menopause, which was not very pleasant for her, but
Jack thought it was "no sweat", as he would say amusingly and frequently, mainly to himself; but Jack
knew Popes were known for spoiling all the fun, so he
had to be on his guard. However, the cautionary
papal counsel would have been better employed advising Della Lovington, who was certainly not averse
to rubbing her legs together so long as Jonas was in
between them, and she was also beginning to suspect
they had not been particularly careful in their
coupling.

Anyway, Martin knew the holiday camp the Splifs
were going to did not allow dogs, and after a week or
two of sulking, he accepted that a fortnight and
Christmas with the Austins might be okay, though he
was mightily pissed off when he heard he wouldn't be
going to the Palace, as there was a corgi he quite fan-

cied. Martin had missed his police dog role and knew also that Jack, he called him Jack now, not Jane, as he was not his master anymore, was concerned there was trouble ahead, and sensed, as only a trained dog can (not that Martin was trained, that was for Nancy boy dogs, Martin relied on natural instinct), he would be needed.

Mandy was a good bitch and she was, after all, a Detective Superintendent, but Martin instinctively knew she was not in his league. Martin knew also that Jack could not see this, as he was an eejit, and so starry-one-eyed where Mandy was concerned that he was often blind to what was going on right in front of his face. This had also been a part of Martin's previous role, to look after Jack when his one eye had been *off the ball*; a regular occurrence, and this still rankled with Martin. Could Jack not see this was how he felt about Rosie the Ridgeback? The bloody hypocrisy, and Martin knew this, being a dog of the world, except in this one area, that is.

SIX

BERYL SEXTON REFLECTED ON MATTERS OVER A cup of breakfast tea. Sigmund Merde had popped down to Portsmouth with a couple of Mandarins during the night. They had kept the two Senior Civil Servants in the chapel overnight, with Siggy monitoring, keeping them semi-comatose, sufficiently aware for them to comprehend the music that played over and over, and for him to mention Education is the *silver bullet* and you mess around with Transport, the arteries of a country, at your own peril, and never sell the *family silver* as a way of feathering your own nests. He spent a considerable amount of time explaining how their plotting and machinations in the corridors of power can affect others, not least himself; these two Mandarins had fully supported Dr Merde's ostracising.

Merde had arranged for the Mandarins to be insulated, prepared for when he wanted them displayed on top of the Banks Mausoleum, the very mausoleum that had been used by the Fascists as a base HQ in their plot to gain access to the Glory Hole; now, that was an irony he looked forward to seeing.

Siggy, and now Jack, were aware this was not a Fascist plot, but extremists everywhere can be manipulated, and nobody knew this better than Sigmund Merde, who had been in the strife-torn parts of the Middle East where *incited* factions fought each other, and, the innocent paid the tragic price. The folly of uncompromising, egotistical belief angered Sigmund Merde, and he could not dismiss it as blind faith either, faith in something unknown, intangible, but a faith that nevertheless insisted normally reasonable people carry out the most heinous of acts. For Merde, it was wise to doubt, foolish to not doubt, and this he told to the two Mandarins, and just so they would remember, he wrote it down in a note and pinned the message to their underpants, just before he left them on top of the Mausoleum as he had to go to the Palace.

———

'OI, RAYMOND BLEEDIN' Blanc, use yer frog legs and 'op over ere wiv some peanut butta, couple of bread vans, mayo and some beetroot, oh, and *free* pints of London Pride while yer at it; spit-spot,' Jack ordered. He felt the need to explain to the Queen, since she appeared overwhelmed, which was not un-usual in Jack's presence, 'Got yer a pint, give us that pansy-arse drink you've got...' and Jack took the Queen's champagne flute, '...I'll chuck it down the sink,' and he did, pleased he'd got the Royal kitchen doing something proper, and all with his *Mary Poppins* magic, and settled down for a bit of sandwich-making, a decent pint, and a chinwag with Siggy and Her Majesty.

This was Jack Austin, barrow boy in residence at the Palace, speaking his own thoughts and Malacop-perisms. He also quoted a lot of films (it's okay, the Queen was aware of Jack's quirks and propensities), TV shows, *Pride and Prejudice* of course, and he quoted everything, generally all wrong and out of context, which contributed to the likeability of the fella, most thought, and if they didn't, he told them so, then they did. However, Mandy, who had just caught Jack up after he'd made a dash from the reception room to the kitchens, dragging the Queen and Ghost with him, thought he was just a loveable feckin' eejit, whether in residence or not, but she knew that in his head, though the lights appeared on most of the time, rarely was anybody home.

'Yes he is, but he's One's feckin' eejit,' the Queen said, enjoying Mandy speaking her thoughts. The Queen, as part of her Royal training, had been briefed on the risks of sharing bath water, and now, with a pint of London Pride in hand, and seeming to quite enjoy the fruity flavours of her capital city's local ale, she observed; the master sandwich maker, by Royal Appointment, Jack informed her, was at work. The Queen watched on, only mildly revolted as it was clear Jack Austin had "a Klingon on the starboard bow" he explained, "a bit of dirt in his eye", although she could have worked it out for herself as his bum wiggled and scratched itself remotely on the corner of a nearby stainless steel counter, which he explained away as "a bit of body popping, darlin'".

A soldier, in his fairy costume and a large pike (not a fish, as that would wiggle and not frighten anyone, although they have a lot of sharp teeth, I think – I need to check my book *I-Spy Fish with big Hampstead Heaths*) in his hand, tapped Jack on the shoulder but looked to the Queen. 'Excuse me Ma'am,' and he nodded to the Queen like she was an insurgent and should not be in her own kitchen, then flicked his eyes back to Jack. 'Sir, you have no right to be here, and we will have to ask you to leave.' General Chaos did not look at all confident in his military assertion or in his poncy uniform, and continued to flick looks to the Queen, then back to Jack.

The Queen turned to her Equerry, smiled her conspiratorial Jane Austin smile she had learned from Jack (omitting the gobshite bit, she'd not quite mastered that yet and Jack made a mental note to teach her), and said, 'Johnnie, be a dear and tell this soldier chap I would like to be alone with Dr Merde and Mr. and Mrs. Austin please, there's a good man, spit-spot.' And to Jack she added, 'There's no need to teach me the gobshite look, Jack, Prince Philip does it well enough for the both of us,' and the Queen tittered right royally.

'Did I...?' The Queen, Mandy and Ghost both nodded, but Jack ignored this, thinking to himself it must be arseycratic nonsense, likely due to in-bleeding, and he began to cut doorsteps out of the loaf, wondering if he could use the end of the pike staff judicially on his itchy backside without anyone noticing or it appearing fishy; well, it was a pike. (Incidentally, for those of an academic bent, a pike does have teeth and if you want to check, it's on page 39 of *I-spy fish with big Hamsptead Heaths,* under the section, *Bottom Feeder*, which Jack could have used right now, coincidentally).

The Queen watched on nervously, secretly hoping Jack would leave his bottom alone, as the one-eyed dipstick lined the bread slices up, ironically, in military fashion, and began spreading liberal amounts of crunchy peanut butter. He then licked the knife and stuck it in the catering-sized jar of mayonnaise, splurged that on the regimented line of doorsteps, licked the knife again and 'mmm'd', then paused, thinking the Queen was maybe starting to look a little green around the jewels.

'Don't worry, sweet'art, all comes out in the wash...' he said and continued, opening the jar of sliced beet-root. 'Beetroot, yer majesty?' He didn't wait for a reply and, with a giant's fork and judicious use of his fingers, he added sliced pickled beetroot, licked the fork, wondered why his fingers were all red, wiggled them at the Queen and gave his best macabre, ghoulish and very scary 'woo-hah', so it looked like he had stained his fingers deliberately, for a joke, but he had to curtail his jokes as there were more pressing matters. He put on the doorstep lids and pressed down. The mayo squidged out the sides, to be scooped up by Jack's stained finger and sucked away. He always kept a hand spare for pressing down; you never knew when anything might need pressing, like Mandy's breasts for instance. The finger was kept spare for his nose and, of course, in the event *Mayo Royale* needed scooping up.

'Jack, please.' The voice wasn't Mandy's, although it could have been, it was Her Majesty's.

'Sorry, darlin', didn't just speak me forts, did I?' said Jack, harrumphing.

'Jack, I would like to talk with Mr Merde, if you would oblige me with your translation of frontier gibberish, please,' the Queen asked, just managing to stop the peanut butter and beetroot sandwich from falling onto the floor. Jack had slid the plate over to her like a Saspirilly on a saloon counter in a cowboy film, with just a tad more force than it really needed, saying, 'There yer go, sweet'art Yer Majesty, get yer laughin' gear round that...' adding, chuckling to himself, '...good catch,' as he realised how he often underestimated how strong he was. Now, that did raise a smile. 'Did I...?' Jack ignored the giggling Monarch as he was starving, having only had poncy food.

'Them nancy-boy canopies would fill nobody up,' Jack said, as he took great lumps out of his Scooby Doo sandwich. He looked at the Queen and Mandy. 'Nem emp tin, luv?' he said, through a mouthful of peanut butter, mayo, beetroot and doorstep bread, which he swigged down with a guzzle of London Pride, and repeated himself, as the Queen didn't seem to quite get the gist. '"Not eating" is what I said; difficult to speak as the peanut butter's crunchy, know what I mean? Sticks to the inside of yer norf an sowf.'

The Queen said she did understand, but her face said she didn't, not that this bothered Jack.

'Shove it over 'ere, luv, if you're not eating it,' and the Queen shoved it, Saspirilly-style, back to Jack but on his blind side – *crash*. 'What was that?' Jack said, eliciting great mirth from Mandy and the Queen and horror from the kitchen staff and various military fish handlers.

Ghost had his nose in the sandwich, looking like this was his first Jack sandwich for a very long time. 'Not eating that, sweet'art?' Mandy looked down at her own untouched sandwich, shook her head and Jack took it; she tried not to show how relieved she was. Jack took her pint also. The Queen, God bless her royal heart and hereditary Hanoverian cotton socks, was drinking hers. She liked London Pride – well, she would; it was her capital city so it was a capital idea, except when she was in Balmoral, he supposed.

'I do like London Pride, Jack, and when in Balmoral, one has a tipple of Glenmorangie.'

'Not bad stuff, but you need to have a go at the Dog's Bollix, lubbly jubbly that,' Jack replied to the Queen, thankfully not with his mouth full, Mandy thought, relieved. "Cept I prefer Len Satsuma.' He chuckled at his Glenmorangie joke and nudged the Queen, who spilt some ale down her royal frock. 'Nah, just kiddin'' Jack said, brushing the back of his hand down the front of the Queen's frock and licking the residue. He knew that with Royal frocks, you always use the back of your hand so nobody thinks you're copping a royal feel. See, Jack knew royal protocol; well, he would, as he'd been to the Palace many times before.

Jack switched to cod Irish. 'I loikes a dropeen of Jameson's meself...' adding in his thoughts, *don't tell the feckin' IRA*. He did laugh at that one. Well, it was funny, or so he thought, and on many fronts, not least the Queen's.

Mandy felt she should stop this hurtling train crash. 'Ma'am, you wanted to talk with Siggy?'

'I did, thank you, Mandy. Sigmund, may I call you that?' the Queen asked.

'Yarp,' Siggy replied, having watched *Hot Fuzz* with Jack on the few occasions he was back in the country, apparently. When Jack tells you something, you have to take it with a generous pinch of salt, as Fireguard says, though this did sound like the sort of thing Jack would do, and with Siggy, and Fireguard too, had he been alive and not in Denmark.

The Queen continued, unabashed, except where Jack had nudged her in a bashful way. 'Well, err, Siggy, although one was not expecting you today, I am glad you came along. I am sorry that until recently, I was unaware of your story and indeed your plight.'

Jack sneaked Siggy's pint as the Ghost's rheumy eyes watered more than usual.

'I have now been briefed and it is quite an extraordinary story. I am convinced there is no way we, that is my government and I, can make this up to you, but rest assured...'

The Queen was interrupted by an agitated Equerry. 'Ma'am, I am so sorry to interrupt, but we may need the services of the doctor. The Permanent Secretary to the Home Office has collapsed.'

Ghost leapt from his stool, Jack nicked what was left of the Doctor's sandwich and with his mouth full, and continuing to drink Siggy's pint of beer, he followed, mentioning he would carry the doctor's drink and food for him. But nobody was fooled by that, and Jack sauntered on, stopping occasionally for a munch and a sup.

'Not in any hurry, Jack?' Mandy asked, as the Queen overtook them both on the outside rail. Mandy knew her man, and she looked at him askance. 'You know what has happened, do you not... Jack?'

Jack looked at his wife and, spluttering ale and sandwich which she brushed from her emerald-coloured dress with the back of her hand, before Jack could do it with the front of his, he said, 'Do you not...' mimicking her manner of speech, '... Uncle Josh, sweet'art?

And yes, I know. I heard Siggy arranging for the band (a string quartet), after about half an hour of us disappearing, to play the theme from Shostakovich's Piano Concerto Number 2, the second movement. Shall we go, darlin'?' and Mandy followed the trail of crumbs, beetroot bits and splashed London Pride.

They arrived into the reception hall to see the guests collected at one end, and on the floor, adjacent to a rather shocked string quartet, was Quentin Bryant, his rotund belly facing heavenward, a lot like Glastonbury Tor. Laid out, the Permanent Secretary to the Home Office was toes-up, his strands of matted hair having fallen away from a clammy pate. Ghost was thumping his chest rhythmically. Jack sauntered up and shoved Johnny the Equerry to one side with a judicious sideswipe of his generously padded hip.

Johnny reacted. 'Excuse me, Mr Austin, you had better stay back.'

Jack farted. He was not going to be told what to do by a toffee-nosed Palace twat, which was of course one of his major failings, that and farting inappropriately. 'It's okay, my old son, I know what this is.'

'You do?' the concerned Equerry replied nasally.

Siggy looked up at Jack momentarily, a twinkle in his watery eye; Jack had missed that mischievous look.

'Yeah, do...' Jack replied, '... it's *Doctor Who*, if I'm not mistaken?' he said, in his *do you not*, posh voice and looked to Mandy for recognition whilst he hummed the tune and everyone could see Ghost pounding the Mandarin's chest to the *Time Lord* rhythm.

Siggy acknowledged it was *Dr Who*, and was well spotted. 'Eet es ack, ellsparted,' he said.

Quentin Bryant was stirring, showing signs of blood returning to his corpulent chops that wobbled to the *Tardis* theme. Jack smiled. He was good at *Dr Who*. Siggy lowered his ministering head to the Permanent Secretary's blimp Mandarin face, and whispered something into a cauliflower ear; the shock was patent on the face that now looked like a wrinkly balloon where some of the air had been let out.

He then issued an order to the equerry, 'Bertyet vac heliobonce, Tonto,'

All eyes turned to Jack, who said nothing as he was too busy bathing in his recent musical success, wondering if he could join the band, and if they had a spare tambourine. So Mandy answered for everyone. 'Medivacuum helicopter, pronto-tonto,' she said, no mean interpreter of frontier gibberish herself, having married a frontier gibbering eejit.

Johnny was onto her like a shot, 'Do you mean Medicav Helicopter, Superintendent?'

'That's what I said, diddli?' she said thinking, diddle I...? *The bath water again.*

SEVEN

It was close on lunchtime when Della surfaced. Jonas was dozing and she looked out of their bedroom window across to Eastney cemetery then flipped her head back to the wounded and exhausted Jonas. 'Babes, there's a couple of bodies in the cemetery.'

Jonas, though drowsy, managed a pitifully painful laugh, his giggling, jiggling his throbbing bullet wounds. He wondered if they would ever heal, but even wounded, he could not resist the lovemaking ministrations of his beautiful Della.

'It is a cemetery, my love,' and he chortled into his pain.

Della rubbed her chin thoughtfully and gazed upon her Gypo. 'Leave the jokes to me, Jonas darlin'. Yer luvvly, but yer ain't got wot it takes, sweet'art,' she responded, shaking her head in a Della loving fashion, which said to anyone else observing, it was a *God save me from feckin' country bumpkin amateurs.*

She walked to her phone on the bed stand, sat on the bed and as she speed-dialled, her spare hand drifted below the sheets to Jonas's bits and pieces, which she fondled as she hummed a discordant tune. Jonas could not help himself. 'Blimey, you cannot hold a tune, are you sure you're not Jack's long-lost daughter?'

Della giggled, thought for a bit, but was needed to respond to an impatient squawking coming from the telephone receiver. 'Jo darlin', it's Della, sweet'art...' as if she needed to identify her voice to Jo-Jums. 'Look, getta coupla woodentops down to Eastney cemetery, will yer, and set up a crime scene, there's a luv. I fink there's two bodies lying on top of a tomb when they should be under it,' and she offered her beaming face to Jonas so he might admire her even more.

Jo responded and not immediately in the affirmative. Della set her straight. 'Look, Jo, I'll see yer down there when it's all set up. I can't do it meself, can I?

I've got some serious fucking to do, yer dozy mare,' and she hung up.

Jonas sighed, and not for the first time wondered if he could keep up with this woman he loved. And what was this about the bodies on a tomb? But one thing lead to another and the bodies, the lifeless ones that is, were forgotten as Jonas ouched into action.

'Christ all bleedin' mighty, Jonas, you're worse than a baby, and 'ere I am, doin' all the feckin' work again.'

———

JUST AS JONAS APPEARED DOWNSTAIRS, Jimbo arrived at the Gravediggers pub escorting Beth Mayhew. The two men acknowledged one another as Jonas took in the look of Beth, a frail lass with a haunted look and black-rimmed eyes, and thought it was hard to see how this diminutive, fragile, spidery girl could have been so vicious and cruel. Della had explained to him, with as much patience as she could muster, which was not much, the effectiveness of brain-washing.

She went on to explain Beth had not necessarily been aware she was being so cruel to her own father, who was still in hospital recovering from a severe beating carried out under Beth's orders, while she watched on, unfeeling, insensitive to the fact that it was her father, someone she had loved and adored as a child, being beaten to within an inch of his life. Whether her father would survive was still unknown. Brian Mayhew had almost drunk himself into an early grave before he was nearly beaten into it by his daughter's henchmen. Jack had said to Jackie he wanted Beth to get better as soon as possible so she could sit by her father's hospital bed; the man lived for his daughter.

Jimbo had the appearance of a full-size either *Ant or Dec*, nobody knew which, as Will, who had been Jimbo's MI5 partner and widely thought to be *Ant*, had been killed in a rocket attack outside Downing Street. Jimbo was not even sure if he knew who *Ant or Dec* were, for that matter. He had missed *I'm a Celebrity... Get Me Out of Here*, missed working with Will, and to date had remained a lone operator and felt this was how he wanted it to remain. It was, however, looking increasingly likely that Della would pair up with him operationally, and he was not sure how he felt about that, either. Della had a rep, and it wasn't one of placid operational karma; she was also known to prefer working alone.

'Della's just taking a shower, Jimbo,' Jonas said, but was distracted as a uniformed police officer stepped into the pub, followed up by a comfortably plump, short woman, who looked like she might own the place any minute, and then she did.

The squat, stout woman spoke. 'Jimbo, how are you...?' She didn't wait for an answer, 'Jonas, I presume?' she said, looking at the giant Gypo, 'I am D.I. Wild, known as Jo-Jums. Can you get Della down here, pronto-tonto, please?'

Jonas looked like a huge Gypo rabbit caught in copper headlamps. 'Err, she's in the shower... err, Jo-Jums.'

'Well, get her out,' Jo answered forcibly, though she ameliorated the vigour by sloping her head in a manner she often adopted with her children, and more than adequately demonstrated she was not intimidated by the size and presence of Jonas, or Jimbo.

Jo-Jums stood four-square and waited. Nothing happened. Jo metaphorically tapped her fingers; this woman was most accomplished and could tap her fingers irritably with her face, for a little while at least. Jo exploded. 'Get her down here now!' Then she calmed and applied an apologetic face that wouldn't fool anyone. 'Please,' she added.

'Alright, alright, keep yer girdle on, Jo, I'm 'ere now.' Della appeared, hair wet, dressed in jeans and a sloppy sweater, and despite her slovenliness, Jonas thought she looked gorgeous, a bit like a young Goldie Hawn. Jo, on the other hand, thought, *how can some women not give a toss and look great?* Jo was a woman who had to work at everything, but was grounded enough to know this is what suited her, what she was comfortable with.

A siren sounded and Jo took great pleasure in the confused look on Della's face. 'Sirens, Jo?' Della asked.

Jo Jums answered the look for everyone. 'Ambulance, not bodies, Della, though they could have been any minute, it's so 'effing cold out there. Two men, middle-aged, unconscious, probably drugged, and they look like they come from a comfortable lifestyle, so we have a conundrum...?' Jo finished off, talking to herself as Della flew out of the pub door, waving her phone and calling back to Jonas to get a fry-up on.

Jo turned on her heels, not so sprightly, and followed on, calling out, 'Della, what are you doing...' and then, '... are you only just having breakfast?'

Della flew across the road, dodging traffic, dashed into the cemetery and headed to where she could see the police cordon, following close on the heels of two paramedics. Jo caught up as Della remonstrated with two constables who did not know her. They were about to get a double-barrelled introduction when Jo lifted the tape and announced, in a now calm and assured voice, though short of breath, 'This is D.I Lovington.' It was enough, and Della stepped through unmolested, though did offer a passing "ner" to the plods.

'Thanks, Jo. Could of 'andled the woodentops meself, yer know.' Della did not wait for a response but barged past the paramedics, took photos with her phone, stepped away and allowed the medics to get to work. She tapped away at the phone and then tapped away with her feet whilst blowing a fog of breath into her fisted hands. 'Feck me, it's taters out 'ere.'

Miraculously, Jonas appeared and wrapped Della in a gigantic sheepskin coat. She cranked her neck and looked adoringly up into the eyes of her Gypo. 'Thanks, love,' she murmured, squeezing his bits and pieces affectionately, eliciting an appreciative smile in response. 'Now, aren't you supposed to be getting me eggs an' bacon?' She looked around, 'Not much more 'ere. Fancy a fry-up, Jo?' Della did not wait for an answer, it was all academic to her, she was going back to the warmth of the pub and a hearty breakfast, and then she needed to sort Jimbo and Beth, but not before she had worked out who the two ice men were.

Jo replied to the rapidly disappearing sheepskin coat, because you could not see Della below the massive garment, 'I'll do the police work then, shall I?'

'If you wouldn't mind, sweet'art. Admin and all that stuff never was my fing,' a throwaway aside as Della detoured and went to see Seb in his shed.

She knocked on the shed door and heard, 'Sexton's Detective Agency,' Seb's sonorous response. Jack had taught him that; he had to do something, didn't he.

'Seb darlin', it's me, Della. Open up, there's a luv, it's feckin' taters-in-the-mould out 'ere,' Della called, stamping her feet and blowing smoke rings with her breath. The door opened and Seb appeared with his cleaning materials in his hand. Della knew the score and stepped inside, removed her trainers for Seb to clean, and then for him to polish away the non-existent marks she had made with her knitted-socked feet, as she padded to his computer array.

On his hands and knees, Seb looked up to where Della stood. He waited, and she looked down. 'I'm not moving from 'ere, luv.' She handed her phone to Seb. 'Do me a flavour, will yer, run these snaps for me. I e-mailed them to yer. Let me know who they are, there's a darlin'.'

Seb stood and put the cleaning stuff down in the allocated place and sat at his computers. Jonas popped his head around the door. 'How long before you want breakfast, Della?'

Della did not look up. 'Give it a mo, and sweet'art,' she looked at him now, 'be a luv and pop along to the chemist and get a pregnancy kit, pretty please with brass injuns on top.'

Jonas stared, open-mouthed. 'Close yer north and sowf, we're not a feckin' codfish,' Della chipped, cod Irish, *Liza Doolittle - Mary Poppins,* she was good, well trained by Jack, 'and shut the bleedin' door after yer, there's a George Raft up me bottle and glass,' and she waved him off.

The computer pinged and Della leaned over, maintaining station with her feet, to see the faces on the screens, recognising them as the two, not quite dead, stiffs. Seb read out the description but Della had already read it. 'Crispin Evens, Department of Transport and Bartholomew Bozoquet, Department of Education.'

'Two senior Mandarins...' Della whispered to herself, hands on hips as she leaned in closer, not expecting a response from Seb, but she got one nevertheless.

'Jack has asked me to monitor the Whitehall Mandarins.'

'He has?' Her questioning face rapidly turned to an angry head. 'Why didn't he tell me?'

'Because you said he was past it,' Seb replied, matter-of-fact, and sent a message to Jack and Mandy.

'Wot you just done?'

'Now Jack knows and you know, so perhaps you will both stop behaving like children and get working on this. I believe this is serious, and I also think someone is about dismantling the Civil Service. Why, who knows, and what is he, they, planning to replace it with?' Seb thought for a bit, then in a quiet and considered manner, added, 'Or... is this just for amusement?' He shook his head, uncomprehending.

'Amusement?' Della was shocked back into a semblance of normality. You rarely heard this type of comment from Seb, but clearly he was onto something. Della pondered, likely tidying up after Jack. Seb had stumbled upon something... thought some more ... and it was serious. 'I'm sorry, Seb,' and she kissed his cheek, 'you're right. I'll be a good girl.'

Seb knew this was not likely to happen but reacted, also unusually for him; he stood up and kissed Della's cheeks. Mandy had taught Seb, who had no comprehension of social skills, to hug or kiss someone he liked, and that was it.

Della left the shed with Seb cleaning up behind her, and she headed back to sort out Jonas, who must be wondering what was happening as she'd not told him when she wanted breakfast and then there was the pregnancy test; though that should be obvious, and Della knew she would likely have to call a family meeting. It was time she met them all anyway, she thought.

EIGHT

IT WAS CLOSE TO NINE THIRTY IN THE EVENING
when the Banana Boys arrived in Portsmouth on a
bleak and dark winter's night, the timing of which,
though not planned, as they had expected to arrive
mid-afternoon, suited their clandestine mission. Well,
it suited their furtiveness, but the wintry conditions
hampered them very much in their frozen proverbial
clandestines. They did have clothing for winter
weather, their mums insisting they wear vests, and
had fleeces with hard-nut intimidating hoods, thick
coats, woolly hats with eye-holes that you can see out
of if you pull them over your face, and of course clandestine gloves. They had the attire, but had left it all
at home, considering it more important to look like
hard-nuts; ironically, those nuts were now hard,
shrunken to the size of raisins, and close to being

frozen off, so the Banana Boys looked stupid, but hard.

They'd had an eventful trip down the A3 from London to Portsmouth, having to summon the RAC breakdown assistance twice, first of all to tie the exhaust back on, and the second time to bring them a drop of diesel as the van's fuel gauge was broken. The RAC man considered questioning the Banana Boys' ability to motor in England, though thought twice when he was given a twenty pound tip.

'I say, I'm jolly cold, and do you think we could get something to eat? I'm a tad peckish,' Jeremy the posh Banana asked, stamping his feet. Nobody knew where Jeremy came from except his dad had been a victim of the recession and been compelled to *downsize*. Keef presumed Jeremy's brain had always been downsized, which would be okay if Daddy had money, but on the street it was a definite disadvantage. However, the massive chip on his shoulder came in handy when violence was needed. Jeremy, refined, sweet like white sugar if you screwed your eyes up, medium height, shorter than the other Bananas, was unusually elegant. He dressed in good quality clothing that was starting to show wear, but at least the trousers stayed up and thankfully concealed his underwear. Jeremy fondled his tousled blond locks as he deliberated on what he fancied to eat.

'We ain't got no money, innit,' Brains replied through chattering teeth. 'I only 'ad a score on me and the fucking RAC geezer took that.'

'Why d'you give 'im twenty quid?' Keef asked, not displaying any effects from the cold as he really was an 'ard nut, a state of being ably assisted by a reduced brain capacity, but Keef did wonder why they had made Brains Banana Treasurer. He also pondered a minor matter of whether they had enough money for diesel for the trip home. You can see now why Keef was leader; he thought of things.

'I didn't mean to, I fort the RAC gave change, and before I could ask he'd buggered off, 'adn't he? Rather frustrating, chaps,' Brains replied, feeling a tad peckish himself, noting this is the way Jeremy would say he was hungry, and for some reason, and just for the briefest of moments, he had a vision of himself as a posh turnip.

'We are about to dig up some money, are we not?' Jeremy observed, feeling his way nervously, pleased he had put the thermal vest on under his Aquascutum shirt, jumper and tweed jacket with leather elbow patches; his mum had insisted.

'Are we not?' Keef mimicked in his refined voice. 'That money's not ours, dip-bloody-stick, it belongs to Big-Knob,' but Keef did momentarily wonder if they could claim expenses. 'We deserve some expenses though, don't we?' Keef asked as if to nobody, pensive, turning to Brains for the authoritative answer, which actually came from Jeremy.

Rubbing his snowball hands and stamping his feet, his extremities the only bits of his body that were hard and not covered by clothing or instructions from Mummy, Jeremy explained. 'Yes.' He nodded, in order to knock a dewdrop from his nose. 'Every venture needs to calculate a residual profit, and that should include the deduction of legitimate expenses, otherwise the people you ask to do things for you, may be reluctant to do so another time.'

Keef thought, *this man needs to meet Fingers' mum*, and not for any criminal coital purpose, either, just so he understood the downsized world and how it worked. 'So, Jeremy, you fink we'd be okay 'elpin' ourselves to a few bob, d'yer?'

Jeremy thought on. His peckish tummy rumbled and he thought maybe a tuna melt Ciabata, washed down with a cheeky Pinot Grigio would not go amiss, and obviously this could very easily be explained away as a justifiable expense to Big-Knob. 'Yes, I think so, and if we explain the logic to Big-Knob's accountant, this could, I feel, be seen as a legitimate tax deductible expense.'

Brains and Shitlegs, looking like real hard nuts in a double pneumonia sense, shivered and tittered, but

Jeremy was on a roll. 'Where would we get a Ciabata and a decent glass of wine around here? Keef, you are familiar with Southsea?' but Jeremy halted, feeling a bony hand slide down and inside the rear of his Saville Row chinos and into his Aquascutum boxer shorts, and ponder, in a fondling manner, on his shivering skinny arse cheeks, more akin to a pair of shoulder blades.

'There is a lovely Italian Bistro in Palmerston Road that would likely suit your culinary tastes, darling.'

Keef reacted to his aunt, Lady Blanche-Teapot. 'Auntie, sweet'art?'

'Keith, now what is going on here?' the elegant Lady replied, lowering her snooty nose from her not inconsiderable height, to take in her nephew's frozen motley crew, apart from the posh one whose bottom and arse bones she continued to caress. Jeremy's only thought was that this elderly woman's hands were warm and felt nice, and he was relieved he had clean pants on; his mum had insisted, even though he had contested that if you were a hard nut, you didn't change your pants every week.

'Auntie, you know Brains and Shitlegs, and the one who's Aristotle yer gropin' is Jeremy. His dad was sumfink in the City until the recession,' Keef said to his aunt who, with deceptive strength, had pulled Jeremy to her and wrapped her spare, aging, bony fingers around the shocked classy delinquent's face, squashing his cheeks so his lips pursed, ready to receive a planted geriatric kiss. All Jeremy could think was that this elderly aristocratic woman was warming his cockles, and he could not stop those cockles reacting.

Lady Blanche-Teapot also sensed the reaction in Jeremy's posh, though fading, trouser department and, allowing her hand to slip further inside Jeremy's clean pants, she allowed her skeletal fingers to continue caressing the posh bum, as her spare hand dexterously pressed the remote control to the garage door that, coincidentally, the tent-pole in Jeremy's chino trousers was already pointing at. The door rose and, with unsubtle finger movements, Keef's aunt steered Jeremy toward the inside of the garage and thence through to the back garden of her house.

The intruder system reacted, flooding the garden with a bright white light, and Keef watched as his aunt guided her hand around Jeremy's rear privates in the floodlit garden, and he asserted his leadership qualities, suggesting the remaining Banana Boys follow. They trudged the length of the garden and reached the back door as Jeremy, following Lady Blanche-Teapot's haughty instructions, began rummaging around the Dowager's undergarments in a futile search for a key, which Keef knew his aunt kept on a string around her neck, in the manner of all re-fined ladies.

But the Duchess, as she was known in Southsea, seemed in no hurry to impart that knowledge to Jeremy. After a passionate moment or two of ooooh's and aaaah's and a particularly ripe, aging, and watery fart, she redirected the search party, huskily chortling, 'Jeremy sweetie, you are in completely the wrong department.' She leaned her aristocratic race-horse head to Jeremy's posh ears and neighed a whis-per, 'Try my tits, darling,' and vibrated her lips, much in the style of a French horse, spit-spotting the face of the vitalised Jeremy.

Jeremy had to admit his hands were warming to the task. Though he had, as yet, not achieved any ulti-mate goal, he was glad he had not worn his gloves, contrary to his mum's advice. His hand, redirected as it was from the Duchess's bottom department, made its way up inside her posh jumper and into the silky blouse, to commence fondling the toy-size sagging breasts that rattled around inside an exotic silk brassier, and sure enough, there was a key residing in the many folds of skin. 'Bingo!' he called out. The ex-citable exclamation and agitation stimulated a reac-tion in the dowager's nipples; in fact, these exertions from Jeremy and his amateurish exploration were having an obvious effect on the Duchess as she snorted steam from her flared, equine nostrils.

The Banana Boys looked on in amazement as their posh confederate searched and fondled, and both Shitlegs and Brains found themselves mildly aroused, never having been with a woman before, being as they were of the ugly variety of gangster, and as an inevitable consequence, they were feeling a tad jealous. Keef of course had been in the Brownies as a lad. His dad had been Brown Ale of the local pack, just prior to being arrested as part of the notorious Seville Orange paedophile mob, and thus Keef was the experienced member of the gang, and imparted any knowledge regarding ladies. He was also used to his aunt making out, so to speak, although he wished she wouldn't do it with his gang members, as she was akin to a Black Widow spider in respect of her chosen lovers, and Keef didn't want to keep looking for new Bananas.

Irritated, Keef pushed past the display of soft and bony porn, and asserted, 'Auntie, can we go inside please? I'm freezin' me fuckin' bollocks off out 'ere.'

At that moment, Jeremy had secured the key with the help of his second hand entering from the top of the deep-cut blouse, and the Duchess obliged by bending down to the back door escutcheon, allowing her face and lips to gently graze the tent-pole of Jeremy's chic trousers, whilst he undid the lock with the key still on the string around her neck.

The door swung open and, righting herself, Lady Blanche flicked on the kitchen lights. 'Now, you boys help yourselves to soup and bread, settle down and watch some television, or go and get your guns and money. I want a little word with Jeremy upstairs.' She tittered and, looking at the gaping mouths of Brains and Shitlegs, whispered into Jeremy's ear so they heard, 'Jeremy darling, how would you like your brains fucked out?'

Jeremy, being refined and brought up in a polite way, until the bankers had fucked the country's brains out, replied, 'Yeth pleathe, I would like that,' his hand fondling the Duchess's bottom.

'Probably looking for the key to the fucking bedroom,' Keef said, in the amusing manner expected of a gang leader.

THE DARKNESS MAY HAVE BEEN VIEWED as a relative blessing for any mischievous machinations, if you were a dim-witted and forgetful gangster, forgetting principally that there were security floodlights of such a brilliance, it made the Duchess's back garden illuminate much as if it were a German Stalag on red alert. These were, of course, the sorts of obvious things Keef and his comrades in villainy often reflected upon when they were being taken away in a police van, but this evening, after they had retrieved some cash, plus expenses, and weaponry from the garden vault, a former Victorian underground ice house, it was not a thought that entered their minds. It was another casual mistake that would rebound on them later, for, if they only but knew, they were being observed.

NINE

AT ABOUT THE TIME OF THE ARRIVAL OF THE
Banana Boys to the Duchess's semi-detached villa,
Jack and Mandy were returning home from the
Palace. Jack, being a sensitive individual, or so he believed, sensed a lingering after-burn following a
stilted conversation with Mandy in a packed train
from London. He sensed also that an inappropriate-
ness to converse in the cab from the station to home
was likely only a temporary respite; a sensible assumption as it turned out. Being a man knowledge-
able in the ways of women, which made him an
extraordinary catch for Mandy, Jack said nonchalantly to his wife, as he headed to the kitchen to get a
white wine for her and a Jameson's for himself, a
snifter so to speak. 'Should we talk about today before
we go to bed, love?' He applied his cheeky, wide boy

smile as he walked on, careful his wife did not see it was a victory smile; he knew she liked his cheeky grin, but he was not so confident about the victory one, that usually rebounded.

'I can see your smirk reflected in the glass, dipstick, and you have not a clue about how women think, but you are honestly, most certainly, one ugly gobshite.'

He loved it when she hurled terms of endearment at him, it made him feel soft and cuddly.

'Soft and cuddly you are, don't switch the light on yet, lover pie.'

Jack turned back to Mandy, having ensured he had removed what had turned out to be a victory smirk; he needed to practice his cheeky smirk some more. You see, Jack Austin really did know women (or so he thought or sensed), and combine this with an innate sense for self-preservation that went hand in hand with this knowledge, along with being a cowardy-custard, he was able to reassure women in a manly way, and, this is why they loved him so much, or so he sensed, as he said, 'Why not? It's dark. And it's not a smirk, it was a smile, the one I know you love, darling,' and he inadvertently followed this up with a victory smirk; the fool.

She knew what he was thinking, obviously, as he had spoken his thoughts aloud, and she could see the victory smirk, but let all of that go in order to press on with police matters. 'Derr, dipstick, can you not see the Duchess's floodlights on and what looks like, if I am not mistaken, the Banana Boys making their way in? Thought you were supposed to be a copper?'

Jack swung his gaze from their darkened kitchen, over next door's garden to the property beyond, now lit up like a premiership football ground for a night-time match and, as a consequence of applying his coppering surveillance skills, he bumped his head on the door. 'Ouch! Shite-on-a-stick. Oh yeah,' rubbing his head.

Mandy giggled at his misfortune and inability to multitask. 'Come here, bozo, let Mummy kiss that better for you,' and Jack presented himself for some feminine ministrations, thinking it was worth a bump on the noggin to get out of talking about what happened at the Palace. She soothed his head, his brow, and kissed his bump, a new one among many older bumps. 'We still need to talk about the Palace.'

'Blimey, did I...?'

She nodded and promptly discarded thoughts of what his current smirk might mean, being more interested in watching what was happening a couple of houses away.

Jack and Amanda lived in a street called Frisian Tun, a cute, chocolate box street, made up of Victorian semi-detached villas in the heart of upper-middle-class Southsea. She always wondered how a cockney barrow boy had managed to get himself such a beautiful house, and in such a neighbourhood, his character being so patently incongruous with the essence of British middle-class reserve that best described the neighbours and least described Jack. But he had, and Mandy, having now married her spiv, was aware it had been a rocky ride as the naturally acerbic cockney wit foundered on middle-class stony ground; pretty much as any normal person would expect. However, Jack was not a normal person, and he persevered, imagining that his neighbours must be dim-witted not to like him and, of course, laugh at his jokes. And then there were his attempts at landscape gardening... He was even thinking of calling himself Gavin (as in Gavin Diarmuid, the famous landscape garden designer), except he didn't want to be known as a Gavin Diarrhoea, in other words, a shite gardener – which, ironically, he was.

'They are dim-witted, love,' Mandy said, agreeing about the neighbours, and Jack felt safe applying his victory smirk, rubbing his head for himself, hoping the bang would not start a brain tumour. Jack Austin was a noted hypochondriac amongst all of his other character faults, which he saw as minor blemishes, and this is what a lot of people did find funny. But not Jack. He could be dying, and who would finish the garden?

He poured himself a cake mixing bowl of Cheerio's that he called "S'laters", and splurged it full of milk and began crunching a mouthful of cereal.

'Haven't you eaten enough today?' Mandy asked, avoiding looking at the mobile feast, as Jack strutted the kitchen eating; multigrain, multitasking?

Jack looked equally perplexed that she should question breakfast cereal at night; she'd not got to the quantity yet. 'Let me finish me S'laters and, despite the patient risks, I fancy sharing the bath water with you. What d'you say?' and he batted his one eye in a manner he imagined to be rugged, masculine and seductive, a bit like Heathcliffe would do to that girl whose name always eluded him.

She giggled at his screwed-up, ugly face, a mouthful of over-spilling S'laters and sauntering back to him, she smoothed his face whilst pushing a couple of Cheerio's, that were stuck to his pouting bottom lip, back into his mouth. 'You run the bath, I'm going to take a look out the upstairs back window, and it's Catherine.' She wrapped her loving arms around him, her trailing hand smoothing his bottom which placated his confused little boy look. 'Catherine Earnshaw, Heathcliffe's love in *Wuthering Heights*, and I'm curious as to what East End of London gang-sters are doing a few doors away.'

Feeling placated and happy to have something to do, like run the bath, not fancying a trip onto the York-shire Moors even though he knew he would be brill-iant at the northern accent, as he had so ably proven with his pigeon fancying (*see Ghost and the Ragman Roll*), he left his wife to do the coppering. He was, after all, an Insultant, and only part-time at that.

There, finally, that's cleared that up. He's not retired, not a consulate but had assumed a role as a part-time Insultant; we still need to divine if he is a full or a part-time spook, or retired?

'They're not East End, love, they're 'Ivver Green, sowf London.'

Mandy was halfway up the stairs, her feminine intu-ition telling her his mind would begin to drift else-where (he'd finished his S'laters) as he looked up her dress, but she still felt he needed telling; that's women for you, and Jack of course knew this.

'I think you mean consultant and did you not retire?'

'I flounced, darlin', there's a world of difference be-tween flouncing and retiring, yer silly mare...' But his mind drifted, and he defied Heathcliffe to stay fo-cused if that Catherine girl, whatsername, had stopped mid-flight and spun her dress so he could get a good look at her suspenders and knickers. Oh, his Catherine was good, and she certainly knew her Heathcliffe, her dirty old northern monkey, and definitely not a Gypo.

'Shut yer face and run the bath,' Mandy answered.

He loved it when he relinquished control of their relationship and let her take charge for a moment or two. It added a frisson of excitement, and not just for him, for Mandy too; as previously mentioned, he knew women and how occasionally they liked to feel they ran the show.

'You have never been in control,' she looked at him from the top step, multitasking, as only women can, unzipping her dress and letting it fall onto the floor, demonstrating how in control she was, before she strode off to the back bedroom, their bedroom. 'Close your mouth, you are not a codfish,' she called as she departed. A brilliant manoeuvre, leaving Jack pleased he had let her take control, and she had even managed to get in a *Mary Poppins* quote.

'Bath, Jack.'

'Righty-oh, sweet'art.' See, that's how you do it; to all intents, Mandy was now under the illusion she was in charge.

'And stop smelling my dress.'

Oh, she was good, and all done without looking back. Jack was convinced women had eyes in the back of their head, and in rare moments of lucidity, it worried him. 'How could you see that?' he asked.

'I could hear your revolting snorting. Blow your nose before I get in the bath, please, and not on my dress.'

'Righty-oh, darlin'.' He was going to blow his nose anyway, just not on her dress. He had a particularly stubborn bogey he obviously could not deal with while in the Palace, although he did think of asking the Queen for one of her knitting needles. Then the train was crowded, but there was no need to tell Mandy and spoil her illusion of control. Jack liked role-playing, and wondered if he had time for a cheese and tomato roll before he had to get in the bath.

Mandy kept the light in their back bedroom off as she padded to the rear window and eased the curtain apart, enough to peek out without being observed. In the Duchess's floodlit garden she saw the Banana Boys, with a new member of the gang, unknown to her, and this new lad was wobbling around the kitchen door, the Duchess's hand down the back of his trousers and having a good rummage, the lad appearing to enjoy the experience. She watched as events unfolded, mildly titillated, and thinking she wanted to get in the bath with Jack, when she heard him let rip an enormous fart. It echoed – well it would, as those of us who understand the acoustic characteristics of a bathroom would know.

'You could have done that somewhere else, Jack.'

He replied with a scientific explanation he thought his wife should have known already. 'It's the poncy food at the Palace, darlin'. It played 'avoc with me innards.'

She chuckled. 'Oh, that's okay then. Just pop down to the kitchen and get me a peg, please,' she called back, preparing her olfactory glands for re-entry into a contaminated bathroom, the Bananas and the geriatric Duchess having now disappeared through their back door. As Mandy turned, her stomach and nose girded, she was treated to a sight equal to what she was expecting to smell, as she saw Jack's naked body wobbling towards the stairs. 'Where're you going?'

'You said you wanted a peg?' he replied, wondering why an explanation was necessary. He turned to face her, holding his hands out in placatory manner, a plea of innocence she thought not at all convincing, thinking his hands may have been better employed covering his bits and pieces. She gestured with her head to the bathroom. He wobbled back, embraced and kissed her, and one thing lead to another, or would have done if Jack had not stubbed his toe on the door to the bathroom.

She was used to this, and used also to seeing him hop around naked, his bits and pieces flopping. Jack's feet stuck out at a quarter to three and were, as a consequence, fair game to any passing door, chair, or other inanimate obstruction. She often thought that at sixty, he would have been used to his feet sticking out by now and have some inbuilt self-protection radar, but that would be to allow a greater degree of life-awareness than should be reasonably attributed to Jack Austin.

After she had kissed his toe better, thinking she could have done with the peg after all, they did get their bath, and the passion over spilled, along with the tsunami of water as Jack wallowed, water-buffalo-style, and still damp, they crash-bang-walloped into the bedroom for a fizzer, their particularly racy form of sex.

Mandy's sublime relaxation after Jack's passionate lovemaking, was only disturbed by his horsey, grumbling struggle to regain his breath, and muffled curses from outside the house. 'Look out back, Jack, see what's happening,' Mandy asked. 'I think the Banana Boys have come back out again.'

'What?' he said, feeling his chest for a heart attack, and thinking he fancied a post-coastal doze; he loved living by the sea.

'Outside, you deaf twat, and it's post-coital. What's that noise?'

Ah, he thought, the passion of the moment may have passed. I did tell you he knew women, but not quite as much as he thought, as he felt he could let that comment go, and settle into his post-coastal doze, sure she was wrong. Coital was something to do with being shy, and he certainly wasn't shy, but he did like to live by the seaside. 'Hedgehogs,' he said and zizzed on.

'Hedge-fucking-hogs?'

He was awake, his previously sated and thus dulled senses now on Fred Alert. 'Yeah, I remember a nature programme on the telly. There was a rat and a hedgehog fighting in an urban back garden, made hell of a racket.' He dozed some more, having cleared that one up for her. He had a natural instinct for calming women, which was why women liked strong men like him, to comfort them, to take control, which he had of course recently, and only temporarily, ceded – there's only so much you can expect of role-playing with an eejit man, she coincidentally thought.

Mandy was propped on her elbow now, and never let it be said Jack Austin, who, as previously laboured, knew women, was slow on the uptake. 'You want to know what happened between the hedgehog and rat, is that it?'

'No, I want you to look outside and see...' she paused to look at his distracted face, the former traces of irritability fading, '...what actually is happening, not what you *think* is happening, and then you can come back to bed and feckin' comfort me, *Tarzan.*'

She raised herself a little more and gave him the stare, which ordinarily would have a galvanising effect on him, but the quilt had dropped further, revealing her wonderfully pendulous breasts and this demanded all his attention, the rat and hedgehog completely forgotten. Jack liked her bosoms. Not too big, not too small, they fitted his artist's hands and he thought of Goldilocks as he gazed on mesmerized. Her mammary orbs teasingly swung at a greater beat as Mandy became steadily more agitated.

'I am very pleased you like my breasts, Rem-bleedin'-brandt, and that your piss artist hands fit, but I want you to look out of the window and tell me what is happening, and before you ask, yes you did... and, I know I am the feckin' policewoman and you are part-time, but I am telling you, look outside, *comprendez?*' Mandy fixed her face, fighting back the smile and warmth she felt for this idiot man of hers, knowing that really, she should look.

Jack loved it when she spoke Gestapo to him. '*Comprendez*, brilliant,' he muttered. 'Ve hav vays of makin you look, yah?' as he stood up, he scratched his bum, skilfully circumventing a particularly nasty pimple that should really have some ointment on it, and made his way to the curtain. She watched him scratching, as he jelly-wobbled to the curtains and wished she had looked herself, but he was there now. He looked out, his bum booming backwards and she leaned back herself; a natural reaction when faced with the possibility of imminent smothering. She had the passing thought that the human body's sense of self-preservation was amazing as she waited for him to assess the situation and report back.

'It's the Banana Boys opening up the old Ice House...' He thought on, which involved another scratch of his bum. Could he not think without scratching something, she wondered. 'Did we put the guns out of action? I can't remember.'

'Jack, leave yer bum alone for a minute, and yes we did, unless we have missed a delivery of more. We also marked the money... Blimey, I wonder where your head is sometimes!'

'Klingon on the starboard bow, darlin'.'

'What? Should I call someone, Father Mike, Spok?'

'No, I can get it.'

She was confused now. 'Get what, Jack? What's happening?'

'I can get the Klingon meself unless...' he tittered. It looked like he had a follow-up as well, she thought, revolted.

'Don't go there, sometimes you disgust me,' she said, thinking she had just saved herself.

He turned back to face her in wonderment. 'I do...?' It was his *don't hurt me, Bambi* face; she recognised it from whenever he knew she had him bang to rights.

She sighed and gave in, like she always did. It was, after all, one of his better faces and that was saying something, considering. 'Please, just tell me what is happening,' she pleaded, wondering at her own levels of tolerance. He rubbed his chin that needed shaving; she could hear it as he scratched harder, rhythmically. '*Doctor Who?*' she asked.

He turned back from the curtain, pleased. 'Yeah, well done, sweet'art, *douze points.*' He rubbed some more and she waited some more; still *Dr Who.* 'They're loading the guns and probably a bit of sausage and mash into a white transit van. We'll get the number from Jimbo's infra-red CCTV tomorrow. Did you say Meesh was down tomorrow? They're driving off... Did you say Keef Bananas and someone we've not seen before went in?' She ahemmed confirmation that Meesh was coming down, and that there had been three Banana Boys plus Keef, as she wondered where Jack's head goes. 'Well, there's only two going off, Brains and Shitlegs, if I'm not mistaken, and we are having Martin. That'll be good, eh? Should have taken him to the Palace. The Queen likes him, and I think he had his eye on one of the corgis. I told him to get his bleedin' eyes tested.'

Mandy knew he tried always to be nonchalant about his dog he had given to Meesh, and the companionship of Martin clearly worked for the poor girl, who had suffered so many traumas in her very short life, but Mandy knew Jack missed Martin terribly. The scruffy ginger Border Terrier had been his constant companion for nearly seven years before he rescued Meesh from the paedophile gang. The dog had been recommended by the police psychiatrists to help calm him. Jack was, still is, a notorious berserker, and sometimes it worked, Martin having many more brain and common sense cells than Jack. If Jack felt the mist rising, signalling an imminent berserking attack, it was suggested he stroke Martin and it would calm him. Now, he stroked Mandy instead, and she was not sure how she felt about that, especially when he said things like, "It'll be alright, girl" and "Down girl," contemporaneously fussing her hair.

'I wonder what happened?' she asked, bringing herself back to reality. She looked at the blur of black hair on the pimply bum sticking out from the curtains and wondered if she should de-fuzz it, then remembered the Klingon on the starboard bow.

'What, between the rat and the hedgehog?' he chuckled, turning to face her and she wondered what was better looking, his ugly face or his hairy, pimply bottom. 'The hedgehog won on points,' and he rolled up laughing and she knew it was game over, but he did seem to be feeling rather well, and quite amorous as he checked his artist's hand measurements.

She responded, trying not to think of the Klingons and which was the starboard side. 'Don't worry, darlin', they 'ave a cloakin' device.'

She thought he chuckled some more, but this was muffled as he decided to give the previously only visual and tactile admiration of her breasts, a more detailed inspection, and she was okay with that, pleased for the hedgehog and okay with her feckin' eejit husband, wasn't she? Temporarily losing control.

TEN

AT ABOUT THE SAME TIME AS THE HEDGEHOG WAS winning on points, a rather disgruntled John Sexton entered his son's pub, the Gravediggers. John Sexton, the size and build of Jonas and still remarkably suave, was a successful merchant banker, but the good kind, if you were prepared to screw your eyes up when you looked at his record. He had, however, redeemed any blemishes to that record, as he, and other doves of the financial world, brokered the deal that spread the nation's debt over seventy years.

He had later remarked to the press that it was pretty much the same as they did with the debt following the Second World War, and condemned the notion of paying back the nation's indebtedness in five years, as the Government had suggested. This rush to clear the books with a policy of austerity caused enormous suffering for the ordinary man and woman, who had nothing to do with the creation of the debt in the first place. The consequent pain to the people was thus relieved by the introduction of the Sexton fiscal policy, the brakes off, and slowly the country was returning to a sustainable growth. But this did not alleviate the hurt, the memory of suffering and, more importantly, the sense of social injustice felt from many different angles and different people. And this was the conundrum John Sexton and his banking colleagues had discussed with Jack Austin.

The Gravediggers was empty except for the Sextons, Jonas and Della, Pansy, Jonas's sister and Angel, her partner, Seb, out from his shed for a rare visit to the pub, Granddad and Mum Sexton, Beryl, a tour-de-force in anyone's book, a diminutive powerhouse of a woman, marginally taller than Della and of a similar bird-like build.

It was clear to anyone who looked on that Beryl had passed her petite genes onto Seb, whereas the giant genes of John Sexton were inherited by Jonas and Pansy. Angel was, as her name suggested, cherub-like, petite and charmingly feminine, and adored her lover, Pansy. And then there was Granddad, the De-Mensa representative of the family, a shell of an old man that hinted he had been the size of Jonas and

John in his prime, but now, grey whiskers sprouted from sunken skin, prominent cheekbones, and from all other facial orifices, making him a prime candidate for the Tufty Club. The milky, rheumy eyes, though difficult to see through, revealed a tacit softness to the old gent, but there was evident the streak possessed of all of the Sextons, one that resided below the surface; ruthlessness, and a strong familial bond. The family was everything and came before anything else. John Sexton was known by all to be a philanderer. Beryl knew this and was wont, on occasion, to have a fling herself; goose for the gander. However, both John and Beryl knew that when it came to the time, it would be the Sextons together as a family; the floozies kicked into touch.

Della wanted to address the family and so smoothed John Sexton's cheek and this soothed the very powerful man's ire, but only temporarily; his rant had still to fully subside. 'Sit yer arse down, John, I want to say sumfink,' Della said, in the closest she came to sensitive Fairy Liquid.

'You want to say something?' John Sexton reacted, swinging his gaze to his wife in what he considered a justifiable tempest. 'Do you know, this woman...' and he straight-arm pointed to Della, '...called my secretary...' He stopped himself and puffed out a great deal of hot air, this time unaccompanied by words, which he struggled to find.

'What did she say to your tart of a secretary, John?' Beryl asked, calmness personified; she had already guessed what was happening and supported Della one hundred percent.

John Sexton raised himself up to his full height, his chair teetering but remaining upright, puffed out his chest, and deflated as he spoke. 'She told my secretary she was fired, that I was retiring, and then she phoned my mistress, Maureen, you know the redhead one from Liverpool, and told her, and I quote, "To fuck off back to Germany or wherever her accent was from", and I would not be seeing her anymore.' He paused, and slouched, hunching his shoulders in despair. There was more, he just did not know how to say it, so Della did it for him.

'Sit the fuck down, you philandering tosspot.' She looked at Beryl. 'Sorry.' She flicked her hands to emphasise she wasn't in the least bit sorry, and carried on. 'I phoned the second-in-command at the bank and told him the fraud squad will be descending and he would receive detailed instructions on what to do if they were not to close the bank down and arrest all of its officers. I have to say this did get the posh tosspot's attention. He has his instructions, and now, John, you will shut yer trap for once in yer fuckin' life, and listen up.'

'I wish I had been there,' Beryl chortled.

Della looked across to Beryl. 'I will fill you in over a cup of splosh tomorrow, but for now, all of you listen, please,' and Della began pacing around the table at which sat the Sexton clan. 'This is the score.' She paced some more and ended up behind the shoulders of Jonas, which she massaged. 'Please say nothing until I have finished, because I might get upset.'

Beryl thought "upset"? "Might?" What was this? But she was only just getting to know the firebrand Della, and she liked what she saw.

Della looked lovingly over Jonas's shoulders into his eyes, and contrastingly, in a soft tone, she spoke to Jonas. 'I'm pregnant. Jonas and I are going to have a baby.' She allowed the astonished looks a little time to rearrange themselves into faces of joy, her hand up, seeking more attention. She got it as her emotions ramped up. 'I am not going to bring a baby into this family if its granddad is off fucking anything with a fanny and staying away all week. My baby will have ever-present grandparents who will, I hasten to add, be taking a full-time involvement, as I can get a bit busy at times. I've tied up all of the loose ends of your business, both personal and financial, John. Your bank is now bullet-proof, so when the fraud squad come a-calling, they will find nothing. Your discreet funds are transferred to a family account; we'll talk about that later.'

She allowed the enormity of what she told them to settle in. John Sexton could not resist a comment, though it came through a grandfatherly grin. 'How did you do all of that?' But he knew it was not Della and glanced over at his son Seb, who shrank into his well-worn wheel-back chair.

'I will tell you sometime, but know this, I will carry on working. And you might as well know this as well, I'm not a copper, I'm MI5, and if any of you spill the beans, I can, and will, wring yer fucking necks. So I therefore need a fully functioning set of grandparents around all of the time, get my drift?'

Della received the shocked grins and nodding in response, as expected. 'Burial (she said Beryl's name as Jack would), tomorrow, you and I will start to arrange the wedding... Well, it will mainly be you, Burial, as I have some serious spook work to do.' She looked at Jonas. 'Shut yer trap, Jonas, I will be careful,' and she waved her crossed fingers in the air.

'I will ask Father Mike to perform the ceremony in the cemetery chapel so Seb can be Jonas's best man. So there you have it, sorted and squared away. Now, I'm taking Jonas to the hospital because I fink his wounds are on the turn, 'eiver that or he's farted again, but I don't want to be a widow before me babe is born.' She looked at her future husband. 'Get your coat, Jonas, my luv.'

She'd finished and Beryl was first up to embrace Della, and then her son, Jonas, who squealed with the pain of the hug. 'Oh, stop being a wimp.' Beryl had similar Nightingale genes as Della, so you can see why Beryl thought Della was right for her son, plus, as a *copper*, Della had decided to let go the fact Beryl had murdered the former Cabinet Secretary, the Head of Armed Forces, the government Chief Whip, and Pomerol, not six months ago, but, as Della had said, "That's all water under the bridge now, we're family" and she hinted she would like to know why all of the Mandarins were copping it.

But that was to be reserved for a cup of tea, and this was all that Beryl needed to hear.

ELEVEN

IT WAS LATE AND ARCHIE POINTE-LACE WAS comfortably ensconced in his West End of London Gentlemen's club, reading the latest edition of *Embroidery for Tofs*; did he ever leave *Bumblin'tons*? The familiar buttoned leather, wing-back armchairs, plush carpet, bookcases stuffed with unread books, would offer any normal over-privileged, silver-spooned individual a sense of secure luxurious comfort. However, Pointe-Lace ignored such things; these accoutrements were his God-given right, part of his heritage, and he gave them all – the surroundings, the money, the embroidery, the power and all of the accompanying trappings – not a second thought.

His mind focused on the latest stitches, but not even his most favourite thing in the world, sewing, in particular needlepoint, could distract him from the bile currently bubbling in his stomach. Anger, a rare emotion for him, which he put down to frustration at a well-conceived and, up until recently, well-executed plan, unravelling due to the shambling interventions of a cockney barrow boy and his wife, and lately, a cocky cockney sparrow.

He had to admit Amanda Austin had a good brain and, in his more generous moments, he would concede she was a good copper, for a woman, but Jack Austin, and now Delores Lovington, were nothing more than burrs under his saddle. But for now, he focused on the barrow boy; the brains, heaven help everyone, of the outfit. Austin had a street savvy, Archie conceded, and he would never ignore such an instinct, but how could Austin even begin to comprehend what he, someone of a universally acknowledged immense intellect, had set in motion? He was aware of only one other person who understood the full measure of what had been instigated, and that person, known colloquially on the street as *Big-Knob*, remained elusive. However, not only did Jack Austin comprehend what he and Big-Knob had done (well, not all, but a significant amount, certainly enough to wreak havoc and destabilise the Machiavellian plotting at least), but Austin was aware, ironically, it was not for the money or anything else that ordinarily would motivate most people. Pointe-Lace orchestrated his machinations for intellectual stimulation and, in his more relaxed moments, conceded it was for personal amusement; he could not answer for Big-Knob.

Archie did not think Jack Austin knew of him, but he did know Big-Knob existed, knew what he was and what he did, but not *who* he was, and neither did Pointe-Lace. Archie even suspected Austin was beginning to comprehend that all he had set in motion was an intellectual exercise. And finally, and this angered him most of all, Jack Austin and his Fred Karno company of vaudevillian, inept, comedian coppers and spooks, and their comic opera antics, had caused the death of his much loved, though foolish, half-brother; blown up in an MI5 Jaguar on Whitehall, just outside Downing Street (*See - A Barrow Boy's Cadenza*).

The fact that the demise of his unbalanced half-brother, Lionel Thackeray, whom Jack Austin had called Len, was due in the main to the dystopian seeds sown by himself, was something that defied Archie's acceptance. He could see this, of course, but the chaotic fallout was not meant to cause any personal harm, which was something Archibald Pointe-Lace had neither foreseen nor intended. If he searched hard enough within his cold fish internal self, he might find a grain of sadness; certainly not remorse, as he had post-rationalised all this as a consequence of a better cause, an acceptable means to an end, what the Yanks called *collateral damage*. He had examined this grain of conscience that irritated, and had enough disillusioned self-awareness to realise this would likely be the grain that created, eventually, the pearl in his oyster. You see, Pointe-Lace was just as unbalanced as his half-brother, buggered and beaten into an English gentleman at Eton, very much as a blacksmith forges his ploughshares; the system intended to create powerful individuals, groomed to rule, groomed for power; their birthright.

Unusually, Archie was aware that any warmth of feeling for others, even for himself, had been knocked out of him with the general debasement that is the mainstay of the elite British Public School system that, in turn, made the elite British men, the men they were, bred to lead. Funny, as it also bred in them a complete and utter blindness; they lacked any of the qualities that would, under normal circumstance, make them natural born leaders, or cause them to appeal to the ordinary man or woman who might wish to be led, and thus encourage them to follow their lead. All empathy, care or charisma, had been repressed out of them and replaced with a divine, martinet arrogance, a conceit that supplanted any natural intelligence, common sense or intellectual capacity. This divine arrogance, in turn, was supplemented with one or two dogmatic concepts that intuitively they knew had to be driven into the Plebs, by a class of individuals who just knew what was best. They knew this because they had been told, ad infinitum, had had it drummed into them as children and young adults, and now they played out this dogma by intuitive force. This force, back in the day, would have been known as *Divine Breath* – it still is amongst this circle of the elite.

Pointe-Lace, however, although a stalwart member of the elite, was a breed apart. He had all of the arrogant superiority and pompous self-assurance, though coupled with an enormous intellect, very much like his late younger half-brother, but Archie had directed his whole being to developing concepts that would in fact disturb the norm, agitate the accepted way of things; the system, but not the Establishment. He would sit in his leather armchair and amuse himself, toying with the Establishment, subtly disrupting the system, the mores of society, and watch on tantalised, as the ripples of discord took effect.

He lived for dystopia, it fed his enormous ego, and ironically, he was sought after by the powers-that-be, to advise on courses of action in both government and civil service circles, how to respond to world events, many such events being of his own consequence. Manna from heaven, and he would chuckle at the naivety of not only the Mandarins who sought, and were comforted by his advice, but for the thought that Big-Knob was under the impression he acted on that person's whim or master plan. It had occurred to him Big-Knob may be thinking something similar, but he discarded that notion as nonsense. It just could not be – and that is divine arrogance, or *divine breath*, in other words, intuitive thought, sent from God, to God's chosen one.

Archibald Pointe-Lace, Archie, known as Buttonhole, for the embroidery buttonhole stitch that was *Pointe lace,* among his Tof brethren, his fellow Bumblin'ton T'tOF's, (Terribly... Terribly Old Farts – you have to say it like you were stutteringly posh with a stiff upper lip – the old is mental, not age related) was sitting in his leather wing-back chair in the first floor lounge of Bumblin'tons. He had a cut-glass crystal tumbler of malt whisky firmly gripped in his already liver-spotted hand, the Glenmorangie swirling and having the life sniffed out of it, his only outward sign of agitation. Ironically, this sniffing and swirling is exactly what Jack Austin did with his Jameson's, but this similarity did not occur to Buttonhole, nor likely would occur to Jack Austin. To anyone else in the club, and there were a few, currently uncomfortable in their own leather chairs, Buttonhole's customary facade of cold detachment was still manifest. However, his ever present smooth feathers were subliminally ruffled; he was disconcerted about what had happened today with Crumb, and he had just heard about Quentin collapsing at Buckingham Palace, at a reception attended by Jack Austin. He considered none of this a coincidence, and Crispin Evens and Bartholomew Bozoquet were late for Embroidery Club.

Pointe-Lace was not a Civil Servant, he would never degrade himself so, and he had no need to work. His life's work was as a modern day Machiavelli, and he took great pride in this. He manipulated and schemed, the Civil Service he considered just one of his many playthings, and now two of his top Mandarins had been played with, and likely a further two sucked into a meddlesome maelstrom. Furthermore, Jack Austin's fingerprints were all over it, and this irritated him, but for now, it was late; he would retire for the night and come out fighting tomorrow.

––––––

THE DUCHESS REAPPEARED STANDING at the kitchen door, her scrawny body a bag of bones contained in an overly suntanned, wrinkled, leathery skin, draped in a gossamer silk nightdress and topcoat. She watched her favourite nephew use his booted foot to menace the cat, which he had on the end of a lead, much as the cat toyed with a mouse. Keef could not see the distress of the cat, he could only comprehend his own amusement. The Duchess smiled as Keef looked up to reciprocate the adoring look his aunt bestowed, a casual kick thrown out in the cat's direction eliciting a satisfying screech.

'Let Thomas go, there's a love, I need to talk to you.'

Keef of course did his Aunt's bidding, and the cat made a mad dash for the cat flap in the kitchen door, only to smash into it concertina-style; Keef had locked the flap shut. This caused great amusement to Keef and Lady Francesca, as the cat tore past the feet of the Duchess and through the open kitchen door in a bid for respite, which was eventually achieved after being tripped by an elegant, aristocratic size twelve foot.

'I sent Brains and Shitlegs 'ome, Aunt, as you asked. What's up?'

'I need you to do me a tiny favour,' and she smiled, pinching her thumb and forefinger. It was as if her whole aged face fractured, the brittle powder coating falling off in scales. 'I need you to dispose of Jeremy for me, there's a dear. He was a nice boy, but he may have been a little too shocked this evening, and well...' the Duchess paused, flapped a hand and allowed herself a sadistic grin that Keef mirrored, '... let us say he will not be telling anybody about it.'

Keef acknowledged and stood to go upstairs. He knew what he was tasked to do and had done it before, which was why he thought upon his aunt as the *Black Widow spider*; often found amongst bananas, ironically.

'Oh, and sleep here this evening will you, Keith sweetie, I have had a message that little Beth may be squealing...' and the Duchess frowned at the use of the street language she had so readily abandoned some time ago, after meeting and marrying Lord Teapot; the frown causing wavy cartoon creases on her high forehead she considered naturally aristo-cratic. 'We also think she is being moved and we need to know where. It will be down here, I think we can be sure of that, and I want you to do me another tiny favour in the morning, so get some beauty sleep, you will need your wits about you.' And she turned on the ball of her foot, clad in posh-slippered clodhop-pers, and waved a goodnight to her nephew.

TWELVE

THERE WAS A BANGING AT THE DOOR THAT WOKE Jack. 'What the feck?' Jack was immediately conscious of a weight on his chest, and checked for a heart attack before he opened his eyes, probably for the last time. He was not alone. Meesh and Martin had crept in and sat on him for a laugh. He looked into the smiley, loving face of the tiny girl and knew she would not think of such a diabolical idea. He knew the notion of creeping into the bedroom and sitting on him was Martin's idea, and he pictured in his mind the little girl and his dog creeping in, tittering to themselves, and it made him smile. Martin wheezed a chortle and offered up a reassuring dog-breath lick in response; yep, his idea.

Where was Mandy, was his second thought, as he energetically frolicked with Meesh and Martin, producing more squeals of delight and growly, mumbled talking and laughing from Martin, and finally he realised Mandy was probably getting ready for work. She had not retired, although she had flounced a couple of times, and sometimes when he had done absolutely nothing wrong. That was the trouble with prima donnas, he hypnotically thought to himself (I think he meant *hypocritically,* so you see, he even thought in Malacopperism). Mandy must have let Martin and Meesh in, he thought again, getting the hang of this thinking lark, recalling Jackie was dropping them down first thing.

But who was at the door now? See, that's thinking for you, and so early in the morning and having narrowly escaped a heart attack; Jack Austin was a consommé thinker. Brushing aside his dog and swirling an arm around the waist of Meesh, he lifted himself up from his recumbent position and switched on his largely ineffective, African Elephant ears that Mandy had said matched his backside. She liked a laugh, she was so like Martin in that respect and coincidentally, she also liked the top of her head scratched and her ears tickled.

He heard a familiar voice and raucous laugh. 'Jo-Jums?' he said to himself as he shooed Meesh and Martin away and out of the bedroom, got up and dressed (well, he put his boxers on and added a shirt with one button, misaligned, but done up) and went to the top of the stairs. At the front entrance lobby he could see Meesh wrapped around Mandy's leg, whilst Martin appeared sexually attracted to the lower limbs of Detective Inspector Josephine Wild.

'Jo-Jums,' Jack called, 'what light from yonder...?'

Scratching Martin's head and simultaneously batting away the over-stimulated hound, she replied, 'Well, it's not to look up the leg-hole of your skanky boxer pants,' and this mumsy woman made like she was retching.

Jack looked down and checked his pants, aware Jo-Jums was a consommé actress, and smiled to himself as he padded down the stairs. 'I've only had these pants on a fortnight,' he informed her and giggled to himself at his rather amusing aside; his asides always amused women. Don't ask, he just knew.

'Jack, go back up, get clean pants and get dressed, and that may amuse us.'

Mandy had spoken, so he turned tail and trudged back to the bedroom to get dressed, reassuring himself this is what he had intended to do all along, and after a spell of admiring his sartorial delegance and toned felt appearance in the long mirror in the bedroom, he made his way back downstairs to the kitchen, where he could hear mumbled exchanges of words, but more worryingly, exclamations.

Immediately, he went to Fred Alert. Exclamations had always done this to him, ever since he was drummed out of the Boy Scouts. It didn't bother him too much as he couldn't do knots, much preferred miles-per-hour, which probably explained his difficulty with string. This morning, he could not think of what he might have done, maybe it was the pants joke, but it was as well to be prepared, so he applied his Boy Scout look, the only thing he had managed before being booted out; he still had the badge for scout looks somewhere.

Jack went into the kitchen mentioning *"Dib dib"* and be *"dobbing prepared"*, three fingers up his nose, multi-tasking an irksome bogy that had been bothering him for days. That fireman hose activity jogged his memory back to the bathroom the previous night, and it was this particular bogey he was going to mention to Mandy, though it was academic as it was now quite loose and he no longer required her assistance.

'Jack, sensible head please or I'll knock you for a sixer,' *Akela* Mandy said, but she was smiling her *I love you, you feckin' eejit,* smile. He liked that smile, it made him feel loved. Realising Mandy should in fact be *Brown Ale,* not *Akela,* he decided it was not a morning for being pedantic or for beer, and zeroed in on his well-used Mocha Pot and set about his morning ritual of coffee-making.

He called back to his pack leader from the sink, multitasking a bounce on Meesh with his swinging hip, so the little girl went sprawling and giggling onto the floor, to be jumped on by Martin. 'Brown Ale, are we still playing that game where we pretend you're in charge, dearest lovely Elizabeth?' He was ameliorating any unforeseen mistakes with a bit of *Pride and Prejudice*; it always worked with women.

Then, before Mandy could answer, he swivelled his attention to Jo-Jums. 'Jo, what light... babes?' using his Shakespeare voice, a change from his *on the bridge in the Steamship Enterprise* voice, classical lesbian (we think he means thespian), sonorous and rising to a crescendo he knew everyone appreciated – well, Meesh and Martin did as they stopped frolicking and looked at him.

Martin "derred" a *Make it so, Captain*. He'd seen all of Jack's Shakespeare before, and he'd never been impressed. Meesh, though, was a relative novice, so Martin whispered into the little girl's ear, multitasking with a lick that had the girl back on the floor in fits of laughter.

Mandy looked at Jo and both women burst out laughing.

'What?' Jack asked. If I had to guess, I would say it was his Gestapo Othello voice.

'It's not Juliet, or feckin' Othello, but Beth, and it's Della, who has gotten onto her balcony and broken the feckin' window, and yesterday afternoon we found two Whitehall Mandarins, alive, just, but frozen stiff, laid out on top of a mausoleum slab in Eastney cemetery,' Jo-Jums answered, her laughter easing a little in order to indicate she felt the subject merited serious attention.

Jack stopped in his coffee tracks, which was quite appropriate as he made his coffee so strong and drank so much of the stuff, Mandy sometimes thought he would be mainlining soon. Jack mused to himself: 'Beth, Della, Whitehall Mandarins...?' he said out loud, pondering, and turned to his Science Officer. 'What tomb, Spok?'

Next, he turned his enquiring look to Jo, a quizzical expression that did nothing to improve his ugliness, and both Mandy and Jo laughed again. 'What?' And he wondered if he should maybe change his style. Granddad shirts used to suit him, and he fancied being more casual in his dress these days, as would be becoming for a semi-retired Insultant. Mandy had already advised against Hawaiian shirts, and as it was still the middle of winter, he'd decided he would fall off that bridge come summer.

'Sit down Jack... or is it Jim, and you will soon be a granddad,' Mandy said, as she allowed Meesh onto her lap. 'Jo has something to say, and I don't want you having an apoplectic fit.'

Jack put on his seriously thinking face, still no improvement, and he wandered over to Mandy to have his bum rubbed, before settling down at the kitchen table to wait for his coffee to bubble, wondering what apoplectic meant, knowing instinctively he probably had it, but was it life-threatening?

'What is it, Jo? Do you not think the shirts will suit me?' he asked, sitting down. 'I suppose Della has countermanded me and is bringing Beth down 'ere?' Jack added, wondering also if he could get up from the table and have his bum rubbed again.

Jo was amazed, and it wasn't about the shirts, but knew she shouldn't be, and quickly gathered in her startled face and reapplied the special reserve fed-up face, especially reserved for her kids and Jack. She knew that in many departments Jack was a bozo, but he did have an ability sometimes to know what is happening, and often before anyone else.

'Jo, you going to tell me? And the tomb, was it the Banks Mausoleum?' His coffee pot began bubbling.

Jo decided to tell him. 'Wear whatever shirt you like, and Della popped into the office yesterday; a sort of post-coital visit...'

Jack thought Jo could be so stupid at times, and he laughed as he relayed to her, 'It's coastal, Jo, you wally, post-coastal...' and sighed about being limbered and working with such eejits.

Jo was not offended or abashed at Jack's outspoken thoughts, she was used to working with him and had done so for more years than she cared to remember. 'As I was saying, Della popped in, post-coastal, likely for some social amenities, and to impart the very sound opinion that she thought you were past it, and maybe you should actually retire and not just flounce in a prima-donna consultant way. She also said she countermanded your orders about letting the people watch the safe house and to follow the watchers back, maybe to this *Myloft* fellow.'

Jo managed a chortle at Jack's made-up name for another Herbert he considered was causing mayhem. The main man even, he had said, but he did put crossed fingers in the air when he had said that. People were convinced he meant Mycroft, but dare not ask; after all, he had labelled the previous villain Norafarty, when he meant Moriarty.

The coincidental irony that *Myloft* was *Norafarty's* half-brother, had still to be revealed to everyone, although Jo and Mandy, both consommé Jack Austin people, thought Jack had more than an inkling of Myloft's identity; he would tell them in his own good time, they supposed, which was always the way with Jack.

Jack was preoccupied, but, on the basis her requests for information would seep into the Austin brainbox by Jackmosis, Jo continued, her eyes riveted on the wriggling body of Jack, evidently struggling with a logistical conundrum; how to get his bum rubbed and get to the stove to his bubbling coffee pot.

'Della did mention also, in her inimitable fruity manner, that although she does not like it when you tell her what to do, this was not the reason why she countermanded you.' Jo left it there, as Jack was chuckling to himself as he dashed to the cooker, stopped his Mocha pot mocha'ing and sped back, presenting his bum for Mandy to stroke. 'Jack?' Jo continued. 'Nothing to say?'

Jack ruminated, which was not a pleasant sight, and as ruminating is a bovine way of thinking, this was of course accompanied by arse-scratching which unfortunately required him to bat away Mandy's hand, temporarily.

'Jack, stop chewing the cud and leave your starboard bow alone, at least until Jo has left, and tell us what you are laughing at,' Mandy said, barely disguising her own amusement and thinking rather than a granddad shirt, he should maybe have a Klingon cloaking device on his head and backside, if they made one big enough.

Jack, ever the pregnantist, returned to his coffee pot, began rubbing his bum on the edge of the sink, much in the way a Romulan would, and out of the corner of his one eye could see Mandy watching his rhythmic backside. 'What? If you won't rub it, I have to use the sink, derr.'

Meesh and Martin tittered at Jack's forlorn look; he was good at looking forlorn, although some people thought it was his spoilt bat face that, ironically, he never did, never having ever been a spoilt bat, although he did like cricket and was going to have a lawn for the garden.

'Come here,' Mandy said and Jack shuffled along the kitchen floor with his victory smirk applied, to have his bum rubbed, while he told Jo and Mandy what he was thinking. Martin sat on Jo's foot to rub his own bum, Meesh snuggled into Mandy's waist, seeking comfort, and Jack, having established his position, leaned into Mandy and whispered into her ear, 'I love you Amanda,' and kissed her lips, gently. The trouble was, by the time Jack got to Mandy and had been overcome by the powerful desire to inform her of his love, and to kiss her, he'd forgotten what he was thinking about, which didn't worry him unduly as he was focused on having his bum rubbed by a gorgeous woman, and then, what colour granddad shirts he would get and whether to get slim-fit or ordinary.

'Jack?'

He'd arrived, it wasn't far from the cooker to the table, and he was already drifting off into a buttock-fondling reverie, so Mandy had to bring him back, fearful of a suspicious amount of movement in his front boxer short department and thinking, *slim-fit?*

'What?' Jack was buying time, using the query as an opportunity to try to remember what he was going to say, without getting caught.

'You were going to say...?' Had Mandy forgotten as well? She did look over to Jo.

Jo obliged. 'Why were you laughing when I mentioned Della?' Jo was exasperated, and Jack wondered why. He always thought she was a good mumsy, thought back to his own mum, who indeed had been a good mumsy, but was also often exasperated with him; quite unreasonably so, he often thought.

'Jack?'

Blimey, he'd drifted off again. 'Well...' a good start, something was coming... (oh shut up, I know what you're thinking, focus on the story and not the bum-rubbing, for heaven's sake), '... I was laughing because this is why I wanted Della to come down and join us.' There, he'd done it, and now all he had to do was to work out how to get his coffee without allowing Mandy to stop rubbing his bum.

Mandy stood, still fondling and caressing. 'I'll come with you to the coffee pot.'

'Did I...?'

'You did...' both Mandy and Jo said, Mandy multitasking with her bum hand to steer her husband to his coffee pot, Jack sporting his smug smirk, not unlike his spoilt bat look he didn't do, unless he was victorious, which he frequently was.

With his hand nervously wobbling, Jack poured coffee into his World Cup Italia demitasse cup, clouds on the cup and grass and a football on the saucer, and having completed that task with a cup and saucer full of black tar, he flicked his head to his bum woman, a bit like a fighter pilot has a wing man, to indicate he was intending to return to the table with cup, saucer and pot. Mandy left his backside and returned ahead of him.

'Oi, me bum?'

'Rub it yourself, I'm not your wing man, and don't flick your head at me.' Jack smiled, knowingly. 'And what are you smirking at, you spoilt brat?' Mandy re-acted, quite shocking him.

'I wasn't smirking and I don't do spoilt bat.'

'Alright, what were you thinking that caused an inadvertent and as yet unidentifiable smirk?' Mandy asked, conceding minor territory; she knew you had to do sometimes in order to get information from Jack Austin.

'Not a smirk... O'Hurra?' Jack said, smirking and wobbling his head to his Communications Officer. He'd decided to demote her from Science Officer as she had stopped rubbing his bum; served her right, and maybe she would think more carefully in a future star date.

'Oh, for fuck's sake tell us... and I don't give a shit about being Science Officer.' Mandy's famed impatience reared its head, but even that would not fool Jack. After all, who wouldn't want to be Science Officer if they couldn't be Kirk with a smirk, and he was Kirk; well, he was if he wasn't Virgil, who, being a wooden-top puppet, never smirked.

'Ooooh dear...' and Jack pulled up his Captain Kirk squirrel's hands to his cheeks to chew some nuts, '... 'andbags at ten paces...' He swallowed some imaginary nuts. He was, after all, a method lesbian and he methodically thought on how he would act some more as an idea struck him.

'What idea has struck you?' Mandy asked, wondering if she should strike him.

He replied to Mandy's enquiring look. 'I was wondering if we're still playing that game, you know, the one where I allow you to think you're in charge, darlin'... Clearly we are?'

Mandy sighed, looked to Jo to acknowledge her responding look of sympathy, and then summoned her dope of a husband. 'Come here, I'll rub your bum, and you can tell us about Della, pretty please with red injuns on top,' Mandy covering all the metaphorical bases, realising too late she had forgotten brass knobs.

Jack went to stand beside Mandy and this definitely was his Kirk smirk, but Mandy and Jo let it go; they were, after all, the grown-ups at the table. Jack presented his bum for caressing and mentioned that Mandy had forgotten brass knobs, and he was now prepared to tell it how he saw it; he just hoped he could remember it all. He looked deep into Mandy's eyes that flared emerald – she was either responding to his sexy smirk or becoming agitated. 'I brought Della down here so she could take over from me...' and Jack leaned into the fondling, thinking he had said enough and could maybe settle down and enjoy himself. He leaned over for his cup, and, after drinking the saucer coffee, as the Kings of Ireland used to do, he sipped some black tar coffee from his World Cup cup.

He looked at Jo and back to Mandy. 'What?'

'That's it, is it, your feckin' eejit majesty? That's all the explanation we are about to get, is it? And when were you going to tell me? And are you retired, or is this a flouncing smirk, not a victory smirk, and the Banks Mausoleum?' Mandy had summarised all that Jo was thinking. There was nothing she could add, so she settled, enjoining Mandy in a stare, both women adopting slanty, enquiring heads, looking for an answer with just a hint of irritation, and I am no smirk expert, but it was likely a Shakespearian *gotcha* smirk.

Jack noticed, of course, he was not an experienced woman man for nothing, and he prepared to answer as he slumped back down into his chair. But which question, Jack was wondering, as he allowed his mind to drift, not realising that inadvertently he had also allowed his smirk to morph; blimey, you have to be really careful with smirks!

Mandy was first to notice the smirk morph and shortly after, a tear forming. She was used to her man crying, especially as they had learned he was suffering with Post Traumatic Stress Disorder, PTSD, but she wondered what had caused this latest facial precipitation. She could not recall any of his known buttons being pressed; she was always wary. Meesh leapt off Mandy's lap and went to Jack's leg. Martin woofed a *God help me* bark and wiped a paw across his furry brow. He'd seen this so many times before. His former master was, unfortunately, a wuss.

Mandy followed Meesh and went to stand behind him and began to massage his shoulders. 'Tell me, Jack, while I give you a rub-down with the *Sporting Life*, please?' she breathed into his ear and kissed his neck.

Jo looked up at the ceiling, joining Martin.

Jack gazed into his wife's not insubstantial nose. He could see right up her nostrils and was wary of an echo, so he lowered his head, the massaging having a sufficiently recuperative effect. She smoothed his head, an Indian Head message without the feathers, he liked them, they didn't tickle, and he turned a solemn gaze to Jo-Jums. 'I'm losing it. Della knows me and has seen and told me several times, 'cept I forgot...' a tiny chuckle, '... she disguises it with humour, but she can see. I'm forgetful, consistently lose my train of thought. I think it's Old-timers.'

Mandy leaned over to look at her man's ugly face and could see the fear behind the horrendous scarring. He had always been scared of Alzheimer's, and it said a lot for her man that he thought of others first. She clumped him. Her Nightingale genes could stretch only so far. 'Why didn't you tell me? I'm your wife!'

He looked at his wife, was tempted to say "are you?" then saw her concerned face; he liked that face, regardless of the staying power of the genes that formed it. 'I was going to... but I must have forgotten.'

Mandy and Jo looked at each other and chuckled; it was funny. Mandy strode to the phone and dialled.

'Who're you phoning?' he enquired, rolling his shoulders and rattling his head, missing the massaging, coincidentally wondering if Mandy had disturbed his hairdo. Then he relaxed, realising he looked good with ruffled hair, which would also go really well with his granddad shirts.

'The doctor's surgery, we're going to get you checked out,' she replied, and began the interminable wait for someone to answer. 'Where have they taken Beth, Jo?' Mandy was demonstrating her multitasking abilities, which served to distract Jack from the imminent doctor's appointment. She knew he hated doctors, and she would have to go with him, to explain to the doctor what the problem was. She'd seen it before. He goes in and tells the doctor he's fine and leaves.

Jack's face became animated. 'Oh no, don't tell me, she's arranged for her to shack-up at the Gravediggers? That will explain the Mandarins across the road in the cemetery, of course. Transport and Education, right?'

He knew the answer before Mandy could explain that Seb had messaged them, and he was up from his chair and headed for the kitchen door before Jo could comment, 'She's down now and with Jimbo... How did you know it was Transport and Education?'

Jo's voice faded when he stopped and turned. 'Jimbo?'

Jo looked at Mandy then back to Jack. 'Christ, Jack, surely you remember Jimbo?' Was the Oldtimers more advanced than they both had realised, Mandy wondered, thinking maybe she should take him to the doctor's sooner rather than later and get his brainbox tested.

"Course I remember Jimbo, I'm not feckin' senile...' stopped, thought, '...yet. Just, I would have thought it would be Tony bringing her down. I asked Jimbo to keep an eye on the Bumblin'ton Club...' more thinking, not a pretty sight, his face, not the club which was an attractive Regency building in St James's, the West End of London, only it was ugly inside, and that was the members, '... so who's watching Myloft?'

'Jack, do you mean Mycroft, and do you know who this is? Because it would have helped if you had said something,' Mandy asserted.

'No, that's the brother of Sherlock Holmes. Myloft is Len's half-brother. Should have thought that through at the time,' Jack said, rubbing his chin, still at the kitchen door, thinking he might have a shave, then scratched his bum to aid his thinking.

Mandy looked at him with loving, yet worried eyes. He was either deep in thought or he had forgotten where he was going. He was scratching his arse so he was likely thinking. Mandy contemplated scratching her own bottom but she had no cloaking device.

Martin got up and nudged Jack's leg with his nose. 'Get on with it, numpty,' he barked, and Jack got on with it, and Martin followed. Martin knew Meesh was soon to be off on holiday with her new family and he was with Jack and Mandy for Christmas. Martin knew, but clearly Jack had forgotten, and this would be him for the next two or three weeks, looking after Jack while Mandy went to work. Martin, once again, put a paw to his furry, furrowed and ruffled brow and woofed a sigh. Why did he have to do everything around here?

THIRTEEN

'JONAS DARLIN', YOU DO KNOW I LOVE YOU, AND I want us to have this baby and be a family together, don't you?' Della whispered. They were in bed and had just made love, which, although mildly stimulating for Della, his wounds made the experience more a painful bliss for Jonas. But, he did love this woman.

'Yes, Della, and I love you too.'

'You do, don't you,' Della said, smooching up to his Gypo ear, and the smooch felt good but he sensed it came with a price-tag.

'Why?' He was starting to get to know Della, and despite the pain in his arm and thigh, he pushed himself up in the bed.

She scratched her fingers through the thick mat of black Gypo hair on his chest and smiled benignly. 'Because I want you to know somefink, honeybun, gorgeous man...'

Jonas sloped his head to enquire what it was that she wanted him to know. 'You should know, because I have said it often enough,' she continued and Jonas racked his brains but still came up blank. 'I do love it in bed with you, you know that, don't you?' He nodded, the smile of a condemned innocent man. 'For Christ's sake, Jonas...'

He battened down his hatches, managing a respectable, "What?"

'... Do I 'ave to do evryfink 'round 'ere?' Della finally answered, a tad frustrated, now on top of Jonas, attempting to sexually reduce her brain capacity and it was not working, as clearly she had to think about doing everything.

'I am injured, Della. It's only a couple of days ago I was shot because of your antics in the cemetery, and the hospital said to keep the thigh and arm still.' Jonas was not in the mood to have Della impugn his manliness, and also wondered if it was really true; Della had told him she was going to become a nurse but in the end became a copper... well, a spook.

Della had a reply, but had to stop when there was a knock on the door. 'Fuck off, whoever it is,' she answered, sensitively. Yeah, Jonas thought, maybe she was going to be a nurse.

'Della darlin', get off Jonas and step outside for a minute, there's a luv.'

'Jack! What the feck you doin' 'ere?' she shouted back, but she had already decided to get off, and now showed some concern at Jonas's injuries.

'Fuck off downstairs, I'll be there in a minute...' she shouted, and started to look at the dressings that were showing signs of blood seepage. She applied her Nightingale face and looked carefully, and Jonas thought, yes, he could see her as a nurse.

'Just a feckin' scratch, yer big cotton-candy pansy-arse,' she said, standing and heading to the bathroom, and Jonas reconsidered her nursing aptitude; he could hear Jack's clodhopping feet disappear down the corridor, along with some distinct chortling, and was that a dog? Maybe Cabbage had come up with Jack, and had Jack been listening at the door? But Jonas dismissed this; Jack was notoriously deaf, and Cabbage, his dog, had no voyeuristic tendencies he was aware of.

———

Jack and Martin had left for the Gravediggers, Mandy was going into work to meet up with Jo and the Commander for a debriefing later that morning. There was a knock at the door; the *Spirit of Liffy* brass knocker resounding like it was cannon fire. It could only be Meesh back again; the child struggled to reach the knocker and as a consequence banged overly hard.

'Alright Meesh, I'm coming,' Mandy called, hopping on one leg and putting a shoe on the raised foot. She reached the door, smiling at what she was expecting to see, but as she released the latch, so the door burst open and smashed into her head. She went sprawling backward and before she could collapse into a heap, Keef Bananas had stepped into the lobby, grabbed the lapels of her jacket and slammed her back into the inner glass lobby door, whilst kicking the front door closed behind him.

Mandy tumbled back and this time Keef let her go. The back of her head cracked into the toughened glass door pane. She slumped, only to have a size ten Doc Marten boot tread firmly on her nose and eyes. She heard the cartilage crumble, blood jetted from her nose and she saw it splatter onto the shirt of Keef Bananas as he leaned over her.

Instinctively she pleaded, 'Please, stop.'

Bananas didn't. He grabbed her jacket, lifted her half off the floor and back-handed her across her face. Mandy's head slewed sideways and she crumpled, tried to stand and was back-handed again. He dropped her and this time she stayed down; she was aware the glass door was now askew and thought, absurdly, *Jack was supposed to have fixed that.*

'You think you're so high and fucking mighty. Not so smart now, are yer?' and Keef kicked Mandy in the ribs.

Mandy knew not to antagonise an ignoramus thug, it only provoked more violence, and so she allowed herself to swoon and the kicking stopped. The faint was only partly feigned as she sensed herself being dragged back into the house. She heard tape being stripped from a sticky roll and felt her arms being tugged behind her. She saw the silvery duct tape roll flash past her eyes as it went to her legs, and finally it was wrapped around her head and sealed her mouth. She struggled to breathe, her nose having collapsed and being congested with snot and blood; she snorted and managed to get air in but it immediately filled up. She snorted again, and Keith got the picture and released the tape. A good sign, Mandy thought. It meant he was acting under instruction, and those who issued the orders wanted her alive; for the time being, at least.

'Not a word or the tape goes back on. Got it, bitch?' and Mandy nodded understanding, temporarily relieved.

She heard an old van pull up noisily outside the front of the house. It sounded as if the exhaust was broken. Keef disappeared, but reappeared shortly after with a carpet roll and Shitlegs. Incongruously, she thought, as she was being rolled into the carpet and then hoisted up to shoulder height that Shitlegs must have come down again this morning.

The carpet was not particularly savoury, and despite the damage to her nose, she was aware of the smell of stale beer, cigarettes and mildew. She snuffled and struggled as she was jiggled through the doorway by the two thugs, to be unceremoniously dumped into the back of the van. She heard the rear doors screech on rusty hinges and slam, the lever click and lock into place. She tried to wriggle and release the carpet roll, but it would not loosen. She realised it must be tied, and despaired as the engine gunned to life and the odours of stale beer, fag ash and mildew mingled with exhaust fumes.

————

SINCE NOBODY ELSE SEEMED INTERESTED, Martin introduced himself to Cabbage with a close examination of her intimate lady parts. Jonas's dog was called

Cabbage, but she was a mongrel Collie really, and a scruffy one at that, but there was something about the bitch that appealed to Martin, who was himself a pedigree, but he was no snob where bitches were concerned. Jack saw the canine attraction, and winked conspiratorially at his dog. Jonas saw and told Martin, in no uncertain terms, "paws off", but Jonas, who knew Martin, but not that well, was lulled into a false sense of security about this hound. Martin had a rep that suited his spook character, he thought – *minternational dog of mystery*. Martin lived on the hedge, and he likely would if he spent the next few weeks with Jack and Mandy. He gave Jonas a cheesy grin; he liked cheese, strong cheddar, none of that French shite, he would say, mimicking his former master.

'Aaaah, that's nice, is he going to give Cabbage one, Jonas? Maybe they should have a room?' Della appeared, chuckling at her amusing aside, as she joined the crowd standing around the flirting Cabbage and overtly stimulated Martin. 'Nice lipstick, Martin,' she said, even more amusingly, as she placated her agitated Gypo with an extended stroke of his face, finishing up with a noisily planted kiss and a raspberry.

Jack gently toed his dog up the backside. 'Later, Martin, we have business.'

Martin gave an old-fashioned look and this softened Jack. He'd not seen that look for a long time, had thought it had gone out of fashion; for dogs, anyway.

'What's up, love, are you not diverted?' Della said, in a Jane Austen amusing manner to Jonas.

'What?' Jonas replied in a Gypo manner, only a little bit like Ted Heathcliffe out of *I Can't Stand Heights*, Jack thought.

Della turned on Jack. 'Jack, Jonas is not a Gypo and its *Wondering Heights,* you dozy bastard, and yes, you did speak your thoughts.' Della eased up on Jack and seemed to be thinking to herself, and Jonas sensed a rebuke; for a Gypo, Jonas was remarkably in tune with the woman with whom he had fallen in love. 'Jonas,' she asked sweetly, intimating that a rebuke was coming, 'did you get rid of that lucky bleedin' 'evver, darlin'?'

Martin knew that look on Jonas's face. He had seen it on Jack's many times before, and he knew that whatever lucky bleedin' 'evver was, it most certainly had not been gotten rid of, so he woofed a "der", and flipped a cheesy grin at Cabbage. Cabbage liked cheese as well, it seemed, and Martin vibrated his lips in the manner of a French horse, just in case it was French cheese the bitch liked. Martin was no expert, but he thought he was in there; he was smitten by Cabbage.

'Can we get on, please?' Jack asked.

Della frowned. She could see the sense in getting on, but did not like being told what to do. 'We will get on when I'm ready. Sit yerself down and Jonas will bring coffee after he's dumped the feckin' 'evver.'

Jonas disappeared upstairs and Jack thought he needed to have a word. It was just not funny seeing a man ordered around by a woman.

'Jack, shut up, and sit down.'

'Righto Della,' Jack replied, knowing he was going to sit down anyway, and when Della's back was turned he stuck two fingers up.

'I saw that, you juvenile, senile old bugger.' Jack had, of course, forgotten that women had eyes in the back of their head, but thought he had her on "juvenile, senile", and he tittered. Della rounded on him. 'What are you tittering about?'

Still tittering, he confidently informed her of her basic error. 'Juvenile, senile?' and he applied his victory, smug smirk. It was good, he'd practiced when Mandy was in the bathroom this morning; he had it spot on, and Martin nodded he had. Della sighed, reconciling her thoughts with an amusing picture of visiting Jack in his nursing home. 'Will you visit me, Della?'

She was about to reply in kind to Jack when her phone rang. 'Jo-Jums, mornin', sweet'art. Relaxacat, girl, I'll be in soon. Get fings going, will yer? I can always catch up and before you ask, Beth and Jimbo are settled like bugs in a rug. I take it you have some woodentops outside?' She smiled; it was her own victory smirk. Jack was proud, he'd taught her that look. 'You didn't bleedin' teach me that look...' but Della was interrupted by Jo-Jums squawking on the end of the phone, telling her to shut up and stop behaving like a child.

'See, Jack?' Della said. 'Jo finks you're behavin' like a kid,' and she reapplied the smirk, but added some brass knobs for good measure before returning to her phone call, all businesslike. 'Jo, what can I do fer yer?' She listened and looked at Jack, who was feeling his face to check the look as there was no mirror. 'Jack, Jo-Jums says Mandy has missed a meeting with the Commander. She left for work this morning, didn't she?'

'Why's Jo ringing you and not...' He stopped and realised Mandy kept his phone for him; usually they were together. 'She hadn't left, but was about to...'

Martin was alerted. He was a sensitive dog, especially if you discussed Jack's looks, but his tail was down; this did not feel right.

Jo told Della she had dispatched a patrol car to the house and would come back to them, Jack was already half out of the door, but came back with some lucky heather on his head. 'Della, you got yer jam jar?'

'Yes.'

'Well, that's lucky.'

FOURTEEN

Pointe-Lace took a call and a rare smile crossed his face, which was noticed by the other members peering over the top of their newspapers. Those sensitive to Archie's moods and looks did not read this as a happy grin. It looked like trouble to them, and the heads ducked behind their papers to avoid being buttonholed.

———

'What? What have you done?' The Duchess was taking a call from Keef. She played her part well. There was always a chance her phone was being tapped, and she was not talking about the police or MI5. She knew her husband's Eton friend, Button-hole, had long tentacles, and her former relationship with Lord Teapot would only stand her in good stead for so long. The problem with Buttonhole, she thought, was he never directly ordered his people but left a lot to interpretation. It was almost as though he delighted at looking to see what they did, reacting to the outcome as if he had never foreseen the results. The Duchess wondered if he really knew what he was doing, but simply trusted in Big-Knob; whoever he was.

———

DELLA DROVE LIKE A WOMAN POSSESSED. Not because they had news of Mandy, it was just her way of driving, and of course everyone else on the road was a bloody nuisance or a moron, and this is what she was explaining to the patrolman who had pulled her up for dangerous driving, on the wrong side of Albert Road, a busy shopping street.

'Listen, turnip,' and she flipped her Met Police I.D. card at him whilst looking back to Jack in the passenger seat, who was just opening his one eye, and returned the manic stare. You had to know Della in order to understand the level of riled that can occur. The patrolman was experiencing normal riled, but to him, it appeared as if he had a madwoman in front of him, and was considering calling this in when Della stepped up to moderate ballistic. The patrolman relaxed just a little as the madwoman who, strangely, had a London Metropolitan Police I.D. card, turned to the grossly disfigured passenger. It then dawned on him the passenger was Jane Austin; he was not the sharpest turnip in the police vegetable patch.

'Jack, am I still a copper or a spook?' she asked, confusing PC Turnip even more.

Jack thought for a bit, felt his face, which was a knee-jerk precautionary reaction; you never knew with Della and looks. 'You know, I'm not sure.' He rubbed his face some more, it was calming him.

Della gunned the engine. Not that she was thinking of a getaway, she was merely tapping her foot in ire. 'Oh, fuck it,' and she stuck the beaten-up old Saab into gear and tore off down the road, leaving the patrolman hopping mad as she'd run over his foot.

Della looked in her rear-view mirror and giggled to herself, oblivious of the chaos occurring around her, as pedestrians and motorists took evasive action. 'Serve the feckin' woodentop right,' she said, as she rummaged around in her jeans, which caused even more reckless steering. Eventually, she produced her phone and speed-dialled with one hand whilst, with her spare hand, she tooted for a car to get out of her way.

'Jo-Jums,' she said into her phone as she bumped up the kerb and knocked over a parking meter, 'do me a flavour, luv, ring whoever you 'ave to, and tell them a patrolman just tried to trip me up. Tell 'em I'll not take action this time, but if they do it again I might get really mad.' There was no reaction on the phone. 'Jo, you there, lovely?'

Jo-Jums replied, 'Della, is Jack with you?'

'Yeah, the feckin' turnip is sitting wiv his eye shut and moanin' on and on. Honestly, I will...' Della paused, sensing Jo had dire news and coincidentally slowed her car down. A following patrol car with blues and twos rammed the back of her. They were jolted but Della was not distracted.

She stopped the car. 'Jo, what is it?' She listened and flipped a look at Jack who was just opening his eye again, as the new patrolman opened the driver door and suggested Della might like to step out. Della spoke to Jack as she obliged the patrolman. 'Jack, someone called Bobby has called at your house, the door was open and there's claret all over the shop. Mandy's not there.'

Jack got out of the passenger seat, remarkably calmly Della thought, and remarked on this to the patrolman, who was starting to strong-arm her.

I may have mentioned before about the Della temperament, but we have, as yet, never seen it manifest itself in its truly sterling colours; I'm not one to dwell in someone else's bedroom, as you would imagine, but I am pretty sure Jonas has this pleasure to come, and I am not sure I envy him that one. When the patrolman comes out of hospital, we could maybe ask him to describe what it feels like to be on the receiving end, but suffice to say, Della kneed him in the groin and tumbled the six-footer over her petite sparrow frame onto the road, and, with her knee on his throat, she whispered gently into his ear, 'Listen, tosspot, feck off back to the Brownies and tell Brown Ale you've been a naughty wanker and upset Inspector Lovington,' and she slapped him playfully on his cheeks a couple of times to affirm the message had been received loud and clear, and his injuries were meant in good humour, of course.

In the meantime, the patrolman's partner was grabbing Della, so it was time he learned about her as well, and she left him sprawled on the tarmac as she ran to the patrol car that was leaving with Jack behind the wheel. 'Oi!' she shouted and Jack stopped. She climbed into the passenger seat and Jack drove off, leaving the two patrol officers standing, a painfully dazed look on their faces, as Jack ran over their feet.

Jack pulled up behind Bobby's car and as a consequence of the narrow street that was Frisian Tun, the serpentine-like lane was well and truly blocked. Jack could see the Duchess railing at Bobby about the perceived inconvenience of the blocking-up of her road, as she described it, stressing this was not the sort of area where police cars stopped, and especially with blue flashing lights.

Della looked at Jack. He was outwardly calm, no berserking, considering his options, weighing up all he knew, and rationalising the situation. She only secretly fumed he had not, as yet, shared all of his thoughts with her, but it would be only a matter of time, or she would run over his feet.

Jack eased himself out of the car with no *oomphing* or complaining, and Della sprung from her own seat realising Jack had his *on a mission* face on; not a smirk in sight. She caught him up, just as he spun the Duchess around to face him, and left Bobby stuttering a warning for Jack to ease up, but the anticipated berserking explosion did not happen. The Duchess looked on at Jack's ravaged face only inches from her own and a gentle shudder ran through her faux aristocratic frame, a slight wobble to her head as she tried to reassure herself of her right to rule in this, her manor. Water off to Jack, who preferred fish to duck anyway, and he allowed his natural irritation at the upper classes to simmer below the surface as he spoke. 'Keef been down, 'as he?' Jack asked, and applied his *how lovely* face that he knew snobs liked.

'No,' she said. He had her. They had seen Keef last night and, if he was not mistaken, he recalled he had not returned to London with the others.

'Oh,' Jack said, 'I thought I saw him last night. Suppose he went home to London?'

The Duchess looked mildly irritated at being caught out, but she was a pro in the non-sexual sense, although he did wonder. 'Last night, he visited me but went home. You'll probably catch up with him in Hither Green, Inspector, I'm sure your colleagues will know his address,' and she looked directly at Della.

Did she know Della, Jack thought? Della was biding her time, the epitome of patience as another patrol car turned up, and Bobby had to restrain the officers from arresting Jack and Della, something about flat feet, but Bobby knew better than to disturb Jack when he had his, *I'm on a mission*, face on; that could morph anytime to his berserking face or, heaven forbid, an unfathomable smirk.

'Lady Francesca Blanche-Teapot, thank you, and I'm sorry for the inconvenience. I will ask these policemen to leave. Oh, you didn't see anything going on at my house, did you? Only Mandy has gone missing and there's tomato fucking ketchup every-where.' There was only so long Jack could maintain a poncy voice, and if you added polite, it became even more of a strain.

The Duchess thought for a while. 'I did see the carpet people take one carpet in and one out, but that is all.' She slipped into snotty cow mode. 'I have to say, Inspector, it did not look like a particularly im-pressive carpet you were having delivered. Not the sort of quality we expect around here.'

'How could you tell?'

The Duchess smiled and displayed a full set of horse gnashers, and Jack wondered if he should pop a Granny Smith in. 'I just know these things, Inspector, and frankly, I would expect no more of you...' She had the bit between her teeth. 'Have you thought of moving to an area more suited to your type?'

Jack was not going to allow himself to be riled by a posh old turnip. 'Thank you, Lady Teapot, I am sure we will not need you any further,' he said and the Duchess returned to her semi-detached villa, to be joined by a number of her sycophants, and they dis-appeared to share tea and likely receive the latest lec-ture from the Duchess.

Jack, irritated, brushed the officer's hand from his shoulder, and now he blew. 'Feck off, woodentop!'

The copper backed away and Bobby hustled the officers away and asked if they could maybe take Jack's patrol car as well. Della, never one to miss a trick, asked if, while they were at it, they could take her car back to the Gravediggers pub and mention to the landlord that the back lights may be defective. The officers looked peeved, and Della added 'pretty please' with menace, and turned to follow Jack into his house; job done.

When Della got there, Jack was kneeling and crying beside the blood-covered glazed door. He thought incongruously that he had been going to fix that door for ages and now he would have to. He was also aware he had been holding his emotions in check, and needed to maintain his calm if he was to help Mandy, but still he wept, and couldn't stop.

FIFTEEN

IT HAD BEEN A PAINFULLY UNCOMFORTABLE journey and Mandy had no sense of time, but it could not have been long on smooth roads, for she soon felt herself being jostled as the van traversed bumpy terrain. Then it stopped and the engine cut. She could hear muffled arguing, a grating metallic growl as the van rear doors opened, and the two thugs debating how best to get the carpet, with Mandy inside, out of the van.

'Unroll the carpet, you fucking turnips,' she called out.

'What?' Shitlegs asked.

Mandy repeated her suggestion and eventually they complied, after which Shitlegs grabbed Mandy by her ankles and yanked her out of the van, causing her skirt to rise, and the bloom of her anger was reinforced by a blush of embarrassment. Not for the first time, she thought she should wear trouser suits to work, but Jack, being Jane, liked her in skirts, primarily so he could look up them of course, and she didn't mind that. Strangely, Keef and Shitlegs appeared to pay no heed to Mandy's indelicate exit from the van, and as they stood her up, her modesty was reinstated.

While they pondered their next move, Mandy looked back into the van. There was another carpet roll there, with still feet, shod in good quality, but worn leather shoes, sticking out of it. During the thug hiatus, she took in her surroundings. She was in a rural yard, enclosed by a hotchpotch of timber and tired concrete block shelters, barns and working sheds. Mandy's senses were alerted by the commencement of a whining, buzzing sound she recognised as a machine saw cutting timber. She recalled Jack saying that not far from Stansted woods, where they frequently took walks, there was a sawmill, and she was convinced this was where she was, but could not see beyond the enclosed courtyard. The yard flooring was part cobbled, but was mainly churned mud which had frozen into ridges, contributing to Mandy's unsteadiness. She was a bundle of nerves, chilled by fear and the freezing cold.

Keef strode off in the direction of what she assumed to be the sawmill, the intermittent whining saw screeching incongruously, agitating a still and frosty day.

'What d'you want me to do, Keef?' Shitlegs called out.

'Follow, you dozy twat,' Keef answered, in the manner of a leader.

'I'm not carrying 'er, she looks bloody 'eavy.'

'Oi!' Mandy said.

'Sorry,' Shitlegs replied, and explained about his bad back.

'Oh, you poor sod,' Mandy replied. 'You could cut the tape from my legs so I can walk. Sound like a plan?'

Shitlegs looked like he considered the plan, stepped to Mandy and fireman-lifted her over his shoulder, and *oomphed* and *aaahed* after Keef, who was waiting at the huge timber double doors. He had removed a scaffold pole that propped the doors, and was discordantly clanking this on the brick paviors that formed an apron to the mill entrance.

'You should have taken the tape off 'er legs and she could 'ave walked, you dozy bugger,' Keef said, as Shitlegs staggered to a halt at the doors and lowered Mandy, and began stretching and arching his back, moaning and massaging as he waddled back to the van to collect the Jeremy carpet, which had no means of self-propulsion.

'Jack can carry me no problem, and he's, what, forty years older than you, Shitlegs?' Mandy said, as Shitlegs returned to the van. She wondered if her nose had grown, but realised it probably wouldn't, as it was probably broken.

'Surely he can't?' Shitlegs called back.

'He can, and has done it often,' Mandy replied. She thought of grinning but it might hurt.

'No?'

'Yep.'

'She's winding you up,' Keef said, coming to Shitlegs' rescue, but not offering any help with the Jeremy carpet.

'Are you?'

'You will see when he rescues me, won't you!' She grinned this time and it did hurt.

Keef punched Mandy in her solar plexus and she doubled up and fell to the floor. The humour of the situation had evaporated and Mandy was violently brought back to reality. She was scared and worried, and why a sawmill? Keef cut the tape binding her ankles and lifted her upright. Despite the pain she was in and the sick feeling in her stomach, Mandy saw this as her opportunity and made to run.

Keef anticipated all of this before it happened and, with grotesque menace and evil pleasure, he swung the scaffold pole and swiped Mandy's legs away. She heard her shin bones crack as she folded to the ground in excruciating pain. She lay there for a while, dazed, unbelieving of her plight and sensing a rising bile within her stomach and, as Shitlegs lifted her, she spewed over him, farted, thought of Jack, then fainted.

———

DELLA HELPED JACK UP, eased him to the table, sat him down and, rubbing his shoulders, she spoke in her caring voice that Jonas had yet to hear. 'I'm sure she'll be okay, we'll find her. D'you know what's 'appening?' Jack nodded, 'Well, why the fuck didn't you tell me?' Fairy Nurse moment was over.

Jack looked up, his one eye red and swollen. 'I fort you fort I was losing it?'

'Yes, well, I can exaggerate every now and then,' she replied, in the nearest she could get to conciliatory and, likely for the first time in her life, not exaggerating. 'Jack, I luv you like a tow-rag dad. I worry about you, and now Mandy. You need me to look after you, or better still, get out of the business and concentrate on being a godfather to Jonas and me's sprog. Now, that is where I do need you.'

Jack looked up from his seat into the beautiful, butter-wouldn't-melt, face of Della. 'You pregnant?'

'I 'ave Jonas's bun in me oven, and that is why you need to look after yerself.'

'Shouldn't it be me saying that to you?' Jack observed, his shell-shocked face portraying mixed emotions.

'You daft bugger. I'll need you and Mandy to look after number one kid, if Burial and John are busy. Now, get yer finking head into gear, and tell me what's 'appening.'

Jack told her and, as he little by little revealed his thinking, she slumped back into a chair, revising her opinion that number one prospective babysitter was losing it.

———

DAI ZEEZE (PRONOUNCED Die Zee-say) was one of those strange fellows, Welsh, but a dyed-in-the-wool Tory, blue, born into a seriously red country. There were many in Wales who were pro the reintroduction of Welsh values and traditions, even independence, and Dai counted himself amongst them. He spoke Welsh as his first language, but to say he was a die-hard nationalist would be to misinterpret his motives. Sure, he was a Welsh nationalist, in a weak-kneed spirit, and if pandering to a Welsh programme got him what he wanted, and quicker, then this is what he was; just not many people knew. He was a hard-nosed Tory, for a limp, wet lettuce of a fop, but at least at Party HQ he was considered an asset in Wales, a country where there were not many Tories prepared to stand.

Dai Zeeze had been brought up by his grandparents who were, back in the day, fierce Italian Fascists; cut their veins, hang them upside down from a lamppost, and Mussolini's blood would come gushing out in buckets, and Dai had been nurtured and succoured at the knee of Grandma and Grandpa Zeeze. As such, Dai's wretchedly pea-sized brain could comprehend only one way in which Wales should go, and it did not have the Welsh people at heart. Zeeze had a powerful self-interest within the only heart that mattered, his own and, blessed with the lyrical Welsh gift of the gab, and an inherent Italian *bella figura* image, he had become a charismatic politico who had soared up the political ladder, and was now a minister in the Department of Health, and tipped for the top.

As luck would have it, as it sometimes does, truth often being stranger than fiction, the Civil Servant who headed up the Department of Health, the Permanent secretary, colloquially known as the Mandarin, was Amlodd Jones. Also a Welshman, also ambitious, but in contrast to Zeeze, Amlodd had a powerful intellect and was an extraordinary man, though very much a behind the scenes merchant, and quite an enigma. People knew not what to make of Amlodd Jones. He had cultivated his fellow Welshman, his junior minister, shielded him and watched him grow in perceived stature; grooming him, you might say. Even though he despised the man and everything he stood for, Amlodd Jones was too canny to say, and cultivated what others would observe and say about his Minister.

Amlodd was also fiercely aware of his heritage, and ironically, his grandparents had groomed him at their knees, their Welsh socialist knees. He was not named Amlodd for nothing. The name in Welsh meant *the Grandfather of King Arthur* and Amlodd viewed Dai Zeeze, (reluctantly, as needs often outweigh common sense), as his King Arthur; a protégé, but only as a figurehead – there was no way he would allow the puppet strings of Dai Zeeze to ever be cut. Amlodd saw himself as *Merlin* in this relationship, the wizard who made things happen. Dai Zeeze could not see this, and Amlodd was determined the man would never live out his less than subliminal ambitions, and profit from his semblance of power.

Amlodd was thought to perceive everybody as a means to an end. You might say, and people did, that he was ideal material for a Mandarin, but in contrast to some of his Permanent Secretary colleagues, his ends were not personal aggrandisement, controlling power, or indeed avarice. In fact, you would be hard pushed to know anything about what Amlodd really wanted. He knew his way around the corridors of power, was secretive, some said sinister, and people knew to stay on the good side of him, and in lip-service they did, because they were creeped out by him, and not just by his reputation. His body was crooked – hunchback, they used to say in the old, non-politically-correct days – and he had a clubfoot to boot, so to speak. He appeared to simper and slime, dressed all in black, and had neither the personality nor the stature to make a stamp for himself, as his crooked frame and diminutive, shrunken, prune-like body meant he was ridiculed behind his deformed back.

He was however, highly respected for his enormous intellect and funnily enough, people thought they used him; used and abused even. But they would be seriously wrong, as shallow political automatons often are, even more so where Ministers were concerned, Dai Zeeze being a prime example of that Ministerial ignorance, only thinly veiled behind a shallow persona of sincerity.

Amlodd had been educated in Wales, in a State school, so naturally and ironically was not cut from the Bumblin'tons cloth, and as a consequence was not suited for that *set* and had never been offered a membership, not that he would have accepted. He had made senior Mandarin status against all of the odds, and he knew all there was to know about Bumblin'tons. He knew Archie Pointe-Lace. He knew of Pointe-Lace's manipulative yet extraordinary mind, the malevolence of the man and knew he was Amlodd's nemesis, and Amlodd would be Archie's; him and Jack Austin, that is.

Archie Pointe-Lace, despite his undoubted subtle credentials as a schemer and Machiavelli, was a man Amlodd respected as one amongst a precious few, and he allowed Archie, or Buttonhole as his silvery-spooned chums called him, to believe he was manipulating him. This is what Amlodd told himself, but Archie was not to be underestimated. Archie was a man not unlike Amlodd in intellectual prowess, or so Amlodd thought, but Archie thought Amlodd was way, way, out of his depth, but isn't that always the way? Arrogance blinds, and Archie Pointe-Lace had arrogance in buckets and spades, whereas Amlodd had something Archie would never have – street savvy, a working class survival instinct – which explained why Jack Austin and Amlodd got on so well.

Amlodd had grown up deformed, debased, and ridiculed on a Welsh council estate in Newport, and had his armour inbuilt, albeit cunningly disguised. Ironically, and from an entirely different mindset, Amlodd thought he was on the same wavelength as Archie. Something needed to be done, but as he sat sipping his tea, reflecting on Pointe-Lace, he thought he heard a sound, a tune. What was that music? He sipped. The tea in his flowery bone china cup had gone cold, but he didn't care. He mused and his mind drifted as the music intensified, beautiful, lyrical, and it gave him a warm sensation and he felt that warmth course through his body, shortly before he passed out.

When Amlodd Jones recovered himself, he was still in his office chair and his secretary was leaning over him, dabbing his shirt to remove the tea stain as best she could. 'Mr Jones... sir, you have a meeting.' Amlodd stirred and looked into his secretary's eyes as she spoke softly to him. 'May I suggest you take a few days off? You must be so tired. I struggled to wake you, and I didn't know you knew Sigmund Merde?'

She answered his questioning look with, 'He has just left, but I suppose it is natural you would meet him. Are you bringing him back into the NHS? I have to say, I think this would be a popular move. You know the nation has taken the man to their hearts. It is even said he will be meeting up with his daughter soon, isn't that lovely?'

Amlodd stared at his secretary. Her voice seemed detached. She seemed like a wooden puppet, her mouth worked by a ventriloquist. Her conversation was fuzzing his mind and so he did what came naturally to him, he agreed with her, and asked, 'Did you hear some music just now?' She looked concerned, and he explained further. 'Shostakovich, the second movement of the Second Piano Concerto.'

The secretary knew the piece but didn't know what on earth Mr Jones was talking about, and told him so. She left after reminding him of maybe taking a break. It would be Christmas soon, but Amlodd was not one for vacations or indeed time off; what would he do with that time?

Amlodd reassured his secretary he was okay and as she turned before going back to the outside office, he asked if she would cancel his appointments, except for Pointe-Lace, and to call the minister, Dai Zeeze, and tell him he was on his way over to meet with him.

He reflected; so Sigmund Merde had been here. He felt his arm, it was itchy. He rolled his sleeve back and saw a small puncture mark; had Ghost given him an antidote? Amlodd knew about the previous four Mandarins, one jogging, one at a Palace reception, and two others, Crispin Evens and Bartholomew Bozoquet, who had been drugged, much like he had just been, and taken from their offices in broad daylight.

The Transport and Education Mandarins were eventually found, chilled to the bone but alive in a cemetery in Portsmouth.

Each Mandarin, now suspected of corruption, had reported they had heard the same piece of music. What did it mean? Was he meant to be taken? Was he suspected of corruption, and had he survived because of the intervention of Ghost? Had he survived, and if he had, why? He was sure of one thing, and that was that he would not be telling anyone, especially Pointe-Lace; after all, this could be his work. Or, he wondered, had he been he left free in order to tell Archie? He would decide when he met him later.

SIXTEEN

THE DUCHESS ORDERED THE DISTRIBUTION OF tea to her entourage in a fine bone china tea service, and her second-in-command, Blossom Bottomley from 32 Frisian Tun, had brought her speciality, concrete fairy cakes. Everything was proper and as it should be. The police cars had gone and the Duchess thought, only to herself, so had the nosy cow Superintendent, and it would not be long before the ill-mannered cockney barrow boy upstart Inspector, followed.

She mused into the future... The Austin house would come onto the market and she could vet prospective owners, to ensure they fitted into *her* Frisian Tun, *her* upper-middle-class idyll. She had a nice professional, middle-aged couple in mind, children grown and flown the nest. Then she thought of the new people at number 23, a poet and his wife. She had erroneously thought they would be acceptable, but now she was wary of poets, especially if they minced and wore berets. She put those thoughts aside – she could deal with them another time and relished the prospect – as she pulled the net curtains to one side and looked out onto a tree-lined Frisian Tun; *her* Manor.

———

DELLA'S PHONE WENT. It was Del-Boy. 'Del, you've heard?' She waited and listened. 'Yes, I've asked Jo-Jums to reinforce the cover for Beth and Jimbo. Jack and I are going back to the Gravediggers now. He's okay, remarkably focused.' Della hung up. 'Jack, shall we speak to Beth?'

Jack screwed up his mouth and Della restrained a giggle at the horrible sight. What *did* Mandy see in the ugly turnip? Then she realised she had just told him she loved him, after a fashion, and so it always was with Jack, she realised.

'Della, ring Jackie, please, she should be with us when we talk to Beth,' Jack said.

Della looked like she did not agree, but the look on Jack's face suggested she should, so she speed-dialled. 'Jackie, it's Della, sweet'art.'

Jack leaned over and took the phone and he swung his head backwards immediately, expecting a right hook to follow. It didn't; was Della maturing? 'Fuck off maturing, you juvenile imbecile,' she said, and clumped him while he was distracted. Jack ignored her juvenile behaviour, but did wonder why he was no longer crying. Mandy was in danger and he had his nearly sensible head on.

'Jackie, you've heard Mandy's been taken?' He listened and Jackie enquired as to how he was handling the news. 'I need to remain stable, it's the only way I can find her before it's too late.' Della could hear an audible intake of breath from Jackie. 'I want to talk to Beth and I think you should be there. Can you get to the Gravediggers now, please? Thank you.' Jack ended the call and handed the phone back to Della.

'What now, man of bats?' Della asked.

'Jackie will be with Beth in an hour, so in the meantime, I think we call in for tea and buns and get yer Uncle Josh 'ed on Della,' and Jack headed a few doors up the road to the Duchess's semi-detached *villa*.

———

Miss Southampton–Meddlesome of number 17 was holding forth to Mrs Constance Crotchet of number 11, principally about what crochet stitches to use on their latest demonstration banners, but generally, the underlying conversational theme was disapproval of the Austins; police cars, indeed, all these opinions, approved by the Duchess, were asserted with complimentary, exaggerated tuts and sighs. The doorbell interrupted the flow of old bat juices, and talk of insurgence and crocheting ceased.

'Major, the door, dahhhhling, there's a sweetie,' The Duchess said, in a manner that would brook no defiance.

Major Newsonse put down his minute-taking pad and made his way to the door, and what he saw knocked him back onto his heels. He began mumbling inanities he hoped would not only sound intelligible, but also disguise his fear, and counter the complementary reaction in his watery bowels. The Duchess was issuing enquiring orders from her parlour, but the Major felt inadequate to the task of a reply. The Duchess frightened him, but this fear was more than superseded by the menace that emanated from the body language and riveting eyes of the visitors; not Jehovah witnesses, although they introduced themselves as such.

The Major remained rigid, his ramrod stance coincidentally assisting in management of his bowels and conveying, he hoped, a trained military posture, indicating, ironically, a readiness to act. Although he called himself a Major, he wasn't, he just thought he should be a Major, and when people enquired about his regiment and where he had served and so on, he would tap his nose, and of course this was sufficient for the middle classes, who believed what they wanted to believe, or what the Duchess told them to believe. The prevailing thought amongst the non-seeing middle class cognoscenti was the Major had been in something secret, likely the SAS, or the Durham Light Infantry, and of course, his passport to acceptance was the fact that the Duchess approved of him. He was their sort, liked embroidery, and this was good enough for everyone in and around Frisian Tun.

Ghost figured it was his role to break the stilted doorstep interlude, as the Major seemed transfixed by the intimidating presence of Abe Hyman, a broad, powerfully-built, squat man, and if you could ignore the patent menace, he was not unlike *SpongeBob Square Pants*, without the grin, or the sponge. He was a powerful and intimidating square box, and Major Newsonse could attest to all of this. Abe was dark in more ways than one, olive-skinned and swarthy. His piercing black eyes were divided by an immense hooked nose, and his stance was one of simmering

threat and imminent attack; Abe was an exception-
ally experienced Mossad agent.

The Duchess, frustrated at being ignored, peered
around the shoulders of the Major to take in the look
of the visitors who had so transfixed her note-taking
Embroidery Club secretary. She shouldered the
Major aside, and such was his weakened condition
that he rolled off the open door and only just managed to stop a full-on collapse and a serious pooing
incident in his mustard corduroys. The Duchess was
not a woman to be intimidated. She immediately
recognised Sigmund Merde as his picture had been
on television almost nightly, but it was the other man
who intrigued her, in a cautionary sense, and it was to
Abe Hyman that she made her first approach.

'Yes?' she snorted to Abe, aloof aristocracy emanating
from her equine pores, and especially accentuated by
flared nostrils, her powerful nose not at all comparable in size, but equally pre-eminent, and a genuine
threat to Abe's.

Abe answered in a clipped, accented tone. 'Keith Bananas, is he here?'

The Duchess took her time in answering, her excuse
being that she was ushering the Major back to the
parlour to continue the conversation on crocheting,
something in which the military man seemed remarkably well versed, and all of a sudden she began to

question the veracity of the Major's military credentials.

'No,' she said to Abe as she returned.

'Do you know where he is?'

'No.'

'He was here last night?' Abe said, in an upturned,
questioning inflection.

After some delay, the Duchess answered, 'Yes.'

Abe was starting to get agitated and Siggy stepped in,
literally, and the lanky bag of bones, asserted itself
into the face of the equally tall and bony Duchess.
He brought a skeletal hand to her shoulder, and
Ghost massaged in a practiced medical manner, allowed his hand to run down the aristocratic flabby
arm, beyond the bingo wings and collected the aristocratic salt and pepper, liver-spotted hand and raised
it to his lips as he bent over and kissed the hand.
'Lady Francesca, how lovely, I have heard so much
about you.'

Siggy lowered the limp hand and rested it on the
Duchess's protruding bony hip, allowing his own
hand to continue its intended journey, travelling back
along the osseous frame, taking a measure of the
Duchess's pelvis, and he smiled. Jack would enjoy
this, Ghost thought, and he would tell him later.

The Duchess looked confused and was further perplexed as Siggy collected her hand again and she was turned into a jiving spin and, placing his hand on the aristocratic bottom, Siggy steered the Duchess to her parlour; the heart of the deadly spider's web. His hand remained on the Duchess's derrière as Siggy guided the floating, horse-like woman to a seat, nodding for her to sit. She did. Abe followed, his presence filling the room, but it was Siggy who demanded the attention of all present. Everyone recognised Ghost, knew of his relationship with Jack Austin and of this man's exploits.

When he had silence, and everyone's eyes were riveted upon him, he started. 'Major, is that the striped, back loop single stitch?' Ghost asked, continuing this rare moment of lucidity.

The major, giving his nice but dim look, his sphincter, fortunately for all, spasmodically clenching, replied, 'Err... err, yes it is, Gho... err... Dr Merde.'

Siggy looked proud that he had identified the stitch, which was not difficult as the Major had a book open on that page. 'Och aye, we nerp eef ananas et licht nit,' Ghost said, and Abe metaphorically slapped his brow and stepped in to clear up the frontier gibberish confusion.

'What the doctor is saying is, we know Keith Bananas was down last night, and stayed overnight. The thing is...' and Abe sketched his hand in the air to incorporate Siggy into the point he was about to make, '... we think he has hurt Mrs Austin and taken her off somewhere.'

This brought a stunned silence, which is what Abe had expected. 'You should know also that we are going to be all over you lot like a rash until we find the Superintendent, and I am not sure how that will fit into your image of this cosy corner of middle-class England... Lady Blanche fucking Teapot?'

Abe turned to leave, but looked back for a throwaway comment. 'Just thought I would mention this... in case you could enlighten us?'

There was a stunned silence, an atmosphere of stitched gloom pervaded the parlour, and just as Abe and Siggy shaped to leave, the doorbell rang again. This time, Abe answered the door to be confronted by two cockneys, one short, beautiful and sparrow-like, the other tall, hefty and an ugly, half blind elephant.

The beautiful one spoke. 'Fuck me, Abe, what's Mossad doing down 'ere?'

'Della, lovely to see you too. Perhaps if you didn't identify me to all and sundry?'

Della apologised, but Lady Francesca's aristocratic lugholes had heard.

———

THE PAIN in her legs was causing Mandy to drift in and out of consciousness. She was in a small store room, and although her nose was congested, it was a floral sawdust aroma she could smell. She was not alone, either. The flashy blue eyes of a man bundled up with duct tape and plastic cable ties, acknowledged her. He was a robust, middle-aged man, dressed in overalls and powdered in sawdust that made his mid-length curly hair look like a talcum-dusted high court wig.

She felt sick, and groaned. The man, whom she assumed was the saw miller, flashed his eyes in sympathy and gestured his head in the direction of what she assumed was the mill area. 'Is that where they are?' she managed. He nodded. 'How many?' He nodded seven times and Mandy said, 'Seven?' and he nodded once to affirm, then shrugged his shoulders; there could be more.

———

'I SAID we would always look out for you, Jack, and we will, and that includes Mandy. I am sorry our man missed what happened to her this morning, we should have seen that coming,' Abe said, as they made their way back to Jack's house, where they were halted by a copper protecting the crime scene.

'Thanks, Abe,' Jack said and, dismissing the constable with a hand gesture, Jack suggested they make their way to the Gravediggers, to see what they could get out of Beth. He did wonder why Mossad would be nearby, but recalled Abe's concern about a right wing conspiracy in Portsmouth, expressed to Mandy and him when Abe had interrupted their honeymoon in France; he'd been proved right on that score. Jack then thought of Bubba French, CIA, who also interrupted their honeymoon, and alluded to a conspiracy within the hierarchy of the British Civil Service, and now his own thoughts gelled. Was there a link? Was there a motive? Was he wasting his time looking for motive? He knew Myloft was playing him, but why, and what was his underlying goal? Was there one? And that made Jack think he needed to speak to Amlodd Jones.

SEVENTEEN

'Jack, I'm sittin' in the front, the back makes me feel sick,' Della said.

But while they argued, Siggy sat in the front. "Ferin' gettin, blomp kidz."

Della and Jack looked on with undisguised bemusement. They understood what he said, you learn Frontier Gibberish at MI5 School, but were mystified about why Ghost couldn't understand why sitting in the front was important as you can pretend you are the driver, and they resented being called "blomp kidz".

Abe wanted to get going, except Jack wanted to sit behind the driver and so did Della. Abe drove off when Jack, in a most ungentlemanly manner, ceded the seat to Della.

'What time is it?' Jack asked.

'Time you got a watch, ugly,' Della retorted.

'Abe?'

'Jack?'

'What you doing down 'ere?'

'Things happen around you, Jack, in case you hadn't noticed...' Abe replied, and Della nodded sagely; it was her sage and onion face, which she usually rolled out at Christmas, '...but it was Siggy who contacted us to let us know you were being targeted by the Banana Boys.'

This was good enough for Jack, so he moved on. 'D'you fink the Duchess is involved?' Jack queried, almost to himself. Siggy turned his head and Jack could see he had a subliminal message to pass on, but right now, Jack was 'liminally retarded and relied on Siggy telling him later.

'Yarp,' Siggy said, in response to Jack's outspoken subliminal thoughts.

'Well, when you tell 'im, you tell me, okay Siggy?' Della asserted, knowing that in this instance, she might need Jack to interpret for her as this was advanced gibberish and she may have skipped that bit at MI5 School, and then she could tuck him up in a nursing home.

'You wouldn't stick me in a nursing home would you, Della?' Jack asked, and Della flicked her eyes to the ceiling, trying to recall if ever she had shared a bath with Jack, and wondering if, just maybe, he was her real long-lost dad.

Abe, not at all distracted by the Della and Jack antics, said, 'It's difficult to say if the Duchess is involved, or just protecting her beloved nephew. I think she knows something, but likely not all... What?' Abe responded to the look on Jack's face, he could see him in the driver's rear view mirror. 'You think she's involved?' He now had Della's attention. Jack nodded but offered no explanation, and Abe and Della left it at that.

Ghost said, "Yernep en sim whey," supporting Jack's theory, which he had not expanded upon, and they drove on to the Gravediggers in silence, avoiding the chaos in Albert Road; a police incident, apparently.

Abe parked in the grounds of the cemetery, beside Sexton House. Della went with Jack to see Seb in his shed, while Siggy and Abe crossed the road to the Gravediggers pub.

Della knocked on the shed door. 'Sexton Detective Agency, how may I help you?' came the sonorous reply from Seb inside his shed.

'Seb darlin', it's Della and I'm wiv Jack. Open up, there's a luv, it's taters out 'ere.'

The locks whirred and clicked and Della waited patiently, but she did stamp her feet, her excuse being the cold, and Jack believed her; he could sense already Della loved this lad, and he was pleased about that.

Seb stepped back to welcome the Della hug and he hugged her back. That was it; it was what Mandy had taught him.

Jack went in. 'Seb.'

'Jack,' Seb replied.

Jack had taught the lad that form of greeting amongst men; and who said there was no difference between men and women?

Seb returned to his desk, where he sat and faced his computer screen while Jack cleaned the floor, though he did notice Seb peeping behind him to see what sort of job had been done.

Della opened up. 'Seb sweet'art, did you think about where they could have taken Mandy?'

Seb spun in his chair. There were tears in his eyes; the lad loved Mandy. 'I have looked at all of the data, looked also at Archibald Pointe-Lace and his assets...' Della looked at Jack, a penny dropped, but she kept her counsel as Seb continued, '... and the assets of known associates, and I cannot find a link. I am sorry, I fear our only hope is Beth, but I do have one or two ideas on how you can probe her.' And Seb explained his thought process that if Keith Bananas had taken Mandy, it would not be to a location the authorities would be aware of, or could trace.

He asked Jack to consider something. 'What if Keith Bananas, or some of his acquaintances, have been fol-lowing you and Mandy, looking for an opportunity? And, if they were, would they look for somewhere nearby to put you, or indeed Mandy? I do not believe they want either of you dead, yet, so it is logical they would put you somewhere secure, and not too far away.' That was it, except he told Jack to think about where Mandy and he would go, or normally could be expected to go; somewhere not crowded, so they could set a prospective ambush.

Jack and Della left Seb's shed and stood around while the locks mechanically whirred shut. It was getting dark, and Jack worried about Mandy being kept overnight somewhere, scared and hurt, cold, if she was out in the open air, and his heart ached. Della could see the emotions portrayed on Jack's ugly face and was amazed he was not running around like a headless chicken.

They headed to the pub.

As they went in, Jack immediately noticed Martin sitting in a corner, and if he was not mistaken, the look he received from the dog was either disgrace or high dudgeon. Martin looked down to the floor, back up to Jack, and applied wrinkly lips that were either a smirk or a grimace, but the hound's eyes did roll – he never could understand his dog when he was in his enigmatic moods.

Jonas saw Jack's confusion and explained, 'He shagged Cabbage, the little bastard.'

The response Jonas got from Jack was not what he expected, neither was it a sympathetic reaction from Della. Jonas still had a lot to learn about the woman he was going to marry, and who was carrying his baby.

Jack roared with laughter and went over to pat Martin's head, whilst Della congratulated Martin. 'Well done, my old son, bet yer 'ad to do all the bleedin' work as well, welcome to the club.'

Martin gave Jack an old-fashioned look, one of his dog's specialities, and it was good, better than Jack's. Gradually, the look morphed on the ginger, grizzled hairy face of the Border Terrier, as if to say, 'Mandy:

what are you doing?' and Martin flicked his head to look at the ceiling above his corner, while his former master had a Roman Catholic moment.

Jonas interrupted to say Jackie had arrived, having previously been to see Mandy's daughter, to offer some reassurances. 'God, I forgot her kids. We will need to get in touch with David as well,' Jack said.

'Done,' Jonas said, 'and David is on his way down from Nottingham. Del-Boy is in with Jackie and Beth,' and he directed Della and Jack to the room upstairs, and they went to meet with Beth, Jack flicking his head for Martin to follow.

Martin needed no second asking. He was fed up with the corner and, giving Jonas a wide berth, he dashed past Della and Jack and flew up the stairs like a rat up a drainpipe, pleased to be away from Jonas's admonishing look that he sensed on his bum. He had a very sensitive bum for a dog, and was painfully aware of this as he made his bid for freedom, the interrogation room, and the comfort he knew would reside within. Martin was good at interrogation. Jack had always used him in the old days, and it felt good to be back in the saddle, sort of post-coastal he thought, in his Maladoggerism way.

Jimbo was standing guard outside the room and acknowledged Della, Jack, and Martin with a nod, as they approached along the corridor, tapped on the door and opened it. Martin sauntered in, Della and Jack followed, Jack squashing through with Della, a joke she did not appreciate, and Martin "derred", though he was encouraged to see Jack was bearing up in what was a strain for everyone.

Martin had to admit also that Mandy's violent disappearance preyed on his mind and he felt this preoccupation may have impaired his Cabbage performance, but she seemed not to mind, and it was just the beginning of the relationship. He cast his dog mind back to when Jack first got together with Mandy, and clearly Jack had been shite in the bed department. Not that Jack could see that, but Martin could; he just had to look at Mandy's face. A dog knows these things, don't ask how, he just does, and Martin considered himself better than most. For a dog, he considered himself blessed in that and many other departments – if he was not distracted, that was.

Jack told Martin to stop muttering to himself, and to go to the back of the room.

Martin slunk off to take up the rearmost position, aware he rarely got credit for all he did; it was a dog's life, except for Cabbage, and there was time. He thought she liked him, but then who wouldn't? He had a way with the bitches. You either have it or you don't, and Martin knew he was a veritable bitch magnet.

Reassured, Martin looked around the room. It was modern, simple and utilitarian, gloomy though. The night had drawn in and the black window stood out against a cream wall, on which an orangey light was shed from two table lamps. Jack paced immediately to the window and drew the curtains and gave Del-Boy an old fashioned look. Martin approved. Everyone in the room was a potential target; one of the reasons Martin pressed his flanks to the wall. He said it was so he could scratch his bum, which had recently been closely inspected by Jonas, but he didn't fool Jack for one minute.

Beth was sitting in an upright chair, her hands dangling at her side, a hint of despair in her eyes as she stared at Jack. Jackie sat beside her, a comforting arm across the shoulders of the frail young woman.

Jackie was wary of how Jack would react. 'How are you, Jack?'

Jack looked confused that this tall and elegant, handsome, forty-something, black, trick-cyclist woman would be concerned about him and not preoccupied with thoughts of Mandy. 'I'm scared for Mandy, Keef Bananas is a cyclepath,' he replied.

Jack peeked back to Martin, who knew he meant psychopath and growled reassuringly, and Jack focused on Beth, fed up with looking at Martin. 'Beth, sweet-'art, I need to find Mandy, and there's strong evidence she's been taken violently. I'm scared she's hurt. Please, can you tell us where they may have taken her?'

Beth looked unmoved, a fixed face, unyielding, no tell-tale signs of emotion. Jackie had previously said this was how the young woman had been, but he also recalled that Jackie sensed she was close to a break-through. If she was, Jack couldn't see it, and was pan-icked. 'Beth, please... I love Mandy...' and Jack sensed tears falling from his good eye, and there was also a hint of a tear in the corner of Beth's eye.

Martin nudged Jack's leg to get out of the way, and Jack shuffled his chair to the side, distracted. Martin leapt onto Beth's lap and gently, caringly, he licked away the first evidence of the tear rolling down her cheek; he was partial to a tear, something about the tang. Another appeared, and he licked that away too, liking the saltiness. Beth's hand rose from where it had dangled, and gently she ruffled the top of Mar-tin's head, who forgot his nurturing and began to enjoy receiving a good scratch, shuffling his head back and forth so Beth knew exactly what to do. He was such a shallow dog, always thinking of himself, Jack thought, thinking of himself and how Mandy would rub his head for him, though he wasn't ginger and his was an Indian head massage, with no feathers.

Beth tilted her head to Jack, and Martin showed he was irritated and let Jack know he had likely spoiled a good scrabbling for him. Then Beth spoke, for the first time. 'I'm sorry...' she mumbled, then more distinctly, showing an inner strength within the girl, '... and Mandy is likely to be in serious danger if it is Keith Bananas who has her. We had several safe places we would go if there was trouble, but the most likely one nearby, where there would be a stash of weapons, would be the sawmill at Stansted Woods,' and she broke down and sobbed, muttering that she was sorry, and Jackie knocked Martin off her lap and hugged the girl. Martin was mightily pissed off. After all, he had done all the work, yet once again he'd been discarded.

He flipped his grizzled and fed-up muzzle up to Della. 'Told yer Martin, yer get no credit, and 'ave to do all the bleedin' work round 'ere,' Della said.

Ain't that the truth, Martin thought.

EIGHTEEN

DEL-BOY AND DELLA SAT AROUND A TABLE, contemplative. Jack had ants-in-his-pants, Jimbo was strutting the strange Gravediggers bar, phone glued to his ear, animated, yet conversing in a hushed tone, every now and then conspiring with a similarly strutting Abe, who made his own calls. Both gave Martin old-fashioned looks as he paced with them.

Martin had one or two ideas of his own; after all, Stansted Woods was one of his favourite walks and he knew of the sawmill, and reckoned he knew it better now he had had a post-coastal chat with Cabbage. Whilst Jonas prepared food for everyone, Cabbage had sneaked Martin into the yard, and although it was chilly and they would have preferred the comfort of Cabbage's basket, needs must, and Martin found he was rather partial to a knee-trembler. The sawmill was where Jonas got sawdust for the pub floor, and as the two dogs metaphorically smoked a post-coastal cigarette, Cabbage was able to let Martin have the lie of the land outside and inside the sawmill.

Eventually Jimbo, Abe and Martin joined the others, as Jonas plonked four beef and one fish stew onto the table, along with a couple of bread vans. 'I can't eat, Jonas, I'm sorry, I want to get going,' Jack said, astounding everyone.

'Jack, I know it will be pointless to say you are not going, but I want you to stay back, and I definitely do not want us, or you, going into the mill until we have back-up in place,' Del-Boy asserted, 'and this is what we are waiting for.'

Martin nudged Jack's leg with his nose. He was irritated that they had not pulled a chair up at the table for him as they knew he liked Jonas's beef stew, but he was distracted from his guttural growling as Jonas plonked a bowl of beef stew down in front of him. 'Why I'm giving you this, Martin, I do not know. You are in disgrace.'

Martin dived his nose into the bowl, only mildly displeased he was not allowed to sit at the table, and began devouring; a dog had to finish his food quickly if he was to return to his begging station, and if he was not much mistaken, this could be the first time Jack gave him some of his own food, and who was this Grace he was supposed to have been in? Maybe that was Cabbage's real name. Was Cabbage a nickname? He made a mental note to call her Grace next time; he liked the name, it suited her.

His stew finished, Martin was back nudging Jack's leg, thinking it was time Jack changed his socks. He didn't like that colour. What was Mandy thinking, letting him out dressed like that?

'Oh, sod this,' Della said, standing up and knocking back her chair, that Jonas caught, preventing it from skittering across the sawdust floor. 'Owzat?' Della remarked, mentioning Jonas could play cricket for England. 'And they bleedin' need him as well!'

Jonas looked back at the woman he loved as he returned the chair to its place. 'You like cricket?'

'What's wrong wiv that?'

'Nothing,' Jonas said, a broad grin spreading across his Gypo face. 'I love cricket.'

'I play good, too, so we may as well get a pub team up, and I suppose it will be down to me to 'ave to do all the bleedin' scoring of runs and gettin' wickets. Jack, get yer 'at and coat, let's go. The feckin' boy's brigade can catch up when their mums say they can go out...'

and Della strode to the pub door, ignoring the be-seeching from Jonas and the pathetic whining resis-tance from Del-Boy.

Martin was at the door first, thinking that at last Jack had grown some balls, even if it was courtesy of Della. They all barged into the back of Jack as he stopped and looked down at his dog. Martin gulped, wondering if he was in trouble for scoffing Jack's fish stew.

'Jimbo, call the cavalry and to tell them we'll meet them up there,' Del shouted, taken unawares at the precipitous action, '...and maybe Jack will have calmed down by then!'

'Del, I'm not sure it's Jack or Della who needs to calm down,' Jimbo said, flicking a look at Jonas, who held his hands out like Mother Superior talking to Julie Andrews, in a "so what can I do about it?" gesture, and probably on the top of a feckin' mountain. Jonas did ask Jimbo to look out for Della, mentioning she was pregnant, and look out for Jack as he was to be number one godfather and babysitter.

Jimbo stopped mid-pace. 'Della's pregnant...?' he ex-claimed, then thought, *And you want Jack as a godfa-ther... a babysitter?* Jimbo didn't know what surprised him most, but knew nobody, except maybe Kipper, the leader of the Portsmouth criminal underworld, could stop Jack from being number one godfather, which was a coincidence, as Jack had borrowed Abe's phone and called his daughter, Alice, and asked her to get her Uncle Kipper out with his own feckin' cavalry, and to meet them at the sawmill.

———

DELLA SWITCHED the headlamps off and allowed her beaten-up old Saab to coast the last few yards into the moonlit Stansted Wood car park. It was where Jack and Mandy would park when they walked in the woods, Jack had explained, not that Della gave a toss. It was some distance from the sawmill; they were taking no chances. Kipper's Jaguar arrived, no lights and purring to a halt, the only noise a crunching of tyres over a frosty, friable surface, to be followed soon after by Del-Boy and Jimbo. They acknowledged Kipper and his associates, Plug and Boz, and the men slapped each other's backs, quietly.

While all this strange human greeting behaviour was going on, Martin slunk off unnoticed; he was in his stealthy Ginger mode. Martin knew these woods like the palm of his paw, except he had not been to the sawmill, but Cabbage had given him the lowdown. Martin pictured the last embrace from the raggedy-arsed mongrel Lassie, and gulped; was he in love with Grace? He'd told his bitch not to worry, he had the skills of a Ginger; stelf, silent but deadly. He could tell Grace was impressed, but then he'd farted, and clearly Cabbage was smitten, or she may have been retching – *girls, eh?* Martin thought; never could read what they were thinking.

Del-Boy surveyed the motley crew assembled in the car park, a mix of deadly criminal power, an MI5 and a Mossad agent, a couple of daft cockneys, and he sighed to the moon, shrugged and asked Jimbo, 'When will the backup get here?' Jimbo shrugged back.

Kipper, the head of the Herring crime family, was a short, tubby, shopkeeper type of man, of a similar age to Jack and with a similar rep; you didn't cross him. He had backup like Jack did, only Jack's was Martin, or more recently Mandy, and both had teeth. Plug was a stringy, lanky individual, deceptively powerful but none of this is what you noticed first. It was his horse-like face with a pronounced, protruding upper jaw, a top lip that curled and teeth that hung down like Goofy and went in different directions, not un-like his beady eyes. He looked like Plug out of the *Bash Street Kids* in the *Beano* comic. Boz was Alice's cousin, not much you could say about him except he was a brick shithouse, who worked the boats in the harbour and a lot of other things as well, but all of these gangsters liked Jack, not least because Alice Herring was his daughter. (*Don't ask, read the other books; what am I, your mum?*)

'Oi Jack, where's Martin?' Della asked, not so quietly.

'Shusssh...' Jack replied in a secret agent way, 'are you really a meat pie, Della? Only we could do wiv a bit of stelf, you know. I sent Martin ahead as a Brussels sprout.'

'A sprout? Martin, a scout?'

'Shusssh, Della.' It was Jimbo and everyone acknowledged his consommé meat pie skills. 'What d'you mean, you sent Martin on, Jack?'

'He's picked up a scent, Jimbo,' Jack replied loudly, like the deaf twat he was.

Della giggled. 'You farted then?'

'Might 'ave...' and Jack wobbled his head, '... it is scary out 'ere in the dark.'

'Where's the sawmill, Jack?' Del-Boy took command.

Jack thought for a bit. 'Well, it's just up the road and down an access lane, or we can approach it through the woods. What d'you reckon, Jimbo?'

'Can't take a chance at being spotted, so we'd better go through the woods. Do you know the way, Jack?'

'Yep, like the palm of Martin's paw,' and Jack set off, out of the car park, through a small stand of trees and across the large swath of land that had long ago been carved out of the wood to form a vista to the aristocratic pile that was Stansted house. The house was illuminated by the moon. It was beautiful and Jack explained why. 'They cut all these trees down to make a vista, Jimbo, and I don't mean a beef curry. You try getting planning permission for that these days, but then that's the arseycrats for you.' Jack smiled. He'd made his socialist point, but he did feel a twinge of guilt as he liked the vista.

Della put her serious head on when she realised Jack didn't know where he was going, and decided she would be a better leader – heaven help them all.

In the meantime, Martin had found the sawmill and, although temporarily distracted by a plethora of yummy poo smells, amazingly, he picked up Mandy's scent in the yard; she'd dropped it? Now, there are a lot of things said about Martin, and many of them are founded in fact, but people certainly had respect for the hound. He was, after all, a devout Catholic, and if he did anything wrong he would feel guilty, and that of course explained the look the dog had when Jack entered the pub earlier. However, Martin knew he would get over it, and probably sooner than he should. That was a quote from *Pride and Prejudice,* one of Jack's favourites and as a consequence of having to watch it so many times with Jack, it was his also, only Martin's favourite bit was when Elizabeth Bonnet played with the dog in the garden, and arsy Darcy looked on after he'd just got out of the bath.

Also, like Jack, he couldn't see anything special about Darcy diving into the lake – something dog and former master agreed upon.

The footing in the yard was treacherous, iced cobbles, rigid ruts and potholes, and Martin stumbled a few times, cursed under his breath and stopped, reminding himself he was a Ginger, and stelf was his middle name; Martin Stelf Austin. He was sure Jack meant Stefan, but his was not to wonder why, just to eat dried crap dog food that was meant to be good for him, and he recalled the beef and fish stew he had just snaffled, and drooled; it dripped, swung like gooey string, then froze. Shite he thought, and wished he'd had his winter fur on.

Martin followed the scent to the big doors in the timber shed. Mandy was in there and something was not right. It was late, dark, and he would have thought the mill workers would have left for the day. There was an orangey glow from under the door and a shadow passed across it; someone close to the door. The door opened and Martin gingered to a dark corner. 'Wot was that?' Shitlegs said.

'S'foxes, yer daft bugger, we're in the bleedin' country, aren't we?' Keef replied. 'Get the wheels and let's get out ov 'ere, we've done our bit, and I don't like the country.'

'What, England?' Shitlegs replied, shivering like a true hard nut.

'No, yer bleedin' tosspot, the country,' but Shitlegs had missed the point, discarded the thought that had not found any fertile ground in his brainbox, and went to get the white van.

Keef held the door open so some of the orangey light could illuminate the way. Martin gingered, his furry flank pressed against the barn wall, well disguised except for his steaming breath; he was in, just as Keef closed the door and the van swung around and the headlamps lit up the yard like a Stalag (a German prison camp – not a type of dog with headlamps, that would be a Lighter, or do I mean Setter – okay, Setter-a-lighter).

Martin's breathing was laboured, he was scared. He sensed the beef and fish stews making a bee-line for his sensitive bottom; he was so like Jack, and not for the first time, Martin wondered if he suffered from PTSD, also like Jack, and made a note to talk this over with Jackie. He heard voices coming from behind the vicious-looking equipment, a huge circular saw on a tilted table... Why was the table tilted? He had a passing thought that it looked like Jack's DIY, remembering him sawing the legs off Kate's dining table, to stop it being uneven; it ended up as a coffee table Jack called a Thacket, after saying "fuck it".

Don't ask, because Martin hadn't a clue either, and what was an Indian coffee table, anyway? Kate could be scary he recalled, and his thoughts returned to his own watery bowls, and a passing thought that maybe he should have skipped the fish stew, but what's a dog to do?

Martin eased his way around the interior of the mill, got his nose out and began blood-hounding as soon as he heard the van with a broken exhaust labour its way out of the yard, the rattling, the putt-putting, until eventually the sounds faded away. He picked up Mandy's scent and sniffed along the ground. The sawdust perfume was redolent of Cabbage, but he dismissed the thoughts and, like a good Ginger, he remained focused and soon he arrived at a store-room. The scent went directly into it.

The previously detached voices got louder, there was movement and a bigger light flooded the space. Martin could hear the voices, but couldn't make out what they were saying. He padded, like his middle name, Stefan, to the side of the store, which was clad with roughly sawn timber boarding and nosed a knot-hole, got a splinter and had to stifle a squeal. His ears twitched as he heard a sniff from inside, then a whimper. It was enough for him to identify Mandy and be aware she was hurt. There was someone else too and Martin could not be sure if he was a guard or another prisoner. He sniffed some Jane Austen to reassure Mandy. 'What light from yonder knot-hole breaks?' Well, it was dog Shakespeare, but would suffice, and neither Jack nor Cabbage was there to correct him.

He listened and heard Mandy's hushed reply. 'That's Shakespeare, you dopy dog, and are you the only cavalry?' Martin felt silly for sniffing his thoughts, but like Jack, he loved it when a woman spoke sweet nothings to him. It was a bit like Cabbage after their first coupling. He could hear her dulcet barks now. "That's it, is it?' she had said. He could tell she was impressed. Don't ask, he just knew these things.

Martin's Cabbage reflections were interrupted by a shouted "feck!" and then a "shite!" and an "oh bollocks!" from outside the sawmill and Martin heard Mandy say nasally, through her miasma of pain, 'Oh no, the feckin' cavalry.'

And all hell broke loose.

There were shouts from the men behind the saw table as they came running to meet the commotion, armed to the teeth. They saw Martin standing to attention, clenched buttocks and a cheesy grin, woofing 'Eeeeeh...' and they stood dumbfounded for a brief moment, trying to reconcile the raucous sound of a motorised vehicle, with a mutt who had a guilty sloping face and wrinkly lips, but this delay allowed Martin the opportunity to run at the first man and launch himself at the wrist of a hand that held a pistol.

A shot blasted out and as the man fell backwards, a flailing hand hit the circular saw's start button. A revving, whirring and zinging resounded, and the bright light, now swinging in the breeze from the opened door, flashed off the circular saw as it spun, waiting grotesquely to eat something, not caring if it be wood or flesh.

Martin dug his teeth in harder, then released his grip as another man made to hit him with the butt of his pistol. Another shot rang out and he heard it ping off the spinning blade as a section of wall, beside the open double doors, crashed, splintered, and then gaped as Jack drove in on a tractor. He'd missed the doors, he never was a good driver and put it down to only having one eye, and later on, he told people he was sure he was heading for the doors.

Della was riding shotgun, tussling to be the driver, a bucket lifted high in front as a battering ram of the tractor, and the headlamps blazing. Jack and Della were not looking where they were going. They drove straight into the first two men, one of whom flung out his arm and screamed as his hand was severed by the saw. Machine gun bullets pinged and panged off the tractor bucket, as blood sprayed.

Jack jumped off and as the driverless tractor swerved, Della launched herself onto two men, stole a gun and shot them. A hail of bullets flew around, almost indiscriminately, as the tractor continued on its chaotic way, ploughing through machinery and baddies. Martin felt a bullet hit his flank and he yelped. Jack stopped for the briefest of moments, reacting to the sound of pain from his dog, but he was berserking, his mist up, and nothing could stop him as he hurtled into yet another man like a human torpedo – well, a relatively speedy whale; okay, a sauntering rhinoceros. Jimbo and Abe followed in through the gaping hole in the barn and Jimbo picked off a heavily-armed man with an accurate shot. Abe locked immediately in hand-to-hand combat with another man, but there were more, and Plug, followed up by Boz and Kipper, was cart-wheeling his arms into a phalanx of five of the gang.

Del had one, spun him and chopped the back of his neck. They were momentarily distracted as a metallic crunching drew everyone's attention. Della had jumped back onto the tractor and dropped the bucket onto the heads of three brutes. Still more attacked, and Della drove into them shouting, 'How many did you say there were, Martin?'

Martin felt a little guilty. This was not what was expected of a Brussels sprout, but he was up again, the adrenalin taking his mind off the grazing wound to his back leg that Jack had said, as he berserked past his dog, was "Just a scratch" but Martin thought was a bleedin' great bullet-hole. Whatever it was, he ignored it as he charged the delicate man parts of another gangster, his jaws closing and taking a firm lock. The man reacted by screaming in a high-pitched manner that reminded Martin of the choirboys in the Catholic cathedral, but then the man began bashing his head with the butt of his pistol.

Martin was eventually knocked off his grip onto the sloping saw table and his tiny legs scrambled, trying desperately to get a grip of the shiny metallic surface, but he was inexorably sliding toward the spinning saw blade, his claws scratching and slipping, legs a blur of scrambling fur, but he was making no ground and was closing on the spinning blade.

Jack leapt for his dog just as Martin screeched. Jack scurfed the scruff of Martin's neck and managed to pull him away, but not before the saw had taken a section of Martin's front left leg. Martin and Jack were both screaming. Jack had his dog under his arm and had grabbed a semi-automatic pistol, and began wildly firing in the general direction of the remaining thugs, round after round after round, until the men were just a heap of bloody pulp, and Jimbo was able to release the gun from Jack's handgrip. Empty of ammunition, it clicked ineffectually.

Martin was quiet in Jack's arm, but, as Jack calmed, so he used his other paw to point to the store, whined, pointed again, farted, then fainted. Jack knew, and laying Martin down, he went to the door, picked up another pistol from the floor, shot at the padlock and remarkably hit it after only four shots, and the door swung open.

Mandy was there. 'Oh, Jack,' she said, then saw Martin. 'Oh, Martin.'

Jack saw Mandy... registered a bloody face, two black panda eyes and crooked, broken legs, and he cried. Those legs were one of his favourite bits of his wife, after her nose, that is, which now looked broken as well. 'Oh, Amanda,' he sobbed.

Kipper appeared. 'I'll get Martin to the vet hospital in Wickham, you look after Mandy,' he ordered and master criminal and hound departed, Martin having regained consciousness, relieved to find he was in Kipper's capable hands and not Jack's incapable ones.

Jack unceremoniously heaved Mandy into his arms. She screamed with the pain as her legs moved. The sound hurt his ear-'oles and he may have unwisely mentioned this, but he had her and he was off, out of the mill, into the yard and, remarkably nimble for a big oaf, he was across the treacherous frozen ground and heading along the narrow, metalled lane to the road. Del called after him that ambulances and paramedics were on the way. Jack heard, but his mist was still up. He just knew he had to get Mandy to a hospital, even if he had to carry her all the way. He was running scared. All the defrayed panic had now risen, gushed, bubbled and boiled, an acidy bile in his stomach.

As Jack reached the end of the access lane, he sensed his adrenaline begin to ebb as his aged step began to falter. He saw the road ahead and could hear sirens in the distance. The moon had gone behind clouds and it was pitch black, the strobing blue lights fast approaching. He stumbled, but kept going. His back was hurting and his breath was scorching his lungs. He wobbled again and Mandy cried, 'I'm sorry.'

Jack gasped but didn't answer. He couldn't think what to say, anyway, and whatever he said would probably be wrong and they would end up talking about it before they went to bed, and more than likely, when he had forgotten all about it and all the brilliant excuses he had thought of, she would then raise it again. Mandy said she promised she wouldn't do that, mentioning double dog doobreys and dib-dib, dob-dob, so he would know she meant it, but she was crying in a blur of pain and a miasma of Jack's steamy breath and spittle.

Jack was slowing. He felt the burn, not in his lungs this time but in his lower back. Excruciating pain was shooting like electric shocks and befuddling his mind, but he kept going as an ambulance pulled up. He wobbled and then stood rigid, leaning backwards to counter the weight of Mandy. He gritted his teeth, locking his painful back and hanging on, looking up into the sky, ablaze from the bright moon as it temporarily appeared from behind incongruously white clouds.

'That's nice, Jack. Romantic. You old softy,' Mandy said.

He looked down at his mangled wife. 'Did I...?'

The paramedics arrived, took Mandy from Jack and lifted her directly into the open ambulance. The doors closed and Jack folded to the tarmac as Jimbo arrived. He watched the ambulance do a three-point turn and head off along the road it had just travelled, and pass another one coming in. The paramedic from the next ambulance jumped out. It was Barry and he recognised Jack immediately; he'd seen Jack injured before and would recognise that writhing lump of lard anywhere.

Barry looked to Jimbo. 'Is he shot? I heard there were a number of shooting victims. I said to my mate, "I bet that's Jane", and here he is.'

Jimbo looked up from the moaning mound of cockney blubber that was Jack. 'No, he's not hit, I think he may have tweaked his back a bit, carrying Mandy...'

Jack responded, 'It's not tweaked, it could be seriously broken, Bazzer... I may become a Perry-eejit?'

The paramedic and spook ignored Jack's pained diatribe, agreed he probably meant paraplegic, but got down to the biz.

'There are a lot of bodies down there, Barry,' Jimbo said to the paramedic as he joined the moaning blob on the floor. 'Not sure if you can do much for any of them.'

'I'd better go and look,' and Barry picked up his bag and disappeared down the tiny dark lane accompanied by Jimbo, as the first police vehicles began arriving.

'What about me?' A plaintive cry from the barely shifting midden heap, as paramedic and spook headed off into the moonlight. 'Nobody cares about me,' Jack muttered to himself and cried, thinking of Mandy, and then Martin.

NINETEEN

HAMLEY'S, THE FAMOUS WEST END OF LONDON Emporium of Toys, is a child's dream. It is also an adult's illusion of a childhood that may have passed, but is clung to fiercely, if, more often than not, held at an emotional distance. But, entry into *Hamley's* can break all but the most resolute, inflexible, emotional barriers; it is a wonderland for children and, unfortunately, people who like to look at children. The shop this day was more than a retail outlet for the latest toys, it was a Santa's Grotto, constructed over four and five storeys of jam-packed illusions; childlike dreams brought to life in the eyes of children and the parents who brought their children, wanting them to experience this fantasy as much as they desired the experience themselves.

If you looked at the faces of the adults, you might be forgiven for thinking it was more a fantasy dreamland for them, for it is reasonable to say that entering *Hamley's* is a poignant experience as well as a jubilation of the spirit, that can make you forget the concerns of the world outside, to live, for a brief moment, in a child's fantasia, and never more so than at Christmas, when life had been so tough for such a very long time.

And there were the sick bastards.

Some children, of course, never grow up. Not Jack Austin or Peter Pan, although there were Peter Pan toys in the magnificent toy shop, which supplied the traditional toy as much as it did the latest fads and fashions. No, some children just never grew-up, could not grow up, and some of those children had children themselves, and not necessarily a thing of joy, and in some instances it would tear your heart to shreds. Such was Maddy and her son Mitch.

The Portsmouth *Evening News* had arranged for a trip to *Hamley's* for Maddy and Mitch, who were residents of a care home that catered for young adults with acquired brain injury. Maddy, who had been institutionalised as an orphan virtually all of her life, was now in this different home as a consequence of a terrible beating; she had the mental age of a very young child. The trip to *Hamley's* had been the culmination of a story being investigated by the *News* journalist Cecelia Crumpet, a departure from her usual stories and articles, as her formal position was Gossip Columnist. She had been researching a story into care homes for challenged young adults in Portsmouth. This more serious genre of investigation was what Cecelia had always wanted to do, but because she was a naturally glamorous woman in her late twenties, her misogynist editor had insisted she predominantly cover frivolous stories of local, and the not so local, celebrities, and the saucier the better; titillation for the voyeuristic public was always in demand. "And there was nothing wrong with Cecelia's picture beside her by-line", the editor always said salaciously, to the constant irritation of Cecelia.

But here she was, covering a story she knew was bigger than anything any national paper had, and way beyond the intellectual pay-grade of her arse of an editor. Reluctantly, her editor had allowed her pretty much *carte-blanche*, because, and the newspaper man still found this hard to believe, Ghost had walked into his office and offered the local newspaper his full story, but only if it was handled by Cecelia Crumpet, and only if it was brought out when it was completed; no phased publication.

The Editor had agreed, obviously, but was frustrated to the point of incandescent rage that his reporter was not allowed to divulge any of her information to him or anyone, and she was to be given full support, physically and financially. He had agreed, of course. This was the biggest scoop of his life, and syndication would not only bring enormous revenues to the paper, it would put the local paper, and him, on the map. His daydreaming mind soared to the dizzy heights of sensationalist journalism, where his local rag would ordinarily be scorned. Interestingly, it was Ghost who had suggested the visit to *Hamley's* this lunchtime, and Jack Austin had nudged the suggestion along with Cecelia.

Cecelia was indeed glamorous, and had a complementary flirtatious and sensual character. She was tall at five ten, a curvaceous dark-haired woman who had to do nothing to herself in order to radiate her sexuality, though she was not averse to wearing the kind of clothes that exploited her figure and good looks. She was a black-haired, *blonde bombshell*, in the Marilyn Monroe mould, although it was not currently fashionable, the preference being for the stick insects on the catwalk. Cecelia had found the stick insect look was not what real men wanted, and as she only wanted a real man, the Monroe blonde bombshell look suited her.

She had the man she wanted already singled out, though he was totally unaware of the impending assault on his senses and emotions, and the subtlety of Cecelia's planned approach, which she knew would succeed (*for this, you will have to wait for the next book, Road Kill - The Duchess of Frisian Tun - and it's a cracker, as is Cecelia*). So, what did she care for the waiflike appearance of women who are portrayed so many times by the newspaper? She reckoned many of these women looked like boys and her feminine senses alerted her to the fact that the fashion editor was more than likely personally interested in the images of little boys; she had his card marked.

Cecelia Crumpet was a fruity woman in many respects; multi-faceted, you might say. And so, despite her pointed railing against the demands of her editor, to cover local and the not so local gossip, she had found her looks and mode of attire could be exploited to get a step in front of some of her gossip competitors as well as the traditional journalists, and she was not afraid to use it. Knowing Jack Austin also helped, but she wouldn't mention that. She had heard from Bernie, the crime reporter of the *News,* that Jack and Mandy had been hurt in a raid last night, and were being kept in hospital. Her blousy heart went out to Jack and his wife, but she knew *Hamley's* was where Jack wanted her to be, where Ghost wanted her to be, and with Maddy and her son Mitch; her news antennae twitched.

This Ghost story was serious, not only because the whole of Portsmouth was buzzing with it since the press conference at Kingston Police station, the one where Detective Chief Inspector Austin had flounced out at the end, but the whole country, and indeed the world, were riveted by the exploits of a man who did so much for others and at a cost so evidently painful to himself. The tabloids were calling him the modern day *Pimpernel*, and so he was, as he miraculously appeared beside Cecelia, and the still patent emotional torment of the man was incised across his skeletal face.

Cecelia had had enough of the story so far to know that these were private thoughts displayed on Ghost's gaunt face, thoughts very likely of his estranged daughter, a girl who would be fourteen now, a young woman, the whereabouts of whom Cecelia's private investigators had not been able to track down. Hopefully, that would be sorted now. Ghost had recommended a very strange detective agency in Portsmouth, one she had never heard of, and even more mysteriously, was not allowed to reveal the name to anyone; the Sexton Detective Agency. She'd checked with Jack and he had agreed with Ghost, which was good enough for her.

Cecelia stood alongside Ghost and Candy, Maddy's carer. Candy had the look of a skinny dimwit but Cecelia knew differently; it was just that this rather demure, brown-haired, skin-and-bone girl, who stood at about the same lofty height as herself, and was of indeterminate age that Cecelia thought was likely around thirty, had psychologically and physically been beaten into submission by a dominating father, so much so that her self-esteem never rose above rock bottom. Why then was this girl caring for Madeleine on a one-to-one basis? Quite simply, it was because Maddy, at just fifteen, had been brought into the same care home Candy was in. Maddy had been admitted shortly after she had been beaten, raped and found to be pregnant. Nobody could get her to talk, but the woman and girl bonded, sharing a traumatic experience, eventually revealing themselves to each other.

The problem was, Maddy had a mental age of about five as a consequence of the assault which left her with a serious brain injury, and now there was the baby boy Mitch, whose hand she currently held. Mitch, in contrast, was a bright boy, and a beacon as to how Maddy would have been if she had not been groomed, targeted, and brutally assaulted. Now aged five, Mitch was as sharp as a tack. Maddy had never told anyone what had happened, except for Candy, and nobody knew who the father was until the day Sigmund Merde met them in the local precinct, on one of the days Maddy was allowed to walk out with her son. Within moments of Ghost talking to Maddy, so her full story was out. He promised her she would forever be with her son and Candy. Maddy and Mitch, along with Candy, will live together always, he had said, and now it looked like this was about to happen, courtesy of the *Portsmouth Evening News*.

Candy held the hand of Maddy, and Maddy held the hand of Mitch, and they all stared at the illuminated toy stage set, waiting for the animated show, the feature of which was the latest toy, *Animatron*, a robot-like doll that, although having lifelike movements, did not bear absolute scrutiny of the intended resemblance of its various guises; but to a child, and in this magical setting, it had the desired effect. They had already watched a set of tumbling soldiers that did not appeal to Candy or Maddy, but Mitch enjoyed it, and Cecelia took photos of the concern in the faces of the mother and her carer, counterpoised with the glee in the face of little Mitch.

She was photographing the scene when she noticed Maddy's face morph to apprehension, and then fear. The damaged woman's facial sinews tightened and tears streamed instantly. Candy clutched the young mother and hugged her to reinforce security, so incongruously offered from the waiflike shell of a woman. But in that moment, Cecelia's camera picked up a steely glint in Candy's eyes and the iron in her soul was revealed. This sense passed to Maddy, and Cecelia's camera, on a roll, caught the transference of emotions of readiness in Candy, and reassurance received by Maddy. Mitch was unaware as Cecelia panned her lens in the direction of Maddy's manic stare, toward a portly city gent in a black blazer and pinstripe trousers, with a balloon face made up of a blotchy complexion, disguised by thick, bottle-bottom glasses in black lumpy frames.

It was like a visual tableau broken only in its transfixed staring, when an *Animatron*, dressed in concert tails, wobbled onto a stage and sat at a toy piano. The toy's head slowly swivelled and looked directly at Winston Mitchell, the portly gent, and an expectant hush descended upon the crowd of onlookers. The concert was about to start and the attempted dash to another place by Winston Mitchell, known as Mitch to his friends, was curtailed by the surged strangulation of the crowd in delighted expectation; children pushed to the front and rubbed against the Mandarin, and his image of fear changed to a momentary semblance of pleasure.

Cecelia caught all of this with her camera, then swung her lens and her own gaze to the *Animatron*, as it began to play. In a sense, it was lifelike, although it was clear the robot was not actually playing the instrument, but the image was a convincing one. She looked around the crowd and the faces showed awe and animated enjoyment, all except for Winston, whose face was drained of any colour; the cheek blotches standing out as a stark raspberry coulis in a bowl of cream. It looked as if at any moment he would collapse, and then he did.

The crowd parted, except for the kids who were transfixed as *Animatron* stopped playing, and the toy's head swivelled to where Winston Mitchell lay. Ghost, announcing he was a doctor, began pumping the heart of Winston, not *Dr Who*, Ghost was in earnest. The Secretary for Social Services, the Mandarin civil servant who had the reputation for taking his job very seriously, continually applauded for travelling the length and breadth of the country, visiting so many Children's Homes, and especially the homes for children with mental defects or brain injury, lay dying. Not even Ghost could save him, but before he expired, people noticed Ghost whisper something, and the Mandarin looked up into the eyes of his son Mitch, and the deep-pool eyes of Maddy. Temporarily alive, she smiled and hummed the tune the *Animatron* pianist had just been playing. She didn't know it, but then she wouldn't, but Cecelia did; it was Shostakovich's Piano Concerto Number Two, the second movement.

TWENTY

CARLY WHEELED MANDY INTO JACK'S HOSPITAL room. They had been expected, yet she still had to jostle for a wheelchair place amongst the family. What is it with Jack and his family, Mandy thought? Which was her family now? 'Well, what can I tell yer? I get hurt, carted off to hospital and still it's me visiting you. Explain that to me, Jack, if you can?'

Mandy, in her wheelchair, had both fractured shins in plaster and stretched out in front of her. She would be in plaster for six weeks and still she had a big smile on her knocked-about panda face. Her broken nose had been straightened, and Jack gazed at it through the crowding family, who parted like the Red Sea. He loved her fireman's hose, and thought her legs looked lovely, if a tad pale in the plaster of Paris.

Did she smile? Jack groaned, because Mandy had a point. 'I like pandas, Mandy. I fink I might call you Ding-a-ling. What're we doing for Christmas?' He sneaked a look to see if he had gotten away with it, and it looked like he had.

Carly, Mandy's daughter Liz's partner, who was leaning on the back of the wheelchair, burst out laughing. Mandy had always assumed Carly, whom Jack called Curly, was the more masculine of the couple, which explained, Mandy imagined, why her daughter was the pregnant one. Eventually, Liz joined in with the jollity and casual banter, relieved her mother had survived a dangerous situation, though not fully intact. Mandy restrained her laugh to a titter; it hurt. Liz, as a consequence of being heavy with child, paced in an uncomfortable manner, unable to settle, and people were affording her as much room as possible in the cramped space; she had inherited her mother's famed impatience.

Mandy's immediate family were there. Liz with Carly, and David, Mandy's son, down from Nottingham and staying with his sister and Carly, and of course there was the ever-present Dolly, the ancient old-age pensioner cleaner, who smelled ever so slightly of wee and lavender polish, an odour that, perversely, Jack loved, and was comforted by; he was a strange man, I tell you, if you hadn't already worked that out by now.

Jack's daughter Alana, who had forgone Jack's wishes she go into a nunnery, was with her man, Josh. Jack had only just gotten used to his daughter living with a man for four years and ignoring his advice that she should shut herself away from the filthy grasp of men, when he had to assimilate the news of her pregnancy, four months, proof, if it were needed, that his daughter had been fiddled with.

Mandy told him to shut up, and he did, for a bit at least.

Having said that, he knew he would be an excellent Grandfevvers, of course. He'd decided he did not want to be known as Granddad or Grandpa, he wanted to be known as Grandfevvers, and Number One Grandfevvers at that; and, as if to stamp his ownership on the name, he claimed he had recorded this formally at Summersent Arse, so Kipper could not beat him to it. Everyone accepted this as just Jack, knowing he referred to Somerset House that coincidentally was now an art gallery, and no longer did registrations of births, deaths and marriages, except Kipper did not know, and was checking to see if Jack had actually recorded this, and if not Summersent Arse, then where? It would be reasonable to say both men, villain and copper, were incompetently competitive.

Jack's recently discovered daughter Alice was there too, with Nobby, her partner. Nobby was also the Police Commander's son, and knock me down with a Grandfevver if she did not announce to the room she was pregnant, also. Jack was mightily pissed off, and not because Nobby had fiddled with his girl, although naturally he had, and furthermore, Nobby had actually fiddled with her before Jack knew she was his daughter to be fiddled with – no, Jack was annoyed because people were there to see him, and now they were all gathered around Alice and Nobby to congratulate them. All except Mandy, who, low down on her wheels, had been left out in the cold as well. Mandy noticed his glum expression. She knew Jack's face well and was the only person in the room who could see the various subterranean visage changes, beneath the ugly bit.

'Good news, eh, Jack?' she said, knowing exactly what he was thinking, because he had spoken his thoughts. Jack shrugged but it hurt his back. He was like a beached whale in his bed and she told him so. His sea mammal mood lightened as his blubber rolled in pain-limited jollity; he loved it when she whispered sweet nothings to him. 'Jack, I shouted that,' laughing and grimacing with her own pain.

'Deaf aids?' He nodded and grimaced again. He laughed and grimaced; they were both consommé grimacers. He loved this woman and was devastated to see her hurt, and he told her so, but likely spoiled the moment by mentioning he may be slightly more hurt than her and may be a parrot.

She ignored his wincing, or exotic birdlike paralysis, and basked in the loving way he looked at her. 'What about Christmas, Jack?' she asked, whilst she had his attention, and, in a consommé way, she had distracted him from the fact that another of his daughters had been fiddled with. She also knew he hated Christmas. Well, he didn't hate Christmas, for he enjoyed it when it finally arrived, just hated the fuss of getting there.

'Christmas?' he imitated her.

'We have to slow down,' she said seriously, as the manic family caroused behind them. 'This has been a hectic few weeks and now we are both injured,' and she swept her hands over her white-cast-encased lower limbs, stretched out before her over to her whale of a husband. Not that he was aware, he was trying to look up her nightdress. He didn't see the plaster. To him, it looked like her legs were dressed in long bobby socks, and this could be quite attractive on a woman in a 1950-ish way, and he liked these fashions and thought of skipping granddad shirts, though they would be quite appropriate now, and going for a *Famous Five* look.

Mandy gave him her special reserve stare. It was special, and generally reserved for him, and he liked that.

He responded with the illuminating news that he needed a wee, and if he did one and it went up in the air, as a whale would spout in the sea, could he get away with it? Mandy giggled, swivelled her chair and pressed the nurse-call button.

The nurse popped her head around the door to see a gathering of unlikely joyous characters, and Mandy in her wheelchair holding a walrus flipper. 'He needs a bottle, nurse, and if you can let me have a pin, I can get his winkle out for him.'

The nurse guffawed, and Mandy decided to suffer the pain and laugh along with her. This had an added benefit, other than embarrassing her husband. It was a moment he enjoyed as it also brought the others back to the bedside.

'Can we clear the room please, Jack needs a wee. I am being discharged so I can meet you all back at our house. Liz and Carly will bring me home and we can talk about Christmas.'

'Oi, what about me?' Jack complained, fitting in a wincing grimace for the benefit of the family, as they may have forgotten he was seriously wounded.

Mandy noticed his actress grimace. 'You're being fitted with an elephant's corset, and until that is ready, you're staying put.'

Jack remembered now, he'd ordered a pink one; he had after all recently had a pink hand cast and then a pink shoulder harness. 'Check when that's coming will yer, luv, only I'd like to come 'ome as well...' he said, adding '...pretty please with brass injuns on top,' so she knew he was serious, then he morphed his loving and adorable, he thought, look, with one of patent sadness.

She knew he was thinking of Martin. 'Martin is okay, though he has lost his front leg below the knee, but they can provide him with a prosthetic,' Mandy answered, looking to gauge his reaction. It was a smile of relief, mixed with a boyish malevolence. 'Yes...' she knew what he was thinking, '... Kipper has ordered a pink one, so you can both be daft buggers together, and Martin is remarkably chipper and recovering well, considering.'

Mandy signalled to Carly and she was wheeled out and the familial entourage followed.

Jack felt alone in the empty room. He thought about Martin, how much pain he must have suffered and began to cry; he needed a wee and everyone, of course, had forgotten all about him. He had to do everything around here, he thought.

'Switch the waterworks off, Jack, you're like a bleedin' girl,' Kipper said, as he poked his head around the door.

Jack flicked his head, permitted himself an actress grimace and mentioned to Kipper he was in a hundred sorts of pain, and he wasn't crying about that. He was most insistent upon that point, and reinforced this by mentioning he wasn't a girl's blouse, either; these were important issues.

Kipper entered the room and allowed Jack to think he had conveyed his message successfully, but Kipper knew, as did everyone else for that matter, Jack was definitely a girl's blouse, and if you asked Kipper's opinion, that blouse had wuss brass knob buttons.

'Martin's okay. Strong dog, and for the record he didn't cry, just the odd whelp.' Kipper went on to talk about the prosthetic for Martin. 'They've made big strides, if you pardon the pun, these days...' and Kipper put his hand up to halt any passing traffic and Jack's giant traffic-sized gob, '... it will be pink, Martin insisted, and he will be allowed home tomorrow, with painkillers. He's managing well, so...' and Kipper flung his hands out like a gangster Julie Andrews.

'Thanks, Kipper and...'

Kipper put his hand up and stopped more galloping gobshite stuff from Jack. 'I have this covered, the vet owes me one.'

'He does?'

'Best you don't ask,' Kipper replied, tapping his nose.

There was a knock on the door and Jimbo popped his head around. 'Yo, Jack, spare a mo?' It was academic as Jimbo was already in, and had Beth with him.

Jack was surprised. 'Beth,' he said, remarkably eloquently or was that elelephantly, bearing in mind the huge lump on the bed that presented itself to the young, and petite, lady fascist.

'Hello,' she replied, nervously looking for a reaction in Jack's eye. Jack could not disguise his surprise, pleased she was talking, genuinely taken aback. 'I'm sorry,' she said as she approached his bed, and Jack, in a subconscious reaction, stretched out his hand. She took it and Jimbo slid a chair under her and she thumped back into it.

'Where's Jackie?' Jack asked.

Jimbo answered, as Jack's and Beth's eyes remained locked on each other. 'She went to your house. She wanted to see Mandy when she got home.'

Logical, Jack thought. Mandy had suffered a trauma, and it was rational that Jackie would go to see

Mandy, but it was as if he had lost all reasoning skill as he looked at Beth. Rather than a young woman, he saw a little girl, a frail child. Not the violent fascist, not unbridled rage; he saw innocence, he saw a broken heart.

'Have you seen your dad?' he asked, and immediately the girl's eyes welled and tears streamed. She nodded. 'How is he?'

'Better,' which caused the tears to roll faster down her cheek.

Jimbo handed her his handkerchief. Something had changed and Jack noticed softness in the MI5 man, but not in the hanky. That was filthy, and Jack thought how lucky it was that Mandy was not here to issue a reprimand; she had a thing about hankies that seemed illogical to Jack.

'He has damage to his body from all the drinking, but they think he will make a reasonable recovery. I sat with him. Told him...' she paused and swallowed emotion, '... I was sorry.'

Jack squeezed her hand. He knew this would mean the world to her father. Ghost had told Jack it was only a will to live that Brian Mayhew lacked, and maybe he would have that now. Jack hoped so.

Another tap at the door. It was Della, and after a nanosecond of staring out Jimbo, she barged past him and went to the opposite side of the bed to Beth. She looked at the girl, not a pretty look, and Jack sensed Della distrusted Beth. Interesting... He was a great believer in The Women's Institute, liked their jam, and the song *Jerusalem*, though not the Establishment behind the words. Della looked caringly at Jack before assuming her default position of rebuke, but Jack stopped her before her mouth motored. 'How are you, Della?'

'What you mean to say is, why has it taken you all this feckin' time to sort out all the filf stuff, Della, after that shambles of a country raid you led? Is that what you wanted to ask me?' She tapped her foot. Jack knew she was not really the admin sort, but he couldn't think what to say. Was this Oldtimers?

Della prattled on, unaware Jack had hypochondriac issues to deal with, '...And did you know I had to stay out there with Jo-Jums for nigh on two hours, in the freezin' bleedin' cold, while scenes of crime set up, and then, they were looking to me for bleedin' explanations? Explanations?' she repeated in emphasis. 'What was there to explain?' She frowned at Jack, 'You know it stinks in the country, and you said Jo was good, but she seems to want me to do all the bleedin' work round 'ere, and I needed to get back to Jonas. You know what I'm like after an operation.'

Jack did. She needed physical release and he had never probed, but someone was always available, he presumed. 'Have you been home?'

"Ave I buggery. There's something wrong with that Jo-Jums,' she said, defraying any emotional interpretation that could be associated with her visiting him before going to get her brain cells seen to, and all of this was accompanied with hand gestures not for the faint-hearted.

She described the Jo-Jums he knew, wanting the i's dotted and the t's crossed. Jack had been there, knew how Della felt, but knew also that Jo needed to do all of this and then she would look out for both of their backsides. He told Della this and he thought she calmed, but still maintained a discreet distance. 'Yes, well, you also said she was fast and efficient. I bet my Gypo will be asleep when I get in now.'

'Maybe he needs to sleep? He might need time for his wounds to heal?' Jack looked at his wrist, at the hospital name-tag loosely wrapped. He shook it and cursed modern technology. 'What time is it?'

Jimbo, sniggering, answered, 'Not sure, can't see the hair or the pimple, but my watch says three in the morning, there or thereabouts.'

'Well, there you go,' Jack said.

'Where what goes?' Della and Jimbo responded, in unison, Jimbo calmer.

'No wonder I'm tired, it's well past my bedtime. Now feck off, the lot of you, and Beth...' he looked at the girl, with a soft eye set in a cabbage patch face, '... come to see me tomorrow, will yer, luv? We can talk, eh?'

The girl nodded as she stood up, and Jimbo put his arm across her shoulders in a fatherly manner. Jack smiled. Jimbo would make a good surrogate dad until Snail got his act together, and he watched the three of them make their way to the door. He called out to Jimbo, having just remembered something. 'Jimbo, do me a flavour old son, get us a Christmas tree, will yer and I'll be yer best friend.'

Della looked back at the whale, her fellow cockney. 'Feck, Christmas...' She showed a childish glee. 'I wonder what Jonas has got me?'

Jimbo sighed, and acknowledged he would likely end up Christmas shopping for Jack, as well as getting him a tree, which he would have to put up for him, especially as Jack was injured. This would not be the first time Jimbo had put a Christmas tree up for Jack. Jack's attempts in the past always fell down, and then, when eventually temporarily stable, the tree ended up crooked and propped with big sticks covered in aluminium foil to make them look Christmassy.

Jimbo could recall, back in the mists before the death of Jack's wife, the look on Kate's face as she looked upon her bozo, who would say, "There you go, sweet-'art, that looks alright, don't it?", with his head slanting to match the angle the tree had assumed, having lost all of its former Norwegian forest dignity. He guessed it was now something Mandy would have to deal with.

TWENTY-ONE

It was early morning, a watery, lukewarm orange sun, colour-washed over London like a Turner painting, wisps of mist chilling the air as Archie Pointe-Lace stepped out to take a stroll. He had sat in his Bumblin'tons wing-back chair all night. He never needed much sleep and knew if he had gone home to his Kensington apartment he would be restless. He was comfortable in his Club environment. It was his territory, as were the London Parks, St James's and especially Green Park, where he walked this morning and contemplated POGROM. The idea for the name came from a clue in, of all places, the *Guardian* news-paper crossword.

Archie did the crosswords of all the broadsheet news-papers and even contributed the odd puzzle himself.

Interestingly, this crossword, that was particularly difficult, had attracted his attention. Not unusually for the *Guardian*, the crossword had been peppered with left wing, socialist riddles, anagrams and cryptic clues. He had always known what he was doing and knew it was an exercise within his head, but all the same, he got a perverse pleasure in wanting to have names, a bit like the military have operational code names. POGROM, the result of a clue, he adopted as his name for his operation... except it wasn't his operation, was it? Except it wasn't his name, was it? The name had been a part of a clue, and Archie was not sure if it had been inserted especially for him. Was he getting paranoid? POGROM was apt, except he didn't want to be cruel, did he? It was an intellectual exercise after all, wasn't it, wondering if all along he was someone's puppet and why was he okay with this? He normally considered himself the Puppet Master.

As he strolled, so he mulled over all of these thoughts, and in particular, reflections upon his ponderings through the night – principally, what on earth was happening? How could these events happen? Were the wheels coming off, and if so, why so dramatically? Not that this bothered him. What worried him was, this was not what he had planned, and although he often set ideas in motion, intrigued and amused to see how they would pan out, this current scenario was nowhere within his mind map.

Truthfully, he wasn't worried about the body count; thoughts of casualties never concerned him, and he certainly never thought of them as *collateral damage*, a crass American expression he abhorred. The Americans, he had always thought, always felt the need to dress things up in words that disguised the horror of events, like, *take someone out*. They could not bring themselves to say *kill, murder*, or *slaughter*.

He recalled his dear Mama, who drank herself to death, and let's face it, who wouldn't, living with his not so dear Papa? His mother would say, "Just one more dwinkee," as if speaking in a childish manner made the drink ineffectual and nobody should worry; but she was wrong, and her drinking had affected him and his half-brother, Lionel. It had been the first time in their lives they had encountered something they could do nothing about, and they watched as their mother slowly, sloshed and slurred, slipped into oblivion each night, eventually to slip into an early grave, and then, in record-breaking time, both boys were shipped off to school to be cold-showered, beaten and buggered senseless, because Papa could not handle things; so much for family.

But none of this bothered him so much as what people would think of him. One person especially;

not that he knew who that person was, but he had his suspicions. What would that person whom he'd heard referred to as *Big-Knob* by some of the street riff-raff who occasionally had their uses, think, if the wheels really did come off? And then what would Big-Knob do? Still he comforted himself in so much as he felt *bullet-proof.* He had constructed an intellectual screen around himself. Nobody could trace anything back to him and, after all, he was the government's most trusted advisor and had been so for many years, whatever the colour of the party in power – he chuckled as he strolled – and whatever party he wanted to be in power at any time; and at that, he laughed out loud.

As he sauntered, now with his thoughts and alien outbursts under control, Archie recalled his meeting yesterday evening with Amlodd Jones. He would have to watch that Mandarin carefully. He had been targeted, his tea drugged, and the music, Shostakovich; Amlodd mentioned he had heard that theme playing and this was not common knowledge. He may be physically crooked and bent and, as a consequence of these physical defects and his nature, the man assumed a weak-kneed, Dickensian, simpering stance, but Archie was not fooled. Jones had an intellect almost as accomplished as his own, and was convinced the Mandarin had worked out what was happening; had he? The man had an instinct, but was it whimsical like his own? Whim did not worry him so much, unless he was combating it in an adversary, and Jones may be just that. It was almost too difficult to focus upon, and he should know, it was one of his own major defence strategies.

Jones, Archie knew, had a survival instinct that enabled him to work the corridors of power particularly effectively, and Archie did worry that Jones had worked out why, and by whom, things had been happening, almost illogically and almost completely under most people's radar. POGROM was, regardless of its potency, whimsical, and should be viewed as such, and would be if it were not being seen to be so dangerous, if it didn't come with a body count; but did it? He knew his half-brother was not averse to a little violence, purchased off the street, and Archie had to admit he had also found this to be mildly stimulating, and it certainly moved things along.

Unfortunately, the street villains rarely had a sense for restraint. Had Jones worked this out? Was that why Jones had called the meeting yesterday, to lay down his own intellectual cards, to call him out; the *Okay Corral*? Whilst interesting and intellectually challenging, it was not acceptable, not at this moment in time. Right now, he had his own cards to play and what would Amlodd do about it? His instinct was to *take him out,* and he chortled to himself as he took a park bench, amused at his American reference, and it occurred to him the CIA had been seeking his assistance. He may be able to help them now and, immensely cheered by that thought, he stood, filled with energy, and began to walk at a faster pace, not back to Bumblin'tons but to Grosvenor Square, and the American Embassy. It was time to be surrogate Puppet Master again.

———

'JACK, YOU AWAKE?' Jackie was seated beside his hospital bed and a doctor in a white coat stood behind her.

'I am now,' and he kicked his brain into gear. 'What're you doing here...?' He thought on. 'Oh God, Mandy! Is she okay? What's happened?'

Jackie reacted to calm him, smoothing his hand. 'Everything is okay. Well, as okay as anything ever is around you!' She smiled, and it comforted him.

'Spit it out, luv.' Jack had a good sixth sense, not that he could remember what the other five were, but his sixth one was good.

'You've got to ease up, Jack, if only for Mandy's sake. She is not as resilient as you, or as resilient as you think you are. I think we have seen you are vulnerable, and I'm worried about you both.' It was Jackie's serious head.

Jack looked beyond Jackie. 'Doc, what you doing 'ere?'

The doctor looked like he had been shaken from a bad dream. 'We... er... I asked Dr Phillips to come... er... in. Er... your records are marked for an alert on trauma, and we received a call from a Dr Samuels?' The young doctor spoke with the raised inflection in his voice Jack had noticed youngsters using these days, very much in the Australian manner of speaking. 'I am Australian, and this is how we talk,' the doctor said.

'Did I...? Australian, you say? Not a Liverpudlian accent?' Jackie barely resisted a giggle, managed a nod and reassured the doctor that Jack often spoke his thoughts aloud, and this was nothing unusual. 'Jim called?'

'He's worried about you, Mandy as well. Maybe it's time?'

'Time? What? What's 'appening?'

The doctor answered. 'You have serious bruising of the lower vertebrae, the lumber area.' Jack thought about a sawmill joke, but the doc was motoring on, maybe Australians had no sense of humour, he reassured himself. 'We are going to take you down to Physiotherapy and you will be taught some exercises...'

The doctor saw the look of horror on Jack's face. It was remarkable the doctor could see this, but he had been medically trained to see beyond ugly, to look for symptoms. 'You will need to keep these exercises up, as we suspect your back will likely cause you difficulty well into the future, perhaps for the rest of your life, but in the meantime, you need to allow the bruising to subside. We will give you anti-inflammatory tablets for that, and the exercises will help with movement. In the meantime, the corset is ready to be fitted and they will do that downstairs also, and then...' he looked at Jackie, '... you can go home.'

He turned to leave, added, 'Good luck,' and it looked like he meant it; he had a serious Liverpudlian look, like a *Beatle*. 'I'm Australian!' and the doc's face morphed from *Albert Schweitzer* to a cheesed-off *Ned Kelly*.

Jack looked at Jackie, his ugly worried face. 'It's okay, I will come with you, then I'll take you home,' she said.

Jack looked relieved. He didn't like hospitals at the best of times and always felt he needed company. Jackie was aware of his insecurities. She still had to work out the source of that fear, but she would, along with all of the other shite this man dealt with in De-Nile, the life-denying river of his Church of Egypt. Or, maybe he was just a wuss; yeah, that was it, and pretty soon he would be lost to Oldtimers, Mandy had suggested, concerned Jackie had not laughed at that.

———

Bubba French was CIA, and looking at him, you would most likely not guess this as he was, many would argue, the American version of Jack Austin, but without the acuity of thinking; Jack always said it was because his brain had been burgered. This tall, portly man was, though, clearly an American, and evidently had his fashion sense steeped in Sixties American CIA style. He wore a checked jacket and ill-matching window-pane checked trousers, Hawaiian shirt, of which only one of the multitudes of colours matched the jacket, slippery grey shoes with decorative brass buckles, and a pork pie hat. He was, as Mandy had said before, "A shite-dressed ad-vert for why you should avoid *MacDonald's*".

Jack had argued that you underestimated Bubba's ability at your peril, although, obviously, he was not in his own league, but then, as Jack had also said, "He was American". Jack always said this as though it was an unfortunate accident of birth, and Americans were to be pitied, but in amelioration, they could con-sole themselves, secure in the knowledge they were not French; *naturellement*.

Bubba had met Archibald Pointe-Lace at the American Embassy before, it was not an unusual event, and at this latest meeting they agreed a plan of action; a meeting at the Home Office. It was also not unusual for Archie to meet representatives of other countries and often at the Home Office. He had been a behind-the-scenes advisor to the British Government for many years, his intellect seen as an asset to throw alternative light on events that could affect the country. However, Bubba, no stranger himself at the Home Office, was wary. Jack had fed him information about certain senior Civil Servants, Mandarins he called them, who had him worried, and this had been reinforced by Archie Pointe-Lace, who expressed similar concerns. But the fat in Bubba's brain told him all was not as it may seem in that state of Denmark, as Jack told him when passing him a Danish pastry.

The CIA had already determined something was happening in and around the Civil Service in Britain, had said as much when Bubba interrupted Mandy and Jack's honeymoon in France, back in November, and this information had been verified to Jack by Ghost. Bubba was pleased Jack was taking it seriously, which was why the proposed meeting in the Home office had been so readily scheduled; they were intrigued.

The Home Office meeting was to be held with Jim Samuels of MI5, whom Bubba knew, and the Permanent Secretary, Quentin Bryant, back at work after a recent scare; he'd collapsed at a Buckingham Palace reception. What was thought to be his heart, the doctors said, was more likely a panic attack. It was of course just this. Ghost knew, and Jack knew, for Ghost had told him. Samuels knew, Jack had told him, and now Bubba knew, Jack had told him, but Ghost had confirmed it, as you never knew if what Jack was telling you was kosher. Oh, and Abe Hyman, Mossad, had confirmed it, so it was kosher, and he would also be at the meeting.

Despite the seniority of the attendees, this was to be a low-level meeting, discreet, and the Home Secretary had asked Archibald Pointe-Lace to lead in her stead. Archie intended to lead anyway, but it didn't hurt to occasionally allow politicians to think they ruled the roost, and at that, he had allowed himself another rare chuckle. Abe had been briefed by Jack that, in his opinion, Archie Pointe-Lace, was not kosher, and may even be a little *puppety*. Jim Samuels knew, because Jack had told him. Ghost knew, but he was not going to be at the meeting. Bubba was not sure if he believed what Jack had told him, but kept a fat-soaked brain on red alert, just in case. Quentin Bryant knew Thackeray was not kosher, but then he would, and he was worried he would have another panic attack, especially as Pointe-Lace had turned up to the meeting with the crooked and scary weasel,

Amlodd Jones, a Mandarin almost on a par with his own level within the Civil Service.

Quentin Bryant knew all of this, he was the Permanent Secretary for the Home Office, but sensed his involvement in the game was up. Ghost had treated him at the Palace after his collapse, and he had whispered, "Pogenromoz in bich nought eee," which Bryant thought meant "Pogrom was a naughty idea".

They settled around the table, in an out-of-the-way meeting room, the aides and PA's having been left outside in an ante-room, and extraordinarily, Archibald Pointe-Lace opened the proceedings. If Quentin Bryant had thought this through, he would not have found this quite so astonishing, but when he had discussed the attendance of Pointe-Lace at this meeting with the Home Secretary, he was not thinking with his highly attuned brain; he had his survival suit on.

'Welcome,' Pointe-Lace said seriously, 'I hope you do not mind, I have invited Amlodd Jones...' and he pointed unnecessarily to the deformed and diminutive Amlodd, whose head seemed to just about peer above the table top, his weaselly hands gripping the edge of the table like a moon man, but with no aerial on his head.

Following his introduction, the deformed Lunar Mandarin relaxed his grip and wrung his hands, a tightening grin displayed on his tortured, creepy face; he was at the grownups' table, he deserved to be here, he had things to contribute; not that everyone would be happy about that, and he knew this.

'I have discussed with the Home Secretary,' Pointe-Lace continued, 'that whilst Quentin's health remains a cause for concern, Amlodd will shadow his position.'

Pointe-Lace sat back and began humming a melodic air, whilst staring upon the bloated, blotched complexion and black beady eyes of Quentin Bryant. He allowed this announcement and the tune to sink in, obviously news to Quentin, and the melodic interlude struck a chord as well, as the shocked look on the face of the Permanent Secretary to the Home Office was evident to everybody. Samuels jumped up – as a doctor, he could see this was no panic attack – and as Samuels got to the Secretary's chair, the Mandarin convulsed, the sinews beneath the rubbery face clenched and Quentin jerked and slumped to the floor.

'Call an ambulance!' Samuels shouted to nobody, but Pointe-Lace had already stepped from the room and alerted the assistants in the anteroom, and returned to see Samuels carrying out CPR. 'This time it is a heart attack,' Samuels confirmed, continuing his work that he suspected would be in vain.

The men stepped to the side of the room as the paramedics arrived and eventually took Quentin Bryant away. Samuels had used the office defibrillator and there may be a chance, but it would likely be a forlorn hope and, Samuels also thought, it was fortuitous that Amlodd Jones had come with Pointe-Lace. Jack had briefed Samuels, explaining Pointe-Lace was Len's half-brother, and also imparted his view: "Pointe-Lace was likely in this up to his clever clogs head, he may even be the puppet-master," though of that he could not be sure. Samuels had concurred. He suspected also that the current Home Secretary would be outgoing soon, to be replaced with Amlodd Jones' man, Dai Zeeze, and he was not sure what to make of that, either. Mandarins were dropping like flies, and unlikely individuals climbed the pole that was currently not so greasy. Still, Amlodd was Jack's man, wasn't he? Samuels was unsure if he felt reassured by that.

There was a gentle buzz in the room, mainly from Pointe-Lace and the simpering Jones, who had ensconced themselves into a corner for their hushed conspiratorial conversation. A secretary entered the room and passed a folded note to Jones, which he read and passed to Pointe-Lace, who pranced, inappropriately, out of his corner to address the meeting. The others retook their seats as Archie reassembled his cold fish emotions.

'I am sorry to say Quentin died.' Pointe-Lace applied a faux sadness to his cod face; he was practiced at this, often in demand for eulogies, probably would do Quentin's, had already worked out what he would say. 'I think a moment's silence?' It was not a question, and all of the men stood and gathered their personal thoughts around the table, heads bowed, not one person thinking of the recently deceased Permanent Secretary to the Home Office.

When the minute was up, Pointe-Lace spoke again. 'The Prime Minister and Deputy Prime Minister are at this moment being informed but...' he paused – respect? Probably not, '... we had already discussed this possibility and formed a contingency plan. Mr Mackeroon had tried to talk Quentin out of returning, asking him to take a sabbatical and recover fully, and clearly he did not heed the advice.' (Pointe-Lace knew why, and Amlodd Jones had a shrewd idea.) 'A little time will be allowed, out of respect, and then there is to be a Cabinet reshuffle. The new Home Secretary will be Dai Zeeze and his Permanent Secretary...' and Archie leaned his head to acknowledge Amlodd Jones, '... will be Amlodd.' Perhaps we should adjourn this meeting until things settle, and reconvene after Christmas?'

A murmur of agreement sounded around the table and the spooks departed, informed of what they had already suspected would happen, aware of all that had just played out in front of their own eyes, but at a loss to know what they could do about it. This, they would decide, and before the next meeting, but in the meantime they left; Bubba for the States, Abe for Tel Aviv and Samuels down to Portsmouth.

TWENTY-TWO

'You sure that's straight, Jimbo?' Jack asked, his stance appearing as an amusing teapot, one hand supporting his back, the other pointing, with his sloped Christmas tree head, to a straight Christmas tree. Something was not right, and he could not put his spout-like finger on it, and then he did; it had no side-strutting. 'Jimbo, you plank, you've forgotten the struts.'

'Oh, that's lovely, Jimbo, thank you,' Mandy said as she wheeled herself into the living room, her stiff white bobby socks pointing at Jack, who was momentarily distracted, convinced if he could bend his back a bit, he would be able to see up her dress, but it would hurt. Jack was a realist, but still he tried, and of course was caught because he moaned; it did hurt.

'Jack look at the tree, it's lovely! We won't need the struts this year,' Mandy added authoritatively, though with a cautioning look to Jack.

Jack shucked his dirty old man reverie and looked at her as if he'd just become aware that his wife was learning-impaired. He returned his gaze to the tree, then back to Mandy, then the tree again and, leaning his head to one side, he said, 'You sure? Jimbo? We won't need the struts this year? I fink we should put them in anyway. What d'you fink? It don't seem the same otherwise, not so festive-like.'

Mandy watched her cripple as he *oomphed* back to the vertical, and decided to throw him a curveball. 'Have you got your corset on?'

'Well, er... no, but then I'm not going out, see?' Mission accomplished, but it looked like more was coming. It did, and so he headed it off at the pass, rather expertly he thought. 'Kirk to Engineering, the tree's fine,' and he looked to Sulu to slip into warp drive for a quick getaway.

'Have you done your exercises?' Mandy was not on the same Bridge, Star-ship or Galaxy.

Jack was caught in the Mandy tractor beam. 'Well, er... no, I need a poo first, see?' He'd saved the day again, and ordinarily would have punched the air in triumph, but that could hurt, and the last thing you need to do, having scored major points, was to wince or even cry. Girls spotted things like that. Experience, you see; that, and he knew women, of course.

Mandy didn't spot anything other than a startled clown, and could hear giggling coming from a kitchen full of experienced Jack people, who had been eavesdropping on the frightened rabbit, fully aware an exchange of this sort between lapin and Mandy would be amusing. They were not disappointed. As the headlamps, which could have belonged to a Romulan battle cruiser, caught the panicking bunny, he sounded Fred Alert, and considered the escape pod in the toilet.

Jackie strolled into the battle-zone, taking up her position as Bones, on the bridge. She had dropped Jack home and decided to stay a while. She liked it with Jack and Mandy's family, it was worth putting up with the shite Jack gave out, but she thought Mandy was bringing that under control.

'Jack, have you been sharing the bathwater with Jackie?' Mandy asked, and Jack looked shocked, and thought, had he?

'Did I...?' Jackie asked, cursing her luck, having caught the habit of speaking her thoughts from Jack; Mandy had said all along that it was contagious.

'Yes, I did warn you.'

'Did I...?'

'You did!' A resounding chorus from the kitchen, and Jackie knew she was bang to rights, but was saved by the bell. It was Jack's phone ringing and ringing; he did not feel like answering it.

Mandy wheeled over, rummaged through his trouser pockets and answered it for him. 'Jim...' she listened, 'okay, I will tell them. Mike on his way? ... Okay, see you later.' Mandy closed the call.

'Jim?' Jack asked unnecessarily.

'Yes, he's coming to check the tree.' Mandy chuckled and heartier laughter sounded from the kitchen.

'Quentin Bryant's dead,' Jack stated, rather than asked, his ambivalence hidden behind a visage of ugliness, a visage that also suggested he needed to attend to his photon torpedoes pretty soon. Mandy was amazed, and not for the first time knew she shouldn't be; her man often knew things before most everybody else. 'Close your mouth, darling, we are not a codfish,' he said, and Mandy snapped her gob shut, knowing full well she would have lost points, but how many?

While Jack whistled *Jane and Michael Banks* from *Mary Poppins*, Mandy enquired, tentatively, 'I will not ask how you knew, but are we supposed to do anything?' She spoke in a pleading tone, hoping there was nothing they could do, as she was tired, and of course legless; another joke Jack repeated ad infinitum; only to be expected, she sighed.

Jack knew exactly what they should do and, risking his life and her limbs, he instructed Mandy, 'Ring Della, tell her to get 'er arse 'round 'ere, tell 'er Mike and Samuels are on their way...' Mandy was about to respond vigorously, when Jack thought of some other things. 'Ring Jo-Jums, Ollie and Stan, get them 'round as well.' He was finished but stretched his hand out. It looked as if he was pondering some more, probably what to do with his hand, which he was waving about like a tart, Mandy thought. 'They can tell us if we need struts in the tree as well,' He added finally.

Oh, that was it.

'I'll get on with that, shall I?' Mandy asked. 'In the meantime, what will you be doing?'

Jack looked at her. 'You're Ohura, Comms, dopy, (she thought she was Spok but didn't say) and I need to have a poo if I'm to do my exercises, and then I have to get the tree struts covered in foil, that tree don't look right to me,' and he flicked a wonky head to the vertical tree, grabbed his phone and skipped off, whistling, *Skip to the loo, my darling.*

Mandy wondered if he had really injured his back, and then he *oomphed* on the first few steps, looked back and received a visage of sympathy from Jimbo and Jackie and a circumspect look from his wife. He ran with the Jimbo and Jackie looks, and continued to skip to the loo, a good poo tune, having looked back at his audience; phasers on stun, obviously.

They all heard the rummaging around of clothes and the first indications of settling in for a long stint. He obviously had his phone out, and Mandy was impressed by his multitasking as she heard him say, 'Siggy, er...' he struggled, '... I know you know, er... one-two, one-two...,' he was off and going, '...can you get round, old son?'

Mandy spun in her wheelchair and called up the stairs, 'Jack, close the door to the bridge, there's a good Admiral.'

TWENTY-THREE

Amlodd Jones returned to his office. He had nowhere else to go, no family inviting him for a seasonal stay, no friends close enough to share Christmastide with. He had long ago reconciled himself to a life of loneliness, enforced by the nature of his deformed body and people's reactions to it. It often amused him to look on as people struggled to be overtly friendly in a *does he take sugar* manner, usually to demonstrate to others in the vicinity that they were empathetic, politically correct, and were unaffected by whatever presented itself to them.

He hated the term *politically correct*; it had dogged his heels throughout his career. He had learned to get a perverse pleasure from the patent discomfort of some shallow people who cultivated his company, courted a tacit friendship even, though not one of those people had thought to invite him to share even the shallowest of intimacies. Over time, he had built a strong position for himself in the Civil Service, and this rise through the ranks came with robust armour, and now he was to be even more powerfully placed, Permanent Secretary to the Home Office, second only to the Cabinet Secretary, and he had his eye on that post as well; with or without his minister, Dai Zeeze (preferably without, but better the devil...and this demon was malleable).

'Have a lovely Christmas, Mr Jones,' his secretary Daphne called, putting on her coat as he passed her by, going to his office. He noticed a bag full of decoratively wrapped gifts leaning against her shapely leg; did he notice her leg more? He wasn't sure. 'Are you okay, Mr Jones?'

He stopped in his tracks, turned his head and took in the picture of Daphne Morris, spinster of this Governmental Parish. She was a comely woman, mid height, taller than him, naturally, mid-forties, slim, a nice figure he thought, brown hair always aggressively scragged back and tied into a controlling bun, and black, thick-framed, oval glasses. She was the sort of female who radiated feminine warmth behind a no-nonsense facade, and he had often wondered how she had made it to the top in an environment of very cold fish. He supposed it was because she was often like the wallpaper, flowery in a bland way, and you didn't notice it. Amlodd, however, both noticed and liked her, but had always suppressed his feelings, dismissing them as pointless, futile, only serving to make his life even more wretched.

Daphne went to pick up the carrier bag of gifts but stopped to look back at Amlodd. 'I heard about Quentin Bryant. I am so sorry.' She raised herself up, leaving the bag on the floor.

Amlodd looked deeper into the brown eyes of his secretary, expanded in size due to the magnification of her spectacle lenses; to all intents she towered over him. He had often wondered, if someone could iron his body straight, would he be of a comparable height to his secretary? 'Daphne, confidentially, we are going to be transferred to the Home Office after the holiday break. I trust you will be okay? I'd like to take you with me.'

Daphne looked at her boss, really looked. She knew what she felt for him, and had often thought that, with a man like Mr Jones, you never knew if you felt sympathy or affection; she felt both at various times. 'Yes, Mr Jones. I thought something like this might happen when I heard the news.' Her face betrayed no emotion, yet she was excited at the prospect of this promotion; it was her Civil Service face, vacant of emotion, almost severe.

Amlodd was always impressed by his secretary's ability to read situations, and in the Civil Service, especially at this level, this required a highly attuned brain; Daphne had that, and this always excited him. They often did the *Guardian* crossword together at lunchtimes, almost furtively, as the *Guardian*, a perceived left-wing paper, was not frequently seen or at least enjoyed in these circles, but this was something they shared, and it made him feel not so lonely.

It was only two days to Christmas and although Daphne would be in the next day, Christmas Eve, it would be for the morning only and Amlodd knew he would have to bear two weeks of brutal solitude. He would be in the day after Boxing Day, a shell of staff only, and nobody with whom he could share a moment or two, even if it was just the crossword. And then there was New Year's Eve.

'Are you off to Rutland for the break?'

Daphne had been Amlodd's personal assistant for a long time and he knew all about her family and her love for Rutland, once dropped as a county as it was so small; later reinstated. She had told him how happy this made the people of Rutland, and how it served to unite a small population. Well, Amlodd knew all about that, being Welsh; bigger than Rutland, granted, but still he empathised with the same dogged grasp of identity.

'Looking forward to seeing your family? Your sister has another baby?'

Daphne liked this about Mr Jones. He took an interest, he wasn't shallow like the rest of her colleagues. It was one of the many reasons why she stalwartly defended her boss to others, so much so, she was isolated herself.

'Yes, thank you, sir, I'm looking forward to it. What will you be doing?' She knew already, and her heart broke for the broken man who stood, bent, before her, his very own Civil Service face on.

'Not much, but I have a lot to prepare for with our prospective move...' Amlodd turned. 'Can you hold on a minute, please?' and he went into his office. He noticed a gift-wrapped present on his desk. It would be from Daphne, and would probably be the only present he would get this Christmas. He collected from his top drawer the small gift he had for her, and returned with it. He tried to straighten as best he could, and proffered the gift. 'Merry Christmas, Daphne, please don't open it until Christmas day, I'd be embarrassed.' He offered an accompanying nervous, diluted smile, a smile that lacked confidence and she could see that. Daphne was not sure what came over her, but she leaned in and kissed her boss on the cheek, lingered, and felt him react.

'Oh, I'm so sorry, sir.'

She waited for a reaction, a rebuke, a smile, she wasn't sure what, but she was not expecting tears. Her boss had always presented his Civil Service armour. She knew there was something behind the facade, but never imagined she would see it. She ventured a touch of his cheek and she noticed an almost imperceptible leaning into her touch. She allowed her hand to stroke his cheek, aware his tears were building, and brought up her other hand and smoothed both of his cheeks as she leaned in again, lifted his face to hers, and this time kissed him properly, on his lips. They quivered.

There was a knock on the door, and abruptly the moment was over. Amlodd rigidly and rapidly disappeared into his office as Archibald Pointe-Lace stepped into Daphne's office. 'Mr Jones in?' he asked, in the abrasive and dismissive way Daphne knew was the advisor's naturally brusque and arrogant manner.

Daphne knew Mr Jones would need a moment to compose himself. 'He has just taken a call, Mr Pointe-Lace, if you wouldn't mind waiting? Can I get you tea, coffee,' she looked at her watch, 'a drink? Mr Jones keeps a good Glenmorangie, sir.' She knew what people like Pointe-Lace liked.

Amlodd poked his head around the door in as casual a manner as he could manage. 'Daphne... Oh, Archie. What can I do for you?' Not for the first time, Daphne thought her boss looked like Marty Feldman, and she smiled to herself. Her dad had always liked the comedian.

Archie indicated with a curt response that he would have the malt whisky, no ice. She knew this, and went to the drinks cabinet and took out the cut glass tumblers as Mr Jones and Mr Pointe-Lace disappeared. Daphne removed her coat, relieved she had managed to control the butterflies in her stomach. She would wait, it was what would be expected of her, but she would wait anyway. She took the drinks in, malt whisky for Mr Pointe-Lace and sparkling water for Mr Jones.

———

MANDY WAS SITTING in her wheelchair at the bottom of the stairs. She could hear the muffled conversation from behind the loo door, and not for the first time wondered about her husband, but dismissed all rational thoughts and focused on his good qualities.

She felt a hand on her shoulder and leaned into her daughter's touch. 'Alright, Mum?'

Liz's face radiated happiness and she was pleased for her, even if she still did harbour reservations about her being in a lesbian relationship. She smoothed the distended pregnant belly of her daughter, felt the movement inside and was tugged emotionally. She was ready to be a grandmother and she thought about it, or at least started to think, because at that moment Jack came out of the loo, still talking on the phone and she tried not to think about how he had managed to maintain the call and do the business, so to speak.

'Oh dear,' she sighed, and Liz massaged her mum's shoulders, "a rub-down with the *Sporting Life*" as Jack would say. Mandy leaned into the massage murmuring, 'That's nice, love...' but reacted to the sudden tightening of the grip. 'What?'

Liz moaned, but calmly responded to her mother, who was massaging her own shoulder now, 'I think the baby's coming,' and it was, and in another spasm Liz called out, 'Carly!' and then her waters broke.

Jack was down the stairs. 'What's up, Liz? 'Cause if you want the bog, I would give the back one a week or two if I were you.'

'Jack!' Mandy said, accompanied by a deft poke with a bobby-socked leg to reinforce the exclamation. 'The baby's coming.'

Whilst all on deck remained calm, Jack all of a sudden became a headless chicken. 'Shit, bang, piss, right. Jimbo!'

'Me?' Jimbo said, knee-jerk reacting to the jerk Jack, and his knee.

'Yes, you Jimbo.' Jack knee-jerked back, but added some brass knobs, which he knew suited his knees.

'Shut up, the both of you,' Mandy more than suggested. 'Carly, get Liz's bag, and Jackie, if you wouldn't mind driving Liz and Carly, and Jimbo, you can drive Jack and me, okay?'

Nobody questioned her orders except Jack, who only asked if he needed to put his corset on for a hospital visit. The Mandy stare sorted that, and Jack went upstairs to get his corset on, tittering to himself because he had gotten away without doing his exercises.

'You can do your exercises when you get back,' Mandy called after him.

———

Archie Pointe-Lace left with no acknowledgement, goodbye, or seasonal wishes. The man just swept past Daphne. She could not care less, she didn't like him. Daphne knocked on Amlodd's office door and walked in, to find the Mandarin leaning

279

back in his chair, fingers steepled, touching his lips. He didn't look up and she thought, even sitting, his body looked twisted and uncomfortable. 'Can I get you anything, Mr Jones?'

Amlodd, with a gentle gesture with his head, indicated for Daphne to take the chair recently vacated by Pointe-Lace. She sat, noticed the empty whisky glass and could smell the residue vapour, which turned her stomach. She waited, and it was some time before Amlodd opened up, clearly challenged by his thoughts.

'Daphne...' He looked at her and she felt a nervous energy course through her body and sensed that something serious had happened. 'I don't know where to start, but if, after I have told you all that I am going to tell you, you want to leave me and work elsewhere, I will understand, and I will, of course, give you the most excellent of references.'

She tensed, her nerves tingling. She was scared, but remained silent. 'Daphne, forgive my language, but there is going to be a lot of shit happening...' Daphne expelled some of the nervous air she had retained; she rarely heard her boss swear or use expletives, '... and in the Home Office, we will be at the very centre. I would also be misleading you if I did not say it could be dangerous for me, and if you were my confidential secretary, as I will want you to be, the danger may encompass you as well.'

He looked up at her. She seemed unmoved. It was not her Civil Service face, he noticed, it was something else, and he realised he had no experience of a woman's intimate faces, so he could not begin to read her thoughts.

Daphne could read him well, and relieved him of some of his worry, 'Thank you for telling me, sir, I still want to be with you.' She left it at that as it was not a conversational moment. She watched his face continue to agonise and she knew not how to relieve the painful thoughts he was processing, because she could not begin to comprehend what they might be, but she said something anyway. 'Amlodd, just say what you are thinking. I am not leaving you. I fully support you, and always will.' She removed her glasses and rubbed her eyes. It was late and she was tired.

He looked into her deep brown eyes as, coincidentally, he plumbed the depths of his soul. He felt she was sincere, and so he screwed up his courage. 'Daphne... er, please let me say what I want to say before you comment.' She nodded, allowed him time to marshal these thoughts that were unusually so difficult for him, and then he stuttered to a start with a nervous laugh.

'Ahah... erm... I have long had the desire to own a cottage on the Dorset coast and, in my wildest imaginings, I have dreamt of you sharing this with me. I know I am being juvenile in my thinking, but sometimes it is only this thought, indeed hope, that keeps me going. I know this is impossible... but... er...' She stopped him with a glance.

Daphne stood up and walked around the large desk and sat on it, almost touching Amlodd's deformed and hesitant body. He quivered. She leaned towards him and once again stroked his cheek and saw again the vulnerability of this high-ranking Mandarin, as more tears formed. She leaned further into his, up until now, closely guarded personal space, and kissed him on the lips and lingered, easing the pressure of her kiss to whisper to him, 'I love you, Amlodd, and if you were to ask me, I would follow you anywhere, and the Dorset coast sounds divine.'

She kissed him again, then sat back upright and awaited a response that was a while in coming. She encouraged it. 'Are you worried what I might think about your body?' He nodded, the response she knew he harboured deep within him. 'Well, don't,' and as if to prove it, she kissed him again, and said he should come to Rutland to meet her family, and she would return with him after a couple of days to prepare for the new office, and maybe they could spend New Year's Eve together?

She'd taken over. Amlodd could now concentrate on whatever it was he needed to focus upon, and she knew also he would tell her, likely over the Christmas break. All of a sudden she felt fulfilled and could see her little Marty Feldman was reborn. He had feelings and he could and would share them with her. He was a man no longer alone.

TWENTY-FOUR

'OKAY, JACK, YOU CAN STOP CRYING NOW, AND perhaps give the baby to Liz or Carly?'

Jack was sobbing into the face of the baby girl as he looked down to his wife in the wheelchair, then across to Carly, who was smiling and crying at the same time, and to Liz, begging with his eyes.

'Alright...' Liz said, '... just a little longer. I'm tired, anyway.'

Mandy intervened. 'Do you have a meeting with Jim Samuels?'

Jack looked as though he had just recovered from a braindead moment, not an unusual look for him, but the birth had been so quick and trouble-free, he'd not had time to think about anything else, apart from people shooing him away – quite unreasonably, he thought, as he was to be Number One Grandfevvers. He couldn't even remember if he'd been able to maintain his wincing?

'You managed that alright, you wuss,' Mandy said, smiling with her eyes, 'but you are *our* wuss, isn't he, girls?' and Liz and Carly agreed. Even the baby managed a gurgle in agreement.

Jack looked at the baby and knew he had to work on this one, as he desperately needed an ally in the female camp. His master plan had started, and he chuckled mischievously to himself, and to the baby, his new partner.

'Yeah? What master plan is that, *Blowfelt?*' Mandy asked.

'Did I...?' They all nodded, the baby gurgled, and Jack knew he had been thwarted even before his master plan had gotten underway.

'Never mind...' Mandy said, lovingly, '... it lasted longer than most of your master plans,' and the three women plunged into laughter as the baby gurgled once more in support.

He handed the little girl back to Mum and commenced his contingency plan. 'And what plan would that be?' Jack looked astounded that he had spoken his thoughts again and would now have to go to Plan

C. 'Plan C?' Mandy quipped, thoroughly enjoying her husband's discomfort.

Jack gave up and sat down. He was exhausted, his back hurt. It was tough, this childbirth lark.

'Yes it is...' Liz agreed.

————

KEEF BANANAS, Shitlegs and Brains squashed themselves into the cramped space of Fingers' dad's shed, aware the filf would be looking for them, but more concerned about Fingers' dad being buried below and likely haunting them as they stood around shivering, trying to look hard, and trying to work out what they needed to do. Ghosts were immune to people looking hard; at least this is what they thought.

'We should lie low for a bit,' Keef suggested, and Brains lay down on the old settee, which was damp and rat-riddled. He was not known as Brains for nothing, but in his defence he had not done his GCSE in subterfuge, it had been in arse-scratching, or so his teacher had suggested and frankly, he had not found it particularly useful in getting on in the world. So much for teachers telling you to work hard in order to get on, he thought coincidentally.

'No, yer plank, I mean keep out of the Filf's way for the time being.'

Keef tried to think of a strategy, looked at Brains, who was now up and rubbing his rat-nibbled rabbit's bum, damp from contact with the infested and saturated settee. You would have thought that, being experienced baddies, they would know how to lie low, but this was the first time they had evaded a capture at the scene. They had heard how things had gone at the sawmill and considered themselves mightily lucky to have avoided it. Fingers' mum had said she would get a message to them, and so they waited, while, they presumed, she shagged her way to Big-Knob. Nobody wondered where Jeremy was; it was a mystery, like a lot of things that happened around them; like, who was Big-Knob, and should a lot of gangsters get their eyes tested as Fingers' mum was no oil painting, for instance?

———

IT WAS close to midnight by the time Amlodd had unloaded his soul and story to Daphne and both felt that in the past few hours they had formed an emotional bond, but now came the awkward moment, and Amlodd had no experience to call upon. Daphne dealt with it for him, and suggested he might like to come back to her place, where they could talk some more. They did, and after some uncomfortable moments, they retired to Daphne's modest bedroom and made an awkward form of love, which was warm, if nervy, and afterwards they slept soundly in each other's arms.

It was good for them, but decidedly not good for the men who had lain in wait outside Amlodd's flat, in the cold, and now the chillingly wet sleet, awaiting his return in order to carry out their orders of aggressive interrogation. Other men were to be even further frustrated, as Amlodd was not intending to turn up to his office in the morning as anticipated, and to all intents, and most unusually, he would have gone on the missing list. The covering secretaries and assistants were to be briefed that Mr Jones was taking his Christmas break, and no, they did not know where.

Big-Knob's plans would have to wait, but in the meantime, Archie was around.

———

THE HESITANT MORNING glory of the day peeked over the horizon to the east. It could be seen from the window of the hospital maternity room. It was going to be a day thankfully without rain or the persistent fine sleet of the past few days, though the puffs of steam from the mouths and nostrils of those early bird people out and about, suggested the air was frigid and the heavy sky, being nudged by a liquid red sun, foreshadowed snow later.

It was difficult to determine Jack's mood as he grunted and moved his legs up and down, as if he wanted to pace, but couldn't get going; *stepping in time*, he wanted to say, but had no chimney sweep sticks. His eyes were fixated, preoccupied in thought, or maybe looking for something he could step in time with? It was difficult to tell, but his mind was definitely distracted, unaware that his trudging, grunting and singing of songs from *Mary Poppins* was annoying.

'Jack, go home and meet with Jim and Mike. Ollie and Stan may still be there, though I imagine Jo-Jums will have gone home. I want to stay with Liz for a bit. Carly can give me a lift home...' and Mandy looked for acknowledgement from Carly.

She got it, and Jackie suggested she would take Jack, but he wasn't listening. In his mind, he was rummaging through Mandy's underwear, but we already know there are no chimney sweep sticks there. 'Jack!' Mandy said, getting the ringing phone from her pocket, 'when have you ever known me keep your telephone in my knickers?'

Jack had, of course, kept his phone in his pants before now, and regularly kept his warrant card in his socks, so it was not an altogether stupid idea. Jack applied the stumped look he had developed as a kid when he had tried his hand at cricket; it didn't work, the look, or the cricket. Fortunately, he was saved by the never-ending ringing bell, and Mandy, waving the offending phone in the air, proposed he might like to take the call.

'Hello,' he said, creatively, bearing in mind he had just been caught metaphorically red-handed. He wondered why he had just done that, but realised he had been looking up Mandy's dress all day and night and there is only so much looking a husband besotted with his wife can be expected to do, he said to himself, reasonably, also bearing in mind that he can argue Oldtimers as a defence, and of course he was a man of action, wasn't he? And this is what Mandy liked about him, didn't she?

'I know, you are, and you can have a look, a rummage, and some action when we get back home, but please, take the call,' Mandy answered, trying not to burst into uncontrollable giggling as it still hurt her panda face.

Jack recovered the situation rather well by running away. He always kept *running away* in his war chest of "get out of things with women". It never failed, and was up there with having a fit, or the good old collapse-into-a-heap, a personal favourite. He was out in the corridor and talking into the phone, which was obviously against the rules, as a nurse was telling him, but, as we all know, Jack is a deaf twat and had his

African elephant hearing ears focused and flapping on the phone.

'I'm really pleased for you, Amlodd. 'Ang on, mate,' and Jack turned to the nurse. 'Yes?' It was his frustrated voice, and the nurse seemed to pick up on this; well, they are trained to be sensitive, you see, which was probably why Della never made it as a nurse.

'Sir, we do not allow mobiles in the hospitals,' the nurse said, unnecessarily.

Jack applied his *I'm taking you seriously* face, which would be a miracle if the nurse picked up on, even if she had a first class degree in sensitivity, because it was just wrinkled lips and screwed-up cheeks, all of which were already screwed-up, even in repose, and I haven't even got to the lips.

'Feck off, there's a love,' and he showed her his *Dr Who* psychic paper. 'Police,' he said, as if this was an explanation as to why he was showing her an old bus ticket. Jack looked at the screwed-up ticket, couldn't even remember getting on a bus for ages, and, worried again about his Oldtimers, recalled this as his excuse for looking up Mandy's dress, and felt a sense of relief waft over his hideous body, which was in fact a surreptitious parp. In hospitals, especially in the corridors where the nurses are wont to patrol, it is always important that parps should be silent so as not to disturb the sick.

'Yes, well,' the nurse replied, choking, 'I think dementia may be a possibility in your case, but please end your call, and you are a dirty old man looking up women's dresses, and maybe you should go to the loo?'

'Did I just speak me forts, nurse?' Jack asked, unnecessarily, waving his bus ticket, just to show her who was boss, or was he a bus conductor? He was flattered she thought him a dirty old man, a regularly used term of endearment by Mandy.

The nurse grabbed the phone, switched it off, screwed up the bus ticket and handed both back to him and said, 'I'm the boss,' spun on her heel and left. Jack could not be sure, but he thought she was chuckling. How could that be, when he had just used his best intimating face?

'Yes, it was intimating, darling. Maybe you should use your intimidating face next time?' Mandy said, and she was definitely chuckling as she proffered her phone to him. 'Jack, why is someone called Amlodd Jones calling you on my phone?'

Jack grabbed the phone from his wife and dived for cover behind Mandy's wheelchair in case the nurse came back. He was not sure, but he thought it could be the one out of *One Flew Over the Sparrow's Thing*.

'*Cuckoo*,' Mandy said.

'I'm not cuckoo. I'm a little stressed – nerves, I fink, from being wounded – and I have just been through childbirth, you know?' Jack responded. 'So...?' But he didn't wait for an answer, instinctively knowing he had won and could score it later. Instead, he turned to the squawking voice on the end of Mandy's phone, at the same time handing Mandy his phone and asking her if she could get it going again, as, for some inexplicable reason, he couldn't remember the passcode; stress can do that.

She "derred". He could never remember the passcode, ever, but she let that go as he was talking to this Amlodd chap. 'Okeydokee, Amlodd, got that... Is Daff there, mate?' He waited and eventually, Mandy presumed, Daff had taken the phone at the other end. 'Daff darlin', about bloody time. Now, you two go off and take a proper break. Look after him, darlin', he's precious...' He waited and giggled a few times. Mandy thought, obviously this Daff was a bit of a card.

'Amlodd, yes...' Amlodd was back on the phone, Mandy guessed as she wheeled closer to try and listen in, and Jack, noticing her move, made to cover the phone with his arm as if she was copying his gnomework (after school work on Fairies). 'I'm meeting Samuels and Mike in a minute, we'll see you after Christmas, have a good one and watch yer back, if you know what I mean, I didn't...'

Jack squirmed and, if Mandy was not mistaken, it was a huge guffaw he was listening to, another joke at her man's expense, she thought. Then she wondered what this was all about, and then, perhaps she would go back home with Jack after all, and she wheeled herself away to inform Liz.

TWENTY-FIVE

AFTER AN INTERMINABLE AMOUNT OF TIME, they returned from the hospital, where there was an extended period comprised of back slaps, masculine cheers and offers of congratulation, before they sat around the table. Mandy was wondering just how Jack had managed to focus all of the congratulatory plaudits on himself. After all, he wasn't the father, only a surrogate Grandfevvers, and she was the actual Grandmother, but here he was, the centre of attention and she wondered if he had donated his sperm, and would she ever know unless the baby grew up to be ugly?

Mandy was already sitting, of course, being wheelchair-bound, and Jack wheeled her to the table, next to him, so he could rub her leg with his spare hand he kept spare for rubbing. Around the table were Samuels, Del-Boy, Jimbo, Professors Ollie and Stan, Father Mike, and Della, who had ants in her pants; whether this was because she wanted to know what was happening, or she was wanting to get back to Jonas and do some more sexual brain cell reduction work, all on her own of course, Mandy was not sure. Jo-Jums had returned, having only had a couple of hours sleep and looking like it.

Samuels opened up the discussion. 'Jack, perhaps it's time to let us know just what is happening, please...' He stopped, thought, continued: 'Will Siggy be joining us at some time?'

'No,' Jack said, 'he's visiting Amlodd's flat, and I expect to hear from him that Amlodd has company. Jack nodded to Jimbo, who had already summoned an MI5 team to meet Siggy.

Jimbo took a call, listened, reported, 'He does have company. It's rather lucky he didn't go home,' and Jimbo chuckled and Jack joined him, although it jiggled his back. Mandy noticed him wince; the bleedin' pansy, she thought.

'Do you really think I'm a pansy, my love?'

'Yes,' Della said, joining Jimbo in a shared response.

Mandy "derred" and looked at Jimbo, who answered her pleading look for rescue back to sanity.

'We have a team on stand-by and they will follow whoever it is, but I doubt we will find out who arranged for the visit. Do we arrest them?' Jimbo asked, not addressing anyone in particular, just airing his thoughts. Not unusual for the people sat around this table, although Jimbo had not had the dubious pleasure of sharing the bathwater with Jack.

Jack jumped in, as if charged with static electricity. 'Arrest them, Jimbo!' he sizzled. 'It will let whoever has arranged this little call know that we have Amlodd's backside covered. He needs to have some protection now, anyway, as he moves to the Gnome Office, so in a way it will be expected.' Jack thought on, and held a hand up to announce the imminence of a thought bubble, and to stop the traffic that looked most likely to be coming from Della's direction, so he swung his hand that way. 'In fact, go in now, take 'em red-handed, it will send an even stronger message, agreed?' and Jack looked around and they all could see the sense.

Samuels nodded, Jimbo returned to his call and the instruction was issued.

'Now,' Samuels said, 'perhaps you will tell us what you think is happening, Jack?' and he put his hand up to stop any interference from Della, and even Mandy. Jack looked, and there was no traffic; of course, he'd already stopped that. Samuels looked at Mandy. 'I know you want to step back, and I have talked to Jack...' he looked at Jack, '... and he wants to do this as well, but we need his assessment of this situation as he has been on this case for a very long time.'

Mandy, clearly agitated, had a list of questions written across her beautiful panda face, so Jack placed his hand on her leg to reassure her. She lifted it off and placed it firmly out of liberties range, and started to address Samuels, but the words would not come. You see, she should have left Jack's hand there, because she might have been able to say what she wanted, had she been reassured.

'What? You spoke? Fuck off, Jack, I don't need reassuring, and this has been going on for a long time...?'

Jack, somewhat miffed at having his hand moved even though this was much to the obvious relief of everyone else at the table, explained, 'This is the continuation of everything...' yeah, he thought that should do it, but Mandy looked like she needed reassurance, '... likely the death throes, at least I hope so, and we need to get in and snuff it out now, it's our best chance.' He wobbled his head, put his hand back on Mandy's leg and looked to her face for a reaction. It came in a double-front, and Jack Austin was not good at double-fronts. He couldn't even undo Mandy's bra properly without help, though in mitigation, the clasp is at the back and he only had one eye, and that couldn't see round corners.

Mandy lifted his hand away, and again placed it firmly beyond liberties range on the wheel of the wheelchair. He thought about letting her tyres down, and she railed at him, again. 'Then why the fuck have you said nothing to me (front one) and who is this feckin' Amlodd bloke when he's at home (front two)...' she stopped, thought, '... or not at home?' She did allow herself a little amusement at that witticism.

Jack appeared temporarily relieved. He certainly liked her witticisms, they ranked up there with her legs and nose. 'I know you do, Jack,' and she rolled her eyes; he liked them as well, though preferably when brightened by exercise.

Samuels stopped Della getting in on the act as she was so obviously itching to do. 'Let's all calm down, and if it is any consolation, Mandy, I am just as frustrated at Jack keeping all this to himself. I also don't want him touching my leg.' Mirth for everyone, except Jack, who not only wanted to touch Mandy's leg, but, if he recalled correctly, she had promised him a rather more intimate rummage when they got home from the hospital, and some action.

'Yes I did, and I am still thinking whether to keep that promise, so be good and spill the feckin' beans, and pronto-tonto.'

'Right-o, love,' and he put his hand on her leg. She sighed and left it there, tapping it occasionally when it squeezed or tried to ascend to advanced liberties.

'Well, bloody get on wiv it, bozo,' Della managed to get in, accompanied by a satisfied grin at Samuels for getting in a verbal punch. She could only remain silent for so long, Jack knew, but did Jonas, he wondered?

'Okay, you know Len had a half-brother...' He was stopped by a "whoa back, Neddy" from Della and this was somewhat more eloquently followed up by Mandy, but not so equine in her phrasing.

'Len had a half-brother?' Mandy asked.

'Yes,' Jack said, neighing, wishing he could get on with it.

'Well, bleedin' get on with it, Dobbin,' Della said.

'Right, I will,' Jack replied, sticking his jaw out in a provocative manner, wiggling it, like he was wobbling on the bit. Della clumped it.

'Oi, that hurt."

'It was meant to, bozo. Mandy, I don't know how you put up wiv 'im?' Della said, with some hand gesticulation not for the faint-hearted. Not that Mandy saw, as her black eyes were up at the ceiling and it looked as though she felt like leaving them there for a while.

'Okay,' Samuels said, slapping his hand onto the table and making Jack and Father Mike jump.

'Jesus, Mary and feckin' Joseph, you made me jump there, Jim,' Mike said.

'What time is it?' Della asked, looking over at Jack's wrist to check his hair and pimple.

'Bloody late,' Samuels said, 'so let's get to the basics and resume tomorrow morning, okay?' It was already technically morning and had been a hectic night, so they let Samuels off that one.

There was a knock at the door.

Samuels sighed and indicated Jimbo should get this one, and after a short time he returned with Jackie who, accompanied by Carly, had a Chinese takeaway and wine; it was game over. Jack got up and returned with plates and glasses. Michael and Colleen followed up shortly after, having just returned from visiting Colleen's parents, and they brought in a curry and some cold beer.

Jack bagged the curry and beer and let everyone else fight over what was left; he was not known to be a gentleman where food was concerned, but he did manage a quick, 'Jimbo, you know where Daff lives?' Jimbo nodded, and confirmed he was arranging to have Daphne Morris's flat covered. 'Better put them on Fred Alert, and Della, darlin', when was the last time you did waitressing?'

They all looked confused, and even more so when he asked Jo-Jums to get a warrant to dig up the Duchess's garden, but they decided to set that aside for the time being, as Jack was at the food and this was something in which nobody doubted his multitasking capabilities.

———

ARCHIE POINTE-LACE RETURNED to Bumblin'tons very late, but the kitchen and restaurant staff had dinner prepared, Brown Windsor soup, faggots, peas, mash and onion gravy and a good claret to accompany it. Unusually, he drank the whole bottle before retiring to his wingback chair, which was not dissimilar in character and radioactivity to Jack's deckchair in the community policing room; nobody dare touch it, move it, and especially sit in it. Not that there was anyone currently in the lounge as it was so late. Archie could not, and would not, ever see the irony. He knew of the barrow boy's deckchair, who didn't? Jack wouldn't see the irony, either, but he only had one eye, and that was totally prejudiced against the wealthy and posh.

The lounge waiter handed Archie a folded note. Archie thanked the man and requested a brandy snifter. The waiter retired and returned shortly after with a balloon glass, swishing a third full with a five star cognac. Archie swirled and sniffed, before he opened the note. He read and gripped the glass tight, the strength of the cut-glass crystal preventing the balloon from shattering and casting aside its expensive contents. The waiter maintained a discreet distance.

'Watson,' (it was Jack's idea the waiter be called Watson), an order from Archie, and the waiter attended.

'Sir?' Watson waited, stiff and erect.

'Speak to Reggie on the reception counter and ask him to rustle up some of his chums, now. There will be some argent in it for all of you, of course.'

Watson didn't know what argent was. He assumed it was spondulics, but checked, 'Argent, sir?'

'Money, old chap, I believe you call it sausage and mash?' Watson nodded to confirm that it was what they would call cash. 'Pull up a chair and I will brief you.'

Watson did, and after a short while he stood and left. Archie swirled the cognac, sniffed but didn't drink. Big-Knob would not be pleased. He made some calls as the weak morning light tentatively penetrated the full-height Georgian paned sash windows, creeping across the plush Wilton carpet. It illuminated Archie's tapping, irritated foot.

TWENTY-SIX

AMLODD AND DAPHNE SAT AT THE SMALL DINING table beside a picture window at the end of her compact galley kitchen. She had a tiny but comfortable flat in Pimlico, and Amlodd felt settled almost immediately within the cosy feminine environment. It was early morning and they drank hot chocolate. It was something they shared a liking for, and Daphne would make it for Amlodd if they worked late. This was not an office and working chocolate, it was an intimate and very close chocolate, and this time they allowed their hands to touch, their eyes to meet and to hold each other's gaze.

'I can't believe this has happened, Daphne.'

'Well it has, Amlodd, believe it. I have loved you for a very long time and waited for you to be ready. You are ready, aren't you?'

He nodded, gripped her hand and squeezed. 'I love you and want you to...' He hesitated.

'What is it, love?' She had a polished Midlands accent he assumed hailed from middle-class Rutland. He was not expert in anything other than the corridors of power, and knew he had a lot to learn about women, but placed his complete faith in Daphne. 'Amlodd...?'

He hesitated as he screwed up his courage. 'Daphne, we've known each other for a very long time and we have gotten to know each other well.'

She cleared her throat. 'Yes, where are you going with this?'

She saw he was going to answer her and it was taking all of his reserves of courage, 'Daphne...'

'Yes, Amlodd...?' She withdrew her hand from his.

'Will you...'

He was interrupted as something was hurled through the window beside them. Shattered glass scattered across the table and a canister rolled across the floor. Amlodd was up, out of his chair that scraped backward, finally toppling over. He grabbed Daphne and, in a moment of rare strength and agility, he collected her in his arms and powered her through to the small living room and to the door and squashed her against the wall, his diminutive and deformed body offering her a semblance of shielding, just before the flash-bang exploded.

The noise was deafening but it didn't have the stunning effect it was designed to cause, except they were both stunned. The flat entrance door burst open and by this time, Amlodd had collected one of the remaining upright chairs and, despite his clear physical disadvantages, managed to smash it down on the head of the first man in. The intruder went down and a following man fired a shot into the ceiling. Amlodd, in a flash, sensed Daphne and he would survive. These men did not want to kill them and, buoyed by that confidence, he swung the chair again and the man's gun went flying across the living room floor.

The gunman was carried on by his momentum and instantly tackled Amlodd to the ground, raised himself and brought his fist back in order to best despatch a haymaker to Amlodd's jaw, which turned to straw as Daphne had collected the pistol and fired. The man dropped, she shot the third man who was entering, and a fourth thought better of the matter, turned tail and ran across the landing and down the stairs, to make good his escape; not enough sausage and mash for this.

It was over, and an extraordinary hush momentarily prevailed. Daphne was rigid, and the peace was eventually disturbed by the neighbours' doors opening and faces peering, nervously, yet energetically calling out, but this was nothing compared to the howling that finally emanated from Daphne.

Amlodd released the gun from her grasp, eased her into an armchair and, with caring stroking gestures, attempted to sooth the rigid sinews of her stiff body. The first man was starting to lift himself up. Amlodd crashed the butt of the pistol down on the man's head and he was out cold.

A neighbour called out to enquire if they were okay and to confirm that they had called the police. This galvanised Amlodd, who went to the phone and dialled, waited, let it ring; it went to voicemail. He rang again. He wasn't looking to leave a message.

Eventually, a sleepy Jack answered, 'Amlodd?' and Amlodd told him all that had happened. Jack was impressed as the Mandarin appeared remarkably calm. Mandy was up beside him, questioning, and frankly not happy that Jack had sped out of the bedroom with not a stitch of clothing on, waving his phone as if, magically, it would dress him – or maybe it was a Klingon cloaking device? She heard him calling down the stairs to Jimbo, loud enough to wake the neighbourhood.

'I'm on it, Jack,' Jimbo shouted back, equally loud and similarly energised. He'd been called by the MI5 team, who had arrived just after the incident and were in Daphne's flat now. Jimbo confirmed this to Jack, and Jack returned the phone to his ear, and Amlodd, his adrenalin beginning to subside, was able to confirm the presence of the MI5 squad.

'What they gonna do, Jimbo?' Jack called out.

'Take them somewhere safe,' Jimbo answered, and Amlodd said he'd heard and ended the call.

Mandy was calling him from the bedroom, but Jack thought that first, he ought to answer the queries from Colleen and Michael, Carly, and then Jackie, who had also appeared on the landing. He put his hand up to reassure them. 'It's okay, just a bit of a *to-do* in London, all sorted, you can go back to bed.' He had them calmed, but they were giggling, 'It's not funny, you know,' he said seriously, and they laughed even more, but he thought he ought to reply to Mandy who was shouting something.

Blimey, he thought, *never a moment's peace*. 'Sweet-'art?' and he turned his ear toward the bedroom, so as to better hear her reply.

'You have no clothes on,' she called out, exasperated.

'What?'

Jackie answered, advancing and directing her response to his largely ineffective jumbo ears. 'You have no clothes on, Jack.'

Jack looked down and harrumphed, and then, rather belatedly, put one hand over his bits and pieces and the other, still holding the phone, to his furry, spotty bum as he shuffled back into the bedroom. They could hear Mandy sighing in disbelief at her man and that soon morphed into raucous laughter, and short squeals of pain, but the giggles had got to her and she felt better than she had done for a few days.

———

ARCHIE REMAINED SITTING, gripping his cut-glass balloon, still swirling, still sniffing, waiting for news. Watson appeared at his side, a folded note on a silver salver. Archie took the proffered note in his non-balloon hand, dexterously unfolded it and read. He put the glass down, stood and, in a hitherto never before witnessed act, Archie bellowed to the rafters. Nobody would know, nobody was in, and the discretion of the staff could be relied upon. He tipped Watson to ensure that discretion. Now, all he had to do was to work out how all of this had happened. He did not believe in coincidence, which was a shame, because all that had happened, or at least the results, had been coincidental, and in truth, such was the way with most things Jack organised. Not that he would admit it, not that he really ever organised anything, or at least nothing with a semblance of organisation.

Archie lowered himself back into his armchair, and this time he gulped the whole contents of the balloon, masochistically savouring the burn as the liquid swilled down his gullet, and he set about trying to comprehend his position. He could understand someone might be watching Amlodd's flat, he had been promoted to the Home Office after all, but he did not expect this to have happened so soon, and certainly not at his PA's flat. Had someone thought this through, and had that person been Jack Austin? Archie knew that, even injured, the Austin mind, as perverse as the thought may be to anyone, still worked, and Archie was one of the few who could respect the barrow boy's thinking; not, though his mentality, and maybe, Archie thought, he needed to, but even Austin could not have reacted so fast, surely?

Archie was resolved, now; he needed to do something about Austin. He was relieved that his wife was effectively out of the game, an inadvertent misadventure by one Mr Bananas, but this had had a providential benefit. He did not want to kill Mrs Austin, but Mr Austin was fair game, and the cockney barrow boy would know this. It was extraordinary that Archie never imagined he was himself *fair game*; he was, after all, a most respected government advisor. However, that blessed *divine arrogance* would stand him in no good stead, as this particular barrow boy was no respecter of posh knobs, and then there was Big-Knob, whose identity remained a mystery.

———

THE MI5 DRIVER WAS TONY, a short man with tight grey curly hair, wire-rimmed national health style glasses, slight, and of a nervously effeminate manner. Amlodd was not sure how he felt, reacting to the commands issuing from someone who looked like Charles Hawtry out of the *Carry On* films, even down to the refined accent and tiny, embarrassed giggles. However, Amlodd and Daphne had been impressed by the way he had dealt with not only with the other MI5 officers but, more interestingly, with the testosterone-fuelled armed police unit that had come charging up the stairs, far too late, calling out in a staccato military fashion, "Clear, clear and clear...".

Tony had told them he had cleared the rooms, and giggled with patently jiggling shoulders, and the armed-to-the-teeth bad-ass merchants turned and bashed and banged their way out of the small block of flats and back into their van, shouting and crunching all the way. Tony said they were probably going back to barracks for their morning *Wheatybangs* and giggled some more.

Daphne settled into Amlodd's spindly arm in the back of the MI5 Jaguar as it whistled and purred up through Victoria, then took a short turn across Buckingham Palace Road, to arrive at an impressive house in the equally impressive, Georgian, Eaton Square; a formal square built around a central garden, enclosed by metal spiky railings. Tony double-parked and hopped out, continually looking all around, his appearance like a jerky, effeminate chicken as he pranced around the car and opened the door.

Daphne stepped out, turned and offered her hand to Amlodd. A door opened in one of the stately homes and an orange light bled across the black and white chequered tiles of an expansive entrance apron and a short flight of stone steps within the portico. Amlodd looked up. Though daylight was due, the sky was leaden and black clouds threatened snow, and he revelled in the thought of a white Christmas with Daphne. Tony showed the couple into the house. The door closed behind them and both Daphne and Amlodd felt as though they could breathe again, and embraced the comforting warmth and sense of security.

Before they could exchange any conversation, Jim Samuels appeared in front of them; he had not long arrived in London from Portsmouth, and had gone directly to the Eaton Square house. He had a meeting later in the morning, but this matter needed dealing with first and, as if he could not have worked this out for himself, Jack had called him to tell him so. Jack had eventually briefed Jim Samuels over a secure line as he was driven back to London. Jack would inform the others later in the morning.

'Welcome.' Samuels knew Amlodd; most Mandarins, at one time or another, meet senior MI5 officers. Jim introduced himself to Daphne Morris. She cautiously observed a man who looked like an older *Swiss Tony*, with Mr Whippy bouncy white hair on a gentle face.

'I'm Jim Samuels and since you have already been vetted for the Home Office, I can tell you I am a doctor, a psychiatrist, but more relevantly, the head of a section in MI5. When you take up your position with Mr Jones at the Home office, you will likely see a lot of me. However, I am sure Amlodd has also now informed you of what has been happening and I am very sorry you have been thrown in at the deep end. I might add, though this may seem insensitive and crass of me, that you appear to have handled the situation very well.' Daphne applied a nervous smile and tried to control her shaking.

'You should be aware also, that this may just be the beginning, though the beginning of the end, eh, Amlodd?' Amlodd, clasping Daphne, nodded agreement. Samuels continued, 'There was another team waiting for you last night at your flat, Amlodd. They have been arrested and we are questioning them. I am not sure they know anything, just hired thugs we think, but by arresting them we have sent a message. Interestingly, this all seems to have been rather hurriedly arranged, and for once this may play in our favour. We have traced some of the protagonists back, and there is a tangible link to Bumblin'tons.'

Amlodd accepted an already-arrived-at assumption, something Jack Austin had also surmised and passed onto Jim Samuels some time ago, hence Watson, put in place to monitor Pointe-Lace. Anybody who had that much influence had to be regularly monitored, which, as it turned out, had been just as well. Amlodd tightened his grip around Daphne's waist and she responded by leaning down and into him.

'Are we safe now?' Amlodd asked.

Samuels shrugged. 'Ye-e-e-s...' He noted the involuntary shudder in Daphne's body. 'We may need to review your plans for the Christmas break, however. Ms. Morris, people will know you intended to go to your parents in Rutland, and they may believe that getting to you might get them to Amlodd. I hope you understand.'

Daphne was smoothing her nerves and thinking, only to herself, now the shaking was under control; she was taking this remarkably calmly. 'I do. Can I call my family?'

'We have people going to your parents' house, and they will speak to them and tactfully explain the situation. We do not want any calls to be made at all. We want you both to stay incommunicado, until we feel it is safe. We will get you back to work a few days after Christmas. You can set up in the Home Office where there will be the incumbent security anyway, and for the time being we will reinforce that. In the meantime, we have a safe house, a cottage on the Dorset coast. How does that sound?'

Daphne smiled, and as she turned to Amlodd, he spoke. 'Perfect,' he said. 'I take it we will not be alone?'

'No, but, under the circumstances, I am sure you will not mind, and my people, except for Jack of course, can be relied upon to be discreet. Now, you must be tired...' Samuels smiled at the unlikely couple. 'Someone will show you to your room.' And at that, someone did appear and the man pointed them to the broad, polished, mahogany staircase, and they set off, with the man following, carrying two suitcases which, they surmised, contained clothes some agent or other had selected from their relevant apartments.

They were shown into a huge bedroom, ornately decorated, with a king-sized double bed. Daphne flicked her eyebrows and Amlodd stuttered a reciprocated wink and opened his arms. She slipped into them and snuggled after their guide had departed.

'What were you going to say before we were so rudely interrupted?' she asked. 'You mentioned we had known each other for a long time and then...' Her words were muffled as she spoke into his neck.

Amlodd shivered involuntarily, enjoying the tingling sensation of her breath and her lips on his skin. She lifted her head for his answer. 'Will you marry me?' he said. 'That is what I was going to ask.' He was not so nervous of the reply this time.

A broad smile broke across her face. 'Yes, Amlodd, I would love to be your wife,' and they undressed each other, clumsily, but that didn't matter. Nothing mattered as they cuddled and fumbled a reinforcement to this new side to their relationship.

TWENTY-SEVEN

'Ally, ally in...' Jack called a meeting. It was the closest he came to admin, and the attendees complained the admin should be done by Jo-Jums next time, as they did not enjoy meeting in Jack and Mandy's garage as it was cold and damp.

Jack was not impressed with the criticism. He had in mind watching the reaction from the Duchess when a search warrant was exercised and her house, and most importantly, her precious garden, was turned over by the filth, none of them Alan Titchmarsh by any stretch of imagination, the extent of their horticultural expertise being a tad south of a *scorched earth* philosophy.

Mandy took a call. 'Right, Jo has set the meeting at the Gravediggers, so we'll meet and have breakfast there.'

There was a healthy rejoinder of support that left Jack mightily miffed. He rather liked the covert nature of meeting in his garage. He also had some stuff he wanted to show people, like his son's old toy Dyson vacuum cleaner. Jack giggled, picking it up and making like he was vacuuming the garage, swerving around the tyres of Mandy's car, but then noticed Mandy looking, and he thought that maybe her car tyres might not need hoovering and that maybe he ought to wince a bit, and he did; you can never have too much wincing.

'Okay, let's go, and Jack, when we get home, if you wouldn't mind doing the hoovering?'

Jack smiled. He was not about to be fooled or lulled into a false sense of security. He knew Mandy didn't let him do the hoovering as he broke the Hoovers, and anyway, he'd arranged for Dolly to clean for them. It was logical that she should come and clean the house if they were retiring, and as a consequence, Jack could no longer give a toss about the community policing room, except for his deckchair. Blimey, what would happen to that?

'Forget your deckchair.' Mandy was irritated, standing on her crutches, the blood rushing to her only-just-

319

mending shins; they throbbed. She looked at her man, still holding the tiny plastic Dyson. 'Is Dolly coming to us? Because if she is, that is the best idea you've ever had,' though she thought, hesitantly, would she like her house smelling of lavender polish and ever so slightly of wee? 'Jack, tell Dolly I will provide her with the polish she needs, okay?' There was not much she could do about the wee, except get super-smelly polish.

Jack smiled. He loved his wife, especially when she acknowledged how brilliant he was. 'Righty-ho, sweet'art, get the lavender stuff, would you? It reminds me of me nan's gaff.'

Mandy "derred" a look to the heavy black sky. How would she manage on crutches in the snow? She left that thought for later, as Stan and Ollie were waiting, Stan's car idling, her wheelchair in the boot. She stole a glance towards the Duchess's garage door. As she looked, it rose on automatic, and the *Duchess-mobile,* a bit like the Bat-mobile only it was a VW space wagon that contained an old bat, exited, pronto-tonto. Now, that was interesting. She was going to miss the arrival of the *search and find* squad. Had the Duchess been tipped off?

———

AMLODD AND DAPHNE lay in each other's arms, it was mid-morning, they had no need to rise and didn't, enjoying a shared warmth beneath the duvet, and the excitement of their new-found relationship.

'I'm hungry,' Daphne said, as she stepped out of bed and padded, naked, to the bathroom. 'Call down and see if we can get some breakfast, Amlodd, and see if I can have hot chocolate as well, please.'

Amlodd looked and admired her beautiful body as she disappeared into the bathroom. She was showing some signs of a little middle-age spread, but was still lithe and shapely, a beautiful woman. He wondered how she would react when he stood naked before her.

Returning, and sensing his look and thoughts, Daphne crawled across the bed to him. 'I will love and adore your body, Amlodd,' she murmured and she slowly pulled back the duvet.

He was nervous, but the effect of the woman he had so long desired, lying beside him, naked, and so clearly in love with him, was all the reassurance he needed. Daphne began kissing his mouth and slowly, she made her way down, lingering across his feeble chest, feeling the hunch of his back and giving him a reassuring smile. She continued down, eventually taking him into her mouth whilst swinging her legs. Amlodd knew instinctively what to do, and they mutually pleasured each other – *ooh err, matron*, he thought, in a Welsh accent.

———

JONAS WAS PREPARING a mammoth fry-up as the spooks sat around the Gravediggers table, joined by Ollie and Stan, spook advisors, and Beryl Sexton, a woman not to be argued with and an experienced mass murderer, (read book four, *Ghost and Ragman Roll* – I could tell yer, but I can't do everything round 'ere).

Jack called the meeting to order but Della said this was her job: "Her rubbadub, her job".

Father Mike stepped in before World War Three erupted. 'You're retiring, are you not, Jack? So maybe Della should start the meeting?'

'Yeah, you old fart, get orf to yer care 'ome and leave this for me to run,' Della added.

'I will run this, Della.' It was Del-Boy, technically in charge of field ops, but he often wondered if he was just the salad dressing.

'Oh, go on then, Blondie, start...' and Della metaphorically tapped her foot. Del looked perplexed, he was not sure how to begin. 'Cat got yer tongue, Del?' Della asked, now actually tapping her foot. Jack asked if it was *Dr Who*. It was, but Della was not as good as Jack.

'Okay, you can start, Della,' Del-Boy conceded.

Smiling broadly, her victory grin, Della started. 'Okay Jack, what's 'appening?' and she giggled. It was funny, but also Jonas had returned with the fry-ups, and was touching Della intimately. 'Jonas sweet'art, are you feeling better?' and the burly landlord applied his Heathcliffe smile; he knew better than to do a Gypo smile.

Now agreeably distracted, Della addressed the table in a polite, inquisitive manner. 'Jack, get on with it, you fucking dipstick,' and she pulled a chair up for Jonas so he could squash next to her.

Jack reciprocated Della's grin. He was already squashed next to Mandy's wheelchair and broken legs. Ghost, in the meantime, had arrived and settled down in a floaty *Pimpernel* way, and took Father Mike's fry-up.

'Please...' Del-Boy pleaded, and Jack felt sorry for the old codger, some twenty years younger than him. 'Well, get on with it because this old codger wants to get home for Christmas, and Siggy, give Mike his fry-up back, please.'

Jack and Ghost put their squirrel hands up to their cheeks, mentioned handbags at several paces, in frontier gibberish, but they did eventually get going, having stored their nuts into puffed-out cheeks. Jack started chewing a sausage he had dipped into

Mandy's egg, breaking her yolk for a joke. He knew she liked a laugh, and he pressed on, mouth full.

'This all started with Siggy... Well, it all started to become known because of what happened to Sigmund Merde.' He had their attention after they had returned their gaze from Siggy, trying not to look at Jack's mouth. 'You recall he was ostracised by the medical profession, but worse, by the whole of society, vilified by the press and all he did was *Treat the body in front of him*.' In just that nanosecond, the thought of the injustice had wound Jack up.

Mandy patted Jack's hand, picked it up and put it on her leg, at advanced Christmas liberties position. It was not a gesture of love, though she did feel a strong affection as he was getting emotional; in reality, she saw it as a measure to protect her sausages and what was left of her egg yolk. 'Leave my breakfast alone, Jack, and get on with it,' she requested in a lovely lady ameliorating manner.

Jack looked towards the door and made to stand and everyone followed Jack's gaze. But nobody was there and when they returned their eyes to the table, Jack was now talking and clearly munching another sausage. Mandy looked; one sausage left. It was a masterly move and, in a kindly gesture, she allowed him his victory smirk as she nudged the master food thief into talking action. She was not particularly hungry, anyway.

'As I was saying,' he continued, stretching for the HP Sauce, 'Siggy had been well and truly ostracised. He has lost his wife and child and the rest of his family wanted nothing to do with him.' He looked across to Siggy, whose eyes watered constantly anyway, but it appeared now as if the dam would burst. 'One person saw through all of the crap, if you pardon the pun, Siggy.' Jack meant the pun on *merde*, French for shit, there clearly was no other joke, although with Jack Austin it often paid to keep an open mind; it could be a *time bomb* joke, he would always advise, and Mandy would concur that the vast majority of his jokes bombed. 'That person...' he paused for dramatic effect, got a nudge from Mandy, so he continued, '... was Amlodd Jones. At that time, Amlodd was a rising force in the Civil Service, in the Ministry for Health. He was destined to become Permanent Secretary, despite his appearance not cutting the mustard, or having been to the right schools.'

'Jack, skip the socialist diatribe,' Del-Boy more than suggested.

Jack did, but everyone knew it would be temporary. 'He's there now, heading up Health, but after Christmas he is to become the new Permanent Secretary for the Gnome Office. His minister, Dai Zeeze, the slime-ball, feckin' creep...' and Jack made like he was spitting feathers, '... will be Gnome Secretary, but we think, hope, Amlodd can control him...' Jack thought, *better the thing you know than the other thing*.

Jack ran out of steam and put it down to lack of sausages, so he nicked Mandy's other one. He licked it so she could not take it back while he was talking; he needed to be able to relax. Jack allowed all of this to sink in, polished off some breakfast, his own, in case Mandy took some; you never could be too careful with food, even if it was cold, but he had the back-up sausage now, just in case.

'Get on with it, and I do not want any of your breakfast,' and she gestured with her head to the floor, 'although Cabbage might like some?'

Jack looked down at Cabbage nudging his leg, recognising a sucker when she saw one, plus Martin had told her how soft Jack was in one of their post-coastal moments. The sucker sighed and put Mandy's plate down for Cabbage. He giggled, ignoring Mandy's look; he knew she liked a laugh, and Cabbage wouldn't mind if Jack had licked the sausage. (Don't ask, he just knew dogs, and of course he knew women, and especially how much they liked their men to amuse them.)

'Very amusing, thank you,' and Mandy sloped a shark-infested grin at him. It was sloped as if looking at a Christmas tree. Jack recognised the look, he could do it himself.

Jack sensed it was time to carry on. 'So, Amlodd got to work investigating and eventually, behind the scenes, Siggy was reinstated as a doctor, but of course by then he was working with us in the hot spots of the world, and a marvellous job he did, too.' Jack nodded at Siggy who reciprocated with a childish grin, eyes still watery, but a smile nevertheless.

Mandy interrupted. 'Working for us?' Del-Boy nodded, and Mandy sighed.

'Yes, well, it sort of worked all round really. Ghost was able to offer expert medical assistance and we got valuable feedback, and that was the extent of it.' He had his honest injun face on, and remarkably, Mandy believed him even if she saw no feathers.

'Okay, Tonto, it'll soon be Boxing Day if you keep on at this rate,' Mandy said, knowing how much Jack liked Boxing Day, and she wondered why, but the reasons would have to wait.

He carried on, enjoying the attention. Mandy knew that because he had adopted his Shakespearian tart stance, adjusting his posture in the wheel-back chair. 'Amlodd, ferreting behind the scenes in the Civil Service, soon discovered a lot of self-interest in various other departments and this was highlighted in the first instance within the Ministry of Defence. Ghost fed back that arms were being readily supplied to both sides of whatever conflict he happened to be in, and before you ask, they were British arms, arms that should have been embargoed and never have received an export licence.'

Jack let that seep in. The table was quiet, and Jack put Della's plate down for Cabbage. He was building a strong bond of friendship here, not with Della obviously, but Cabbage, which was important if Martin and she were getting close.

'Jack, Martin is not building a relationship with Cabbage,' Jonas asserted. 'I am firm on that, aren't we, Della?' Della didn't look so convinced. Instead, she "aaahed" and looked lovingly down at the dog that was scoffing what was left of the enormous fry-up she had no intention of eating anyway.

'If I may continue, I need to get Mandy home and check her legs.' They all quietened, except for a silent expression of sympathy for Mandy from Jo-Jums, Beryl and Della. 'I am sure that by now, you are beginning to realise why many of the Mandarins in top departments are turning up compromised, or in certain situations dead. Natural causes, I might add, though a little bit of Shostakovich may have helped.'

Everyone knew about the music, and by now had guessed this was likely the only input Jack had had into this masterly plan of counter deceit. 'So, Amlodd, or should I also say, Daphne Morris, as she was very much a creative assistant to her boss, discovered all of the shenanigans going on and identified the resultant effects. It may now be dawning on you all...' and Jack counted his fingers and thought just for a brief moment about picking his nose.

'Leave yer hooter alone, please,' Mandy pleaded, to the continuing relief of everyone.

Jack decided he could ignore this and continued, 'Transport – why did transport contracts not go to English bidders? How come alternative bids just pipped the British contractors, and why were the British government so wedded to the open tendering procedure of the EEC, when clearly other countries flouted those rules? Yes, deceit; yes, shenanigans, which basically amounted to corruption, and British jobs were lost to the continent and America. People suffered, became frustrated, they could do nothing. A nail in the British economic coffin, not that this bothered the people with their fireman hoses in the trough.' Jack stopped to sip some cold coffee and nodded to Jonas.

'More tea, coffee?' and Jonas disappeared to the kitchen.

'So we have Transport, Defence... what about Health?' Mandy asked.

'Almost every department was tainted, because it was now clearly demonstrated that the Mandarins could get away with it. Only Amlodd appeared to stand in their way, and funnily enough, it was thought Amlodd was the puppet master. This is one of the reasons why he has, up until last night, remained immune, untouched. Amlodd even allowed Ghost to drug his tea and let it be known generally that he had heard the Shostakovich, and people thought he was in the so-called club, which incidentally we believe is known as POGROM.'

Jack paused. 'And here is where I was mistaken. I must be getting old, Della, because it should've been obvious after we realised Archie Pointe-Lace was Len's half-brother. Len was motivated by socialist values. He was clever, but he had been steered. We sensed it, but we should have seen it, and he would only have allowed himself to be steered by someone close, someone he respected, of equal or higher intellect...' and Jack did a *taa-dah* gesture, '... one Archie Pointless. Is he Big-Knob? Who knows?' Jack sighed. 'It should have been obvious this was a war with subliminal casualties, a war waged on an intellectual level. It was a war on which a small number of people would capitalise, but that was not the *raison d'etre*.' Jack restored himself with fresh French blend coffee, hence his use of French that nobody, except maybe Mandy, realised.

He continued, his tongue sticking out to cool the scalding. '*Pogrom* means an act of organised cruel behaviour done to a large group of people, in this case the whole of Britain, but it had the unfortunate luck to spill over to a vast majority of the western world. Not deployed because of religious factors or race hatred, as most historic pogroms, but...' and he paused to emphasise his point, '... for intellectual delight, amusement, stimulation, or perverse pleasure. The greater the dystopia, the greater the pleasure, and subsequently the fantastic opportunity presents itself to be able to rebuild society. But how? Whoever is behind this thinks he knows best; divine arrogance? They used to call it *Divine Breath* in the ancient world, in other words, *intuition* and the ability to see it and react to it. All bollocks of course, and the consequence of a warped mind, a brilliant mind, but nevertheless warped and it must be stopped, and I believe our man here is Archie Pointe-Lace. He is ideally placed as an independent advisor to government, all departments, and almost bullet-proof. Am I right, Siggy?'

All eyes swung to Ghost who was nodding, but the breath had been taken away from all of those around the table, especially Father Mike, who could see now what torment Jack Austin, his long-time colleague, had been carrying around inside him and for so long. He knew Jack well enough to know he could not externalise his theories until he had them at least partly resolved in his own mind.

'Jack, the other departments?' Mandy asked, 'What about the Treasury? Are you saying the credit crunch and the subsequent recessions were somehow or other also down to POGROM? I can't recall the Treasury Permanent Secretary's name on our radar, and is Pointe-Lace, Big-Knob?' Jack smiled at his wife. He adored her, loved her mind and ability to cut to the chase. She smiled back at him, but was that brass knobs she had added? It was. 'And while you're at it, how did you know about POGROM, and why have you not mentioned it before?'

Jack answered, 'POGROM was something fed back by Amlodd Jones and his assistant, Daphne Morris. They had surmised something from the Guardian crossword and don't ask me how, just looking at the black and white squares gives me an 'eadache.' Mandy knew this to be the case. Looking at anything generally gave Jack a headache, he preferred to guess things and make things fit, a bit like buying his clothes, she supposed.

'I put them in touch with Seb...' he flicked his head in the direction of Seb's shed, '... and together, they read something between the boxes and came up with that.

Amlodd let the name slip a couple of times at meetings, lunches, with other Mandarins of equal status. He sensed recognition and that was it, his message had gotten through. Ghost pushed that further when he tickled the sensitive spots of the Mandarins who did come onto our radar. He got a reaction and, over a period of time, we knew.'

Ghost nodded.

'Transport I've mentioned, as with Defence. Health, we think, was about an inexorable creep to privatisation; the feckin' bastards...' Mandy brought Jack back to reality with a reality check stare. He carried on, 'Education, likely something to do with private Academies and the handing over of capital estates for nothing, no money exchanging hands, at least in the open... Social Services, the Mandarin who died in Hamley's...'

They all nodded, recalling the incident and the article written by Cecelia Crumpet. She had highlighted the direct relationship of abuse and cruelty in the Children's Homes, and how it could be firmly laid at the feet of that particular Mandarin.

Jack continued, 'He was running the paedophile network we smashed.' (See book 1 - *Cause and Effect*.) 'He used his visits to care homes for children to mask his vile acts and expand his network, his contacts. The Crimes Against Children unit are onto that now, and yes, we need to nail Treasury, because we believe it was they who caused the crash and convinced the government to bail the greedy bastard bankers out, when the sensible option would have been to bite the bullet, jail the feckers, let the banks got to the wall and ride out the storm, pretty much as Iceland did. However, Basil Moneybags, the Mandarin...'

Mandy stopped him. 'Do you mean Basil Montbeag?'

Jack nodded, applying his, *of course, you banana* look. 'He has proved more astute, more resilient than the others, and we need to think of another way to get to him. Ghost, John Sexton and I have had some thoughts, and then there must be a bank or funding institution behind all of it and we have ideas that revolve around the City Company, Bellands, (*Wait for: Dead No More – Rhubarb in the Mammon – to be published*).

'We can discuss that later, but the main thing is to close in on Archie Pointless and bring him down, as he is, probably for the first time in his life, panicking, or at least twitchy. He is vulnerable. I have to say he does not have the charm and appeal of his late half-brother, darlin',' Jack said, looking at Mandy as they had both had liked Len, 'but...'Jack stopped his discourse as Beth had wandered in and stood beside Jimbo. They had formed a bond, and Jack was pleased about that, but they needed to be circum-spect about what was said in earshot of the girl.

What they would do about her and all of the things she had done, he left to his Church of Egypt doctrine, but something would need to be done, that was for sure.

TWENTY-EIGHT

ARCHIE, FOLLOWING HIS UNCHARACTERISTIC rant, stoically absorbed the news that Reg and his cronies had failed. Those captured had been taken by the police, likely MI5, Archie thought. It crossed his mind that maybe he could use his contacts to delve into that pot and find out more, but he was only too aware they could all be traced back to Bumblin'tons. Despite his intellectual prowess, Archie sometimes could not see what was right in front of him, as is often the way of dastardly dicks. Jack had pointed this out when they had decided a long time ago to plant Watson in Bumblin'tons, before they were aware of any unscrupulous dealings by Pointe-Lace.

Archie was not bothered about the capture, or its ability to direct investigations to Bumblin'tons. He considered himself bullet-proof, but instigating the moves using men from his Club had been an error, and one uncharacteristic of him. He would need to watch this behaviour, a rant and a knee-jerk, all previously unheard of, yet the anger still bubbled within him. By way of a distraction, he turned his mind to more immediate issues, staffing the Gentleman's club for the festive season, as key members of the serving and support staff were now assisting MI5 with their enquiries, and this is what preoccupied his thoughts, and those of the Chief Steward, Watson, who irritated Archie further.

'For God's sake, man, phone an employment agency, it can't be that difficult.'

The Chief Steward was not a man to be intimidated. He had reserves of experience in dealing with worse characters than the irascible Pointe-Lace, but he did know when and where he should show respect, it had been a part of his training, and for the time being he demurred to this senior member of Bumblin'tons.

'Sir, I have already taken the liberty of approaching the principle agencies, and it is a difficult time and... well...' The Steward was clearly showing nerves at imparting bad news.

'Spit it out, man.'

Archie was known for his intellect and arrogance, not patience, and offered up a stare from behind his newspaper, that he rattled to demonstrate his ire. He had it open to a breaking news story of *A Shoot-out in Pimlico, London*. Archie could not disguise his irritation – not that the Steward was interested in interpreting any gestures or thoughts from Archie Pointe-Lace. He, on the surface at least, had his own problems, and this, in the scale of things, was massive, even though it was a fortuitous situation his principle other boss had already capitalised upon.

'Sir, we have a dilemma.'

This did get Archie's attention. 'And that is?'

'The only staff I can get is a rather elderly chap...' He did not have time to finish.

'That's okay, just get on with it.'

'That is not the difficulty. If the gentleman has experience, and I am told he does, age will not be a problem. It's just...' Archie gave the steward a stare over the top of his half-moon glasses and, undeterred, Watson imparted the devastating news, '... the only other members of staff I can get are two women, one waitressing, the other in reception...' and he allowed the shock and awe to rumble like an impending thunderstorm over the senior member.

The thunder and lightning struck. '*What?*' It flashed and crashed on. 'Insupportable! Not acceptable! A *woman?* Women...? At Bumblin'tons?'

The Chief Steward took a discreet passing pleasure in the patent discomfort of Archie Pointe-Lace, and the prospect of women in an exclusive West End, Gentlemen's Club, one of the last bastions, and Watson knew Pointe-Lace would view that bastion as one that would need defending at all costs. But could Pointe-Lace countenance a less than efficient service over the Christmas period? It looked like all of these thoughts of balance were passing through Archie's mind and in the end, the steward knew, personal comfort would outweigh the tumbling of the barricades, which could be rebuilt.

'It will have to do, but keep it quiet. A one-off.' Archie looked at the steward. 'Okay?'

The steward nodded and left to attend to matters. It had all panned out exactly as Jack had suggested it would, but he knew Jack from the old days, and was worried about how this would now truly pan out, *pan* being the operative word, as Jack would be in the kitchen. They could not risk his well-known face being exposed at the front of house; it would be recognised by many members, and he would frighten the rest. He had not met Della yet, the MI5 man had that dubious pleasure to come, and he hadn't a clue who the other woman was, whose codename was Burial. He assumed she was on the contract killing side which, funnily enough, was not far off the truth.

———

JACK TOOK A CALL, laughed, hung up, stood, clapped his hands and made everyone, especially the still frail Beth, jump. 'Right,' he said, rubbing his hands together as if this was all the explanation everyone needed. The meeting was winding up anyway and nobody wanted to hurt Beth, or indeed to discuss sensitive matters in front of the young lady, who seemed to be slowly on the mend. Jack knew he would have to ponder what action the authorities should take, but he would deal with that another time. Right now, he had chips to fry, and he considered the gist, if not the detail and totality of a plan, had now been conveyed – at least this is what he told them.

Jackie led Beth away.

Jack sat, then he stood, and Cabbage mimicked him, attentive to see if any more crumbs of edible comfort were to be coming her way, though, if she were honest, she was not feeling at all well. As Martin would say, "a bit Tom and Dick", and, although she had no experience of such matters, she thought Martin, the little ginger imp, had done for her. How would she break the news to Jonas? Della, she knew, would be okay, understanding even, as she was also expecting. Cabbage liked Della.

'Right, let's put Christmas on 'old for a bit. We have some catering to do. Della? Burial?'

Mandy looked up at Jack, shocked again. Her toes, poking out of her plaster bobby socks and wrapped in a pair of Jack's revolting socks, wiggled with irritation. They twitched, having only just calmed following Jack clapping his hands, and her look of dismay morphed to annoyance. 'What? What do you mean, put Christmas on hold? And Della and Beryl?'

Jack blew out a sigh and Mandy clenched her nose as he had sausage breath, but she was prepared to put up with that to listen to the explanation which she knew must be serious, as this also meant postponing the looking at, and feeling of, her intimate lady parts, something Jack had never allowed himself to be distracted from before.

'I mean, darlin' we 'ave to put on 'old me rummaging of yer lady parts as well as Jesus's berfday, okay? Della, Burial and I 'ave a job at Bumblin'tons...' He thought on. 'Rather fortuitous really, Daff shooting those blokes, who incidentally were all staff at the club. They need temps now, and urgently. And, 'old yer 'orses, girls, and fasten yer girdles, Della and Burial will be the first women through the portals of the Gentlemen's club, ever.'

Jack smiled. He was looking forward to the prospect and had clearly dismissed any thought of Christmas, which Mandy knew never rose highly on his radar anyway. "It's for the kids," he would say, though you wouldn't know it, the amount he ate and drank. But, intimate relations with her? That, he did care about. So this was serious.

Jack could see the smoke signals from his wife, and so, expertly, he headed this off at the pass. He put his hand up to deflect any verbal abuse that may be inadvertently, and unreasonably, directed toward him, and he set about explaining. 'This is our chance, sweet'art.'

Yep, he thought, that seemed to have done the trick. Mandy was quiet, though she did have her mouth open, he noticed, but no words came out. It must have worked, and who said Jack Austin didn't know women? He farted in their general direction, then checked he hadn't actually farted, as experience told him this could break any spell, however cleverly he may have woven it. And then he thought of embroidery and Pointe-Lace – a buttonhole stitch, if he was not mistaken, and he rarely was, of course; how many times had he been called a sew and sew? And then there was the Duchess...

He was so preoccupied with that thought, he completely missed the whirlwind that was Mandy's eventual riposte. He later put this down to the fact she was sitting in her wheelchair and he was standing, and nothing whatsoever to do with him being a tad deaf.

Mandy could see her riposte had fallen on particularly stony ears, both of which stuck out like taxi doors on a brick shitehouse, and thought perhaps there was nothing she could do about it, but did ask, 'How long, Jack?'

Jack seemed to snap out of his reverie. 'How long's what, love? If you don't know by now, perhaps you should open yer eyes next time?' and he guffawed at his amazingly witty aside, and could see how it had immediately relaxed Mandy; he was good for her.

Mandy did laugh. 'How long do we postpone Christmas for?' Mandy persevered, knowing she would get a guess that was likely to be in the realms of fantasy.

Jack looked at Della and scrunched his face, which made no visual difference, maybe just a little uglier. 'Bout a day? Christmas Eve, what d'yer fink, Della? We just need to tickle the wasp's nest with a pointed stick and scarper, what could go wrong?'

Della scrunched up her own face. It was beautiful, cherubic almost, and Jonas, who was about to assert this was their first Christmas together, melted like the wet rag Gypo he had become. 'Yeah, reckon so...' She looked at Jonas. 'I'm sorry, Jonas, luv, I know this is our first Christmas together, and next year we'll 'ave a sprog for you to bounce on yer knee.' She looked at the large man who was so besotted with her and then glanced at Beryl. 'I will calm down then, sweet'art, I promise.' Del-Boy and Jimbo giggled. 'What?'

'You, calm down? That'll be the day,' Jimbo replied, risking life and limb, but Jack could not see why they were questioning this, and told them he would also be quietening down. Now, that did raise a laugh, including Cabbage, who thought about her next year, puppies, and would Martin stand by her, but instinctively knew Martin would; it would be in his Catholic blood, and of course Jack would kick him up his backside if he didn't.

'He'll stand by you, Cabbage,' Jack said, and Cabbage "derred", barking her thoughts again, and she looked forward to sharing a bath with Martin, although Martin had already said he didn't like baths, saying there were serious associated risks.

———

EARLY ON CHRISTMAS EVE MORNING, Amlodd and Daphne were covertly delivered to the Dorset coast, and the cottage. It was cold and dark, no urban light pollution, a raw and gloomy countryside, the car headlights dazzling off falling snow and the thickening white blanket.

The cottage was an old army house, not what you would call picture postcard. This was all army territory around Lullingstone, which was beautiful, picture postcard. Neither the serviceable, unromantic cottage nor the military surroundings mattered to Amlodd or Daphne, for they were with each other, and occasionally, as daylight asserted itself through the heavy snow clouds, so they looked out at the picturesque army manoeuvre fields and ranges. They could filter out the image of a staged military combat, and the *Danger*, skull and crossbones signs; risks of unexploded ordinance were the last thing on their minds.

They talked about getting married, and grinned when it was suggested that if they wanted to go out for a walk, someone would go with them, and to avoid the ranges; *der*. They had no intention of going out, they wanted time to be intimate, to be in bed together. They had plenty of time ahead of them to indulge a shared love of country walks. It also didn't matter that they had a limited wardrobe. They had dressing gowns, military issue, itchy hair-shirt stuff, and that was also okay, amusing even. Otherwise, they had the clothes in which they had arrived, and a hastily packed suitcase each, with clothing and personal requisites selected by a monkey MI5 man, and none of it mattered, not a jot. Their love, desire, and frustration, pent-up for so long, was now released like a champagne cork. They were blissfully happy.

They stayed upstairs, coming down occasionally to the kitchen where they grazed, if they didn't take trays back to bed. Someone had put up an artificial Christmas tree, wonky, and defective lights, but they appreciated it. The cottage had beautiful, if dangerous, ethereal panoramic views, and in the distance they could see a slowly shifting, murky, grey sea, occasionally blanketed out by falling snow. There were three MI5 men and one woman attached to the house. One man inside the house, one outside, and in a nearby outhouse that had been fixed up in a rudimentary style, were a man and a woman, a couple ostensibly holidaymaking. It would serve to keep a distant look over the approaches to the cottage, and to cover the perimeter, and to this end Flora and Johnno took frequent walks, hand in hand, whatever the weather threw at them, and it was not being particularly obliging this Christmas Eve, with biting, blustery winds driving progressively heavier snow.

It had snowed just before they had arrived and it lay deepening on the already frozen ground, the white crusting adding to the scenic quality. The clouds were heavy with more of the stuff, and whilst this would make patrolling difficult, it would have the beneficial effect of making it easier to see at night if the clouds would oblige and permit the full moon a stage upon which to illuminate the crisp white land-scape. They were not expecting trouble, but it paid to be wary, and so they were, and would capitalise on all of the assistance nature could provide.

TWENTY-NINE

AT ABOUT FOUR IN THE MORNING, coincidentally, as Amlodd and Daphne were leaving London for Dorset, so Jack was preparing himself. 'Yes Jeff, no Jeff, egg, chips, bacon and beans, two slices and a big mug of tea... Jeff... HP sauce, Jeff...?'

He was practicing his Gordon Blue cooking phrases as Mandy helped him buckle up his corset. He could do it himself, she had seen him when he thought she was not looking, but he liked her doing it, and she could also make sure he had his pants on the right way round, which helped when he wanted a wee, and afforded her a chance to give him the occasional, reassuring fondle.

He may consider himself a hard nut, but Mandy knew her man needed continual reassurance, and coincidentally, he looked like he needed it now. He was crying. She was used to this as well, but could not think what may have brought on this current bout. 'What is it, love?' she asked, in a fond and reassuring manner.

Jack knew not only was he safe physically with Mandy, he was secure in the knowledge he could share his thoughts and worries, and his wife would not abuse that privilege, never take the piss. 'I was thinking of Bambi.'

Mandy stifled a piss-taking giggle, which caused her lips to vibrate, and then she could hold it no longer and let out a resounding roll of laughter. He looked hurt, and so she reapplied her caring face with an accompanying apologetic fondle. 'How so, love?' she asked in Japanese, knowing her use of a colourful language would reassure him. Was he thinking about having venison for Christmas?

'Hai, anji-son,' Jack replied in Welsh, thinking he ought to get some practice in before meeting Amlodd. 'I was thinking of when the huntsman killed Bambi's mum.'

Mandy found it even more difficult to stifle her laughter, but, as we have previously said, she knew her man and she was a woman of amazing inner strength. Well, I suppose you would have to be to live with Jack Austin, a man who did not like the penguins in

Mary Poppins, but had an anxiety as he liked the song *A jolly 'Oliday wiv Mary*. He had not mastered the *fast-forward* buttons on the DVD player as yet, so had to watch all the bits he didn't like, like *Step in Time*. He cried at *Tuppence a Bag,* and said, to whomever could be bothered to listen, or he had cornered, he'd known the granddaughter of the Piccadilly flower seller when he was a lad, and he had.

'Forget Bambi, there's a love,' she said to him, in the tone of a mother putting her fretting child to bed, 'you have to focus on getting the bad guys.'

Mandy marvelled at the incongruity, aware also that Beryl had said she would get a few of the machine guns she had, just in case. Knowing he would be going into the path of danger, it was she who fretted, but it was only a London Gentlemen's club; how iffy could that be, apart from their policy on women members? Then she reminded herself of how many other benign situations Jack, and she, had been in that had turned out to be chaotic, and more often than not, evolved into a bloodbath.

She would have felt reassured if he had been taking Martin, and then she fretted as to just how the dog was. The veterinary hospital had said Martin was faring remarkably well, walking on three and a half legs. It would be a while before the final prosthetic leg could be fitted, but Martin was in remarkable fettle considering, walking well on the temporary leg and was insisting he be released home for Christmas; he didn't want Jack opening his presents or eating his treats.

Mandy sighed as she did up the last buckle up of the pink corset. It pinched and squeezed his waist so he farted. 'Ooops, twist,' he said. He liked pontoon, but hated playing cards. More incongruity? You forget, Jack Austin is an enema, which fortunately had not passed his lower lips that morning, especially as he had been talking about "bum navigation". Mandy thought he meant colonic irrigation, and tried very hard not to think about it.

Jack looked around at his wife and she giggled like a squeaky balloon releasing tight air, pinching her nose, pressing her lips together as she gave his parts one last fondle, before hoisting the *Sloop John B* sail, his jumbo boxer shorts. He was grateful. He couldn't bend, but Mandy was thinking she didn't want him farting again. It was bad enough when he did his exercises, and she intended to take issue with the doctor as he had suggested Jack might need to keep these up for the rest of his life.

———

In London, the frosty air was filled with a light, swirling snow, the sky leaden and threatening. It was this Christmas card view that greeted Archie Pointe-Lace as he stepped out from his Kensington apartment building. Striding into the weather, he felt the chill on his recently shaved cheeks but was determined he would not let the weather, or anything else for that matter, destroy his light-hearted disposition, and he paced energetically in a military manner into the blustery snow, spinning his furled umbrella.

Archie was not the sort of man to linger and absorb the rare beauty of the picturesque setting of the Albert Hall and its surroundings. Flakes settled and melted on his number-ones, his best bib and tucker, his armour, so to speak, a Knight ready for the tilting yards. He was dressed to the nines, the full Monty, you might say, black, wide, chalk pinstripe suit, double-breasted with expansive lapels, black shiny shoes slowly being slushed by snow, black bowler hat and a military-style camel hair coat, his city boy's umbrella and finally, his trademark yellow rose buttonhole. He had a yellow rose delivered every morning, a tradition, and if the rose did not arrive, and in time, he was mightily peeved, and didn't everyone know it.

He stepped in a lively, surefooted manner. He was in a good humour. Overnight, he had rationalised everything and, as is the way of all good sociopaths, had concluded nothing was his fault and he could present, if ever asked, a reasoned and rational argument that would quite naturally carry the day for him. However, just to make sure, he was going into the Ministry of Health to meet Amlodd Jones later this morning, to assert his case, to lay the ground. So this was why he was dressed in his number ones, and why he paced with a jaunty demeanour. Image and body language said everything, before you proffered a well-reasoned and intellectual argument. He was confident he would put things into place today and enjoy the Christmas Break, cherishing a private thought of his leather wing-back chair in which he would be sitting, reading, and observing the game as it rolled out, tweaking every now and then when he felt it needed an insightful prompt. But first, a hearty breakfast at his Club.

———

SLEEP DID NOT RETURN for Mandy. She recognised fear in her collywobbles, for her twerp and not for the first time wondered why she had married Jack, but comforted herself that they had talked – well, she had talked – and she was convinced he had listened, and agreed this would be it. He, and maybe she, would retire, and he had reassured her it was about to be over. She was comforted until she saw his concealed crossed fingers behind his back reflected in the bedroom mirror, which explained why he was not rubbing her. She had thought that odd at the time.

Mandy bumped her bum down the stairs and hoisted herself into her wheelchair (which was parked conveniently, without the tyres deflated as Jack had said he was going to do for a laugh), grateful nobody had seen her indelicate descent.

'Well Mandy, I must say I quite enjoyed watching that,' and Jackie, the trick cyclist from the Isle of Lesbos, grinned at Mandy's shocked reaction. Jackie headed off to the kitchen, suggesting she would make breakfast, and Mandy wheeled herself to the table.

'Worried?' Jackie asked unnecessarily.

Mandy nodded. 'Why, I can't be sure. He's only going into Bumblin'tons, and will be out of the way in the kitchen. Heaven help the diners!' Mandy laughed as she pictured the posh misogynists throwing up and forced to sit on the toilet all Christmas. Jack was not best known for his culinary hygiene, he believed it all contributed to the flavour of his gastronomic compositions. Yuk!

Jackie left the counter and massaged Mandy's shoulders in a reassuring *Sporting Life* way. 'He'll be okay, he has Martin with him.'

Mandy looked astonished and Jackie explained Martin wanted to be there. Kipper had collected him and it was Kipper who was depositing them all at Bumblin'tons. Mandy looked really worried now, for

Martin as well as Jack, and Jackie said she had spoken with the vet who had said Martin had a temporary prosthetic, painkillers, and would be okay if he rested, and both women giggled.

'No Father Mike, on God Squad duty for Christmas, I suppose?' Mandy nodded. 'I thought that was all a front, a bit like your Community Policing squad?'

Mandy nodded again. 'So did I, once,' and both women smiled, with a hint of concern for Martin, and Mandy noticed she had completely forgotten her worries for Jack. That was the *Sporting Life* for you, a miracle horse-racing paper with similar powers to the Church of Egypt.

THIRTY

'GOOD MORNING,' ARCHIE SAID CURTLY, avoiding eye contact with Beryl, who was woman'ing the reception counter that, by all things holy and revered in Bumblin'tons, should have been manned. 'I will have my usual table for breakfast, see it is set up for me, woman,' Archie directed.

'You will have whatever table we have ready,' Beryl replied, taking no prisoners.

'I beg your pardon, madam?'

'My pardon is granted,' Beryl replied, smartly gripping the edge of the reception counter like she was ready to pick it up and launch it at Archie, who was stunned and making no move to any table.

'Oi, mush, you want breakfast, then get yer arse into gear or you'll miss it. We pack up at half nine.'

It is fair to say Archie looked as though he had been kicked up his posh backside by a beautiful, though maleficent, angel, and then was, as Della toe-poked him. And, multitasking as only women can, which members of Bumblin'tons would not know, of course, she looked at her watch, then back to Archie, offering a not particularly subtle suggestion that if he didn't move, she'd leave her shoe up there next time.

Archie did move into the dining room, looking every bit as scared as a First World War soldier going over the top for the final push, knowing his chances of survival were next to none. There was an irony there, as, in the murky past, Archie's Great-Grandfather had been a General and had sent many men to a sure and certain death, in order to gain ten yards that would be lost, along with another shed load of men the following day, on yet another final push. The irony, however, was lost on Archie as Della gave him a final push to a highly inappropriate table.

Della knew which table was Archie's, it having been previously pointed out to her, but Jack had suggested Archie needed to be put off balance, so she made a deliberate show of ushering him to a different table, away from the full height Georgian sash windows, into a gloomy alcove, adjacent to the waiter station, no trains coming, and giggled, but Jack wanted him seated close to the kitchen doors as well.

Archie was not amused, and may have mentioned it to Della.

'Shut yer bleedin' trap, you Uncle Josh ponce, sit down or you'll get nuffink,' Della said, accompanying this with a shark-infested smile. She looked at her watch and suggested Archie get a move on. 'I've not got all bleedin' day, what d 'yer want?'

Archie mumbled his reply, 'My usual...', thought, and added '... please.'

Della ruffled Archie's perfectly set hair. 'Good boy, and what is yer usual, dopy?' and she lifted his chin with her index finger so he was forced to look directly at her.

'Err...' Archie was out of his comfort zone. This woman's finger, light as it was in touch, felt to him like it was branding his chin, and although on his territory, he was certainly floundering, which coincidentally Jack had suggested he might cook for lunch; he liked fish.

'Come on, tosspot, what yer 'aving?'

'Egg, two sausages, two rashers of bacon and fried tomatoes, wholemeal toast and butter... and black coffee, please?' Archie replied, cautiously, unaware what sort of response he would get.

'There's no effing sausages.'

'No effing sausages?' Archie mimicked, wondering where that voice had come from, feeling his throat for his refined voice box.

'I'm terribly sorry, sir, but we do not have any fucking sausages this morning,' Della responded, mimicking Archie, who was now bogged down on territory that resembled the Somme where he normally ran the roost, from afar of course, and in a comfortable wing-back.

'We always have sausages.'

'Not today.'

'Why?'

'Because.'

'Because?'

'Because.'

'Because what, woman?' Archie exploded.

Della clipped him round the ear. 'Don't you talk to me like that, sonny, or you'll be on the naughty step, understand?'

Archie nodded, and was unable to resist a look over his shoulder to the stairs. 'Can you tell me why there are no effing sausages, please?' he asked, not realising how close he actually was to the naughty step, but now aware of a continuing distraction of shouting from the kitchen, something like, "Yes, Jeff."

Archie stood up, filled with righteous anger, and his chair toppled as he strode off in the direction of the noise source, but he only made a few yards as Della tripped him. It was a doozey, and he went flying into the decorative Chinese zigzag screens. She made a mental note to score that and let Jack know; it had to be worth at least a hundred points.

Archie, recovering himself from the floor, could not reason with himself, especially in the short distance from the dining room to the kitchen, and without his wing-back chair, where his natural poise and grace would reinforce his divine arrogance. His good humour had rapidly deserted him, and all in the space of fifteen minutes. He was also unaware that this disjointed imbalance was about to be further knocked out of kilter, as he entered the kitchen and took in a sight he never could have imagined.

His first comprehended spectacle was a few remaining sausages on the floor, being eaten by a dog with an outsized pink-plastic-covered bandage on one of his front legs, a Border Terrier if he was not mistaken, and this dog was enjoying what should have been Archie's bangers. Even more incongruous was the fact that the dog had a Waitrose supermarket plastic bag on each of his other feet, and another bag, suitably sculpted and appropriately cut out with eye, nose, ear and mouth holes, on his head, and tied with a big bow under his chin.

Archie stood open-mouthed and Martin barked some *Mary Poppins*, suggesting, "He should close his mouth, he is not a cod fish", and, by way of a health and safety aside, "has he not seen hygiene measures in a kitchen before?" Martin was completely unfazed by the dramatic entrance of Archie Pointe-Lace and, if you think about it, he wouldn't be fazed, as he had lived with Jack, the King of Drama Queens, for most of his eight years. So Martin continued eating the sausages, knowing that if he didn't, someone else could grab them off him at any time, and he wasn't thinking about Archie, he had in mind Jack.

So, Archie's prima donna display was never likely to upset this dog, who was Roman Catholic. But because he was fed up with the guilt thing, he was thinking of becoming a Buddhist, principally for the meditation and humming, not the orange suits; that was Gerald Kitchener and those daft clothes would not go well with his ginger fur. Martin had often thought he should take up meditation and had mentioned this just the other day to Cabbage, shortly after they had had sex, and quite reasonably, he felt the need for a post-coastal nap, but unfortunately, Cabbage wanted to talk about the future. God, did not bitches appreciate the replenishing strength a dog can get from a bit of meditation, and it most certainly wasn't post-coastal sleeping!

Jack was there now, in Archie's face, as the real chef reacted and told him to mind the bacon. 'Feck off, Jeff,' he called back, thinking Cordon Wamsey would have liked that one.

'I'm not sure that Gordon Ramsey would want to be involved in all of this,' Archie said, waving his poncy, prima donna, Nancy boy hands about. He took a step back as Jack's bacon grease breath was intruding into Archie's personal space. Of course Jack was eating more bacon than he cooked, but, as he had explained to the real chef, "You have to test it, don't you?"

Archie took in the look of the sous-chef. 'And you are?'

'The sous-chef,' Jack replied, and as if to attest to the veracity of the claim, he did an Indian Towpath dance and looked out of the window to make sure it didn't rain; it certainly seemed to have made the snow fall harder. Jack was impressed with his Sioux Indian Medicine Man magic, and pointed this out to Martin, who was rarely impressed with anything his master did, but did wonder if maybe he could medicine up some more dog paracetamol. His leg was okay, it was just he had a headache, what with Jack shouting "Yes, Jeff" all morning.

Archie was not convinced, not being one to put his faith in Medicine Men or weather forecasters, it would seem. 'Do I know you?' he asked, in a posh turnip voice.

Ah, Jack thought, *he must have spotted my eye.* 'I don't know, d'yer read *Vogue?*'

'*Vogue?*' Archie replied, even more perplexed, and Martin, who had finished his sausages and was looking for some bread to mop up the grease and HP sauce on the floor, barked a "der", and sighed some sausage dog breath that must have reached the nostrils of Archie Pointe-Lace, if the stepping back and retching were anything to go by. Mind you, he could just be looking at Jack's face, Martin thought, so as not to feel offended, and he doggy guffawed. Archie took an even bigger step back. Perhaps not, Martin harrumphed.

Jack spiralled in a very effeminate way. 'Fashion model' he said, and pointed the toes of his right leg, extended and shook it all about, and elegantly brought it back to his shin, flounced a bit with fairy flapping hands as if he was about to fly off, and mentioned the publication, *Ballet Weakly*.

Martin thought the emphasis should be on the weakly, and Jack gave his dog an old-fashioned look. Martin harrumphed again. Martin knew he was good at harrumphing, and made a mental note to demonstrate this to Cabbage when he got home, where, he suspected, he might need it often. He was quite taken with Cabbage, she was lovely, even for a mongrel Collie. Martin was, of course, a pedigree Border, but he liked a bit of ruff, he always said, laughing at his joke, and Jack always laughed. Mandy thought it was funny – well, she did the first time, anyway.

'Why are your flies undone?' Archie enquired of Jack, thinking he was pleased the "effing" sausages were off, along with the rest of the breakfast now, as he took in the sight of a more than rotund, greasy, slovenly sous-chef, also with a Waitrose bag on his head, and then swung his gaze back to the Waitrose-bagged hound.

Jack thought he would demonstrate some of his temperamental chef stuff he had been practising. Not that Mandy seemed to appreciate it but, as he had explained, he was a method lesbian (Martin thought he meant Thespian, but then again...).

'Feckin' 'ell, mate, where you bin? It's Jeffin' 'ott in 'ere, and me bits and pieces are over -'eating.' That seemed to do the trick, Jack thought. Now, if he could only master the cooking bit.

Archie was revolted. Turning to the giggling cherub waitress, he insisted, 'This is not funny, woman.'

Della socked Archie with a convenient ladle and he went spiralling and flailing backward, seeking stability with one hand in a catering size tub of lard.

'Oi, I was going to put some of that on the cat's boil,' Jack said, sharing the joke with Della, while Martin looked around for the cat, thinking a bit of post-perennial chasing would be nice (I think he meant post-prandial?). He liked to chase a cat or two after eating, although he would have to concede cats more often than not got away, and this one was likely to get away this time because he was seriously wounded, and limped.

Just as the sous-Jeff and dog righted themselves from their mirth, a man stepped into the kitchen through the back door.

Now, Jack is often accused of being unobservant, but he did notice the Kalashnikov the man held, and furthermore, this communist gun appeared to be pointing at him.

'Oi, what 'ave I done?' he innocently pleaded, not unreasonably he thought, knowing he had done absolutely nothing and wasn't it always the same, he got the blame for everything. Della agreed. She also got the blame for "everyfink", and she also "'ad to do all the work round 'ere".

'I do all the work round 'ere, Della,' Jack said, offended, making his case quite plausibly he thought, but Della had no time to react with a counter argument, as Beryl came in and fired off several bursts of her M25 machine gun – at least we think it was an M25, it could have been another motorway, but the resultant effect was there was no counter left for Della to argue with, and the stainless steel extract canopy over the cooking range fell onto the gunman's head and knocked him out, but not before he let off a salvo of his own, which shot Archie's foot off.

Martin leaned to the collapsed Archie Pointe-Lace, and managed a comforting woof, the gist of which was, *I know what that feels like, and he could recommend the new pink plastic feet.*

Jack picked up the Kalashnikov and accidentally, as Jack and guns do not mix (*see the previous books, which you should have read anyway*), shot out the kitchen window.

'Well, that should cool it down a bit,' Della laughed. 'You can do yer round the houses up now, the flies are gathering around yer 'ampton and it's not very pleasant.'

'What, the flies or me 'Ampton Wick?' Jack asked, not unreasonably, as he adjusted his dress; not that he was wearing a dress, although he had worn the occasional ballet tutu, and if you don't believe me, you only have to look up some back issues of *Ballet Weakly*.

'Bofe,' Della said, giggling, beginning to enjoy herself. Della was a woman who lacked subtlety, and Jack may have mentioned this a few times, but she might not have heard his whispering aside, behind his grubby, cowardy-custard hand.

Archie was screaming from the floor. *The bloody wimp*, Jack thought, *one scratch and he cries like a baby*. 'It's not a scratch, it's my whole foot,' Archie cried, a reply to Jack's outspoken thoughts, and shouted a painful plea. 'Ambulance!'

'Who are you calling an ambulance?' Jack answered, bringing a little humour to a situation he sensed needed it. He had a sense for these things, don't ask, he just does; he knows how to defuse many things, his specialty being atmospheres. Bombs, he left to the Nutters.

The gunman was starting to recover. They knew because they could hear the scraping of the stainless steel canopy across the tiled floor, so Jack kicked him in the head for good luck. 'That's for luck, mate,' he said, just in case the man didn't realise why he had been kicked in the head.

The man said, 'Oh,' so that was okay, he knew now.

Della kicked Archie in the dodgy, non-existent foot and Archie screamed, and Jack was getting a bit fed up with this cry-baby, 'Look, mate, it's only a scratch, I've 'ad a lot worse, ain't I Della...?'

'You, yer bleedin' wuss, you're worse than clever clogs 'ere – well, clever clog now, I imagine.'

Archie didn't seem to get the joke. Either that, or he had no sense of humour. Jack looked and reckoned it was no sense of humour, but we all know that not more than thirty minutes earlier, Archie had been in a good humour, which goes to show what can happen if your foot is shot off. Something to bear in mind.

Jack sighed. He never got any symphony around 'ere, and Archie was certainly getting on his wick. 'And, don't fink I'm going to pick you for my football team,' he said to a writhing Pointe-Lace. Della did think that was funny, and there was an added bonus in that Jack and she would be lucky for the rest of the day.

Watson poked his head around the door. 'Okay?' he called.

'Okay, Monty,' Jack called back.

Archie, in between crying, said 'Monty?' (See, I told you he was clever.) 'I thought you were Watson?' Maybe not so clever?

'This is Monty Python,' Jack answered, and Watson sighed and looked at Archie writhing on the floor. It was difficult to see what was HP sauce or tomato ketchup, though there was a lot of claret.

'My name is Eric Ser-pent,' Monty said, 'the rest you can work out for yourself, as you're supposed to be so fucking clever,' and Watson kicked Archie's dodgy stump – for luck, you understand and everyone did understand. Even the bloke with the stainless steel canopy on his head, now at a rakish angle, said he understood.

'Right,' Jack said, clapping his hands and rubbing them. Everyone jumped, except the man with the canopy on his head, and Archie of course who, upon reflection, could have hopped. 'Let's close this joint down. Della, call Del-Boy, let 'im know what's 'appened and we probably ought to get Brains 'ere to 'ospital,' and Jack started to crouch in front of Archie, in order to best converse with the man.

This took a little while and was accompanied by major grunts, *oomph's* and senior citizen passing of wind. Jack was wearing his corset, you see, and crouching like this was also one of his exercises, which ordinarily he would do after he'd had a poo, and as he had left home so early... Jack explained all this to Archie but it looked like the toffee-nosed twat was more focused on his foot, or lack of it. *Lightweights*, Jack thought, and everyone agreed. Well, he was down now, a bit wobbly, so Martin fixed himself under Jack's bum, to provide additional stability whilst affording him access to a sausage that seemed to have found its way under a counter. It was covered in Archie's tomato ketchup, which Martin found, like an excellent claret, enhanced the flavour somewhat; they were not particularly good sausages. Martin had had better.

Now relatively stable, Jack reached out to Archie's blood-soaked, chalk pinstriped jacket lapel, and plucked the yellow rose and discarded this to the floor. Archie, in his pained miasma, was confused, and Jack stuck his finger into the buttonhole slot in the lapel, slid it right through and tugged. Archie followed the lapel, a questioning look on his now very pale face.

'Buttonhole,' Jack said. 'Pointe-Lace...'

Watson interrupted to say the ambulance and Del-Boy were on the way.

'What's yer point, Jack?' Della asked.

'My point, Della, is just that Pointe-Lace is an embroidery stitch for a buttonhole – correct, Mr Thackeray-Mayhew? Because that is your name, is it not? And it is through the *Guardian* newspaper crossword that you communicate, as well as the small ads in *Embroidery Now?* I am correct, yes?'

Martin had eaten his sausage and most of the yellow rose. He discarded the thorns, they tasted too sharp, and was finding Jack's bum too much of a physical burden. He was used to the psychological burden, and occasionally he bore the physical weight, but don't forget, Jack was wearing the corset and this was heavy, and Martin only had three and a half legs. Well, that was Martin's excuse and so he let everyone know with a squeal.

Jack was not impressed with his dog and told him so, because he had a window of opportunity to interrogate Archie before the ambulance came, after which people might say he was taking advantage of the man being hurt, which he was, of course, though he was doing it with excessive delicacy. Jack nudged the bloody pulp of a foot stump to prompt an answer to his last question (excessive, maybe not so delicate?). Martin sighed, he could see Jack's point, but Della, observing the situation and thinking nobody, except possibly Mandy, who needed a bleedin' medal and her brains and eyes tested, would want Jack's bum on them, was able to slide a stool under Jack's behind, and Martin made a limping run for it.

'Yes?' Jack asked again, but Archie was losing it. Jack pressed, not the foot, but this was an option not to be ruled out, 'Archie, tell me. The game's up for you now, so spill the beans, old chum or...' and Jack raised his foot, which was a lot easier to do on a stool than on Martin, who wriggled and moaned a lot.

Archie did respond. 'Yes...' grimacing in pain '... you have it right. How did you know?'

Jack resisted a smug look, he could do that later, and he pushed on with asking the questions that had been on his mind for a very long time, since yesterday. 'Was the instigator for your brother and you, Professor Mayhew? Is Brian Mayhew your father?'

Della looked completely stunned, and rapidly reviewed her opinion that Jack was losing it. He was a dipstick, no doubt, but this was clever stuff and she made a mental note to kick Jack up his arse. Don't ask, it was Della's solution to just about everything; girls, eh!

Archie confirmed Brian Mayhew was his father and the inspiration for the socialist agenda, which had been so readily and radically taken up by the half-brother, Lionel Thackeray. Then Jack asked the million dollar question: 'Is Beth Mayhew your half-sister?'

Archie nodded. 'Yes.'

'And is she, for want of a better expression, master-minding this latest right wing conspiracy?'

'Yes.'

'Is she Big-Knob?' There was a hush, and Archie thought long and hard.

'I don't know,' he said finally, and Jack believed him.

'D'you think your father is Big-Knob?'

'He could be, but nobody knows. My father took to drink after my mother died, ironically from alcohol abuse, but he controlled it for effect.'

'Did he invent the story of Beth's surfboarding accident?'

Archie managed a smile in appreciation of a scheme well executed. 'We both did, and it enabled Father to be close to the military establishments he wanted to manipulate. He'd had enough of career politicians mismanaging policies, inventing this and that excuse, not understanding anything about what they were about, except how to further their careers and feather their nests. This is why he also organised the Mandarins, which, I have to say, needed very little prompting, as they had their own self-interest agenda to follow.'

Jack noticed that explaining the machinations of their scheming was acting like a drug on Archie, dulling the pain the man must be feeling. He'd seen this effect before, not least in himself. He asked another question. 'POGROM. What is that?'

'Apart from the *M* standing for Mandarins, it stands for nothing other than a relatively amusing aside to a chaotic manipulation of society, except we never meant for any physical harm to come to people, but I suppose, upon reflection, it was inevitable. Lionel assured us it was all for the "greater good", you know...' and Jack did, Len had said just that to him in a hotel in Lyme Regis. 'Eventually, Beth ran with the cause and became very good at it, but she did not have Lionel's sensitivity, and I did detect that she gained a certain pleasure from causing pain to people.'

The paramedics arrived and began muscling in, but Jack sat his ground. 'In a minute, mate.' He looked like he would brook no argument, and the paramedic decided he could begin by taking some vitals from Archie, and looked for his foot, which was pretty vital, while Jack asked one more question. 'The Duchess, Lady Francesca Blanche-Teapot, is she involved? Is she Big-Knob?'

Archie laughed out loud, which surprised everyone. '*Her?*' he scoffed. 'She's nothing other than a meddling old fool, but we were able to use her via the contacts in *Embroidery Now,* using her house as a temporary base, and Beth found it useful to use the

Banana Boys. I take it you know Keith Bananas is Lady Francesca's nephew?' Jack nodded he did, as he eased himself back.

The paramedics took charge and Watson stepped in to winch Jack to his feet. He made a show of it as well. It was not as if he was heavy or anything Jack thought, but he allowed that he was awkwardly positioned. Jack's back hurt, which was a combination of a serious injury and an uncomfortable sitting position on the stool. He'd been okay sitting on Martin, and he would take this up with his dog later. He had been tense as well, which would likely have caused his back to stiffen, he imagined. He was appalled by the cruelty of Beth in beating her father as she did. And for why? Was this something that Brian Mayhew had agreed to, also for effect, like the drinking? Because if he had, it had everybody fooled.

Del-Boy arrived with some of his cavalry and took over, easing out the local plod who had been pressing to get access to the club, but were being held up by some MI5 muscle Jack had invited, for a bit of support and Christmas money, he had said. They knew Jack, and knew it would likely be lots of support and no Christmas money.

Della put her arm around Jack's shoulders and squeezed him. He looked at her and she kissed him on his ugly, wrinkled cheek, and blotted a tear with her handkerchief. 'Blimey, Jack, you don't 'arf impress at times,' she said, then she bashed him. 'Don't suppose it would have killed yer to let me in on this, would it?' And she roared a laugh.

'Should I call Jimbo and Jo-Jums and tell 'em to take Beff into custody?' Jack nodded, and Della speed-dialled Jimbo. 'Put a guard on Brian Mayhew as well?' she asked Jack, as Jimbo came on the line, and Jack nodded again, feeling very sad. He'd liked Snail (Jack's name for Brian Mayhew) and then, later on he had warmed to Beth. They had both well and truly hoodwinked him. Still, he would get over it, and probably sooner than he should, and he felt better, as he always did after a bit of *Pride and Prejudice*. Maybe they should prescribe Jane Austen on the NHS, he thought.

Jack took the opportunity to take stock. Archie's confessions had confirmed many of his suspicions, and there was a lot to run with. He would need to press Brian Mayhew, who, as a Professor of Economics, almost certainly could have nobbled the Treasury Mandarin. He thought maybe Ollie and Stan could suggest a way forward there. But who was Big-Knob? His gut feeling told him it was Brian Mayhew, but this did not seem right. Then again, he had Brian Mayhew pegged for the mortuary not so long ago, and he recalled how the doctors were suggesting his recovery was coming along better than they had at first anticipated. Ghost had suggested Brian Mayhew may be drinking himself to death. Maybe he had been wrong as well, and then again, Beth had stood by and overseen her father being beaten to within an inch of his life. Was all of this staged? Surely not? Or was this a case of the younger child carrying on the father's work, regardless of how the father fared?

And what was the father's work? If Len was to be believed, it was an almost benign way of getting society to correct itself for the greater good, but for Beth, there was a completely different motivation altogether, there had to be, and he was almost certain Beth was Big-Knob. But would they ever know? And how important was it to know, anyway? So long as it stopped... So long as *she* was stopped.

It was quiet. Even the paramedics had stopped to listen to Jack's spoken thoughts, and they all looked to Archie, who nodded and, as the morphine took effect, smiled. He had to acknowledge the fact that his adversary, Jack Austin, albeit a cockney barrow boy, was more than his equal.

They took Archie away, some MI5 minders' accompanying the paramedics, though Jack did point out he was not likely to run away, and the local police swarmed in and completely missed the joke.

'Time to go home, Della,' Jack said, 'Christmas with our families, that's nice.'

'What about all of this shite?' Del Boy asked, and Jack left the reply to Della; she was, after all, his protégé.

'You're admin, Del, and I'm not your feckin' protégé.'

'What, all on my own...?' Del complained, like a spoilt brat. Did he stamp his foot? 'And I wasn't even here, so how can I know what happened?' Del spread his hands out like he was Julie feckin' Andrews on a mountain.

Jack was getting fed up, and threatened Del he would tell the Mother Superior on him. Del looked puzzled, so Jack helped him out. 'Watson was 'ere, he'll help you, won't you?'

Watson nodded to Jack, wondering how he had gotten caught up in all of this.

Del looked around him. 'Who's Watson?'

Watson sheepishly put his hand up. 'Watson – well, Monty Python...' Jack explained for Del.

'Snake,' Monty said, confused himself, and Jack thanked him, and Monty let his eyes roll to the ceiling but brought them straight back down, along with Del's, as Martin was sick on Del's shoes.

'It's the rose,' Jack said, 'Martin never was keen on flowers, glutton intolerant, I think. You coming, Della? Burial?' Jack called back, as he walked out, managing a wince here and there just for good form, and the three of them and Martin went off into the gathering snowstorm.

Martin still had the Waitrose bag on his head, but the others were not at all prepared for the snow, so they hopped a cab to Waterloo Station; well, Martin hopped, the others just stepped in.

THIRTY-ONE

THEY WERE ABLE TO GET ONTO A PORTSMOUTH train pretty smartly, and as soon as they were settled, Jack called Mandy to tell her they were on their way home and to get Jimbo, after he had locked up Beth, to put the struts on the Christmas tree. He'd been worried about that all day and was about to get into a heated debate about why he was more worried about the Christmas tree than the shoot-out in the Bumblin'tons kitchen, but Martin was nudging his hand.

'What?' Jack asked, irritated, because he had not yet told Mandy to tell Jimbo the struts had to be covered in aluminium foil, to make them festive.

'Get the feckin' Waitrose bag of me head, bozo,' and Martin shook his head so the bag rattled and Jack hung up on Mandy in order to get the bag off Martin's head.

Jack's phone rang. 'Jack, you hung up on me.' He detected Mandy was a tad miffed, as could all of the other passengers. Martin whined and hid under the seat. He knew he would get the blame, he always did, and he had to do everything around here.

'Hello, luv,' Jack answered lovingly. Mandy went ballistic. That was not supposed to happen, and he thought he might need to revise the handbook he intended to write when he retired, *Women are from Venus and Men should make a run for it...* a short book, with lots of pictures and big writing, so men would actually read it.

Because Jack was busy making a mind map for his new book, he had completely missed the point and content of Mandy's telephone call. 'Are you listening to me?' she asked irritably, so all the carriage and possibly the train driver could hear.

Jack looked for help and the passengers nodded. 'Of course I'm listening.'

'What did I say then?'

The other passengers were able to whisper what she had said. 'You said you wanted to get into me pants and 'urry up 'ome...' He smiled his gratitude, but the passengers were in hysterics as a tirade ensued, which hurt his ear.

One of the things in his self-help book for men would be to encourage an early onset of deafness, and to always hold the phone at arm's length – a simple strategy, but you would be surprised how many men forgot this rule. Mandy calmed, it was safe to listen. He did not hear his darling's tones now. Instead, he heard the dialling tone. She'd hung up, which he thought rude and put it down to her minipause, from which she suffered, and he knew exactly what that was like as he often forgot things when pausing, and fully expected her to call back soon if this was one of them mini things.

He tapped his fingers on the phone, waiting, and Martin re-emerged, Waitrose bag still on his head, looking a bit dishevelled. Jack lifted the bag off and Martin leapt onto his seat. Jack decided to ignore everybody and look out at the snow-covered landscape as it whizzed by the train window. The phone rang, and he let it ring, for two reasons; one, it would teach Mandy a lesson, and two, the vibration on his lap was rather pleasant.

'Answer the phone, numpty.' Martin was always there for him, and Jack liked this about his dog.

'Sweet'art, I accept your apology and we can make it up tonight in bed, lubbly jubbly,' and he rubbed his hands together and, as a consequence, dropped the phone on his lap. Della rummaged around Jack's man parts to retrieve the phone for dipstick. 'Oi, Della, Mandy might see.' He realised his mistake immediately, but it was out there now, and so he bathed in the chorus of applause, as if this was a deliberately witty remark. He was often witty without realising it, and presumed himself to be a natural wit.

'Twit,' Della said, handing him the phone, 'it's Jimbo, not Mandy, and I imagine there won't be any making-up sex for you tonight, dip-feckin'-stick.'

Jack was sad and Della looked as if she was taking pity on him. 'D'you fink Mandy will be upset? After all, I've done nuffink,' and he held his hands out in a pleading manner. Della clumped him and pushed the phone to his defective ears.

'Jimbo, has Mandy told you to put the struts in? Put the tinfoil on first, it's easier that way.' He looked around and bathed in the glory all Christmas tree erectors feel about this time of year, a seasonal thing, like salt and pepper.

'That's seasoning!' Jimbo shouted, knowing Jack was a deaf twat, and the phone would likely be a yard or so away if Jack had thought it was Mandy calling. 'Jack, I need you to listen...' Jimbo asserted, waiting as he could hear Jack discussing salt and pepper with the other passengers. Jimbo had cultivated the art of patience in his dealings with Jack, but not much. 'Jack!' he shouted and Jack returned to the phone, sensing Jimbo was losing patience.

'Hi, Jimbo, I was talking about newspeppers...' Jack guffawed, and the other passengers joined in, realising now, if they hadn't already, that Jack was a natural twit.

Jimbo could be heard chuckling, but the moment for levity was over. 'Beth has escaped, and Brian Mayhew has done a bunk from the hospital. Del-Boy suggested I talk to you. Why is that?'

'Because I have a conversational way and I'm a natural twit.' Point made, he ducked, anticipating a clump, but Della got him on his way back up. Jimbo practiced his patience, awaiting Jack, whom he knew relied on his attics (antics), to marshal his thoughts then come back with an idea he would suggest he'd been thinking about for ages. 'Look, Jimbo, I've been thinking for ages...' told yer, '...Brian Mayhew, or Beff, may be Big-Knob, and if I am thinking correctly and for long enough, they may try to get to Amlodd Jones as he will be the only one who could nail Brain. Beth, of course, we have bang to rights.' Jack left that thought in the air while he tried to think of something else he had been thinking of for ages.

'Brian? You mean Brian Mayhew?'

'That's wot I said, diddli?' The passengers were shaking their heads. Martin woofed "Brain" Jack ignored them all; he had important things to think of for ages. He clicked his finger and thumb, which meant, one, he had an idea, and two, Della had to rummage around his private trouser department for his phone again; you try clicking your fingers to a eureka moment and keeping hold of a phone!

'God, do your flies up,' Della suggested, shuffling his bits and pieces around to get to the phone.

'It's 'ot in 'ere, Della, *der...*' he replied, sloping his head to a Christmas tree angle, '... give us the phone.' He snatched the phone while Della zipped his flies, which prompted sighs of relief all round, though some titillation too, Jack suspected, as Della was drop-dead gorgeous. Though of course if you said that to her, you would likely drop dead as she could be a bit temperamental, and you would certainly be wanting to hold the phone as far away as possible when talking to her, and Jack made a mental note to brief Jonas on that one. Maybe he could sell him the first copy of his book?

Della nudged him gently. Jack wondered if this was her Nightingale persona that Jonas had mentioned? 'Jack, please talk to Jimbo.'

Being polite, he ducked just in case, but she clumped him on the way back up, again. He definitely needed to practice that.

'Jimbo...'

'Yes...' Jimbo answered, but Jack was stuck.

Christ what was he going to say, he thought, as the train pulled into Guildford station, 'We're at Guildford, Jimbo, get us an 'elicopter, will yer,' closed the call, jumped up and began to leave the train.

'Oi, what we doing?'

'Getting out, Della, yer plank,' he answered and wondered if Della should have her IQ tested, and so did Martin; he was already on the platform with snow falling on him, wondering if Jack had any more of those Waitrose bags he kept for crime scenes. Jack was always prepared. He had been a Girl Guide before being drummed out – not for being a boy, but for being ugly, stupid, and shite at knots.

THIRTY-TWO

SHITLEGS STRUGGLED TO OPEN THE SHED DOOR. He was frozen stiff, a known weakling, and snow had accumulated. Fortunately, the Banana Bandits were skinny as rakes, so could squeeze through the narrow gap. Fingers was outside, laughing. Brains squeezed out first. 'Don't suppose you fort of clearing the snow so we could open the fucking door?'

Fingers dobbed Brains on his nose. Fingers was a nice chap if you could see past the psychopath, but there were pressing matters. 'Big-Knob's been in touch.'

'Who'd yer mum shag to get that message?' Shitlegs asked, and Fingers dobbed him. Who'd be a baddie? But then again, Jack was being clumped a fair bit today and he was a goodie, although the Banana Boys viewed him as a baddie; it's confusing on the street.

'What did Big-Knob want?' Keef asked, as he was the leader.

Fingers answered in his OCD hyperactive manner that in the old days they used to call ants-in-yer-pants. Jack Austin still used that expression, as developments in modern day psychological evaluation had completely passed him by.

'Big-Knob said to say yer aunt's gone on the run, and the filf 'ave dug up all of 'er gardin and she ain't best pleased about it. 'Er pride and joy, I presume?'

Keef acknowledged it was, and began to worry about the bodies he had buried there, the cache of arms and Big-Knob's cash. He wasn't worried about his aunt, she was more than capable of taking care of herself, and it would be difficult to pin this on her as the filf, a couple of doors away, would likely tell everybody it was his Banana Boys who hid the arms, money and the bodies. However, things were going to be difficult, and he knew who to blame for this fiasco, Jack fucking Austin and his missus, and he swore revenge. He already had some squaring-up to do with Jack Austin, what with the Poles being brought into the neighbourhood; he knew just how much his aunt was upset about all of that as well. You do not upset Keef's aunt and expect to get away with it, was the message Keef was trying to convey to Fingers just now, but everybody had dropped off listening to Keef's rant, preferring to nurse their pneumonia instead.

'Finished?' Fingers asked.

'Yeah,' Keef replied.

'We've work to do.'

'We do?' Brains asked.

Fingers contemplated dobbing Brains again, but chose to be informative. 'Me mum wants yer to get down to Dorset, you 'ave to kill some people.'

He had their attention now. They liked killing people. The thievery and getting caught was only a sideline, the real money was in killing people. They could barely contain their excitement.

'Who're we killing?' Keef asked, by way of making conversation, as was his turnip manner. Real contract killers would ask about where, what were the risks, what money was in it, and then who, but that was the Banana Boys for you, and Fingers fully expected them to complete the task and be killed, or at least captured, and if they didn't, he would finger them to the filf, by way of an ironic gesture, or kill them himself. He'd already got another gang to replace them, and funnily enough, the leader was also called Keef –

Keef Bozoquet – and his dad had been the Permanent Secretary for the Department of Education until being dismissed in the past few days. An incentive for the Bozo boys, who wouldn't see the irony in avenging the department of Education.

Fingers explained the set-up at the Dorset Cottage, information that Big-Knob had passed on to his mum via the criminal bloke she was shagging at the time. Some of the detail and risks may, therefore, have been lost in the number of translations between not the brightest of thugs you were likely to meet, but they had the address and knew it was in the country and that it most likely smelled. The bit they had forgotten was the bit about the MI5 minders, so you see the system of communication set up by Big-Knob was severely flawed... or was it? Maybe Big-Knob wanted it to fail? Nah, that can't be the case, Fingers thought, and anyway, he had asked the Bozo Boys to follow the Banana Boys to make sure they did the Biz, and for the Bozo Boys to do the Biz on the Bananas if they didn't get killed or captured.

What could go wrong? Two gangs, with hardly a brain cell amongst them, were headed to the frozen white plains of darkest, though it could be moonlit if the snow clouds would permit, Dorset, and needed to get this done as soon as possible in order to get home to put their stockings up on the mantelpiece, before Father Christmas got there.

I am aware there is no such thing as Father Christmas, and even if there was, the Banana Boys would probably get nothing as they had been very naughty, but you just can't tell bozos – which, coincidentally, would apply to the Bozo Boys, too, as they also had stockings to hang, and this may have been preying on their minds as they set off.

———

THE TRAIN DEPARTED GUILDFORD, leaving Della, Beryl, Jack and Martin a forlorn picture, lonely as a snow cloud on a snow-blown platform, the dim electric light beginning to tinge the snow orange as daylight faded.

'Feck me, it's taters,' Della complained.

Jack shushed her, he was thinking, 'Should have put a vest on.'

Jack's phone went, and kept going. 'Phone, Jack,' Beryl said unnecessarily, except for deaf twats preoccupied with getting helicopters.

He answered. 'Just get the fucking helicopter will yer, Jimbo?'

'What? What helicopter? Where are you and when will you be home?'

'Mandy sweet'art, can we skip your apology until I get home? I need to get this helicopter organised,' and he hung up.

The phone rang again. 'Jimbo, the helicopter. How many times...?'

'Jack, you hung up on me,' Mandy said and if Jack had to guess, she was likely having a mini-pause event as she seemed a tad irritated. Probably flushing as well, he thought.

'Look luv, why don't you have a little lie-down, eh? Martin's sure it was you who hung up on me.' Jack looked at Martin; in trouble again, thanks to his eejit former master.

There was a beep-beep in Jack's ear. 'Sweet'art, gotta go, call waiting,' so he hung up and pressed Call Receive. 'Hello.' Nothing. 'Hello?' Still nothing.

'Ha-fuckin'-lo,' the porter with his wheelie wagon, which was going beep, beep, said. "Hal-fucking-lo to you too, and get out of the way."

Della was seriously wobbling her head, she enjoyed that.

'It's not funny, Della, I fink I have a stalker call.'

Della, Beryl and Martin enjoyed that. To imagine anyone would stalk Jack! The angry porter was still trying to get past a deaf twat. Della pushed Jack to the side and the porter and his electric cart went by but ran over Jack's foot. 'Ow!' he shouted, and it looked like he meant it.

'Jack, you wuss,' Della remarked, grabbing his phone that was ringing.

'If that's Mandy, tell her she hung up on me, and I'm seriously injured and might not make it,' and Jack feigned a faint.

'Shut it, yer bleedin' actress, it's Jimbo and he wants to know where to direct the helicopter and where are we all going?'

A circumspect Jack looked for the candid camera. 'Not Mandy, calling to apologise?'

'No.'

'Oh.'

'Jack.'

'Yes.'

'Helicopter?'

'Give us me phone and when I've sorted this I want you and Burial to tell me about the mini-pause thing.' He grabbed the phone. 'Jimbo, pop around to me house and tell Mandy she definitely hung up on me, and put some struts on the Christmas tree, it don't look right to me. I'd do it meself but I'm seriously injured.' He hung up and Della and Burial sighed.

The phone went again. Della grabbed it and answered. It was Mandy. 'Hello, Mandy.' She listened. 'Look, I'm not getting involved. Hang on, Jack is gesturing, although he could just be picking his fireman's hose...' and she passed the phone to Jack.

'Darlin', fort you were going for a lie-down? Anyway, Jimbo'll be round in a minute to put some struts in the Christmas tree... Hold on, sweet'art, you can apologise in a minute. When Jimbo gets round, tell him we're at Guildford station and need to go to the cottage in Dorset where we have Amlodd and thingybob holed up. I fink Beff knows where, she probably fluttered her eyelashes at Jimbo, the twonk. Anyway, we need to warn the lads on the ground, and Flora, I suppose, although I've never been keen on her... Hang on, Della?'

Della grabbed the phone. 'I've never been keen on her, either, but you need to know her name is Marge...' She paused, thinking... 'Or is it Flora and we call her Marge? Oh, buggered if I know, but by the time we get Jack home, we will have briefed him on the menopause. Okay, sweet'art, now you go and have a lie-down, dear,' and she hung up.

'Good, sorted. Now, where's the fucking helicopter landing?'

'I thought you'd sorted that?'

'Do I look like admin, Della? Tell 'er, Burial, I'm not admin.'

'Della,' Beryl said, 'Jack's not admin,' and she giggled. She'd not had so much fun since she'd machine-gunned the Head of the Military, The Cabinet Secretary, Pomerol, and someone else she couldn't remember... oh yeah, the Government Chief Whip.

The phone went and Beryl grabbed it from Della and she briefed Jimbo that they were intending to go to the Dorset cottage as they feared for the safety of Amlodd Jones and his secretary, Daphne Morris. 'And we need to move pronto-tonto,' she told him.

Jimbo confirmed a helicopter from the traffic police in Portsmouth had been dispatched, and Del-Boy would be meeting them down there.

Jack flicked his fingers at Beryl, a gesture she did not appreciate. He was oblivious, no change there then, but she did give him the phone.

'Jimbo, is the pilot Top Gun?' Jimbo confirmed it was the same pilot used on the Fort Cumberland Op. 'And I need protection for Mandy. I fink the Banana

Boys might get the 'ump about what we did to his aunt's garden, especially as we think she was not directly involved, but eh, she must have known something?' and Jack hung up.

'Sorted. Anyone fancy an ice cream?

THIRTY-THREE

Mandy answered the door to Jimbo and Father Mike. She was expecting them and was thankful Jimbo would be staying over. Mike was doing Midnight Mass at the Cathedral and she'd hoped to go with Jack, but that looked unlikely, though the bonus was that Liz and Carly were home with the baby, and together, they would go to Mass.

'Mike...?' Her eyes were pleading.

Mike responded with an arm around her shoulders. 'He will be okay, is that what you were worried about?' She nodded. 'And you'd like me to bless the baby?' She nodded again, tears close, but held herself in check to answer the door again. It was Fatso and Maisie this time, making social rounds and saying they hoped to meet Mandy and Jack at the cathedral later. They had a cuddly knitted Sea Bass for the baby, and told Mandy not to let Jack eat it.

Mandy looked around. All of her and Jack's family were there, except her son David, and he was on the way. Michael, Jack's son and his girlfriend, Winders, were organising drinks and finger food, with Alice and Nobby helping. Alice's pregnancy was starting to show and she had discarded the bandages and wore her scarred face, which was work in progress, with a pride similar to her dad. Alana, Jack's daughter, was seated on an armchair, with Josh on the arm, his arm draped around her shoulders. Just Meesh was missing, and she had spoken on the telephone to Mandy, saying she was having a lovely holiday with the Splifs and she missed Martin; well, who didn't? Mandy didn't mention the fact that when Meesh got home, Martin would only have three and a half legs – well, three and a pink one.

It was a moving moment for Mandy, all the family there and the strong, comforting presence of Father Mike beside her. Funny, she now appreciated his beatific omnipresence, whereas there had been a time when she had resented his relationship as a spook and a long-time friend of Jack. Now, it was all water under the bridge. She whispered a small prayer. 'Keep Jack safe, and bring him home, please.'

Mike clasped her hands and helped send the prayer up to admin, as Jack would say, not that he believed, but they shared a spirituality. He joked that they were soul mates, and Mandy believed they were.

'To Dad, get home safe, and very soon,' Michael toasted.

'To Jack, my love,' all eyes on Mandy, 'and the feckin' Christmas tree that for once is straight with no struts,' and everyone saluted Jimbo's erection.

The mirth subsided as Jackie and Gill arrived, continental-kissing everyone. 'He not back?' Jackie asked, unnecessarily.

Mandy breathed deeply and Jimbo steered Jackie and Mandy into the kitchen, which, for the time being was empty, except for the all-pervading smells of Michael's beautiful baking. Father Mike followed and Jimbo spoke. 'Jack is in a helicopter on his way to the Dorset coast. There has been a major altercation at Bumblin'tons. To cut a long story short, Archie Pointe-Lace is Archie Thackeray-Mayhew, Professor Mayhew's son, half-brother to Len and, hold onto your horses, half-brother also to Beth.'

Jackie processed this information. 'A family affair...' She thought on. 'Did Jack know all of this?'

'We think Jack has long suspected something like this,' Jimbo answered, 'but Professor Mayhew was a bit of a shock. The pair of them, Beth and Snail, have been very good at pulling the wool over all of our eyes.'

'Who is Big-Knob, Jimbo?' Jackie asked.

Jimbo hemmed and aaahed for a while and rubbed his chin noisily, thinking he needed a shave before Mass. 'Beth's back in custody and has reverted to her old cold self. She will be taken to London. Brian Mayhew is under arrest and back at the hospital for checks. His condition is such that he will be released into custody in a few days. And as for Big-Knob? We don't know, and we're not sure if we will ever know.

'However, we can see Len had been wound up by his dad, the professor, and spurred along by his half-brother Archie, but, as Jack suspected, Len's motivation was altruistic, following Jack's socialist diatribes that first caused Len's concepts to gel, and this presented a great opportunity for the professor. A beautifully simple model for civil dystopia, an intended benign social pogrom. We think Beth came into the active fold sometime later. She was certainly the hard-nosed one, and showed no remorse for the hurt she caused, even to her own father. So Jack's conclusion is that Beth is Big-Knob. However, I would be very surprised if we get an admission.'

'Why are Amlodd Jones and his secretary a target?' Mandy asked.

'Jack says because Amlodd first sensed something was happening after the treatment of Siggy, and together, Daphne and Amlodd assembled the jigsaw, and as a consequence, they have a lot of hard evidence on the Mandarins and their cohorts, and have been sharing all of this with Jack. We know Beth issued orders to the soldiers, likely the Banana Boys, and possibly another crew we think are the Bozos, and now, with nobody to countermand the order, two gangs could be on their way to Dorset. So, Jack and his MI5 team and local tactical units are heading there now. It's cold, dark, and nobody knows what will happen, but the team on the ground have been warned, and are ready.'

———

IT WAS cosy in the cottage. A log fire burned, a hint of wood smoke suggesting the chimney should be swept, but it was a pleasant, homely smell. Daphne cooked, Amlodd helped, and they marked the commencement of their domestic life together with a bottle of wine. Bliss? A little, but following the message from MI5, the atmosphere in the house had adopted a nervous energy of readiness, which took the edge off.

The doors and windows had been secured while Amlodd and Daphne looked on. Outside, there was a broad expanse of yard in front of the cottage as you approached from the road, illuminated with garden lights, decorative more than functionally defensive. The back garden was dark, black, the moon unable to break through the heavy clouds that were still issuing weighty flakes, which were accumulating on the frozen ground. Any chance of resurrecting the yuletide spirit was lost when the two officers in the cottage revealed sophisticated weapons, machine guns Amlodd knew had a name but could never identify. As a boy in the valleys of Wales, he had never had a fascination for guns. His upbringing had been artistic, poetry, tinged heavily with a political bias.

Chas, one of the MI5 men, stoppered the wine bottle, a prudent measure. Amlodd and Daphne did not disagree, but a glass or two may have helped their nerves.

'You're sure they are coming?' Amlodd asked.

'They're coming,' Chas answered, dourly, focused, no time for chit-chat.

A tap on the window, three plus one, the signal that either Flora or Dave, who had drawn the short straw, were patrolling. Poor buggers, out in this weather Amlodd thought. They were prepared inside the house as well, with outdoor clothing and survival rations, in case they had to make a run for it and were left outside for the night. Again, it was prudent, though the thought of it caused bubbling sensations in the guts of Amlodd and Daphne.

A phone vibrated on the table. Chas picked up, listened, ended the call and pocketed the phone. 'They're here.'

The silence was unnerving. Amlodd and Daphne were assimilated town people, used to traffic noises, sirens, shouts and laughter, angry drunk voices... it was all meat and potatoes to them. But silence, until you hear it – or rather, don't hear it – can be truly unnerving, as can be the pitch black of no light pollution. They could hear the phone vibrating in Chas's pocket. He answered and listened, closed the call. 'Another gang has arrived, we may be up against eight men.' He clicked his weapon and it both scared and reassured Amlodd and Daphne.

The quiet tension was shattered as a helicopter hovered, enjoined by a staccato crashing sound of automatic gunfire. A glance out of the window showed muzzle flame illuminating a group of men like dancers in disco strobe lighting, as they fired into the air.

The shooting stopped. The helicopter could be heard moving away. 'Fink they're here, Top Gun,' Jack said, as he watched Beryl prepare her own weapon.

'No bleedin' kiddin', Tonto,' Top Gun replied into his mic.

Top Gun, the police pilot, had known Jack many years, and despite everything that was said and widely believed, he did not owe Jack one, but was prepared to come anyway and had called via the Marine barracks and collected some additional machine guns and Major Laugh, who also did not owe Jack. The Cumberland Fort team were back together and they high-fived, except Jack, who didn't know what that was, so Della clumped him with her five and Martin licked it better. Martin's licks were known to be remarkably efficacious for clumps, and he had been licking Jack for nearly eight years, if you took off the time he had been licking Meesh better.

A few fields away, Top Gun put the helicopter down and they waited while Jack was sick. Martin considered eating it but was not keen on carrots, though he was aware they would help him to see in the dark. Martin was also aware everybody was looking, so he woofed that Jack was a tart, but knew his former master was scared; he had seen it so many times.

'You okay, Jack?' Beryl asked.

Sniffing, wiping away tears, he grunted hoarsely, 'Not sure I can take any more of this, Burial.'

The team looked on, concerned. Beryl eased Top Gun and the major to one side while Della observed, weighing up whether or not Jack needed a technical nudge to get him going again. 'It's okay, Jack, we're here for you. Stay back, leave the rest to us, eh?'

Jack croaked an okay, and Della had her confirmation, this was real. 'Yeah, stay back, wuss,' and Jack appreciated her kind words.

Major Laugh interrupted as he handed out Day-Glo orange survival suits, designed to show up in the sea. Beryl helped Jack put a suit on. He did say orange didn't suit him. His attempt at humour encouraged them as they looked at him in his orange onesie, twiglet arms and legs sticking out; not so much Tangerine dream as Satsuma nightmare.

Martin was appointed guard dog, which he was not pleased about. He was further disgruntled, wondering where the feck was his survival suit, but he knew marines didn't like Border Terriers, preferring poodles, so they would not have a suit for Martin. They moved on, Martin in a sulk, nursemaid to a wimp, and they belly-crawled to a ridge and looked over.

Two transit vans were parked facing each other, and the dipstick occupants had left their headlamps on so they could be observed. The two gangs were expressing their rivalry in an animated fashion. They had come to blows, like an ice hockey match where the players throw down their gloves and skin and hair flies. It was icy underfoot and, as a consequence, they were generally slipping, swinging, and missing each other, but this altercation did allow the MI5 external team to make their approach unobserved. After a few minutes of grunts and the occasional sock, the noise of which carried in the still of the night, the two warring gangs were surrounded and a polite request issued from Dave the spook, to the effect that they might like to give themselves up.

Cue pandemonium. Immediately, the Banana Boys dived under their van. It was second nature for them to run and hide, and often in the silliest of places, but this time their hiding place had merit, principally because it was the only hiding place around, except for the Bozo van and that had now been shot to ribbons, was on fire, and at risk of blowing up, so everybody scattered, except the Banana Boys, who hopped in their van and made a stuttering getaway.

They had escaped twice now, a Banana record (not to be confused with a *Bananarama* record).

The Bozo Boy's van blew. 'Cor, did you see that, Della?' Jack said, and Della and Beryl decided not to clump him. That was close! At last Jack's moaning was paying off.

From their ridge, they could see the MI5 team flat on the ground, while the Bozos limped a retreat to the nearby barn conversion, only to turn as they faced a salvo from the two MI5 *holiday makers*. Like panicked hares, they headed to the cottage, and Jack mentioned it was a bit like those pinball machines, as the Bozos swerved in another direction to avoid fire from the cottage and then yet another change of direction. The MI5 team were using their firepower to corral the gang.

Beryl, who had no patience, released a salvo and took out the Bozo Boys' legs. They didn't move anymore, except for a bit of wriggling, which you would do if your legs had been taken out by a machine gun, and Jack knew, as he had seen Archie wriggle just because his foot had been shot off.

It was over. Jack remained motionless, except for one motion, a little accident in his bottom trouser department when Beryl's gun went off.

THIRTY-FOUR

JACK WADDLED IN THE DEEPENING SNOW, following the marine, a police helicopter pilot and two feisty women. Martin, on his three and a half legs, kept Jack company in his own waddling manner. 'What's the time,' Jack called out, looking at his bare wrist.

'Time you got a watch, it's nine,' Della called back.

Jack checked, shook his wrist, his hair past a pimple was slow. 'Probably needs winding,' he muttered. Martin didn't laugh, he'd heard them all before.

They were met at the cottage door by Chas, who stepped out of the way so Amlodd could shake Jack's hand. 'Jack, is this it?'

Daphne stood beside Amlodd. 'Come 'ere, Daf,' Jack said, arms out.

'Not on your Nellie,' Daphne replied, 'you're rancid.' The game was up on the trouser deposit.

'I've gotta give those back to the quartermaster. What will I say?' Major Laugh said, only mildly irritated, enjoying Jack's predicament.

Jack applied his prima donna face, which was better than his wimp one and mentioned to Daphne that he required her to direct him to the bathroom; not that he needed a bath, but he certainly needed a poo. They suggested he might take a shower afterwards, and Jack replied that he would consider it. Then flounced.

Della called Father Mike. She wanted to let him know everyone was okay. She mentioned her concern for Jack, which impressed Mike, and informed him the Banana Boys had gotten away. She called after Jack, still waddling his flouncing ascent of the stairs, 'Jack, Father Mike says he's taking the family to the cathedral for Midnight Mass. He wonders if you'll make it? I think he was suggesting you should, be-cause Mandy wants to see you.'

Jack flicked his head, an encouraging sign that he was on the mend. 'Probably wants to apologise for hanging up on me,' he answered nonchalantly (yep, he's on the way back), and he flounced into the bath-room, for a poo, and then to find some bottom wear, as his day-glow trousers, and the ones underneath, would not be appropriate for a cathedral; Jack was most particular about church-wear.

———

THE BANANA BOYS eventually made it back to Fin-gers' dad's shed after a scoot around Dorset looking for baby sheep; there were none to be found. Fingers had telephoned them to say the game was up and they should go on the lamb. Unfortunately, the Ba-nana Boys did not realise it was an American hard-nut expression for run away, a bit like if you go to the bathroom in America you don't have to have a bath, you can just have a wee, but if you miss the toilet it is generally advised you go on the lamb – it all ties up, a common language, so not to speak.

'I'm gonna get that fucking Austin,' Keef said, and he would have paced up and down in a rant, except it was congested in the shed. Nobody realised that if they just chucked out the damp, rat-infested settee, there would be room for ranting and pacing. How-ever, they would not then be able to lie low. They de-cided to split up and go their separate ways and meet up in the summer, or somewhere they had heating. So they all went their own ways, together, until Keef told everyone to stop following him and to fuck off, and they did, bleating, as you would if you were on the lamb.

———

'DAFF, I chucked me trousers and pants out the windah, the foxes can 'ave 'em,' a recovered Jack commented, as he came down the stairs like a commando, just the tails of his shirt disguising his embarrassment.

'Jack, you don't have to walk like a commando if you have no pants on,' Major Laugh said, and he would know, he was a commando and wore no underpants; probably given them to the foxes in Portsmouth, Jack thought. 'I do have underpants, and commandos do not mince, well, not all of them,' Major Laugh replied, striking a balance and a striking pose, tittering to himself.

They said their goodbyes to Amlodd and Daphne. Jack was weeping, which he explained, was because he was pleased Amlodd and Daphne were getting married, and also because his exposed varicose-vein-riddled legs were getting pneumonia.

'Not because you were scared just then?' Daphne hit the mark.

The tears came faster and harder. He hugged Daphne but spoke to Amlodd. 'Yes, I can't take any more,' and, as Amlodd was now Permanent Secretary to the Gnome Office, he informed him, 'I am going to retire.'

'Jack, I don't need to know that, but I wish Mandy and you the very best of health and happiness.' The two deformed men cried to each other, and as Jack bowed low to embrace Amlodd, his shirt lifted and Daphne saw Jack wearing what looked like a pair of her knickers. They were extremely tight and displayed every nook and granny.

After a few more sniffles, Jack joined the team yomping back to the helicopter. He had his day-glo trousers under his arm; nobody had the heart to tell him he should have left them for the foxes, but they could see, and mentioned, that Jack's spindly day-glo legs had enormous goose bumps that stood out like chicken eggs, on top of his varicose veins.

He climbed into the helicopter and Della grabbed his trousers and chucked them out of the helicopter, for the foxes. 'Jack, you feckin' stink,' Della remarked, stating the obvious for everyone, except for Martin, who thought it was rather nice and snuggled up to his master's lower regions, offering warmth with the occasional efficacious lick.

Recovering his spirits, following those kind words from Della, and in no patent danger – until he saw Mandy, that was – he reverted to form. 'Put the 'eater on, Top Gun. I'm on a promise with Mandy after she has apologised, and I want to be able to find me willy when I get home.' There was no answer forthcoming. It had been a long day and everyone was exhausted and settled in for the helicopter ride.

'When will we get there?' Jack asked.

'About 11.30,' Top Gun replied, except Jack didn't hear as he was a deaf twat, and didn't have his head-phones on. Della clumped him, put his headphones on and smoothed his wrinkled cheeks. Jack would never understand women, and what he never under-stood was that they struggled to understand him. So you see, there is a clear need for him to write that book, *Venus and Thingy*, which he considered would likely be a more catchy title, and if he was retiring, he might now be able to do it, and he imagined being lauded by all of womankind at some poncy reception.

Della leaned over, removed his headphones, and clumped him. 'That's from womankind,' and Jack thought maybe he was finally getting through, and though it might be a painful exercise, he needed to persevere for the sake of *man*-kind.

THIRTY-FIVE

''Urry up, Top Gun, it's nearly midnight!' Jack shouted, not realising he didn't have to as he was speaking into his mic. Top Gun reeled from the assault on his ears, and the helicopter veered. 'Oi, steady on, I'm already a bit tom and dick, and I might need another poo.'

Top Gun was going as fast as he could into a strong headwind, but soon they hovered over the Catholic cathedral and after a while, several irate drivers got the message, halted to provide a clear stretch of road, and the helicopter landed. Jack bailed out, on a mission, mentioning this to a number of disgruntled drivers who could not summon their Christmas spirit for a loony in just a shirt and girl's knickers. He had to get into church in time for Mandy to apologise, a quick pray, and home to bed. 'Lubbly jubbly,' he said to himself, rubbing his hands as he jumped from the helicopter, only to be snagged back; he'd forgotten to take his head set off. He handed them to Della, ducked and she missed, but he bashed his head on the helicopter door.

Sometimes life never cut him a break, not realising it was a full time job for Jack's guardian angel, who on this occasion was a tad behind as there had been a head wind. Blimey, who'd be an angel, except you get lovely sparkly wings, but the hat is just a silly golden hoop so you look a twat. The angel suggested he shut up and get into the cathedral as he was late, not realising the sentiment was shared in Heaven, where the celebrations for Jack's retirement were just getting underway, and, it was also the Guvnor's birthday – *Christmas*.

The Cathedral was packed to the rafters for the biggest show of the year and as Jack ran in, he collided with a cow, mooing and ruminating on the miracle of Margie (a holy Margaret angel and not a Magi, as is generally passed off as perceived wisdom), standing in a full-size, stage set, stable. There was the possibility Jack fecked, if the shocked faces on the children gathered there, and on Father Mike's holier than thou gobshite visage, was anything to go by, as Jack took in the Naivety set, staged with live animals and live children, and thought, *I'm dead meat*.

The children laughed as Jack removed some particularly itchy straw from Daphne's knickers. *Kids*, Jack thought, *who'd 'av 'em?* Then he realised he had had some and was about to have several grandchildren, and this brought a broad grin to his special Christmas face. At this time of year he applied his best joyous face, which came with a sparkle from his eye, enhanced with glitter in the redundant eye socket. It was a bit like the tree struts; if he didn't do it, it didn't feel like Christmas.

He looked up at the rude conflagration, laughing and rolling about in the aisles. He may have said out loud that this was a holy place and maybe they could shut the feck up, he couldn't remember, as he was looking around for Mandy, and then, where was Father Mike? 'Just like the Holy Ghost to disappear when I need him,' Jack said to himself, aware it must be nearly midnight and he needed to get some joyousing going, sing a few Christmas caramels. He looked at his wrist and remembered his hair past a pimple was slow and he'd not reset it.

Father Mike reappeared and made Jack jump. 'Blimey, Mike, get yerself some Christmas bells round yer ankles, will yer.'

Mike desisted from comment as he lifted a spare cassock over Jack's head. Jack contemplated leaving his hands inside, for a laugh, but eventually allowed his arms to be passed through the armholes, in the spirit of goodwill to all priests who were men, and, turning in a strutting model manner, Jack admired himself, wondering if he could have been a priest. But at that moment of daydreaming wonderment, the cow stepped back on Jack's foot and shat a pancake on his other foot. He contemplated hopping, steam rising off his unscathed and more than usually malodorous foot, instead he sighed, but in a Christmas way.

'Shoes off,' Mike ordered, hardly able to contain his angelic mirth, and Jack contemplated taking the shoes off and chucking the smelly one at the Father, but he dutifully did as he was told and, as he bent down to untie his cow-shite-ridden laces, he was goosed by a goose, who was having a gander at his bits and pieces up his cassock, and may have made a goosey derogatory remark about Daphne's knickers, but Jack didn't speak Goose so he couldn't be sure.

He did, though, leap into the air, which was very much appreciated by the children, and their beatific faces, so enjoying themselves at his expense, made Jack melt. Oh well, he thought, but just then the cow clumped him with her tail. 'Feckin' women', he said out loud, and was greeted by a summary intake of breath from the conflagration.

'Sit, Jack,' Mike instructed, pointing and shoving him in the cassocks, and Jack went to where Mike steered, which was over to Mandy, who was sitting in her wheelchair in the aisle. She'd not saved a seat for him. Maybe she was angry, he thought. Maybe it was he who should apologise; yep, that would be it, he thought, and he went up to her and the guardian angel, who incidentally was called Moses (well, Jack was Church of Egypt), caused the conflagration on the pews next to Mandy to divide, like the Red Sea, and a seat appeared for him, just like that. Not that Jack appreciated the miraculous event, he thought it was because he was important.

He leaned down to Mandy's ear. She was pinching her nose, so he pinched his own. It must be the funny voices game she often played when she went into the bathroom after him; (*for the benefit of my American readers this not when he had a bath*). 'Sorry I hung up, my luv,' he whispered in a squeaky voice, and she replied, in an equally squeaky voice, but in a more elevated register because she was a girl, that she was sorry, also.

Jack stood up, released his nose and declared to everyone, 'It's alright, she's apologised.'

Mandy looked way, way up, to the nave ceiling and, speaking to Moses, called it a draw as he nudged, in a smelly way, past her and into his seat. 'Jack, what happened to you?' she asked, but he told her to be quiet, he was having a quick pray. She giggled, and all of a sudden felt a lot better. She was impressed as Jack did appear to be praying, because his lips moved and she could hear him; in fact everyone could hear him. Even the lambs looked up as Martin arrived, having had the cow poop removed from his ginger fur by Father Mike's assistant bell ringer, and the hound "derred" at his master, his expression saying "praying again?"

'What's up?' Mandy asked; it was her midden miasma-tinged face.

Jack looked back at her, an amazed look on his Christmas Joyous visage. 'You just wouldn't Adam and Eve it...' he replied, appropriate cockney slang for church. 'My gradian angel apologised for the helicopter door, but there was a headwind. Said they were all pleased I was retiring.'

Mandy skipped the shite – the cow shite and the bullshite – and got straight to the nub, which Jack knew was a place in France, so was alerted. 'You're definitely retiring?' Mandy asked, and coincidentally felt a sense of elation, because he looked serious. This wasn't his April Fool's look, it was his Joyous Christmas one, albeit without the glitter or foil-covered struts.

'I yam, darlin', just you, me, the kids and grandkids. I've even informed the Gnome Office.'

'You have?'

'I 'ave, that was my final job. I 'ave Daphne's Alan Wickers, and they're a bit bleedin' tight in places, I don't mind telling you, and need to get them back to 'er, then that's it.'

Mandy pinched her not insubstantial nose and went in for a kiss. 'My best Christmas present ever, love, and I'll ease Daphne's knickers off for you when we get home, okay?'

Jack smiled, his best Christmas present ever as well, that and her apology of course, major points that was.

'Her-hum.'

'Oh, fuck off, Mike, and get this show on the road, will yer? Daff's drawers are bleedin' killing me, and Mandy wants to ease them off, dead slow like, when we get home.'

The conflagration rolled up, not bothered they had missed the birth of Christ time. Jack could have told them Christmas was a tad late anyway as there was a strong head wind, but why show off his celestial contacts.

'Quite right,' Mandy said, pinching her nose again, going in for the killer kiss. Jack loved this woman, and

Mandy thought, just as bloody well, and apart from her eyes and nose departments, she loved him with every fibre of her body.

'Just as well,' Jack said – they both needed a bath but Mandy still had her very stiff bobby socks – oh well.

THIRTY-SIX

'WOULD YER LOIKE A DROPEEN OF JAMESON'S, Father?' Colleen was waving a tumbler of Irish whiskey in front of the nose of the yet-to-be-defrocked Jack, and acting out the role of *Mrs. Doyle* in *Father Ted*, 'Aaah, go on, go on, go on, go on... go on, go...'

'Right, Windahs, a creditable performance,' Jack answered, as he took the whiskey, swirled and sniffed. It was not the same. The earthy smell he loved so much had a tad too much cow pat. Mandy had made him take his shoes and socks off and leave them outside, but Jack didn't want the foxes to have his tan brogues, so he tied them up with string and looped them over the back gate, but there was still a very evident pong, and he put this down to the liquid consistency of the cow poo, and its propensity to splash upward. He had remarked that in the country, a place he was not a particular fan of, one was aware of such things.

'One, aware...?' Mandy mimicked in her best *Queen of England* voice, and he knew he was done up like a kipper. He leaned back and enjoyed the moment, then saw the tree sparkling in a very vertical manner.

'Where's Jimbo? That tree don't look right to me,' and he sloped his head, and the whiskey he had sipped oozed from the side of his mouth, proving once and for all that he was no multitasker.

'The tree is fine. Have a shower and dump your clothes out for the foxes.'

Jack looked at his wife as if she was mad. 'I have to return Daph's Alan Wickers and, if I recall, you were going to help me off with them?' He smiled his victory smirk; he'd practiced, and it was good.

Mandy wheeled herself over to the disgraced Vicar of Christ and ducked her head under the cassock to the great amusement of the family as they looked on. Jack blushed. Was that a first? And Mandy had missed it. They could hear some murmuring from beneath the cloth and they could see Jack doing a little Ali shuffle, hear muffled squeaks, mention of a jumbo arse, and Mandy eventually emerged with Daphne's knickers and asked Michael to chuck them out for the foxes, convinced Daphne would not want them returned.

'Right, well, you will have to explain that to Daphne,' Jack said, returning to a more normal colouring that suited his victory grin better.

'Stop smirking, Jack.'

Jack looked shocked. 'I'm not smirking, it was my victory grin, you just missed my smirk because you were otherwise engaged.' He smirked again, and realised, once again, he was done up like a kipper and decided to go for a shower.

While Jack was singing his deckchair Italian operettas in the shower, the family gathered around the vertical Christmas tree that Mandy considered a lot better without the struts. The conversation was stilted, not uncomfortable so much as lacking in energy. It was late, and intuitively Mandy saw Christmas happening around them. She and Jack had done nothing to contribute to the festivities or even the presents. Mandy had already got presents for the children long before the season kicked in for Jack, which ordinarily would be around Boxing Day, but was feeling bad because she had got nothing for him. She knew also that he would not care at all.

Mandy skipped her depressing thoughts, because she harked the Italianate Christmas Carol whistling getting louder, which heralded the approach of Archangel Jack down the stairs. 'Hark, it's the fucking heralding angels...' a curtailed remark plus an intake of breath when she saw him present himself to her wheelchair. The stifled and muffled titters were audible. Jack was, as normal, in a shirt with one button, misaligned, but at least secured, and his clean Christmas boxers. It was the bulge at the front of them, however, that had everyone's attention.

'What?' he said to the family, spinning around to offer those at the back a better view, and returned to present his crotch level with his wheelchair-bound wife's head.

'Jack, please, it's Christmas,' Mandy said, trying to get the childish smirk off his face.

'It's not a smirk, it's a smile that says I love my wife, I adore my wife, and I'm looking forward to retiring with my wife, if you pardon the bed pun, not the bed pan...'

He chuckled at his witty remark that left everyone else, not least Mandy, stony-faced, and was about to continue when Mandy stopped him with a hand gesture that extended to a lucky dip into his underpants to collect his phone. She stopped with her hand nestling in the family jewel department as she remembered that she had his phone in her hand bag. What was this, then? And slowly, she brought her hand out with a felt box – at least this is what it felt like – flipped the lid and saw a beautiful ring, a contemporary design in predominantly silver, with a gold central band that held a deep green emerald.

Mandy's breath and speech faculties were taken from her just as Jack, her feckin' eejit, *oomphed* into a kneeling pose beside her, took the ring and slipped it onto Mandy's ring finger. It nestled there, a perfect match for her silver and gold wedding band. 'I love you, Amanda,' he said, as he turned the ring gently on her finger.

'I love you... too,' was her choked reply. Mandy, of course, could never remain speechless for long, and soon she was looking for an explanation. 'Jack, this is lovely, but when did you...'

He halted her with a kiss, which shut her up. 'I telephoned Barbara Tipple...' Jack was a personal friend of this highly talented jewellery designer who had shops in Portsmouth and London's Mayfair. She had designed and made the wedding ring, which explained why the eternity ring matched and fitted perfectly.

'When did you telephone Barbara?' Mandy, naturally, did not let him finish, and in many ways he liked this about her, as often he would start a sentence with no idea what he was going to say.

'I telephoned her after our honeymoon. I wanted her to design the ring for when I actually retired, and after all that has happened these past few weeks, and today, and I'll tell you about that later, I knew my time was up. I need to get the Oldtimers checked out, and I do not want to waste any time not being with you. She hurried up the making of the ring, and when I was in London I collected it... I said you'd pay her later,' and he waved his body backwards, as if defending his head for an imminent attack, and laughed, as did everyone else, and the spellbinding moment was over, in true Jack style, with a shite joke.

Mandy reflected, *I wonder if he meant that? Surely not...?*

Jack returned to his feet, *oomphing* and wingeing, telling everybody about his bad back and how a daft cow had trodden and shat on his plates of meat, and things were indeed returning to normal, but Jack nearly always had an ulterior motive, and the *oomphing* was emphasised. 'Someone give me an 'and to get Mandy up the stairs, only me back's playing up,' and he *oomphed* and aaahed to reinforce the point.

Michael, Nobby and Josh got up to do the honours, but Nobby had a question. 'What is it, Nobby? Ask away, then we do not talk about the case throughout Christmas,' Jack said, smiling at Alice's man.

Alice shuffled to stand beside Nobby; obviously it was a shared question. 'Why, Jack, why...?'

No need for further explanation, everyone knew what was being asked. They wanted Jack to offer some reasoning as to why Snail, Beth, Len and Archie did what they did. Jack looked at Mandy and scanned the whole of his family, just missing Meesh. He lifted Martin onto Mandy's lap and kissed his dog,

'Get off, yer feckin' Nancy,' Martin woofed, joking. He was a card, his former dog.

Stroking Mandy's hair, Jack leaned down and gave her a reassuring kiss.

'I know you're not a Nancy boy, Jack, but you could be a eunuch if you don't get on with it,' urged Mandy.

Jack smiled, his best loving one, which you had to be an aficionado of ugly faces to fully detect, but Mandy was, and she smiled back at him and nudged him with a bobby sock to get him going.

'Nobby, in mediaeval times, powerful men, more often than not Church hierarchy or Kings, believed if their instinct or intuition told them to do something, it was a whispered instruction from God. They called it *Divine Breath* and it had to be obeyed. Today, we call this arrogance and blind pompous faith, to imagine a person has a God-given right to do something, regardless of the pain this might cause anyone else. We sometimes call this these days, "for the greater good".'

'Aye, that's the feckin' Tories for yer...' Colleen said, and wondered why she had said that, and why the Scottish accent. She'd not shared the bath water with Jack, but she had with his son.

'Likely is why,' said Jack, smiling at Colleen, he liked her. His son had made a good choice and if she was a socialist, even better.

'Jack, please...' Mandy asked, fatigued.

Jack continued, 'Snail, Brian Mayhew was a professor at the London School of Economics. He did not necessarily have a radical plan for revolution, but he hated with a vehemence the career politicians who steered a safe middle road, or even worse, a radically dystopian doctrine, weak, and completely unaware of what real people needed, what really needed to be done, "for the greater good".

'Brian Mayhew believed the party system and the culture of career politicians, groomed in the colleges, emerging with a pre-fixed doctrine, would eventually destroy this country. He wanted a non-party system, politicians who debated the merits of a policy and could not be whipped into something they did not believe in. He even put this to the powers-that-be and was laughed out of Downing Street. Unfortunately, it was a Labour Government, but then I don't know why I say that because, essentially, I agree with Snail. I am not really a party man, either. I have beliefs I follow and espouse at every opportunity.'

The sigh suggested everyone knew this already.

'Well, anyway, Brian Mayhew wanted to sow seeds of disruption. He saw it as "nudges" to make people think. Archie, his son, a man of astounding intellect, not unlike myself...' the resulting moan, Jack read as a sign of agreement, '... Archie was already involved in advising government departments, civil servants and ministers, so the system existed to sow the seeds of dystopia they called *"Pogrom"*, slowly at first, a little here and a little there. Len took off on his own socialist mission, and if I was being particularly creative in my pig sty thinking, I would say Len's death was arranged by Beth, who had her own particular right wing, fascist agenda. To be fair to Brian and Archie, they never saw this as the ultimate outcome, but Len was family, and this meant everything to them, but not so much to Beth.

'Beth said something to me in the Gravediggers that made me jolt. She whispered, "Divine Breath" and that was when I knew everything, and guessed she

430

was probably Big-Knob. You see, what Brian Mayhew wanted was altruistically right. In my view, anyway. The problem is, all around them were people who could not comprehend what was happening, and these people attached themselves to the coat-tails out of self-interest, and after a while, this gathers momentum and it's difficult to stop.

'The Mandarins, they had power and wanted more, which is also why Brian Mayhew dropped out, seemingly after his daughter was killed in a jet ski accident. He drank, yes, but not to the excesses we imagined. He was there to counsel Beth, to curb her violent right-wing excesses. She considered this her own Divine Breath. He tried, but failed, and she had him beaten to within an inch of his life, and felt no compunction. She was, you see, doing God's will. Mad as a bleedin' 'atter, of course, as was Brian in the end.'

Jack lubricated his dry mouth with a swig of whiskey and continued, everyone around him hanging on his every word, which held no trace of Oldtimers.

'Archie, well, he did his work for savage amusement, his Divine Breath persuading him that he had a right to question everything, regardless of the consequences. He saw the ideas as they came into his head – also as *Divine Breath*, I suppose. Ironically, Len was the only sane one, and he tried hard to curb the hurt done to people, but in the end, even he couldn't stop it. So you see, all of this mayhem occurred because one man believed it was his divine right, his *Divine Breath*, to question the system. The further irony is, he was right, just wrong in the way he went about it.

'So the question is, can we ever change the system? New Politics? Who will laugh and make jokes at the system, sort of a... *Dadaism*...' Mandy could hear his mind ticking over, he had another plan for fuck's sake. He continued, '... who knows? But it will not be me doing it, as Amanda and I are retiring off into the sunset to enjoy what time we have left together...' Mandy sighed with relief, maybe she had not read the signs right? '... to live life to the full, and of course, I have the garden to finish and I don't mind telling you, I've some brilliant ideas there.'

They all groaned, but knew they would have to let the ideas pan out and afterwards pick up the pieces, as it seemed, even in retirement, Jack Austin was going to be a force to deal with.

'Oh,' he said as an afterthought, 'I also want to be known as Dick from now on, and Mandy will be Duck. Okay, Kirk out.'

He signalled to Nobby to get Mandy to the transporter room and up the stairs. Nobby leapt into action, not sure what to make of what had been said, as Jack disappeared at warp speed, excited as Mandy had promised him a rummage. He called back from the top of the stairs, 'And Nobby, find the feckin' struts, that tree don't look right to me.'

'Jack!' Mandy called to him, as he slowed and ascended the remaining stairs with a modicum of actress wincing.

'Dick,' he replied

'What, Jack?' she replied.

'It's Dick, Duck.'

'Duck?'

He ducked as if dodging a flying bullet. 'I'm Dick, you're Duck,' he carried on.

'Jack!'

'Dick, Duck.'

'Duck, Jack?'

'Dick, Duck,'

'Duck you, fucking Dick,' and Mandy wished everyone a Merry Christmas, as Nobby and Josh carried Duck up the stairs to be rummaged, by Dick.

———

DELLA HAD her first Christmas with Jonas and the Sexton family. They had arranged everything and she didn't have to do a thing. And Sigmund Merde? He met with his daughter, in time for Christmas. Jack and Amanda? The Kind Hearts and Martinets conspiracy over, will they slip into a cosy retirement? No?

———

No

———

Definitely Not

———

Follow Jack and Mandy, as Dick and Duck, in the new series, *The DaDa Detective Agency:*

It has often been said to me that Amanda and Jack Austin are akin to a modern day *Jeeves and Wooster*. An astute observation, and though not intentional, it did inspire the next series, where Amanda is the decorous, finely poised and adroit *Jeeves,* cosseting and protecting, the chaotic cockney barrow boy, *Wooster,* Jack Austin.

The Kind Hearts and Martinets conspiracy over, Jack and Mandy go forward, in their retirement, as *The Dick and Duck Austin, Detective Agency,* henceforth known as:

THE DADA DETECTIVE AGENCY.

BOOK 1 OF THE NEW SERIES - THE DADA DETECTIVE AGENCY

ROAD KILL - THE DUCHESS OF FRISIAN TUN

Where narrative threads from the five books in the *Kind Hearts and Martinets* series are exposed as nerve endings, all of which are twitching and aching to play out a role in the future; revenge. Jack and Mandy, unwittingly centre stage.

An au courant, romantic comedy, crime thriller.

A droll and saucy insight into the Middle Class, Haut Monde, and Geography...

Tales of a reclusive England, with:

The Journalist, The Professor, The Synchronised Swimming Instructor, The Fish Wife, The Dame, The Actress (really Jack Austin), The Geography Teacher,

The Gossip Columnist, The Spy, The Police Inspector, The Man from the Council,

The Priest, The Knight,

The Super-grass (deceased), The Gangster, and,

The Lady Blanche.

———

Book 2 of the crime thriller series **The DaDa Detective Agency**

RITE JUDGEMENT – 'UMBLE PIE

The conclusion of *Road Kill* sets the scene for the DaDa Detective Agency to impact on the world of Establishment, deal and double deal, murder and conspiracy,

the darkness just a breath away,

a *Rite of Spring...*

Merde and Mandarins: Divine Breath
ISBN: 978-4-86752-555-5
Large Print

Published by
Next Chapter
1-60-20 Minami-Otsuka
170-0005 Toshima-Ku, Tokyo
+818035793528

31st July 2021